THE OTHER SIDE OF THE PILLOW

Presented by

Cyril Gillion

Product of

CGpublishing

The Other Side of the Pillow
CG Publishing

Publisher's Note:

This book is a work of fiction. Names, characters, places and incidents are products of the author's imagination or are used fictitiously. Any resemblance to actual events or locales or persons, living or dead, is entirely coincidental.

Manufactured in the United States of America

I S B N
978-1-4243-3406-3

ACKNOWLEDGEMENTS

First and foremost, I want to thank the person who gives me the ability to give thanks; that is the one and only, the creator of all, God himself. When I'm trying to formulate the simplest sentence at three in the morning, only God can put those fingers to work.

I also want to thank these individuals for supporting me during the preliminary stages of this book: Erika Brown, V. J. Prophet, Anna Johnson, Janine "Knowledge" Mitchell, Porsha Robinson, Antinal Thomas, and Corey Crosby.

To Keith Sanders and everyone at Marion Designs, thanks for taking a cover idea and transforming it into a work of art.

To Garette Cassells (an extraordinary playwright), I appreciate your input and guidance on the side of marketing.

To my sister Toccara, thanks for critiquing my work when it was nothing more than scraps. Wouldn't trade you for another sister on the planet.

To my grandparents, aunts, uncles, and cousins, I could fill an entire book if it took thanking all of you.

For those of you at Affiliated Computer Services, thanks for sticking in there as you anticipated this novel to drop.

I've gots to give a special thanks to the woman at Subway … uum … Ms. Silveradore … Salvadere … Heck, I never can get your name, but when it comes to giving me the hookup at lunch, you always prepare a helluva sub, and that's all that counts.

To my cousin Eunice Gillion, thanks for all the talks. God works in mysterious ways and I know he's working through your work. Can't wait to see you on the bestseller list.

To Bridgette a.k.a. *Gorgeous*, thanks for being there from the time I picked up the pen until the time I put it down. You are truly a gem, indescribable. And to me, an acknowledgement without you is like a novel without words…

Last, I want to thank Kenneth and Shirley for putting their chromosomes together to create that sixth son, Cyril Miegon Gillion. I don't know whom idea it was to keep the saga going, but if I was a betting man, I'd say it was Kenneth. Thanks dad!!

The Other Side of The Pillow

<u>Prologue</u>

She points the rifle beneath his loins, perfect aim, the barrel pressed against his genitals.

She's a sharp-shooter that's ready to kill. A six-year-old child who just witnessed her mother get brutalized before her eyes, battered by the hands of her stepfather.

"Put down the gun, Angel. Please baby ... put it down."

That was the voice of her mother, screaming from the other side of the room with blood pouring down her face. But at this moment, Angel was ignoring that bloody voice, and within a five-minute span, the little Angel has metamorphosed into a little menace, has finally come to a point where she could not only care less about the consequences, but could now look the repercussions directly in the eyes.

Her mother cries a bucket of tears. *"Please Angel! Listen to me and put the gun down!"*

"That's right, Angel. Be a good girl and listen to your mama. You don't even know how to use that damn gun."

Angel slightly raises her brow to give a wicked stare, and she cocks the rifle the way her stepfather had demonstrated to her in the past, gets ready to give the instructor his own tutorial.

Mama cries some more, continuing to fill up that bucket. And after minutes of constant shrieking, the cries start to take a toll on Angel –

pain chasing pain through the same bloodline – and the pain suddenly becomes too burdensome for Angel to handle, too heavy for the heart of a six-year-old; so she hesitates, fidgets, and with the blink of an eye, the gun is quickly stripped from her possession and now owned by the hands of the enemy, her stepfather.

He grabs her, turns her around, and he raises the gun towards his daughter's temple.

"Bastard!" her mother screams. "Let go of my daughter!"

He smiles. "Not until you open up that safe."

"I already told you that I don't remember the combination."

"Don't remember, huh? Well let's see if a bullet will make you remember," he says, restraining his daughter firmly.

Mama comes closer. Walks towards her daughter as if she's walking through flames.

"Don't come any closer!" he yells.

"So what are you gonna do, Travis? Kill your own daughter?"

"Stepdaughter," he replies, pressing the gun against Angel's temple to give a no bluffing sentiment.

Mama looks at her daughter. "It's alright Angel … mama's gonna get you out of this."

"Not if mama doesn't open up that safe she won't. I'm not kidding, Betty. Give me the combination or Angel will be—"

"Okay okay okay. 5-5-6-6-3. Now let go of my baby!"

Never letting go of the hostage, he unwinds the combination, and soon he stumbles across the cocaine that he's been looking for, a white Christmas packed in zip lock bags.

He samples it; smiles while taking a whiff of the devil's pie, but he realizes that the taste has a different tang to it. Bittersweet. Nowhere near the product that he's so readily come to love.

He snaps. "This isn't dope!"

"Yes it is."

"You think I'm stupid, Anna? Huh? Think I don't know what flour is when I taste it?"

"Flour?"

"That's right woman … flour! Now where's the real powder?"

"I don't know."

"What the heck you mean you don't know? Either it's here or it's not."

"They … they … they must've switched bags."

"What?"

Cyril Gillion

"Someone must've switched the bags while I was counting the money."

"So are you saying we got robbed? Is that what you're trying to tell me?"

Paranoid, she fumbles over her words, terrified of seeing the leopard push its way through her husband's veins. "We can fix this honey. All we have to do is—"

"That's it!" he says, raising Angel into the air while drilling the gun into her cranium. "You've got five seconds to give me the dope or else Angel's brains are gonna be splattered all over this damn apartment. One!"

"Please baby don't do this. Just let her go and I'll—"

"Two!"

The screams become more intense, but before the count concludes, Angel bites his wrist in midair, breaking herself free from her stepfather's arms. She rises to her feet and runs into the arms of her salvation, those arms of her better half.

Gunshots are suddenly fired.

Shots chasing the backside of Angel.

Death chasing the dorsal of life.

****

1

I awake with the imaginary gun in my hand, sweaty, pointing it directly at the white walls of oppression.

I am in jail. A step up from prison. A boxed in hell-on-earth that was waiting to place me into another box.

The top bunk is where I lay. Four feet of space that forces me to wake up hallucinating every half hour, bunched on top of a muscle-bound woman that went by the name of Taboo. Opposite from her, I'm nothing but this petite brown-skinned sistah with long hair, no blemishes, a playground for my cellmate to explore.

To some – to the ones that know me best – I'm known as Angel Inghram, an ordinary girl from the projects whose main determination in life was to be a lawyer. But to others – the ones that only saw my mug shot on television – I'm known as the ultimate slut, bitch, whore, and oh … that's right … skank.

Murder was the case that they gave me, or should I say the case that I was about to be convicted of. Just eight hours ago I stood before the judge in an orange jumpsuit, hoping he would look at my police record and realize that the murder was only an accident, that the only thing I ever murdered in my entire life was a stray dog and that was only because it ran in front of my car while I was in a rush to get to class one morning.

First person I called was Mr. Stern, one of my college professors who supposedly hooked me up with some attorney named Patricia Dawson. But due to the price that she was charging, I'd say it was far from a hook-up. I mean here I was, twenty-four years old with a criminal record as clean as satin sheets, and the best the judge could offer me was bail set for a hundred grand – the type of cash I haven't seen in my entire life – but you can bet your bottom dollar that I was going to get it from somewhere.

I guess the million-dollar question is why did I kill him?

Well it's simple. I had been raped. Forced to kill a man because he was seconds away from killing me. And the only person who was able to witness it was an eighty-year-old veteran, a man who probably wasn't sensible enough to testify on my behalf.

All that kept running through my mind was my mother, how she once told me to build laws instead of break them. That was the last thing she said to me before her death, March 2, 1989, the same day my stepfather took her life while she was simply trying to save mine.

The ring.

I remember the ring more than anything. 22Karat Gold. Sterling Silver. Cold metal pressed against my mother's face as he beat her in front of my eyes, constant nightmares of knowing I wasn't strong enough to pull the trigger when I had the chance.

Seems like it was just yesterday when I was sitting in that dreadful courtroom, waiting for the judge to throw the book at him, watching him smile as he was awarded second-degree murder for only ten years, BS to the utmost degree.

Worst thing about it was that he died in prison, never got a chance to make it through those ten years. Word has is that after serving five he got stabbed to death by someone who was once an enemy of his on the outside, some drug lord that he owed debt to for over ten grand. The night of his death, I remember crying myself to sleep, not because of him dying, but mainly because I wasn't able to take his life the same way he took the life of my mother, and returning the vengeance is something I wanted more than life itself.

Life after my mother died was like living in death.

I lived with Aunt Terry. Since my birth father died while mama was pregnant with me, Aunt Terry took care of me until the age of eighteen, and that was only because no other family members were interested in raising an antagonistic six-year-old girl.

Our house was in South Miami. Scotts Projects. A gruesome place that only had one way in, no way out, and not even the police would enter after dark.

Living with my Aunt Terry was no cakewalk either. She was a religion freak. One of those family members that'll make you go to church from sunup to sundown, like being a Christian was equivalent to being a slave.

We never saw eye to eye.

While Aunt Terry dreamed of me being the first woman minister in the city, I had different plans in mind, bigger rocks to climb. I wanted to be a lawyer, the top female prosecutor around. And I literally mapped out my future on how to achieve my dream, even went to three different schools in three different cities to achieve it.

With every bridge I crossed, it felt like I was getting one step closer to my mother, like I was piecing her life back together with every exam I passed, but never did I imagine being detained by the same system that I spent my entire life trying to become apart of, especially when I'm only a week away from taking the bar exam, the last bridge before encompassing that world of litigation.

"Inghram, get your ass up. You have a visitor."

That was one of the prison guards, coming to release me out of my cell so I could have my thirty-minute talk-time with my significant other, the last person I wanted to see at this particular time.

His name was William. William Randolph.

Although he was the second man I ever dated, he was first in every other category, the first man to get into my mind, dig into my heart, made me look at love in a different perspective.

There was an age gap between us. Sixteen years to be exact. While I was a girl of modern times, William was a man of ancient; a man that has no tolerance for hip hop because he feels it only corrupts the minds of youth.

William was also as spiritual as they come (just like my Aunt Terry), the type that once lived a life of crime before deciding to ride that chariot of Christianity, destined to enter the pearly gates of what they call heaven; a place that has no address, no landmark, no where on a practical map.

That was our crossfire, the one and only thing that placed us on different sides of the fence.

While William saw Christianity as a savior, I saw it as nothing more than a scheme, just a big melting pot of hypocrites that profit off

Cyril Gillion

their own beliefs, hoaxing people into thinking that ignoring certain doctrines would only lead to their demise.

Though we had different insights on the spiritual tip, I still loved him unconditionally. And with three months of consecutive dating, it was a love that has come so sudden, often scared me at times.

Along with being a spiritual man, William would rather slit his tongue before ever saying any type of profanity, but once the guard escorted me around the corner, I could tell that William had already put that spirituality on hold, because first thing he said to me was, "Don't worry, Angel! I'm gonna get you the hell out of here. And when I do … he's a dead man!"

"Too late, William. He's already dead."

"Well I'll kill 'em again," he replied with fists clasped. "Are you ok?"

"I'm fine. Just a slight pain in my side."

"Did he leave any marks on you?"

"Yeah, a few on the right side of my thigh."

"Good."

"Good?"

"We're gonna need as much evidence as possible to get you out of here. When is the first hearing?"

"You're a little too late for that. The first hearing was yesterday."

"Were you granted bail?"

"I guess so, if you consider a hundred grand as bail … how did you know I was here?"

"I went to your apartment. Figured I'd come over to apologize for our argument. But when I got there, the whole place was sectioned off in Dutch tape."

In a sense I was happy to see him, but I was more afraid of being seen under these conditions. Us communicating through a glass wall. Over a telephone. Felt like our love had suddenly become barricaded.

"Why didn't you call me?" he asked.

"How could I?"

"What do you mean how could you?"

"Thought you were upset at me."

"Being upset is one thing, Angel, but keeping you out of danger is another. If God hadn't given me the inclination to go over your apartment and check on you, who knows how long it would've been before I knew what happened."

"Yeah, well maybe your God should've given you that inclination before I was getting the crap beat out of me. Maybe he should've—"

"Let's not start this, Angel."

"No William, let's start. Where the hell was your God when I was being thrown around my damn apartment?"

"He was right there with you. How else do you think you're still alive?"

"I'm still alive because of the old faithful pistol. Because I followed my gut instinct. But if your God was so just and powerful, he would've prevented me from getting raped, and I wouldn't have to be sitting behind this damn window, talking to you with my hair in some messed-up corn rolls."

I dropped the phone for a split moment, tried to grab hold of my composure; gathered some lungpower before my asthma leaped out the bag.

I am a nervous wreck internally, a puzzle of pain that's unable to be put together. Humpty Dumpty collapsed in a million pieces.

It's no secret that William is broken up as well and he gives me a look of uneasiness as if he's afraid of presuming this tug-a-war of words, both of us waiting for the other to continue the conversation.

Stepping outside of my vehemence to savor the moment, I tell him, "I'm sorry, William. I wasn't trying to—"

"It's ok, Angel. No need to apologize. I guess it's easy for me to harp on God's goodness when I'm not the one behind bars."

I give him another apology, one that runs deeper than words; would apologize until the end of time if it meant spending another day in his arms.

I tell him, "I didn't mean to snap at you, William. It's just that I want to get out of here ASAP, whatever it takes."

He says, "Leave that responsibility up to me. I'll get you out."

"And how is that? Did you not hear me say my bail is a hundred grand?"

"Ten percent of a hundred grand is only ten grand. That's not so bad."

"Not if you're Donald Trump. But where in the world am I supposed to scramble up ten grand?"

"Like I just told you. Me."

"You?"

"Yeah, I think I can get my hands on that type of money."

"How so? You barely have enough cash to take me out to dinner, let alone bail me out of jail."

"Trust me, Angel. I'll get the money. You just make sure that you—"

Cyril Gillion

"Two minutes left," the guard intervened.

"For Christ's sake!" I snapped. "We just started talking."

The guard sneers. "Two minutes!"

William tells me, "It's okay, Angel. I'm gonna get you out of here. But promise me you'll stay focused while you're inside. The bar exam is next week and I want you to be ready."

"The hell with the bar. I'll just take it next February."

"No!"

"What?"

"You prepared to take it next week so that's exactly what we're gonna do. We must not loose focus of the main objective. You'll just have to study in jail."

I look at him as if he's gone nuts, and all I can say is, "Are you nuts? Incase you haven't noticed William, I'm about to be on trial for murder and my mind is nowhere near equipped for taking any type of exam. Besides, even if I was in the right frame of mind, how am I supposed to study in here?"

"Simple," he replies, reaching into his briefcase to grab a large textbook.

I smile.

The textbook is the preparation guide of the bar exam, the same one that I saw online a couple weeks back.

William drops all four hundred pages of the textbook on the table.

"When did you get this?" I asked.

"Never mind when I got it. Just promise me you'll study."

I smile again. Smile at my man. Smile as time closes in on us and we realize that the moment is as limited as our words.

"Can you do me another favor?" I asked.

"Anything."

"I want you to call my best friend, Cuqui. Tell her that I'm gonna need her to get on the first plane to New York and it's important that she don't erase any recorded phone conversations or messages on her cellular."

"What's on the cellular?"

"All the evidence that I need for the trial. And when she comes, tell her to make sure she brings my Aunt Terry as well."

The guard taps me on my shoulder, causes a discomfort to settle within me as time bullies its way between William and me.

William gives me a hard stare. A comforting stare. Stares at me as if everything is going to be alright, although we know it's not.

He mutters, "We're in this together, Angel. And I know you don't wanna hear it, but I'm praying for you. Praying for us both."

That moment ends. So does the time. Takes us back into our separate worlds.

A half hour later my world consisted of a swarm of jailbirds that were all waiting for food, a line longer than the one in unemployment. I stood in between two heavyset women that were larger than life, trapped in between two levels of funk.

I was hungry. Felt like my stomach was throwing an endless temper tantrum, steadily cursing me out in tenfold.

The cooks were serving roast beef. Or at least that's what they said it was. But after seeing a large pot of unprocessed ground beef, I guess roast beef was all they could label it as.

Side items were a combination of old broccoli and mac-and-cheese. Macaroni in one pot. Cheese in another. I guess they expected us to mix them together and be thankful for our blessings.

One of the inmates asked, "Could you put a little more broccoli on my plate?"

"Roll your fat ass down the line!" the cook replied.

Once getting my tray, I glanced into the over-packed cafeteria and found a seat in the corner by myself. Women stalked me like I was the new girl on the block, and from the way that they were hissing in my direction, you would've thought a man was strolling the scene.

Eventually, my cellmate Taboo, found me. She pulled up a chair with three of her friends trailing behind her in the shadows.

Two of them were just as large as her. Short hair cuts. Tongue rings. Dyke appeal. Definitely dyke appeal.

The other girl was a little bigger than me. Same complexion. But only she had piercings-galore and a tattoo that read, *Dead already*.

Minding my business, I sat up straight in my seat, turned on my no-nonsense glare, strapped on my I'll-slap-a-bitch face before I became the bitch that got slapped.

"What's up with ya?" Taboo asked.

"I'm chilling."

"Mind if we chill here with ya?"

"Guess not," I replied, chomping away at the roast beef.

She turns to the other inmates, grabs their attention as if she's the leader amongst the bunch. "Eh y'all. This is my girl, Angel. Why don't y'all show her some love."

                              Cyril Gillion

Instead of speaking verbally, they nod their heads to acknowledge my presence, as if saying hello would be breaking the code of confinement.

While the other girls talked amongst each other, Taboo discreetly gave me the low-down on what each girl did to get locked up. Sherice and Taz had gotten busted for robbing a convenient store. But it wasn't the robbery that got them locked up. It was how they beat down the cashier after finding only twenty-five dollars in the drawer. The smaller girl, Dynamite, was in a more messed up situation than I was. Word has it that a drug deal went wrong and she tried to make an escape for the border, but in doing so, she killed two cops in the process and wounded three more. Plus she was supposed to be a habitual offender, which meant she had a first-class ticket to the big house.

To symbolize the murders, Dynamite wore two teardrops under her eyelids, and from observing the other women, it was obvious that Dynamite was supposed to be the badass in the group.

I tried to find my place amongst this crowd of women, but never could I see myself blending in, not unless I quickly developed a pseudonym that could harden up my name.

No one ever asked me my reason for being here, but I could tell that word spreads quickly, because the first words that came from Sherice's mouth were, "So I heard you popped someone."

"Who told you that?" I replied.

"Don't matter who told. In here, there's not too much I don't know."

Taz laughs. "Pretty little thing like you actually killed someone … get real."

"So is it true?" Sherice persisted.

"Somewhat," I replied. "Depends on how you look at it."

"Man or female?"

"Excuse me?"

"The person you popped. Who was it?"

"If you must know, it was a man."

"She only killed him because he was about to bust open that little cherry of hers," Dynamite added, her voice as harsh as sandpaper. "It's not like it was pre-mediated. Isn't that right, Angel?"

I ignore ignorance.

"You see Angel, real murderers mark what they kill," she says, pointing to her engraved teardrops.

Taboo speaks on my behalf. "Who gives a damn if she killed a man, woman, or a damn dog in the alley? She's still sitting up in this hellhole with the rest of us."

Silence rests on the table as I can feel the tension flaring, and between the five of us, there was enough estrogen to cause a holocaust.

Dynamite asked me, "So where you from?"

"Why?"

"No biggie. Just inquiring."

"Miami."

"Is that right?" she says. "I'm from down that way too. What part you from?"

"Scotts Projects."

"Whaaat? God knows it's a small ass world. I used to stay in Liberty City."

"For how long?"

"All my life. Grew up right around the corner from Southside Park."

"What high school you went to?"

"High school? Girl, the highest school I made it to was Franklin Middle School."

We laugh. Laughter somehow sparks a connection between us, and Dynamite no longer seems so intimidating.

Finally able to let down my guard, I decided to take off the no-nonsense mask and I stepped back into my normal costume, the Angel Inghram who's far from a female gangster.

I ask Dynamite, "So why'd you leave?"

"Warrants."

"That's it?"

"Hell yeah, girl. MPD was all over me about a burglary that went down on 78th and Branden ... Some nigga was sitting on fifteen kilos, had the dope stashed in the backyard of his grandma's house like no one would notice. Can you believe that? Fifteen kilos in the backyard of an old lady's house ... So peep this right ... One day I saw his grandma carrying the dope in the backyard, looked like she was attempting to bury it in the dirt. So you know I had to get her ol' ass right ... shiiiiiiiiiit ... old lady or not, I was still planning on robbing that lady blind. But I wasn't about to do it alone. I couldn't take that chance. So I gathered up a couple of them Zulo niggas from lil' Haiti and told 'em I'll give 'em half the profit if they went in and grabbed the kilos. I told 'em I'll be waiting in the get-away car."

"And they actually went for that?"

                    Cyril Gillion

"Hell yeah. You would've went for it too if you had a chance to split fifteen pies amongst three people ... shiiiiiiiiit ... that's enough loot to buy three Johnny Cochrans."

"So did y'all get the money?"

"Most of it. We were riding-out with twelve keys until those niggas got greedy and wanted to go back for more. But after going back, that ol' lady was waiting for us with a glock that was damn near bigger than she was, and she knew how to use it too. That lady didn't waste any time blasting those Zulo niggas and she would've shot me too, but I was already down the street by the time her old ass got outside."

Taboo said, "Girl, you mean to tell me that y'all went up in there with no heat."

"We had heat. But our heat wasn't hot enough for the heat that she was packing ... That ol' lady had the kind of heat that'll put a hole through your stomach. And what makes it even worse is that she was able to identify me to the police which mean them pigs were on my ass like I was Carmen Sandiego."

Humoring this horrible story, I ask Dynamite, "So did you leave?"

"Haven't you been listening at all, little girl? I may not be blessed with a degree, but I do have enough sense to know that you don't stay in town after being involved in a drug case with two dead bodies lying around. Girl, I packed up them twelve pies and tried to drive my ass to Mexico. And had it not been for that damn tail light, I would've made it all the way."

"Tail light?"

"Hell yeah. After the police pulled me over, they took about a half-hour to do paperwork for one lousy ticket. So I'm like, all this paperwork for one little ticket. What I look like? Bo Bo the fool or something ... shiiiiiiiiiit ... and it's obvious that they were up to something, because time they came back to my car, both of them had their hands on their pistols like they were fixing to straighten me. So I had to make a choice 'cause I wasn't 'bout to let them niggas pop that trunk and not only steal my pies, but lock a bitch up for ten years or more ... so I took my chances ... I pulled out my strap and gave them a taste of their own medicine ... shiiiiiiiiiit ... I blasted both of them pigs and got the hell-out-of-dodge, rode that '83 Caprice about a hundred and twenty miles per hour. And really, I didn't even know a Caprice could go that fast until I actually started flooding it... Next thing you know, I'm on a high speed chase with about ten cops and a helicopter flying over me. Them police cut my ass off right before I got off the exit and had every gun in America pointed at my car, everyone ordering me to get out the car with my hands up. So you know I'm a ride-or-die chick right? shiiiiiiiiiit ... I pulled out my strap and started blasting away at all them pigs, helicopters too; I didn't give a damn. Next thing you know, they're throwing my ass in handcuffs, reading me my rights, and I'm suddenly sitting up in here with y'all whoes ... know what I'm sayin ... In just the blink of an eye my whole world got messed up ... but it's all good though. I popped two of them pigs, so I guess I can still sleep at night."

She gives a light smirk, somewhat scary, as if killing people is equivalent to stepping on ants, a craft that she's mastered in life.

I don't know how much of the story was true, but you do have to wonder how she claimed to shoot at so many cops and not only manage to still be alive, but come out the battle with nothing more than a scratch.

Ten minutes later she was still rambling on, catching me up on some things that were popping back in Miami, and everything that came out her mouth was either related to selling drugs or robbing someone.

Finally taking the conversation to a new avenue, she said, "I wonder why we never knew each other?"

"Probably because you were too busy robbing people while she was in school," Taz said.

"I didn't hang out much," I replied. "And when I did, I only chilled with one person."

"And who was that?"

"Cuqui."

"Who?"

"My best friend named Cuqui."

"Nigga or chick?"

"A female."

"Oh ... well I probably wouldn't know her. I don't usually do whoes."

No reply.

She carries on. "I remember the fish market being in your part of town. I used to go there everyday to snatch up some catfish. Remember Mr. Gately?"

"Yeah," I replied. "Doesn't he work there?"

"Not anymore he doesn't. He was just killed a couple months back."

"Really?"

     Cyril Gillion

"Yep. Overdosed on some bad weed."

"I used to roll with his nephew, Sheldon. You know him? Kind of tall. Lanky."

She tells me, "He died as well."

"For real?"

"You mean you didn't know about that? Girl, where the hell you been at? He got smoked in a drive-by about two years back."

"Heck, is anyone alive these days?"

She laughs. "That nigga used to be mad cool. Always rode in the flyest ride around. Used to date my cousin, Terrika. You know her?"

"The name doesn't ring a bell."

"She has a brother named Tom. They are my cousins."

"Nahhh. Don't ring a bell either."

"How about Trevon? You must know him 'cause y'all stayed on the same block."

"Kind of short and heavyset?"

"Yeah, that's my cousin too."

I ask, "Are you related to the whole city of Miami?"

"Haven't you heard? We run that city."

"That's good to know."

"From Opa Locka to South Dade, my fam' is well known. Hell, I even got people here in Brooklyn. Ask anyone and they'll tell you 'bout the Ross's."

"Who did you say?"

"I said Ross. We're all across the globe."

The name throws darts at my soul, changes the tone of the conversation. For that is the same last name of my stepfather, the murderer.

Wandering if she hung from the same tree as the bad apple, I tell her, "Your last name sounds familiar."

"Yeah, I knew you'd recognize it."

"Do you know of a Travis … Travis Ross?"

"Of course I do. He was my uncle. First person to teach me how to cutup coke. But he hasn't been with us for nearly twenty years."

"Is that so?"

"Yep, he went to prison."

Those darts are steadily flying but I find the strength to ask, "Why did he go to prison?"

"For killing … second-degree murder … Had it not been for that crack-head wife of his, he would've still been with us today. She used to smoke up all his yayo … would smoke it by the packs … and since my uncle was the type of man that never let a woman come before his paper, he had no choice but to put her out of her misery. My uncle did mad time for that murder too. But if you ask me, her freeloading ass deserved it anyhow."

As she talks about my mother, I can feel myself turning red, and while I stare at the smile that lies on Dynamite's face, I try to keep my own dynamite from exploding inside, but before I can do so, the dragon within me has already busted through my internal organs, ferocity seeping through my pores, rage filling up that beaker, and as that beaker overflows, I leap across the table with every intention of doing a 007 on this bitch, reaching at her throat like a patient that reaches for insulin.

Taboo caught me before I could grab hold of Dynamite, but I still managed to catch a grip of her weave, damn near tried to yank it out of her scalp.

"Get this crazy bitch off my hair!" she hollered.

More girls try to pull me back, each using all the strength they had to keep me from pulverizing Dynamite.

"Stop pulling me back!" I screamed. "I'm gonna kill 'er! I'm gonna kill 'er!"

I broke free from their arms and eventually caught the neck of Dynamite, started choking her on the table like I was squeezing a chicken for dear life, drilling her face into the plate of roast beef.

The guards rushed over. It took three of them to release my hands from her throat; took God himself to tame that dragon within this little body of mines.

"Inghram, we got something for that little nasty temper," they said, dragging me out of the cafeteria like an untamed beast that was locked in chains. With two holding my arms and one grabbing my legs, they took pride in dragging me to the hole, throwing me into the bottomless pit.

One hollered, "You wanna fight somebody? How 'bout you sit in the hole and fight these darn walls!"

I stayed in that hole for hours, all alone, nothing to tamper with but a rusty razor that lay in the corner.

Trapped in the middle of four dark walls, I lied on the ground and looked to the ceiling, took the time to redo my corn rolls that were falling out of place.

          Cyril Gillion

A light beamed through one of the cellular bars, atonement creeping through a little hole, just enough brightness for me to get a foretaste of freedom.

I ponder over that freedom. Pondered over the possibility of going back to my normal life, journeying back to the only world I've come to know, and then I pondered about wicked thoughts, about reaching my freedom, about a hole that could lead me out of this hellhole.

Once again I observe my surroundings.

The razor.

It pierced an inclination inside of me, carved the seal off that criminal mindset.

With a cell that had a circumference of forty feet altogether, a diameter of fifteen, eighty-six square blocks covering the walls, and each block going at a six-inch radius, my freedom looked closer than ever, as if I was looking through a microscope.

If time was on my side, I could chisel my way through these walls, crawl into the laundry area, then scurry through the gauge room that leads to the corridors of my freedom. Freedom that hides between a swarm of NYPD and a barbwire fence that sits twenty feet in the air.

"Inghram!" the guard yelled, busting back through the door with hard boots and a flash light.

I snap out of my criminal world and hop on all fours like a puppy that awaits its owner. The guard stares at me with an evil scowl, daring me to return the grimace.

"Get yourself together!" she demanded. "You're getting out on bail."

2

A Year Earlier

If I'd known a relationship would cause me this much strife, I would've turned lesbian a long time ago.

Those were my thoughts as I sat at the dinner table in despair, dining in the finest restaurant in upstate New York.

It was my birthday. Twenty-three years of a celebrated existence. Damn near felt like forty.

The scenery never appeared so calm, lights never seemed so dim, and the most raucous sound was the wine sauce that was sizzling from the medium-well cooked steak.

I was here with Kevin Armstrong. My lover. A guy I've known since elementary school, used to live on the same street while growing up in Miami. With him no longer being that skinny kid who used to chase me around the house with paintballs, Kevin was now taller, of course bigger, manly features, manly charisma, ALL MAN. And with two hundred and twenty pounds packed inside that 6'4 frame, he was emerging as one of the top football players around, a potential lottery pick in the NFL draft.

"Here are some fresh scallops for you and a Chicken Parsela for the lady."

That was the voice of the waiter, the only black man in the restaurant besides Kevin and me, and from just ten minutes of being there, the waiter was already eyeing me down, enough eye contact to start an epidemic.

Not your average waiter, he was actually handsome, more handsome than Kevin, too handsome to be serving customers and collecting tips. And even with an apron tied around his waist, he wore it like a three-piece suit, like he was born with a niche for servicing women.

"Care for anything else?" he asked.

"Naw partner, we're straight," Kevin said, placing his arm around my shoulder to show ownership.

The waiter continues to stare as he walks away, starts undressing me with his eyes. I stared back at him. Rode that stare like a ferrous wheel in the park. And from all the pain that Kevin has took me through, I had every reason to keep the stare going strongly.

For our relationship was at the last breaking point. The point where one party is full of bliss while the other party is contemplating the quickest way to jump ship.

I was that other party; a woman still tugging at the string of love yet wandering what it would be like to let it loose, and five years of kinship will keep any woman tugging at that string, hoping she'd grip it back someday with both hands.

I'd given our relationship the ultimate evaluation. And that evaluation wasn't based off what we've been through, but more so on what was soon to come. I evaluated us from that blood pumping, clogged artery, gossiping son-of-a-bitch friend of his that never lies.

His heart.

A year ago I would've said our hearts were on one accord, beating in sync, as if we knew the thump in each other's chest. A year ago if someone had told me that Kevin didn't love me, I would've went to the grave trying to defend my man.

I thought I knew my man. Thought I knew his heart. But for some reason, the things you don't know are always the things that hold the most weight, plus they are the same things that sneak up on you like a thief in the night.

My thief – the thief that took Kevin from me – was a football. That was always his true love, a talent that I always thought I could stand beside, but never thought I'd be standing behind. Ever since Kevin found out that he could be a potential lottery pick, his personality had done a complete three-sixty for the worse, and no longer was he that high school boy who was eager to change the headlights on my Honda Civic. He was now a target. A collector's item. Not quite celebrity status, but strong enough to have me replaced at any given second, our love now lingering on a floating raft.

"This steak taste horrible!" Kevin says aloud.

"What's wrong with it, Kevin? Thought you said you liked your steak cooked medium-well?"

"Angel, does this look medium-well to you?"

I love Kevin dearly, but at the same time I hate him. Biggest thing I hated was his softness for alcohol. He was a liquor bottle waiting to spill. Drunk so much to where it nearly ended his career, almost put him out of commission. He gets it from his father, a man who died from an overdose of powder, killed around the same time that my mother died. His father and my stepfather used to be hangout buddies, would often hit up the old spots in Miami to gamble their money away, then come back home angry, liquor all over their breath while waiting to tear up anything in sight. My stepfather would often release that wired up energy on my mother, beating her night after night without any recollection of what he'd done the next morning.

Kevin's father would do the same, and that's what attracted me to Kevin the most. We understood each other. Shared the same struggles. Cut from the same cloth of pain.

But now everything has changed. Switched seasons. Winter has turned to spring. Summer dresses as autumn. And just like the seasons, Kevin has gone from a guy who never drinks, to a guy who drinks on special occasions, to seldom drinking, to an uncontrollable addiction that needs therapy to cease.

Now, through Kevin and that liquor bottle, I no longer see the little boy that I come to love. I now see his dad; see my stepfather. And through that double mirror, I see my mother; see myself.

Kevin bites some more of his uncooked steak, tries to get into it, but with every bite he hates it more and more.

He soon gets fed up, his face turning into lava.

"Waiter!" he yells.

The waiter comes over with a sleek stroll, the same waiter that was eyeing me down earlier. His eyes go back from me to Kevin as he smiles. "Can I help you?"

"Yeah, help me by cursing out your cook," Kevin replied. "This steak takes like a hard brick dipped in teriyaki sauce!"

"Excuse me?"

"I asked for my steak to be cooked medium-well."

"Is that not medium-well?" the waiter asked.

"Hell no! More like well burnt."

                    Cyril Gillion

The waiter hesitates, gathers his composure, and says, "Ok sir. I can take care of that. How 'bout I bring out another medium-well?"

"How 'bout you refund my money. My money plus an extra steak-to-go."

"Excuse me?"

"You hard of hearing or something? I said I want my money back, plus I want the meal re-cooked. And tell your—"

"Kevin!" I said, intervening.

"What?"

Trying to bring down his loud tone, I whispered, "Treat the man with some respect."

Kevin shushes me with his hand, blocks me out like a parent does a child, and he continues to display his true blackness inside this white establishment.

He rants to the waiter. "Listen here! Either you give me back my money or get your damn manager."

The waiter gives an upsetting scowl, wants to retaliate, but his conscience reminds him of the percentile of black men that are unemployed in this city.

Not wanting to be another statistic, he says, "No problem sir. I'll get you the manager."

Minutes pass as me and Kevin sit at the table in silence.

Looking at him as if he missed a class on home training, I'm not only embarrassed to be with him tonight, but I'm embarrassed of being his woman in general.

It wasn't long before the manger came stomping towards our table in full stride. He was a white man in his mid forties. Medium built. Thick mustache. Carried a hairline so receding to where you could see his thoughts.

Those thoughts matched his serious demeanor as if the customer wasn't always right in his eyes, looks like he was already upset before ever hearing the whole dilemma.

"Eh brother, why are you over here causing all this friction?" the manager asked, his face beaming perplexity.

Kevin grew rigid. "What did you just call me?"

"I called you brother," the manager said, launching back. "It's been a while since—"

"Stop right there!" Kevin said, rising from his seat. "First off, never in your life are you to call me brother. You got that?"

Not backing down, the manager matches Kevin's aggressiveness, and they stand nose to nose like two leopards in an open field.

I turn my stare in fear of what's about to happen, and once I turn back around, I see two fists flying in the air, both fists opening up to lock pinky fingers, now wiggling the index finger, shooting the bird, locking thumbs, and twisting each other's wrist. Then, they turned around to lock pinky fingers again, did that thing with their thumbs, bumped shoulders, shot the bird again, and finished it off with a double backslapping handshake.

Frat brothers.

My mouth drops to the floor as Kevin smiles. "I can't believe it's been three years," he said.

"Four years if you're counting the summer of '03.

"So when'd you start running this joint?"

"About a year and a few months … you still playing football?"

"Yeah, I'm in the expansion league. They feel I have a good chance at being a first round pick this year. Possibly a lottery."

"Humph. Looks like you've been catching more than a football lately," the guy says, looking in my direction.

Finally getting the urge to acknowledge me, Kevin says, "Angel, meet Tim. He pledged with me at Albany State."

I said, "I never knew you pledged Alpha."

"That's the point, Angel. You weren't supposed to know."

Tim says, "No need to worry, sista. Kevin wasn't man enough to pledge Alpha. He bought his way into the organization."

They laugh.

Tim asks me, "So what's a beautiful thing like you doing with a chump like Kevin?"

"Coincidence."

"Must be one hell of a coincidence. Did you go to Albany State as well?"

"I went to NYU. Now I'm at Brooklyn College studying law."

"Brooklyn Law huh? That further makes me wander why you're with this chump … So how'd you like the food?"

"Excuse me?"

"The food. Did you enjoy it?"

Hesitant with my response, I wanted to tell him the truth, like how the vegetables need a little more seasoning and the rice couldn't tie Uncle Ben's shoe laces, but instead, I swallow that truth and tell him, "The food was great."

Kevin adds, "Would be even better if we had another bottle of wine."

"No, Kevin. One bottle is enough."

 Cyril Gillion

"Come on, Angel. If a man can't drink on his woman's birthday, then when else is he supposed to drink?"

Tim looks at me. "It's your birthday?"

"Damn straight," Kevin says, intervening. "So hook us up, Tim. Tell that ignorant waiter of yours to bring me a few more bottles of that good stuff and we'll be straight."

Thirty minutes later, Kevin had finished chatting with his fraternity brother about ol' times.

The night was starting to unwind.

Kevin had already ate another sirloin, an order of lemon salmon with red beans and rice, and compliments to his friend Tim, our table was hooked up with five bottles of wine, four of which Kevin had already downed.

While he drinks his liver away, I was still upset, still bothered from the way he treated the waiter earlier.

Looking tipsy, Kevin asks, "You wanna try dessert?"

"Nope."

"Come on, birthday girl. I'd tell Tim to hook us up with some cheesecake. And I know how much you love cheesecake."

"Yeah, but who's to say that you won't make a mockery out of the key-lime pie."

"What's with the attitude? Do you wanna go somewhere else?"

"You damn near embarrassed that waiter to death, Kevin. And quite frankly, I'm not sure if I can endure any more of your craziness."

He snaps. "The hell with the waiter, Angel. Had that nigga not been so focused on you, he probably would've gotten my order right."

"Ok, so you go on a madman rampage, all because you thought another man was looking at your woman?"

"No, Angel. I went on a rampage because I was disrespected."

"Disrespected?"

"Damn right. That waiter wasn't the only person who was looking around. You were scoping him out just as hard, made me feel like I was sitting in between two peeping Toms."

I tell him, "You're imagining things."

"Don't try to play me, Angel."

"I don't have to, Kevin. You're already playing yourself. Been playing yourself the whole night." I try to back off a little; lower my voice. Don't want to flood the engine with too much intensity, too much anger.

I look at the people around me. They're not looking directly at me, but they do notice me. They notice us. Appearing as the only blacks in the joint, we stand out like two colored folks at a Klu Klux Klan rally.

I switch up the tone, look at Kevin with liquor on his breath; tell him, "I'm sorry, Kevin. It's just … sometimes, it's like you're not the Kevin I used to know."

"Yeah, well maybe I'm not."

"What?"

Gulping down the wine like he's in a shot-glass contest, he says, "You know what Angel, there's no sense of even speaking on it."

"What do you mean no use of speaking on it? Are you stressed or something?"

"Stressed is not the word."

"Then what is it?"

He drinks some more wine, shakes his head in agony. "Fine, Angel. It's you."

"What?"

"You asked me what the problem was. So there you have it. You're my damn problem."

"Me?"

"Yeah you … we haven't had sex in months."

"You're acting like this because of sex?" I look around the restaurant to ensure that no one is listening. "Okay … forget about it, Kevin. How 'bout we talk about this later?"

"No, Angel. I'm tired of waiting to talk. Tired of waiting period. We're gonna talk about this shit right now. We're gonna—"

"You're drunk."

"What?"

"You're drunk, Kevin."

"No I'm not."

I reach over to snatch away the wine glass, but he swats my hand away. "Leave it alone, Angel! I already told you that I'm not drunk."

"Yes you are. And when you're drunk, your temper starts to flare."

"Any man with desert-dick would have a temper!"

I want to go off on him, want to slap him for saying that. But I remind myself that he's incoherent, that the bottle of wine is the one who's really talking; a bottle making him say things that he'd dare not say when all of his senses are stirring.

 Cyril Gillion

Sense he put it out there, I'll admit the sex part. We haven't had sex in a few months, been so long to where I couldn't recognize his penis if it was staring me in the eye. But truth is, our sex life has become incompatible, far from lovers that are insatiable. Instead of taking his time to work all the areas that used to stimulate me, he now rushes it like a man does a woman on the street, loving me with his dick while I love him with my heart.

But no longer was my heart into it. Not by a long shot. And truth of the matter is, no matter how much I try to fake it, the vagina can never do what the heart won't allow.

He goes on to say, "I don't know how much I can take this Angel."

"Take what?"

"Walking around like a horny toad. I mean let's be honest. You need me more than I need you."

"What?"

"That's right, Angel. Incase you forgot, I'm the soon-to-be-lottery-pick, the next Warren Sapp, women stalking me, people interviewing me, everyone asking about my personal life, about all kinds of stuff. That's me. Not you."

I could retaliate to this animosity. Could take this thing to war. But I keep trying to convince myself that the man across the table is not really my man, not Kevin, keep telling myself that the liquor has him at a handicap, and in the rules of battle, you never go to war with the handicap.

So I sit and wait. Wait for him to continue. Wait to see what he's about to say next. How far will he take the conversation? Will he unravel any hidden truths? Tell me that he was only riding this love thing for the ride, perhaps because he was already traveling that road, and his next stop is only a block away. Alcohol will always make a person say how they truly feel. Would bring the truth out of a terrorist.

He goes on to say, "All of these women coming at me, backs all out, butts hanging to the floor, breasts popping out their shirt with my initials written all over them. All of this booty around me and I have to turn my cheek like Martin … Luther … damn … King."

Not yet Angel. Don't strike him yet.

He says, "Do you know how many times I wanted to screw another woman within this last month?"

Those words sting at my heart like killer bees, and I can't help but to say, "Enlighten me?"

"Too many to count. But every time I get the urge to have sex with another woman, I think about you and I no longer can do it. So tell me, Angel ... why aren't we having sex? Are you giving my stuff to someone else?"

"No."

"Then why aren't we fucking?"

I snap. "Simple! Sex is supposed to be enjoyable!"

"What did you just say?"

I want to take back my comment, want to bury those words in a place where it can never slip out again. But those words have already come with a certain price; a price non-refundable.

Kevin shakes his head, liquored to the core, but he's coherent enough to say, "I've gots to be one of the dumbest niggas in New York. All of these ample opportunities I had to get laid ... women in my hotel after football games ... God knows I should've—"

"Why are you doing this, Kevin? Don't you know how close you are to—"

"Leaving."

"—getting left ... I should've left months ago. Had it not been for school, I would've been long gone, would've packed my things and got on the first midnight train to Florida."

He lays aside the bottle of wine, shuffles his shoulders, and lets out a laugh. He laughs as if my words are meaningless, worth pennies, and I don't have the courage to walk out the door, leaving him with nothing but hookers and a football to lay-up with every night.

He says, "A couple months, Angel ... you wanted to leave me for the last couple months ... well try years ... try wanting to leave a person for the last couple years. That's where I am with you."

I swallow those words, words rushing down my throat like cannonballs. But instead of firing them back, I say, "So why the heck are you still here? Why haven't your tired butt left?"

"That's the point, Angel. I can't leave. Can't leave the woman you love ... can't run from your own heart."

A year ago I would've fell to my knees from hearing those words. But with another birthday, I'm now older, a little wiser, and strong enough to tell him, "I don't believe you?"

"Huh?"

"You don't really love me, Kevin."

"You crazy? You have the audacity to tell me that I don't love you. Woman, I traveled the globe just to be with you."

"What are you talking about?"

"Why else would I accept a scholarship to Albany State when FSU was offering me a full ride?"

                    Cyril Gillion

"You told me that Albany was one of the top colleges on your list."

"I only said that because you were going to NYU. I would've said anything to keep us together."

I stand my ground; tell him, "I'm not buying that. If you love me so much, you wouldn't continuously cut me off at the ankles when I try to get involved."

"Involved with what?"

"The football practices that I can never attend. The games on the road. Or even greater, how come every time we go out, we have to go to these high-class uppity restaurants, places where you know you'll never run into other players or other women that be all up in the crack of your butt? Huh? Is that some type of football code or something? To have a woman but only in secrecy. Hell, even your frat brother was surprised to know you had a woman."

He acts as if he's oblivious to these allegations; gives the stare of an innocent convict in a courtroom.

Then he shakes his head in dismay. "Is that what you really think, Angel?"

"That is what I know."

"Well since you know everything, know that I brought you here for a reason."

"And what reason is that? To constantly bitch about an uncooked steak!"

Rage set in his eyes as he realizes how much are relationship is on the rocks, and as that loose cannon explodes within him, he slams the fork on top of the dinner plate. "The hell with this, Angel! I was gonna wait till later but I guess I have to show you now. Guess I have to show you how much I really care!"

Drawing much attention to the both of us, he rises from his seat, slings the chair from the dinner table to free up some space, then he reaches into his coat to pull out a tiny black box that's outlined in gold trimming with a ribbon on top.

"What are you doing?" I asked.

"I'm doing what I should've done a long time ago."

He gets on his knees, face flushed, and I look around while he grabs the attention of the entire restaurant.

"Get up," I whispered. "Get up from off your knees."

"No, Angel. You want seriousness. I'll show you seriousness."

He flips open the little black box, reveals a rock-diamond so grand to where you would've thought it was carved from Mt. Everest.

Radiating like electricity on ice, the diamond forced others to gather around for a closer visual, pulling them in like a cyclone affect.

Voltage runs through my heart as I whisper, "Kevin ... Kevin please get up ... this ... this isn't the time."

"This is the perfect time, Angel. And I don't care how many people are looking. I'm gonna show you how serious I really am this time!"

Afraid of what's about to happen next, I tell him, "Don't do it, Kevin. Don't do it."

"Do it!" screamed some guy in the restaurant. "Go 'head and do it!"

I closed my eyes to wish this wasn't happening, and by the time I opened them up, the ring was already parallel to Kevin's chest, his eyes starting to water.

We're now surrounded.

Waiters and waitresses are hovering over our necks, and one of the waitresses is carrying a cake in her hands, all smiles, looks like she had intentions of singing me happy birthday until Kevin stole the show.

Kevin puts the icing on the cake and mutters, "Marry me, Angel ... Please baby ... make me the happiest man alive and marry me."

He grabbed my hand tightly, tears welting in his eyes, put me in a *no breathing zone* as he waited for a response.

He cries.

I'm at the verge of crying.

I try to hold back the tears. Try to fight back. But a tear slips down my cheek, leading a path for others to follow.

He'd finally said those words; words that some women go a lifetime waiting to hear are words that I want to escape right now.

I was in the hot seat. The electric chair. Feels like I'm sitting in a pile of ants.

Not knowing what to say, my speech starts to slur, and my words drift out as, "What. Should. I. Say?"

"Say yes, baby. Just say yes," he replied.

"Say yes!" screamed a bystander. "Yes!" screamed another.

But I couldn't say yes. Couldn't say no either. Both words had their own mishaps. Both could cause calamity in ways that I've yet to phantom. Nevertheless, time was ticking and I had to say something. Had to say something while inquiring ears were waiting to hear.

"FOR CHRIST'S SAKE! JUST SAY YES!" someone screamed again.

     Cyril Gillion

I turn back to Kevin. Tears flowing down his cheeks. The word *yes* blending in with the sweat that leaked from his pores.
"Sorry Kevin but I just can't do it … not tonight."

3

It's been nine months since the night with Kevin. Nine months since I refused the immense diamond that would've curled perfectly around my finger.

I'd relocated again. I was now living in Brooklyn, New York; the bottom portion of the melting pot.

Kevin and I haven't talked since that night. Neither party was ever brave enough to even pick up the phone. Word has it that he got selected in the NFL draft, but then again, if he did get selected, I'm sure his egotistic ass would've called to brag about it by now.

Although I could care less about ever seeing him again, it still didn't stop me from getting depressed every once and awhile, and between getting over him, working a dead-end job, and trying to balance school, I somehow developed a drinking habit that was out of this world. What a coincidence?

On top of that, I was still having the endless nightmares of my stepfather, the same nightmare that existed for the last eighteen years. Thinking that time would cause these nightmares to lessen, they'd actually worsened to the second power, and now they were so bad to where I even purchased a pistol, no intention on using it, just needed one near me in order to sleep peacefully at night.

 Cyril Gillion

People often wondered why I never sought counseling. Why I never let therapists instruct me on how to handle these issues; put the past behind me.

I say what for?

Why waste my time and energy on some textbook scholar, just so they could tell me something I already know, resulting in thousands of dollars that'll be missing from my pockets? Never saw the point.

As I settled into my living room, I checked my caller id. There were fourteen missed calls. One was from my professor and the other thirteen was from an unknown number.

I checked my voicemail as well. Thirteen messages:

"Bitch, why haven't you called me back … oh what bitch, you take your ass all the way to New York, go to your little brainiac school and forget about your girl … you damn disloyal bitch!"

I knew that voice from anywhere. That was the voice of Cuqui, my best friend that was always leaving crazy messages. I deleted the message and played the next, but this time the person was laughing and lots of static was in the background:

"Bitch, I'm leaving this message just incase in case you didn't get the last one … you're still a disloyal bitch … I've gotta give you the 411 on something … I guess the only way to reach you is to call from an unknown number, so when you get this message, call me back. It's Cuqui … and one more thing before I forget … bitch you better—"

The call ends.

I chuckled as I got in the shower to freshen up.

Cuqui has been my best friend since third grade, so good of friends to where we often thought we were related by blood. Her name was pronounced the same as the cookie you eat, only spelled differently. The name comes from her Spanish father, but considering that she's one of the blackest women in Miami, who knows if that was her real father or not.

She was shorter than me. More proportioned. A woman that often wore her hair as a natural. With a tenth grade education, Cuqui never graduated. She dropped out of school to pursue her career in cosmetology; *costoligy* is what she would call it because she could never pronounce the word. When we were little, she stuck by me through everything. From lying to authority to middle school fights, she was there. And even if I was winning, she'd help me stomp the girl that I was beating.

Cuqui was no stranger to family quandaries herself. As a twelve-year-old she stabbed her uncle for trying to molest her, damn near caused a family affair with her aunts and uncles. She's been shipped from relative to relative ever since, seeking someone who'd be able to handle her rage. The continuous moving allowed her to see things the average girl didn't see, and although she was never a killer in the classroom, her street savvy could get her more than some women with a PHD.

Personality wise, Cuqui and I were like oil and vinegar, totally different but a perfect blend.

We had the same drive but different ambitions. While the pursuance of school led me up here, Cuqui was working on getting her own beauty shop in Miami. I'd constantly ask her to move here with me but she often refused, told me that Miami would always be her only home and the only way to pull her away was to literally tie her up and put her to sleep.

Looking at New York make me dread the fact of ever going back to Miami. I haven't been in a year. Not that I didn't want to. Just didn't have the time. Last time I went it seemed like the same people were up to the same tricks, the same shit but a different toilet. Everyone was either getting pregnant and working at Burger King, or working at Burger King and getting pregnant. Every now and then I mentally travel back to that epoch of me being a little pimple-faced girl with big hair bows, playing in the streets of Miami. But the more I reside in that dream, the more I see the cries of my mother and then my deliriums finally become a reality. No more could I stomach that place; a place where I shed more tears than smiles. Therefore, I had to get away. Far away. And separating myself from that place was a strategy that took years to execute.

But with every step forward lies a stumbling block.

My stumbling block was getting used to Brooklyn; a place that was different from Miami, much different from the condo that I used to share with Kevin in Manhattan.

As a woman in Brooklyn, I had to adapt quickly, had to learn the rules of this city. And first rule I learned was that everything in Brooklyn was centered around one word and one word only.

Hustle.

From adolescence to false teeth, everyone had some type of hustle, and it took me awhile to realize when I was the one that was getting hustled.

My first hustler was a Turkish man in a yellow cab, a face of total innocence. Like the true tourist I was, I'd jump in the cab, telling the cabbie to take me to my usual destinations. He'd total up the number

                                   Cyril Gillion

of miles I was traveling, factor in the cost per mile, and the moment I thought I was close to my destination, he'd take me on a ghost ride by strolling me through the same old spots. After fifteen minutes of going through a maze and fifteen more minutes of luring me into a taxicab confession story, he'd end up dropping my ass off around the block from where I initially started, smirking and pointing to the meter that read $18.50.

Something told me to bite the bullet and get a car, but that was worst than walking. The driving in this city was so bad to where you would've thought there was a buy-one-get-one-free-deal on driver licenses. Brooklyn is the only place where a person will park their car in the middle of an intersection, exit the car, leave the keys in the ignition, flip the bird at the cars behind them, and skip across the street to go on a talking spree with a friend or foe.

Because of the chaotic atmosphere, I started to become a homebody, but being at home was just as worst. My apartment complex was Brooklyn Estates, far from the estate that I pictured. Here, I was paying $900 dollars a month for a place with no installation, ceiling fans that couldn't blowup a balloon and walls thin enough to hear someone snoring. Not to mention the proprietor lied to me about the interior design. Over the phone, he told me that the place was top of the line, completely furnished. Blown away, I was completely ready to lounge in the apartment of reverie. But the moment I entered the vicinity, it was obvious that I got hustled like never before, because the only thing that was completely furnished were the walls. Walls furnished in lots of dirt that took days for me to scrub.

After getting out the shower, I wrapped a towel around my waist and opened the window blinds of my apartment. While looking out in New York City, I saw the old man, Mr. Rutherford, staring at me from across the hall, eager to catch a glimpse of my bare breasts.

I closed the blinds back shut.

Mr. Rutherford had to be at least eighty years old, and the pervert must've been craving for some younger women because he'd always wait until his wife went to sleep before getting the nerve to be a peeping Tom. I used to get very angry. Even went as far as calling the police for sexual harassment, but when the cops recognized my physical address as being in one of the worst parts of Brooklyn, their only response was, "Lock your doors and try to keep your windows closed."

The Other Side of the Pillow

He was one of the crazy people that lived around me. Truth of the matter is, everyone living in these apartments was some type of crazy, and if not crazy, then outrageously ghetto.

My neighbors were a perfect example of what ghetto was all about. They were a mixed couple that needed some serious patching up. It was a young black woman, Mona, and an older white guy named Pete. Besides Mr. Rutherford, Pete was the only white guy living in Brooklyn Estates, but because he was dating a woman as beautiful as Mona, he was highly respected. On the other hand, Mona was as gullible as they come, a chick that'll believe anything you tell her. Every night she'd come knocking on my door at one in the morning, asking to borrow a spatula. There's no telling what type of kinky stuff that her and Pete was doing with that spatula, but I know she wasn't flipping no damn pancakes with it for certain. She'd always ask me for it right after using me for some advice on her cheating ass boyfriend. She wanted to leave him, just never had the courage. I'd often come to her apartment, sit down with her and indirectly tell her how stupid she was for letting a good-for-nothing man like Pete use her. Every time we talked, we'd rehearse our lines of how she could step out the relationship. I would pretend as if I was Pete who was coming home from work, and she'd practice her alibi for leaving. After our rehearsals, I thought she would be eager to send him packing, and I was proud of myself because I thought I'd given her a backbone, thought I put so much fire in her ass to where she could've shitted brimstone.

But one woman's insight is another woman's ignorance.

In this case, that ignorant woman was Mona. And the ignorance showed the moment I left her apartment, because soon as Pete came home, Mona would transform from a tough Sistah Souljah to a no backboned having little girl. And the white guy must've been hung like a horse, because in only a thirty-minute span, she was back at my house, smiling like the sun, asking to borrow another spatula.

In spite of everything, I still kept her in my circle of associates. After all, she got me my first gig in the city; put me down with a job that totally contracted my character, but still a job.

I was a phone sex operator. That's right. A student by today – call girl by night – one of those women that men talk to at the wee-wee hours of the morning, thinking they're speaking with Janet Jackson, but the realism is that a man or woman could be sitting behind that curtain.

My place of work was called Club Ding-a-ling.

                    Cyril Gillion

It was the top call center in Brooklyn, the melting pot of unadulterated phone sex, and for the men that were calling, it was by far the most expensive.

Like any college student, I hated my job. And like any student I needed money to not only pay classes, but also pay bills. At Club Ding-a-ling, I worked off commission, every dollar based on your average talk-time. The test was to see how long you could keep a man on the phone without making him climax too quickly, or as Mona would say, 'Who was the best at burning a man's orgasm.'

My call girl name was Angelic Puss, a name crowned to me by the other girls who worked there. They said it symbolized a combination of innocence and wickedness, sort of like an angel in a devil's dress. I despised the name at first, but after seeing how much of an ear-catcher it became to the clients, I guess you can say it kind of stuck.

Some of the girls called me baby puss. Not because of my age, but mainly because they thought I had no clue about sex, except from what I heard through girl talk, and considering that Kevin was the only sex-partner I ever had, I was considered a virgin in their eyes. They knew about my goals, about me wanting to be a lawyer and all. I guess you can call them my sponsors because they pushed me to never quit school so I won't end up as a fulltime call girl for the rest of my life.

From working with the girls at Club Ding-a-ling, I learned more about men within this last month than I've learned in the last five years. Each man wanted to be stimulated, but each had their special tactics for getting off. Most of the men were nice, but every now and then you'd come across the guy who treats you like dirt, the guy who thinks your whole life consists of sitting behind a desk and attending to his sexual fantasies. The only way to keep my sanity was to remind myself that it was only a job, not an occupation, and in this realm of work, the job was always ninety percent mental, ten percent spoken words. Once that ninety percent drops to eighty, you're dead. Dignity lost forever.

I loaded up my laptop and checked my syllabus for an update on the course outline for one of my litigation classes. Just from viewing the class layout, I was instantly traumatized by countless assignments that were due for the semester. With a 1400 SAT score and a worthless medal that read Suma Cum Laude, I was under the impression that Law School would be as much a breeze as undergrad.

I was dead wrong.

Nonetheless, this last year at Brooklyn Law has been more challenging than I ever imagined, forced me to use more than ten percent of my cerebrum.

Tonight my assignment was a five-page paper that was just assigned yesterday, due tomorrow, a paper asking my views of the death penalty which I've yet to write.

Was I for the death penalty? Damn right I was. And anyone who ever witnessed a homicide would also agree.

Just like capital punishment, the laws of motion says that the only way to stop an eighteen-wheeler truck from speeding is to lineup another truck from the opposite direction, making sure it's driven with the exact same speed and velocity. If not, that eighteen-wheeler will keep on rolling, smashing the other truck on its ass, still terrorizing anything else that surfaces the road. Moreover, when it comes to murderers, imprisonment never stops a person from moving; it only decelerates their truck-like attitude. And what's the use of trying to slow down a criminal when you can stop them completely?

In the midst of my thought process, I heard loud knocking on my front door.

I checked the time. Eleven p.m. Too late to be opening my front door at this time of hour, especially in a place like Brooklyn.

With the slightest idea of who the person was, I asked the knocker for their name, but no one ever spoke out.

I proceeded back in my room to finish my paper, but before I could pick up the pen, I heard it again.

Knocking.

Loud enough to ricochet my eardrum this time around.

Still there was no answer. Neither was there a face through the peephole, only a circle of darkness.

Becoming extremely fed up, I threw off the chain lock, released the bolt lock, detached the bottom lock, flicked on the porch light, and before I slung the door wide open, rage caused me to yell, "You either better be the police or a butt naked Allen Iverson. Otherwise, get the hell off my—"

"Sorry, ma'am. We were just trying to sell some cookies."

To my surprise, the knockers were two little boys with big brown eyes.

I said, "I'm sorry children. What type of cookies you selling?"

"We're selling Girl Scout cookies."

"Girl Scout Cookies? Neither one of y'all are even girls."

They sighed. Then they dropped their heads to the floor.

      Cyril Gillion

Remorseful of my sudden actions, I calmed myself and said, "Okay, what kind of girl-scout cookies are you selling? Got any Samoas?"

"No ma'am. But we do have these peanut butter brittle cookies that I'm sure you'll enjoy. And we also have some almond crisp."

"Really?" I asked.

"Yes ma'am."

"Can I take a look at your merchandise?" I asked.

"Sure, ma'am. Help yourself."

Staring at their smiling faces, I instantly saw flashbacks of me and Cuqui, saw those days of us going door to door, we both trying to make a couple dollars to buy ourselves some pop sickles and rollups.

They were so little. So cute. Eyes that'll make a prisoner cry. And to top it off, they had perfect manners that I never possessed at their age. But in this neighborhood I had to remember that everyone was a potential hustler, including children.

Not giving into their smiley faces, I decided to give them a quick interrogation, had to make sure their hustle was legit and I wasn't been hoaxed.

I ask, "Are you boys in school?"

"Yes ma'am we are."

"What grade level?"

They hesitated. "We're in the 5th grade."

"Fifth grade. That's wonderful. And do you boys like school?"

"Yes ma'am."

"What's your favorite subject?"

"Lunch."

"Do you smoke?"

"No ma'am."

"Drink?"

"No ma'am."

"Who's the president?"

"Uuum ... Bush."

"What's the genetic make-up of the formula E=MC2 and who originated it?"

"Uuum…"

They carried looks of bewilderment, as if they wanted to strangle themselves for knocking on my door. But through the struggle, they never lost focus of their objective.

"So are you gonna buy any cookies?" the taller one asked.

"Sure."

"Great!" the other surmised.

I said, "Just tell me the price and I'll be all set."

They hesitated, said, "It's only $9.50."

"What did you say? Did I hear 9.50?"

"Yes ma'am," one consummated. "Just the low price of 9.50."

Thinking that they were trying to hustle me, I said, "Do I look stupid or something?"

"No ma'am."

"Do you see the words *Angel is stupid* written in bold letters across my forehead?"

"No ma'am."

"Do you smoke that fiery stuff?"

"No ma'am."

"Then why are you trying to hustle me?"

One was petrified as the other spoke lightly. "We're sorry, ma'am. We're just trying to raise money to go to Disney World."

"Disney World? I've already been there and trust me when I tell you that it's not what it appears to be; Mickey Mouse is much shorter in person."

Showing puppy faces that signaled pity, the boys sighed heavily. An unutterable remorse bloated my veins as their poignant eyes mirrored my hostility. I felt like trash. I bled internal guilt. I wanted to apologize a thousand times over.

"You boys have to forgive me," I told them. "I do realize that you're trying to do something positive and at least you're not out trying to rob someone. When I was your age, I used to do the same thing. So I have no right to get mad at the price that you're setting."

It was obvious that they could give a rat's ass about my childhood stories. There intentions were set out to make an extra buck. And how could I blame them? They were only fifth graders.

The shorter one asked, "So are you saying you're gonna buy some of our Girl Scout cookies?"

"No honey. But I have a better idea. How 'bout you keep the cookies and I'll give you both a tip so you can split the $9.50 for yourselves. That's $4.75 each."

"Are you for real, ma'am?"

"Yes I am. Just wait here a minute. Let me get my purse from the bedroom."

Ecstatic to do a good deed, I strolled into my bedroom to get my purse. While searching for money, I could hear the boys slapping hands as if they were already in Disney Land.

     Cyril Gillion

Then I heard whispering:

"Eh man, did you see what she was wearing ... that bitch ain't have on no clothes ... she got some big ass titties ... she was smiling at me ... yeah right nigga ... She was smiling at me ... nigga you must be dreaming ... how could she be smiling at you ... you're retarded ... I wanted to milk them titties right then and there ... if you weren't with me, I'd be spanking that ass tonight."

Terrorized of the constant chitchatting, I looked into the mirror and realized that I was only wearing a bra, wanted to kill myself for forgetting to put on a shirt.

I was beyond embarrassed.

Those little babies had seen my bare flesh. Ten-year-old kids that wasn't old enough to view pg13.

Scurrying to the dresser to snatch up the biggest t-shirt that I could find, I reached deep into the closet to grab a heavy trench coat from my high school years. I wiped the dust from it, buttoned it to the top, and held my breath as I presumed back to the front door, only to see the kids smiling as if I was their personal playground.

Flashing the money that I'd promised, I told them, "Now I want you boys to spend these nine dollars wisely. No candy or cookies."

"Don't worry, ma'am. We will."

I split up their nine dollars, divided the quarters. "That's $4.75 for you. And $4.75 for you. Now what do you boys say to Ms. Angel for being so nice?"

They looked at each other, gave little smirks, and then they looked back at me. "We say you fell for the oldest trick in the book. Stupid bitch!"

They laughed and ran down the stairway. I tried running after them but the sleeve of my coat got caught in the banister and all I could do is yell out profanity as they stuck-up their middle fingers from afar, running down the street.

That was the second time I got hustled around this area, yesterday by a drug addict and today by little children. But I guess that's Brooklyn altogether, a place where you either hustle or get hustled.

So I'll let them have their victory, at least for now.

But payback is a bitch. And I heard she bites hard.

$$\underline{4}$$

The next morning I awoke from a gruesome nightmare, pointing my gun towards an alarm clock that read 7 a.m.

I was late for class.

Not your average class, this was the class of Professor Stern, a professor who was just as strict as his name.

I jumped out the bed and made my shower a quickie, had to race against the faucet before the water got cold. Inside these apartments, I sometimes thought the meter had a mind of its own, because seconds after turning on the shower, it seems as if the hot water would take a break, quit its job, and tell the faucet to kiss its ass.

Dashing into my room for a towel, I quickly headed to the dresser to bra my babies from getting sick. These breasts have gotten bigger since me and Kevin split, and I was now at a point to where I was self-cautious about sporting them around. The constant chants of men yelling *Eh Red* had turned into *Eh you, the one with the big titties*, and now I hated my breasts so much to where I was thinking about getting a breast reduction. However, I couldn't afford to do that, at least not now. These breasts did a lot more than just sit-up and look cute. They've paid my rent. Put food on my table. Both has opened many wallets and maxed out credit cards galore.

My ass had gotten bigger as well, but it still didn't measure up to my top half. Within the last six months I began to get lucky, felt like

                          Cyril Gillion

I'd won the winning ticket of the ass lotto. The size three that I wore for so long was now up to a size seven, and after all those squats, I was finally able to wave farewell to the junior's section in JC Penny's, no longer afraid of heading into the gap and placing my hand on some apple-bottom jeans. That made me happy. To know that my white girl's ass had suddenly bridged the gap of sisterhood and those days of feeling like my breasts were laughing at my butt are long gone. I was finally starting to get what I wanted. To be proportioned. Finally able to see my breasts take my ass more seriously.

Grabbing all my belongings, I left to go to class.

Brooklyn University is fifteen minutes driving distance – ten if you're traveling the subway – but at this hour, you were looking at an even twenty.

A year in the books and I still feel like a little fish in a big pond, a southern bell that's yet to adjust to this fast paced life.

By the time I reached Smith Street, the multitude of people was beyond ballistic, bumper-to-bumper traffic but only on foot.

I was constantly getting hissed at by every man imaginable, a large tax bracket of men ranging from white-collar to blue-collar to blue-collar to no-collar. And no-collar was the guys in beat-up tank tops, street-corner-hang-out-guys that were prying for the next victim to hustle, preferably women.

Once arriving to class, I was twenty minutes late.

Professor Stern was in the middle of a lecture on globalization and procedure rights. I tried to make a beeline to my seat while his back was turned, but in the midst of speed walking, a voice told me, "Ms. Inghram. Stop right there."

I stood stationary, turned around. "Yes."

"Where are you going?"

"I'm going to … to sit down."

"Sit down?"

"Yes."

"And just where to do you plan on sitting? All of the seats are taken."

I look at the four empty seats in the back, but before I can state the obvious, he says, "Those seats are for the students who came on time. Unfortunately, I don't have any more seats for late students."

I wander if he's only jiving, but his facial expression is serious.

He tells me, "Get here on time and you can claim your seat. Until then, you must stand."

The Other Side of the Pillow

And like that, I have no choice but to stand in the back of the class, an example for other students to think twice about ever coming late. If I was a man I'd say he has me by the balls. But I'm a woman, an angry bitter woman at that. And right now, he has me by the tits.

Legs burning, a forty-minute class period felt like a lifetime.

After class was over, Professor Stern collected the assignments that were issued on capital punishment, and while I exited the classroom, I heard my name again, louder this time around.

Fear caused me to stop in my tracks, turn to face the general, and sure enough, Professor Stern was waiting for me at his desk, his arms folded.

He tells me, "Pull up a seat."

And that scares me even more. A seat means a drawn out conversation, a lecture, but I don't hesitate to do what Simon says.

I ask, "Is everything ok?"

"Why don't you tell me, Ms. Inghram? Is everything ok?"

Damned if I answer, I decided to plead the fifth.

He goes on. "I've been looking over your transcript."

"You have?"

"Yes, I have. And it appears that you've been amongst the top ten percentile since freshmen year in high school."

"Yeah … I mean yes … I was, wasn't I."

"Records show that you were not only a national merit, but you graduated Magna Cum Laude in undergrad."

"Just trying to build the portfolio," I said, thinking this conversation may actually turn for the best.

Professor Stern slouches back in his chair, legs crossed, and he runs his fingers across a shabby beard as his eyes go back and forth from the transcript to me.

Then he drops the transcript on his desk, his full attention now focused on me, his eyes dissecting my body language.

I wait for him to mention another one of my accomplishments, but instead of giving me that satisfaction, he says, "Let me ask you something, Ms. Inghram."

"Yes."

"In this class, would you consider yourself as one of the top ten percentile students?"

I hesitate with my answer. "Is that a trick question?"

"Do I look like the type of Professor who gives trick questions? Answer the question, Ms. Inghram. Either you are or aren't?"

       Cyril Gillion

His expression tells me that he wants an honest answer, but my conscience begs to differ.

I decided to tell him the truth anyhow. "I would."

"You would?"

"Yeah ... I ... I would certainly consider myself as one of the top ten percentile students in this class."

Reaching into his rolodex of graded papers, he flashes an assignment that I wrote last week, a paper asking my views about the judicial and legislative branch. The paper is notated as a failing grade, the letter "F" written as large as the American flag, and there are red marks spread throughout the entire paper, more bloody marks than that of a crime scene.

Professor Stern sits the paper on my lap, giving me a better visual of that crime scene.

He tells me, "What the hell is this?"

"It ... it looks like my paper."

"No, Inghram. It's crap. Crap that I won't tolerate from a student who claims to be in the top ten percentile." Then he grabs the paper that I wrote last night. "I tell you what I'm gonna do, Ms. Inghram. I'm gonna read this paper – the one about your feelings on capital punishment – and if I think the paper deserves a "B" or higher, I'll allow you to re-write that bull crap from last week. However, if this paper is as crappy as the last one, I recommend you drop this course why you still have the chance, because my assignments will only get tougher."

Getting clarity, I ask him, "Are you gonna read the paper right now?"

"Right here. Right now. Right so you can see it."

I swallow hard, look around for Ashton Kutcher because I must be getting punk'd, but as he reads my paper, I realize that this is not a joking matter – no Ashton Kutcher – and Professor Stern continues to look back-and-forth between me and the paper, multi-tasking between an undetermined score and my undetermined destiny.

I sit in silence; wait for the devil to finish playing with brimstone.

He reads and stares. Reads and stares. Reads and stares.

After reading, he stares at me some more, never speaking, watching me like an algebraic equation that's waiting to be formularized.

I swallow hard; give him the look of a student who's unaware of her fate.

Ten seconds pass and still no words.

I want to make the first move, want to ask him what he thinks about the paper, but I realize that this is a game of chess. Not checkers. And in the world of chess, patience is always a virtue.

He picks up the red pen of blood, writes a B+ on the paper, and tells me, "Good job, Inghram. You've got an 89%."

Calming my nerves, I start to breathe an untimely breath.

Professor Stern finally lets me leave, but before dismissing me, he hands me the paper that I had to re-write; tells me, "Are you considering taking the bar?"

"Haven't planned on it."

"Well plan on it. You've taken courses on contracts and torts, right?"

"Yes."

"Good. The MBE part of that exam is mostly made up of those two courses. Don't wait until the summer to take the test. If so, you'll fail. Better to take it now while the brain is still cooking."

I don't respond, only nod my head to pretend I'm listening. After the lecture, I walk to the door like I'm walking for my freedom.

Then I hear my name again, thunder at its darkest hour. "Inghram!"

"Yes."

"And before I forget, try getting to class on time for now on. Otherwise ..."

Cyril Gillion

_5_

Two hours later I had ditched the business suit, the professional dressed schoolgirl, started changing into some mid-thigh tights with a white halter-top.

Getting ready to conduct a different style of business, I was at a place where most women dare not to go, the gun range.

I've been coming here for a year. First introduced to it by a magazine in Books-a-Million, and I've been a victim ever since.

At first I was scared to come. Hell, its one thing to carry a gun, but firing is a different story. Takes a real woman to load up a clip and put an AK47 to use.

The gun range is this fifty-foot combusted place that sits isolated. A pool hall lies to the right and a Catholic Church is a block down the road. People would get up on Sunday mornings, go worship and pray to their Gods, then come to the gun range to shoot at their leisure.

But one person's leisure is another person's salvation.

Some people go to an altar for their salvation. Some go to therapists. Some go to priests.

I come here.

Not only was the gun range a place where I could clear my mind, but it was my place of revision. My temple. And like all temples, all places where humans come to lay their transgressions, I'd bring my troubles here every Sunday, bring that huge bag of burdens that is soon emptied into a two-inch clip and pushed by a trigger.

Every week I brought a different goal, a stronger will to compete. Six months ago that competition consisted of a hundred gunslingers that were all working towards a common goal, a goal of who could win first place for being the best shooter.

I came in tenth place. Six months before that I came in twentieth. This year I'll surely finish as a finalist.

But today's competition was not against others, but more so against myself. The test was how many times I could accurately hit a male manikin at three different pressure points before the timer sounded, and for the past two months, I've been trying to beat my own record, twenty-four landed shots in two minutes.

In total, there are nine different shooting blocks, four-feet apart. Between each block is a berm to restrict bullets to a specific area. Inside those blocks lies a headset that is used to lessen the sound of the exploding bullets. Most people wear those headsets. Guess they prefer not to hear that sound of death. Unlike them, I never wear it. Never felt it was necessary.

Prepared to kill, I stood in front of my favorite block – block number four – right in front of the bulletproof window where people often restocked on ammunition.

I locked eyes with the male manikin that was a hundred feet in front of me. When I first started that same manikin was only a fifty feet – the distance for most beginners – but now I'd doubled that distance, quadrupled my determination to put as many bullets in him as possible.

I picked up the gun, a chrome semi-automatic that had two chambers of death. Each chamber holds approximately five bullets, and after each shot attempt, the gun has to be re-cocked in order to continuously do its damage. I had forty bullets total, ten bullets resting in both chambers while the other twenty waited to be reloaded. I set the timer at two minutes, put both hands on the gun, and stood in my shooter's stand as I waited for the clock to move towards the twelve.

The timer sounded.

Ten shots are aimed at the head of the manikin, the first pressure point. I have perfect form. My legs are bent, shoulders arched, but I only manage to land four of those ten shots, the other six missing so badly to where you would've thought I was a beginner. That's always been my weakness. I'm a sluggish starter. Never been able to jump out the blocks, but always capable of finishing strong.

                    Cyril Gillion

I continue to cock the chamber as I fire another eight shots, and that is where I usually start to feel it. Three of those shots land accurately. Two do a royal flush to the cranium. One flies north. The other south. One barely makes its mark.

I fire two more. Still don't connect. Miss badly. And I'm now in the hole, one minute left on the clock, have to land fifteen more bullets in order to shatter my record that seemed damn near impossible to break.

My next five shots are perfect, but time becomes relentless and those fifty seconds has turned to forty-five, forty-five turns to forty, forty chases the neck of thirty-five, thirty-five to thirty; time is tossing the baton to time.

I reload, cock back the chamber, land my first shot at his right nut, my second shot at the other, but the third one goes off the beaker, and that causes me to become more ruthless, more furious, and most of all, more careful.

I take another shot, capitalized on the fourth attempt, nearly blew the dick off the manikin.

I shoot and shoot and shoot. With every shot, I get meaner and meaner. Show no mercy. Shoot as if I have a chip on my shoulder, a female gladiator on a conquest to take all.

Each shot takes me into a higher rhythm, an unreachable peak, and the adrenaline runs through me like Marion Jones down the stretch of a hundred meter race.

The gun gods are on my side.

There's one bullet left in the chamber, five seconds remaining from that inconsiderate, son-of-a-bitch called, Time.

I hold for those last five seconds. Tighten my grip. Take my time and look into the eyes of the manikin – those eyes of my stepfather – and as I am the pistol, I hear my mother screaming her heart out, *"Put the gun down, Angel. Put it down!"*

Eighteen years later, those words are still daggers to my heart, bullets to my soul. But now, after eighteen years of soul searching, I'm finally strong enough to release the little ammo that's left in this chamber of death.

I fired at the manikin. Looked at the clock.

Another record broken.

<u>6</u>

**Later that night I had to work the graveyard shift at my part time job,
Club Ding-a-ling.**

I was more than a half-hour late and all I heard when stepping
through the door was, "You're late!"

That was the voice of Dexter, my boss. He was one of those
bosses that didn't care what came out his mouth and if you dared to
talk back, he'd threaten to fire you at any given moment.

Dexter was a heavyset man. Middle aged. A bald spot in the
center of his head with a large tattoo on his arm that read, *My world.
My nut.*

As mean as Dexter was, he was also just as lenient. Took me a
minute to realize that his hard demeanor was nothing more than a hard
shell on the outside but jelly in the middle. Within my short period of
working there, I'd already become one of his favorite girls, and our
conversations would often go far outside the work place, talking about
everything from the death of my mother to the death of his daughter.

He monitored all of our calls. Mines especially. He'd even bring
me into his office in between calls, just to tell me how much I'd
progressed.

"Angel!" he yelled. "I've got three calls waiting for you in queue.
Hurry up and get your ass on the phone."

"I'm not in the mood for your BS today."

"I don't care what type of mood you're in. Menstrual cycle or no menstrual cycle, you're now on my watch. And on my watch, you either get down to business or go home."

Behind me sat an older woman named Vicki. She was the veteran of the group. The mother of the PSO's. She taught me the ropes on what to say to most of the callers and how to draw the line between persuasion and being overly provocative.

Everything around here was a competition. Who could get the highest talk time? Who could get the most red-light specials? Who was the best impersonator? It was competition that caused much drama, especially considering that your hourly wage fluctuated every week.

"Baby girl!" Vicki said. "You plan on picking up your line or what? Two calls have been waiting in the queue for three minutes."

I picked up line 6. A guy named Tom Bonniker was calling from Ohio, Texas.

Transforming into my sexy PSO voice, I uttered, "You've reached the gorgeous Angelic Puss and if your name is Tom, I'm waiting to do some incredible things."

"Is this Angelic Puss?"

"Of course baby ... who else?"

Tom was one of my regulars. A married man who hates the fact that his wife is never around.

He says, "I've missed you so much, Angelic Puss. I've been trying to reach you earlier, but I kept getting that other girl named Peaches."

"Don't worry baby. I'm here now. Are you on a cell phone?"

"Why'd you ask?"

"Because a phone cord is only going to interfere with what I have in store for you."

"And what is that?"

"Tonight, I'm going to do whatever your wife doesn't do."

He hesitates and begins with, "What about head. My wife refuses to give me head anymore."

"What? What type of wife is that?"

"I know I know. It's like she never has any time. She's always working at that damn hospital."

"Is that so?"

"Yes, and when she is here, it's like she never wants sex. I don't know if she's screwing the doctor or what, but I'm losing my mind."

Tom likes it when I'm aggressive, so I tell him, "Guess we're gonna have to teach your wife a little lesson … so ease off those little shorts big boy."

"They're already off."

"Already?"

"Yes."

"It's yes ma'am to you."

"Yes ma'am."

"Now I want you to go into the bedroom and get one of the lotion bottles that your wife has on the shelf."

He hesitates, says, "Which one? Jergens or soft skin?"

"Jergens."

"Got it."

"Now dump out the contents."

"What?"

"Dump out the contents in the lotion bottle."

"Uuum … I don't think that's a good idea."

"Tony?"

"Yes."

"Do you want this oral pleasure or not?"

"I do."

"Then don't stall me baby. Angelic Puss never likes to be stalled."

"I'm not trying to stall you. It's just that the bottle has yet to be opened. My wife will be very upset if she comes home and notice that I've tampered with her things."

"Tom, who wears the pants in your household? You or your wife?"

"I do."

"Could've fooled the hell out of me. Do you bring home the bacon?"

"Yes."

"Put food on the table?"

"Yes."

"Buy toilet tissue when more is needed?"

"Yes."

"Then open that damn lotion bottle and dump out those contents!"

He doesn't reply, but I do hear him moving around like an addict on speed, rushing to live-out his oral fantasy.

Meanwhile, lines 7 and 15 were ringing off the hook and some callers were waiting in queue for five minutes or more.

Tom said, "Angelic Puss. I've emptied the bottle. Now what?"

"Slowly slide that shaft in these jaws of paradise. But be gentle. These jaws are just like the lotion bottle … tight … not wide enough for your pickle."

"Do you really think I have a pickle?"

"Yes baby. Thicker than Kosher."

He squirms.

I ask him, "Can I call you Mr. Kosher?"

"Yes."

"Yes ma'am!"

"Yes ma'am."

Pretending to intake his shaft, I started making exotic noises, lots of grunting, personifying those sinful sounds while I threw up internally.

Mr. Dexter was monitoring my call from his office, giving me a thumbs-up. From the way he was smiling, you would've thought I was a black Monica Lewinsky, queen of fellatio.

I tried to smile. Tried to take his thumps-up as a compliment, but who wants to be complimented on doing a good blowjob.

In the midst of my sloppy slurping, I heard a voice appear on the line, a voice that interrupted the foreplay between me and the caller, Tom Bonniker.

Tom, are you nuts! Hang up that phone and get your little pecker out of my Jergens bottle right now!"

"Baby, I was only trying to——"

"Are you on the phone with those sex women?"

"No."

"You're lying Tom."

"I'm not lying."

"Yes you are you little bastard. What I told you about those little slimy sluts. All they wanna do is get your money and—"

Click.

I could do nothing but laugh. Then I glanced at my talk-time for that call. 14.06 minutes. Not bad but could be much better.

I picked up line 15, grabbed a call that was waiting in queue for twelve minutes. Atlanta, Georgia.

My voice goes back to its original tone. "I've been waiting all day for a manly voice to appear on the line. Please tell me that this is him."

The caller says, "My name is Pensy."

"Penis?"

He chuckles. "No, Pensy."

"Okay Mr. Pensy. Well tonight you are, *Mr. Penis*. And what is it that you're looking for tonight?"

"I'm looking for a plus size woman. A woman that's big in all the right places."

"How big do you like 'em?"

"Extremely big. Sumo wrestler type big."

"Well Mr. Penis. Guess tonight is your lucky night because you found that sumo woman, all 320 pounds worth of pure flesh."

Wanting to get a visual of the caller, I asked, "And what about you? Are you my sumo wrestler type of man?"

"Actually, I'm a thin guy."

"Thin?"

"Yeah, one hundred and forty pounds."

"And you like big women?"

"Love 'em. Don't think I've ever been with a skinny woman in my entire life."

"Sounds like fun. The thinner the man the thicker the package."

He's smiling. I can tell he's smiling. And as the floodgates open, he asks, "So how big are those breasts of yours?"

"Big enough."

"And how big is big enough?"

"Big enough to burp you," I replied in an orgasmic voice.

He becomes more courageous and says, "I wish I was there right now ... I'll show you how those breasts are supposed to be handled."

"Would you handle them with care?"

"Tender loving care."

"Show me."

"Show you?"

"Show me how you'll handle these melons. Talk is cheap."

Journeying that flight of imagination, he hisses through the receiver; a bad version of what he thought was erotica. In the midst of his lewd conduct, Cammy and Tasha were laughing behind my back, both trying to listen in.

Cammy said, "Babygirl, put him on speaker phone."

"Okay," I replied, readjusting my headset.

The caller said, "Angelic Puss?"

"Yes."

"You still there?"

"Not going anywhere, baby."

"Good, because I wanna try something new."

"Anything you want."

 Cyril Gillion

"Can we do anal?"

"Excuse me?"

"Anal. I wanna try anal."

"Okay, but just so you know, no man has ever broke that seal. But I guess you can be the first."

He tells me, "No, I don't want to give you anal. I want you to give it to me."

"Excuse me?"

"Been a while since I've received it and my wife isn't up for experimenting."

His comment tears up my stomach, makes me wish I would've kept my job at Save-a-lot.

Speechless of how to respond, I decided to mute the caller for a quick moment. To me, this whole thing is sickening, but it's entertainment for the women around me, my co-workers that are listening in. They can tell that I'm nervous; it's written all over my face. And above all, I think that's what amused them most.

Tasha eventually pulls me out the rabbit hole and decides to give me some help with the call. "Ask him if he got the KY jelly," she said.

"Do you have the KY?"

"No. I don't like lubricant," he replied.

"Really," I said, looking at Tasha for more help. "Well how do you like it?"

"I like it ruff. Want you to pound me very very hard."

Laughter resumed amongst the other girls as they had a party in the background.

One of the girls said, "Tell him to get on his knees and prepare for the talliwacker."

"What?" I replied, muting the caller again. "What the hell is a talliwacker?"

"Girl just say it!"

I clear my throat, hesitate, and in my best voice, I tell him, "Get on your knees and prepare for the ta … lli … wacker."

He says, "I'm already on my knees."

"You are?"

"Been there the whole entire time." He hesitates and asks, "What type of strap-on are you wearing?"

"Huh?"

"Your strap on? Describe it."

Tell him that it's black.

"Shhhhhhh. Quiet down. He can hear y'all."

The Other Side of the Pillow

Tell him that you have a nine inch jelly penis.

Naw girl. Try saying curved. Tell him that your thing is thick and curved.

"Shhhhhhh. I got this."

I bring the mouthpiece closer to my lips, spectators watching my every move.

I tell him, "I have a sexy looking rod and it's very very moist."

My girls laugh. *Bitch, are you crazy? What type of penis is that?*

The caller asks, "Does it have veins?"

"Yes baby … are you ready for me to put it in?"

"I'm ready."

"You sure?"

"Yes."

"Tell me with some conviction. Convince me that you want this rod of plastic."

"I'm ready I'm ready I'm ready!"

"Okay then. Here goes the—"

Click.

That was the finger of my boss, Dexter, disconnecting the call, spoiling the party.

He rants, "What the hell is going on out here?"

"Nothing," Tasha said as the girls continue to laugh. We're just showing Angel the ropes. That's all."

"Well while y'all are showing Angel the ropes, I have other clients waiting in queue. Now get those asses back on the phone."

Just like that we all got back to work.

I took about four more calls the remainder of the night. Three of them were calls that were well over a half-hour, boosted my average talk-time up to 15. 5 minutes.

This was my part-time job. My school outside of school. My second life.

7

After hours, I found myself catching the subway home alone, something I never usually do.

I made a detour. Instead of going straight home, I caught the subway downtown – no intention of partying – just wanted to stroll through the nightlife, and considering that there was no class in the morning, I was also looking for the nearest liquor store to grab a bottle of greygoose.

Once reaching downtown, cars flooded the streets like it was five o'clock rush hour traffic. Bright lights were beaming everywhere I turned, seemed like Christmas fell onto the lap of November.

People of all races had packed the streets. Some going into clubs. Some hanging on benches. Shish kabobs being sold on sidewalks. Some dancing. Others rapping. Ministering. Skateboarding. Everyone performing their own hustle to earn an extra buck at two in the morning.

I made one wrong turn and I was on Saxon Blvd, a street darker than midnight.

It didn't take long for me to realize that I'd suddenly stumbled into the ghetto, dumped into the loophole of danger.

The only people walking were drunks and crack attics and I guess I fell into that category as well, because I was this close from turning around until I saw that liquor store; figured I'd come to far to turn my back on the bottle of greygoose.

Standing in the liquor store were two men. Both black. One wore his hair in a ponytail, the other in braids.

They had brown bags in their hands; both were drinking liquor in the liquor store, even though the sign clearly says, *No food or drinks inside*, and the cashier – a short elderly Indian man – didn't seem to mind their rudeness, or maybe he was just too terrified of sending them back outside. Huddled in front of some bottles of dark liquor, they posted up as if they were protecting their favorite drinks.

Something told me to just forget about the greygoose and walk out the door, but before I could turn my glare, the guy with the braids had already marked me as his territory, and he started staring me down like an undiscovered diamond in the desert.

He carried a liquor aroma. Baggy jeans. Doo rag. Wife beater shirt. Owned a straggly pair of sneakers that were beat-up and half laced, used to say Nike before the *N* got torn off.

I turned my eyes elsewhere, started running my fingers through some Vodka and Jamaican rum.

"Eh lil' mama?" he asked, coming over in my direction. "What you drinking tonight?"

"Excuse me?"

"I asked what you drinking?"

I ignore the question; continue to look for my favorite bottle of alcohol.

The greygoose sat on the third shelf, two remaining bottles that were stacked on top of some Courvoisier, bottles too high for my reaching. As I struggle to grab one of the bottles, he grabs it first and tells me, "Reaching for this?"

"In fact I am. "Mind letting me have it?"

"Mind telling me your name?"

"Never mind. Go 'head and keep that bottle for yourself." I reach for another bottle, but he grabs that one too. "Look here!" I snapped. "I'm not in the mood to be screwing around with some nigga about a bottle of liquor. So if you're not gonna pay for that bottle, I suggest you give it up."

"Damn shawty. All I asked was your name."

"The hell with that chick," his friend said from afar. "Give her back the drink so she can go 'bout her business."

Trying to get out of there as quickly as possible, I paid for the drink and told the cashier to keep the change.

 Cyril Gillion

After my departure, relief settled within me, but fear still lurked around that corner. I strutted 162nd Avenue as quickly as possible, walked that road like the street was my competitor. I did everything possible to take my attention from what was going on around me. The drug dealers. Addicts begging for money. Pimps yelling from afar. Some trying to bait me. Others being downright ruthless; everyone acting as if I was their next masterpiece in disguise, their night walking mistress.

A car sped up beside me and stopped on breaks. Tinted windows. Bright beamers.

I tried to walk faster, but before I could put these little feet in motion, a tall muscular man grabbed me by the shoulder and raised what looks to be a gun towards my chest.

My brain goes into relapse.

"Get in the damn car!" he yelled. "Get your ass in the car!"

I couldn't move. Couldn't think. Attempted to run, but couldn't think.

Never loosing focus of his visual, he glances over his shoulder as if he's watching for possible bystanders. He yells, "Are you deaf, bitch? Didn't I tell you to get in the car?"

I try to hand over my purse. "Here! All the money that you want is inside."

"What?"

"My purse … my purse … take it!"

My comments anger him more, and the gun quickly goes from being pointed towards my chest, now pointed towards my neck, now towards my mouth, now down my throat.

"This is your last time, bitch! Get in the car!"

I waste no time crawling into his passenger seat, a cold seat of dark leather. Checkerboard design. Evil squares with wicked intentions.

He slams the driver-side door, smashes that shielded glass within me, leaves my soul broken into little pieces while he speeds down Saxon Blvd.

Anxiety rushes down the back of my halter-top, hijacks my feelings, infiltrates my thoughts.

It's silent in his death-mobile; the only sound lurking is the air-conditioner that's chilling my bones.

He drives fast. Drives recklessly. Drives like he's driving me to an unmarked cemetery.

Shit. That is the only word that comes to my brain, a word spiraling so fast to where my breathing quickens, each breath trying to outrun my lungs that are in desperate need for an asthma inhaler – and my respiratory system has now become its own administrator; a system that is no longer regulated by heartbeat but now by turbulent terror.

I crawled up against the door. Hugged the window like it's the last thing I'd ever set hold to, and if I could, I'd cover that window with bold letters of, **HELP. PLEASE HELP**.

"Put on your seat belt!" he demands. "I don't need anyone dying on my watch."

I buckle up but sit there confused, wandering why a person would kidnap someone but still force them to abide by road rules.

Fear causes me to glance at him from the corner of my eyes; watch him as he place the wrapped gun beneath the seat.

Gambling with words of death, I ask, "Where are you taking me?"

He doesn't answer, leaves me wandering whether I'd have a watery grave or a burial of ashes sealed in a jar.

I have a smorgasbord of questions but I dare not speak again, couldn't get my lips to tremble if the jackpot was waiting for me in the trunk.

Through the shadows, I can't make-out the kidnapper's face, but I do catch a glimpse of his wardrobe. He's wearing a brown-collar shirt. Black dress slacks. Black hard bottom shoes.

Gospel music plays in the background. Kirk Franklin. And I'm now confused more than ever. Don't know if he just came from a church function or if he's getting ready to plead God's forgiveness before determining my fate.

The kidnapper speaks. "Where do you live?"

"Huh?"

"Your place of residence. Where is it?"

"You kidnapped me to take me home?"

"Just tell me darnit!"

"112th and Brookeville. Blue apartments. Two blocks up from the police station that sits on the corner. A block down from Shoneys. A Citgo gas station across the street where you can drop me off."

Minutes pass. No words.

Just when I'm starting to breathe again, he gives a light chuckle, and I'm right back on pins and needles, have no idea what he's laughing about. Don't want to know. Don't want to ask.

He says, "No need to be afraid. I'm not going to hurt you."

My conscience tells me that he could possibly be telling the truth, that I should relax and let down my guard, but my sub conscience overshadows that notion and refuses to let me step out of that armor just yet.

He says, "Seriously, you need to relax. I only want to get you home safely."

I ask the stranger, "Am I missing something?"

"What do you mean?"

"Five minutes ago you had a gun to my head, forcing me into your car. Now all of a sudden, you want to do a good deed by taking me home."

"If you think I wanted to kidnap you, then you're sadly mistaken."

"Then what would you call it?"

"I saved you from getting robbed."

"Excuse me?" I asked, looking at him like the crazy kidnapper he was.

"While you were walking, I saw two men trying to sneak up behind you. They both were anticipating on snatching your purse."

"How do you know?"

"Because I shined the light on them while I was driving up. Good thing I took this road tonight, because had I went down Bloomingdale, only God knows what could've happened to you back there."

My mind tells me a million things.

I try to convince myself that this is only a nightmare, that I did my usual and went home with Mona after work, that I never caught the subway and took a trip downtown, that I never went to the liquor store and walked that dark road, that I never was forced into this man's ride by gunpoint, that we're not really exchanging words at the moment, and this whole ordeal is just a figment of my imagination, a continuous nightmare that'll soon be over.

I ask him, "Why should I believe you?"

"Because you're not dead."

"I'm not dead yet."

"Trust me lady, if I really wanted to kill you, you'll be close to peeing in your pants." He gives another bone chilling laugh while I ask, "If someone was really about to rob me, then why'd it take you so long to say it? I mean, what type of deranged psycho pulls a gun on someone to save them from danger?"

"Pretending to kidnap you was the only way to get you into the car."

"But what if you had screwed up and shot me for real?"

"I wouldn't have."

"How do you know?"

"The gun wasn't loaded."

"I don't care if the gun was loaded or not. Accidents do happen you know."

"Not in this case."

I tell him, "How about this. Let me out this car and I'll walk the rest of the way. Thanks for your concern, but save your time and energy."

"You're not going anywhere."

"Excuse me?"

"I'm not letting you out this car."

We approach a traffic jam, looks like an accident lies ahead, nothing between my freedom but space, opportunity, and the latch that opens the door.

I reach for the handle but the child lock is on, and I suddenly start to panic, start turning into a ferocious leopard that's trapped in a cage, a crying toddler that can't escape the crib. "Let me out this damn car! Let me out right now!"

"Scream all you want but you're not going anywhere little lady."

I fidget. Twitch. Fidget. Twitch. "Thought you said this wasn't kidnapping."

"It's not."

"Well it sure as hell doesn't seem like it!"

"I'm just trying to get you home safely okay. It's 3 a.m., gruesome on these streets, and quite frankly, whether you know it or not, you're nothing but a walking rape target to these pigs out here. And I'm not about to put you in any more danger than what you were already in. I'm not gonna have that on my conscience."

I try to calm down; try to do everything possible to put my franticness on hold.

He lessens the speed of the car and says, "Tell you what. If you don't believe my intentions were to protect you, I'll prove it to ya."

He reaches under the seat to grab the gun that's wrapped in a dark cloth, but before he gets a chance to remove the gun from its fabric, my frantic state does a double-take, sparks me to reach over and attempt to grab the gun from his hands, but his grip is too strong, and we're now tussling for possession, pulling at the gun on both ends, and in the midst of our tussling, an explosion occurs, but instead of it being the sounding of a gunshot, it's nothing but a large banana that busted all over the steering wheel, an imitation gun that was concealed beneath that cloth.

I go berserk. "What the hell is this?"

"That's your loaded gun."

"You mean to tell me that there was a damn banana underneath this cloth the entire time."

"Unfortunately, yes. And as you can see, it's not even loaded."

He laughs aloud, gives the look of the Joker who just played another trick on Gotham City.

I don't know whether to feel upset, relieved, or just plain stupid for allowing someone to frighten me with a piece of fruit, but as his laughter continues to relish, I have no choice but to laugh with him, for humor is all that can keep me from strangling him at the moment.

He turns his glare towards my wardrobe and says, "What were you doing walking on that street anyhow? Were you working that street?"

"Working?"

"Yeah, that's one of the busiest streets for women."

Realizing that he'd indirectly called me a whore, I take off the smiley face and give him the reaction of an insulted woman, shoving his arm into the steering wheel.

The car shift lanes.

He gains control of the steering wheel and says, "Woman, what are you trying to do? Kill us?"

I snap. "I'm not a hooker!"

"Yeah, well you're not sane either … and if you weren't hooking, then what were you doing?"

"Not that it's any of your business, but I was coming from work."

"At three in the morning?"

"You never heard of the late night shift?"

"Not dressed like that I haven't."

I tell him, "What about you? Since you're so focused on inquiring about my life, let's talk about yours. What are you doing dressed up at three in the morning? You a pimp or something?"

"Do I look anything like a pimp?" he says, turning on the light to give a better viewing.

I can now see his face. Finally able to see the man behind the darkness. The kidnapper.

To my surprise, he has a face that I never expected to be so handsome, perhaps the most handsome face I've seen in Brooklyn.

His skin is fiery-brown with a clear tone. Brand-new complexion. Looks like a face that was just pulled fresh out the box with a receipt.

He has a goatee. Watermelon lips. Eyes that are brown as autumn. Shiny as asphalt.

Those eyes are his most extravagant asset and as I look into them, they dare me to turn away. Double dares me. Flirts with me at all angles. Heaven trapped in little balls.

He also has a baldhead. Smooth and glossy. Looks like he once had a contract with head-and-shoulders or could've posed for men's aftershave products. The itch inside dares me again. Dares me to rub that head of his, but then I remember that we're still in that phase of stranger-hood and I'm supposed to be answering a question.

He smiles. "So tell me."

"Tell you what?" I replied, taking my eyes away from those lips.

"You still think I'm a pimp?"

"Do you want me to be honest?"

"Please."

"Any man that can lure women into a car with a banana, gots to have pimp tendencies."

"Well I'm not. I have a nine-to-five like everyone else."

"And what might that be?" I asked, praying that his occupation would match his looks.

"I like to refer to myself as a restaurant nutritionist provider."

"A what?"

"A restaurant nutritionist provider."

"So in other words, you're a waiter."

"Guess that's another way of saying it."

I chuckle. "Are you ashamed of your job or something?"

"What makes you think I'm ashamed?"

"Because of the way you described it. I mean come on … Nutrition Provider … Why must you try to intellectualize your occupation as a waiter?"

"I'm not trying to intellectualize anything."

"Like hell you're not. Men are forever labeling their jobs as something more powerful. Just the other day, I ran into a guy who said he was a Technical Support Agent. It wasn't long before I realized that technical support agent only meant working in a call-center for Sprint. I mean, why can't we all just be comfortable with what we really are?"

His expression says I've insulted him, and his beautiful eyes go from sunup to sundown, his gaze reverting back to that scary looking man who first ordered me into the car.

He tells me, "Your job title is not always what society says it is. It's what you feel you are in your heart. And I see myself as more than just a person who waits tables. That's all you can see from the outside looking in, but actually, that's only half the battle."

    Cyril Gillion

I look at him as if he's lost his mind, and I have no choice but to ask, "Are you serious?"

He sneers. "Very serious."

It was interesting to see how a person could be so defensive about an occupation that really means nothing on the corporate ladder, one who's technically considered a failure in the modern world of commerce. In my head, I tried to give him the benefit of the doubt, convinced myself that although he waits tables for a living, it was only a job, not an occupation, only a stepping stone to something more innovative.

He says, "There are millions of occupations that are looked down upon, simply because of how the public label them. But really, their contributions go far beyond their labels."

"Well then Mr. Have-a-Heart. What would you label a garbage man as?"

"A sanitation engineer."

"What about a mail man?"

"A postal carrier."

"A stripper?"

"A burlesque stimulator specialist."

We laugh.

Minutes later we approach my apartments, Brooklyn Estates. I remind him to drop me off across the street, right next to the Citgo Gas Station.

He says, "What is it? You afraid of getting dropped in front of your apartments?"

"Don't forget that this is kidnapping, remember?"

"Well maybe I can kidnap you another time?"

That comment catches me by surprise. He smiles.

I smile back. "That's okay. Don't know if I should be hanging out with strangers."

"Everyone's a stranger at first. Besides, I'm not asking you out on a date if that's what you think."

"That is what I think."

He reaches into his glove department and pulls out some sort of brochure that reads, *Getting Down for JC*. Then, he hands it to me and mutters, "Just in case you're interested."

I drop it back on his lap. "Sorry, but I don't get down for anyone. Especially not some JC."

He giggles.

I ask, "Something funny?"

"Yeah, sorry if I wasn't clear, but JC means Jesus Christ. My church is hosting a youth convention next weekend and I just want to know if you'll be interested in checking it out. I promise you won't be disappointed."

Thinking he's full of BS, I tell him, "That's ok."

"That's okay meaning *no* or that's ok meaning *ok*.

"That's okay meaning *no*.

"What is it? Are you seeing someone?"

"I guess that's one way of putting it. I'm married to my schooling. Don't have time for men. Definitely don't have time for a church gathering."

"Seems like you do have time for something," he says, looking at my brown bag of greygoose. "You plan on tackling that whole bottle tonight?"

"If needed, yes."

"Well I tell you what? How 'bout you just think about it ... by the way, my name is William. William Randolph. And your name?" he asks, extending his hand to greet me.

I shake his hand. Never felt a hand so soft. So inviting. And although I have to let the hand loose, I want to clinch it like I'm holding a parachute for dear life.

He says, "Well…"

"Well what?"

"I nearly save your life and you can't even tell me your name."

"Oh yeah," I tell him, stepping out of that trance. "My name is Angel."

"Angel what?"

"Angel is all you need to know at the moment."

"Okay then, Ms. Angel. Maybe we'll meet again, hopefully under different conditions. And maybe next time I'd be lucky enough to get your last name."

I stare back into those tempting eyes. "Maybe."

Cyril Gillion

8

As I break stride into my apartment, I instantly bombarded the kitchen with an urge to dulcify my lethargic state.

Two messages lie on my voice mail. I refused to check either one. All I cared about was opening that bottle of goose and getting one notch below intoxication, eradicating that heavy load from the week I just endured.

The house was a total mess. Clothes and shoes were scattered everywhere you turned, and it got even messier after I dropped my skirt on the living room floor, only left wearing undergarments that became a peeping zone for the old man across the balcony, Mr. Rutherford. I closed the curtains and turned off the lights, but before heading towards the bathroom to set my bubble bath, I made another trip towards the kitchen to grab some imitation bubble formula, a large bottle of dish detergent.

I came back into the bathroom with some inscents – blackberry of course – sat them on one side of the tub, the grey goose sitting on the other, ran my bath water to a sultry temperature, fired up some candles, stepped outside of my undergarments, jumped into some nakedness, settled into the exalting bowl of rapture, tub euphoria.

As the dish detergent birthed bubbles, I filled the glass with greygoose.

I drink and drink and drink.

I'm not a drunkard. Just a school-girl alcoholic.

Drunkards can't control their liquor.

Alcoholics can.

Drunkards amuse other people.

Alcoholics amuse themselves.

Drunkards drive recklessly through intersections, get raped in alleys, urinates in their own vomit.

Alcoholics such as I, know exactly when to put down the bottle.

I drink and drink and drink.

William. William Randolph. A man who pretends to be a man of God. Loves his job as a waiter. Different than other men I've ever come across. His name kept spinning through my mind. Ran circles around the membrane.

Those hands.

I kept seeing his hands. Reminisced on how it felt to touch them – the after effects – would re-introduce myself a thousand more times if it meant shaking those hands again.

I drink and drink and drink.

William. William Randolph. It's like he was in the tub with me right now. Butt Naked. Thought I saw him through the bottle of greygoose. My little rubber ducky. The two of us popping bubbles while watching the suds disintegrate.

I fought the phantasm of those hallucinations; kept telling myself that this was only a figment of my imagination, delusions creeping through the back door of reality to hold my sanity hostage.

The shit didn't work! And as those hallucinations subside, it didn't take long for William to start pouring liquor on my breasts, caressing one of my nipples, pinching the other, pouring on some more liquor, all while letting the greygoose sizzle down my belly, down my cherry tree, down unto his lips that sat above the water.

He kisses that cherry tree. Tongue-kisses it gently.

And just like that his tongue went back up north, back up my navel, back up my stomach through those pearly gates of bosom.

His tongue was so wicked. Wicked with a rhythm. Wrote its own rhymes. Sung a chorus around my breasts as he stimulated those nipples with symphony. I wasn't ready for this action. Tried to convince myself that I was still a virgin. Still pure. Still that butterfly in its cocoon. I decided to hold back and tell him that it was too soon, that I wasn't prepared to touch my toes (or have them touching the bathroom ceiling), and I finally started to push him way. Told him to ease up. Slow down. Let loose of my nipple.

                      Cyril Gillion

Let.

Loose.

That.

Damn.

Nipple.

He fought back. The liquor fought back. With greater force he pulled my legs apart to go deep sea diving beneath the bath water, hooked my clit like a fish that was going upstream.

That made me yield to him, made me surrender. I let him take charge. Let him have that fish. Let him force those dirty words out of me like, "Sex me William. Sex me Mr. Liquor Bottle. Whoever you are, stranger or no stranger, please hurry up and sex me before I get sober. Sex me with no questions asked and no showing of identification."

I started to become the aggressor. I grabbed his penis. Grabbed that grande liquor bottle. Shoved all twenty dollars of it into my tight little tunnel, breaking the seal that has been locked away for months.

I liked that feeling; loved it. Loved the way the bottle took advantage of me, made love to me, felt like paradise in a glass as we moved in motion, in accordance with each other, sexing on cloud nine, trying to reach cloud ten, repeating that cycle over and over until my orgasm subsides, until this tub of ecstasy ran dry.

I lay back in that tub for minutes. Maybe even hours.

The bottle of greygoose was half empty and Mr. Liquor was now resting in my stomach, curling around my abdomen, made me feel sicker than a dog.

I stood on my knees and puked in the drain; puked until I couldn't puke no more.

I'm never drinking again.

Feels like I'm lying in a pile of knives. Would die a million times before ever putting my lips around another liquor bottle.

I suddenly became mad at the entire world, but most of all at my self, started rethinking those thoughts that I fight every night.

Why didn't I pull that trigger and kill my stepfather? Should've murdered him like he murdered my mother. Should've been there for mama. Should've been there for myself.

Should've. Would've. Could've.

Those words flood my head like irrigated streets, makes me wonder if this so-called God will ever bring the love that mama had given me in the past.

I then thought about Kevin, about his feelings that I pushed to the side. Did he still love me or was I just leftover lunch? Was he now with another woman, some football fanatic that was more interested in his career than I was? I wonder what would've happened if we stayed together. How my life would be in the next ten years. If he would've convinced me to give up my dreams and be a stay-at-home wife like my mother, living a life of pampering babies and house cleaning, waiting for him to walk through the door while dinner sat cold on the table.

I didn't want that life. But I didn't want this life either. Life itself felt like a big gamble. Poker play. You can't win for loosing.

And then I cried…

    Cyril Gillion

9

I remain in this tub of dish detergent, naked, a tub that used to be a torrent of ecstasy hours ago.

My head was spinning out of control, each neuron doing a pop-a-wheelie through my frontal lobe.

It was 7:15 am.

I rinsed off the remaining subs and got dressed, threw on some overalls before heading to the coffee shop to study.

At the coffee shop I was as regular a customer as the coffee that was brewing. Not only was it a quiet place for studying, but the lattes were free before eight.

I stumbled in there the same time I do ever Saturday morning, smelled the same scent of the old man who sat in the corner reading his newspaper. Here, the manager did more hiring and firing than Donald Trump, and as I sat down, I saw a new waiter strolling the scene. The waiter was in his mid-twenties, slim, spiky hair with yellow highlights, and I couldn't tell whether he was Spanish, Mexican, or Italian; looked like Tiger Woods with an apron tied around his waist.

Smiling in my direction, he licked his chops as if I was fresh coffee that was waiting to brew.

"Hey gorgeous," he said. "Can I get you anything?"

His accent spoke a poetic lingo but face was completely cursed.

I said, "Guess I'll have a vanilla soy latte with sugar. Much sugar."

The Other Side of the Pillow   69

"Whatever you want, Sweetness. Care for anything else?"

"Thanks but no thanks," I replied.

"Are you sure you don't want anything? Nothing at all?"

"I'm sure."

"Sugar?"

"No thanks."

"An extra cup?"

"No."

"Mind if I put a little cream in your coffee?" he asked, licking his lips, loading his little pecker of ammunition.

"Hell no! All I need is my damn soy latte."

He walks away.

I lay my head on the table, needed a quick minute of rest to soothe the hangover from last night. Professor Stern was giving a linguistics test on Monday and I had no idea how to prepare.

Before I could raise my head to prepare a thought, I felt a slight rub on my shoulder along with a voice that said, "Hi Sweetness, here is your coffee." Snarling, I clasped my fist, pulled back, and right before hitting the waiter where it hurts, I noticed that this wasn't the waiter at all, and instead, it was the face from last night, William Randolph.

I could've died.

Out of all the men walking around in New York City, why did he have to walk into this coffee shop, especially when I'm dressed like a rainbow, breaking the ethics code of colors.

Wearing rugged jeans with a white t-shirt that swallowed his massive pecks, he was masculine in every sense of the word, looked like a black superhero that was coming to serve justice.

Before I could wipe the ash from my lips, he asks, "Do you always make a fist at people who bring you things?"

I freeze up. "Huh?"

"I'm talking about the coffee," he added. "You don't seem too happy about it being delivered. Or is it just the deliverer?"

"I think it's just the deliverer."

He takes my response literal and without saying another word, he turns his back, walk towards the exit, and as he walks in a slow stride, I contemplate on yelling, Wait. Please. Come. Back.

Just when I think he's about to exit, he turns right, heads towards the cashier, picks up another cup of coffee, makes another right, and starts heading back towards my table. Never asking permission, he sits beside me as if he didn't care if I was with someone or not, and if I was, there'd have to be a party of three.

　　　　　Cyril Gillion

Then he looks at his watch. Looks back at me. Stares at me as if he appreciates time.

Smiling, he raises his cup of coffee. "I want to propose a toast," he said.

"A toast?" I asked, looking bewildered.

"Yes ma'am. A toast."

"Mr., I don't know where you're from, but where I'm from, we don't use coffee to toast. We use wine."

"Coffee is originally derived from the word *Quawah*, which is the Arabic term for wine. So if it's not too much to ask, can we finish toasting? All I need you to do is raise your cup."

Thinking I wasn't the only one who drunk too much last night, I play along with his game, and I raised my cup of coffee – wine – whatever the hell it was that I was drinking this morning. I didn't know if he was out to flatter me or simply push my buttons, but regardless of both, he was testing me for certain.

I say, "Tell me, Romeo. What the heck are we supposed to be toasting to?"

"We're toasting to tragedies."

"Excuse me?"

"Tragedies that we encounter."

"At first I was only kidding, but now I'm truly convinced that we really are from two different worlds. In my world, people toast to positive things: Anniversaries. Reunions. Birthdays. Normal people don't toast to tragedies."

"In order to honor the good times, we must first appreciate the bad, the tragedies that come before the enchantment. That's why I toast to tragedies. What's the beauty of watching the sun rise if you never saw it set?"

"Quite interesting. Wish I could look at life the way you look at it."

"And how is that?"

"Awkward. Very very awkward."

We share a mutual smile. The first thing we've shared so far. And together, that smile is more warming than apple pie, coffee without the creamer.

He glances again at his watch, looks like he's pressed for time.

I ask, "Gotta be somewhere?"

"Not really. Why'd you ask?"

"It's just strange that a man would consistently look at his watch for no reason at all. And I don't see any Movado or Rolex hanging from your wrist, so what's the purpose?"

"The purpose is I just won twenty dollars."

"Excuse me?" I asked astonishingly.

"I just won twenty dollars in five minutes."

"Twenty dollars for what?"

"Twenty dollars for keeping your attention … I made a bet with the waiter that I could hold a conversation with you for more than five minutes. He swore that your attitude stinks and you'd dismiss me at the drop of a dime. Looks like I won. But since this was a collective effort, I guess I can say we won."

"Is this supposed to be a joke, because if it is, you may want to buy yourself a better sense of humor."

"I assure you that this isn't a joke," he says confidently. "Watch, I'll show you."

He looks over at the waiter, signals a thumbs-up and some other type of gesture, perhaps a money signal. Had this been five years ago I probably would've cursed his ass out, but with age comes a bigger conscience, and at the moment I was too embarrassed to let profanity run its course. Instead of getting all hostile, I smiled in his direction, then softly uttered, "So where's my cut?"

"Your cut?"

"That's right. Business is business. And since you rendered my services for your benefit, I suggest I get fifty percent. Or maybe, I'll–"

"Hold on a second. So you're actually cool with this?"

"Cool as a fan. I mean when you really think about it, we just met yesterday, which means you have no obligation to care about my feelings because I damn sure don't care about yours. Now where's my cut?"

He changes his expression. "Ok ok. I was only kidding."

"Kidding huh? And why should I believe you?"

"Like you said, we barely know each other. So what reasons do I have to lie?"

"The same three reasons why all men lie to women … Ass. Ass. And more Ass."

He laughs aloud and takes a sip of his coffee.

Unintentionally, my eyes started to wander and I caught a glance of the bulge in his pants, tried to look away before he caught me looking.

He drinks more coffee.

  Cyril Gillion

I peeked again just to ensure that my 20-20 vision wasn't lying, wanted to make sure his package was as bulky as it appeared to be.

It was.

The package looked like it had a mind of its own. Was well worth the view. Well worth the possibility of him catching me stare.

When I looked up, I met eyes with his, a deer trapped in the headlights.

He said, "Do you like what you see?"

"Huh?"

"Your eyes, they're wandering. Do you like what you see?"

"Yes … I … I … like your jeans."

"My jeans?"

"Yeah … Your jeans are nice. Very nice. Every man should own a pair of jeans like those."

"That's funny because I thought I looked like a bomb this morning. These jeans are faded, rusty, and they're probably older than you."

"Yea, but above all, they have that rugged look. And that's a good thing. Too many men are walking around with jeans that are cut, ironed, and creased better than us women. Nice to know there are men who still dress like men these days."

"So I take it that you like the blue-collar type of man."

"I like any man who fits the qualifications of a real man. That includes taking care of his household, handling responsibilities, and when needed, he's not afraid of getting his hands dirty."

"Hmmm. Guess that means you don't have a problem with your man missing a shower every now and then either."

"Correction. There's a thin line between a rugged man who isn't afraid of getting his hands dirty, opposed to a man who is just plain dirty. I don't know of a woman yet who would fraternize with a dirty man, but a man who's rugged can get more coochie than tampax."

He laughs aloud. "Is that a hint that I could get those goodies if I wanted them?"

"No. That's a reminder to never miss a shower."

We shared more laughs, slick comments, all the buttery stuff that people do during the preliminary stages of a getting to know one another.

He soon picked up my criminology book, started skimming through the pages. "I take it that you're studying law," he said.

"Indeed I am. Third year student at Brooklyn Law."

"I had a feeling you were in law school or something of that nature. I bet you usually attract men like a magnet."

"Actually, men are usually intimidated when meeting me."

"Really?"

"Heck yeah. It's like after finding out that I'm in law school, the conversation suddenly goes sour, and men either start fumbling over their words or changing the subject to something related to law, as if all I care to talk about is politics. It's crazy because I can almost sense when it's about to happen."

"Really? So what have you sensed about me thus far? Do you see a man who's intimidated or one who's overly confident?"

He looked at me impatiently; all ears, waited to rebuttal against either answer I'd give in return.

I was in a lose-lose situation. Truth is he seemed overly confident, but then again, telling the truth doesn't always set a person free, especially when it comes to men.

But in this case, lying could be worst than the truth.

If I said he was intimidated, he'd probably try to prove the complete opposite, never allowing me to see the real man behind the man, the real flesh behind those pecks. But then again, truth or no truth, I may never see the real man anyhow, and that could possibly be an advantage for us both.

I continued to fumble with the question, then after a thorough examination I ricocheted the question in his direction, asking, "Why don't you tell me yourself. Right now, are you feeling intimidated or confident?"

He says, "That's not fair."

"What's not fair?"

"You can't answer a question with a question."

"Why not?"

"Because you just can't."

"According to who?" I asked, struggling for straws.

"According to the dictionary, Mr. Webster. Last time I looked up the word *answer*, the definition never mentioned the word *question*.

"What makes Webster's definition any more factual than mines?"

"Because it's the dictionary. That alone makes it more factual."

"But the dictionary was written by man."

"And?"

"And, if it was written by man, it doesn't necessarily make it factual, doesn't make it certain."

"Well Ms. Technical, if you want to look at it in that sense, then nothing in this world is for certain."

                        Cyril Gillion

"That's right. The only thing in this world that is certain is the uncertain."

He argued, "No. Based on your philosophy, how could we even be sure that the uncertain is certain? Because if the uncertain was certain, it certainly would contradict the notion of what certainty really means."

"What?"

He gasps for breaths. So do I.

We both were so adamant about proving our points to where we would've argued with our own argument had it meant defeating the other.

The average man would've been passive, but he was far from the usual type. I think that's what I liked about him most; I liked his toughness. Liked the way he was so headstrong. And no matter how old a gal gets, she'll always be rude to the cute boy with freckles.

He eventually called for the waiter; asked for two additional cups of coffee without my consultancy.

I told him, "More coffee doesn't guarantee more company."

"Well you can't blame a man for trying."

"Exactly what is it that you're trying to do? Get a number, perhaps a date?"

"Maybe my intentions are to get you drunk."

I laughed. "Drunk off what? Coffee?"

"No. Drunk off wine, remember?"

"Is that your only solution to getting women? Intoxication?"

"Of course not. The normal fish would've bit the pole a long time ago. However, a true fisherman understands the depth that he must go in order to catch the right one."

"Humph, so now you're comparing me to a fish."

"I wouldn't say fish … I see you more as a shark. One that's nice and tender, full of protein, a fisherman's fantasy."

He lets out a smile, and then he stares at me. Stares into my eyes as if he could see right through me, as if he knew I'd masturbated to his shadow the night before. There was no use in fighting the flattery, no sense in running from it. And his constant flows of sweet-nothings were starting to mean something.

This whole situation was strange. To know I was flirting with the same man who kidnapped me at gunpoint, better yet banana-point, is hard for me to grasp, even harder to digest. Some people say that the first week of getting to know someone, instead of meeting the real person, you're actually meeting their representative. Now I'm not one to challenge that saying, but in this case, if the saying is true, then I don't care if I never meet the real person because the representative has already knocked him out the picture.

My curiosity started to fluster and I wanted to get to know this representative a little more, wanted to chip through his wall of inquest.

I said, "Speaking of fish, how many do you have wiggling from your hook?"

"Depends."

"Depends on what?" I asked, hoping a logical explanation would back his response.

"Depends on what you consider wiggling. I talk to lots of women. It's a natural instinct. But don't get it misconstrued. I'm not some type of male gigolo if that's what you think. I'm just a man who grew up around all girls, which means communicating with women is second nature. So when you say wiggling, you have to be more specific."

I suck my teeth. "Whateva negro. Stop trying to be naive. When I say the word *wiggling*, I'm not referring to some general conversation that you have with Jane Doe over coffee and doughnuts. I'm talking 'bout a little bumping, a little grinding, and a whole lot of pushing."

He laughs, says, "Cool … I didn't know you wanted to talk grown-talk at eight in the morning, but since you've already put it out there, I guess I have to be honest. In my adolescent years, I used to have a lot of woman. Used to catch more tail than the whole cat kingdom. But five years ago I had a life-changing experience. It was something that brought me closer to God. However, although it changed my life for the better, it hasn't been the most attractive thing to the ladies. Now it feels like women run within five minutes of meeting me."

His last sentence caused my eyebrows to flare, and my conscience suddenly spoke out loud, told me to immediately stop the conversation, grab my belongings, and run out the door like hell. But another voice intervened, the bad conscience, convinced me to ride that road of curiosity a little longer.

I took a closer look at him. I tried to find a recognizable flaw. Searched for the butter that was hiding behind that glowing smile.

How old was he?

His shirt said twenty-five, pants said thirty, and depending on whether he wears glasses or not, he could pass for thirty-five.

Older than thirty-five meant trouble. Been around the block. A man that age could have a graveyard of skeletons.

Before I could utter a word, he says, "If I recall, you said you was a third-year law school student, right?"

     Cyril Gillion

"Yes, why?"

"No reason," he replied apathetically.

"Let me guess. You wanna know my age but is afraid of stepping out of line."

He chuckles. "No need to ask for your age. I already know. I knew the moment you stepped out my car last night."

"Is that so?"

"Women over twenty-five don't usually have the words *Baddest Bitch* written on the face of their cellular. So on a good day, I'll give you twenty-four and that's being fully dressed in stockings."

I could've disputed his answer, but to rebuttal against the truth would only make me look more immature than what he already portrayed me to be.

I tell him, "I guess you're right. I'll be twenty-four in few months. But my cell phone says as much about my age as your shoes say about yours."

"What's wrong with my shoes?"

"Nothing I suppose. Not unless you're over the age of forty."

"Excuse me?"

"That's right," I consummated. "The. Big. Four. Zero. I mean come on. Track shoes with a fresh pair of jeans. Younger men are not sporting that type of gear in the new millennium."

He doesn't reply, gives me a sideline glare, and the confidence he possessed earlier has now seized, as if the number forty had suddenly struck a nerve.

I knew right then that my sense of humor was no where near funny, and his expression told me all I needed to know, that if he wasn't forty already, the number was a few steps from knocking on his door.

He soon admits the truth, that he really is forty, and as I subtract our ages, the mathematical difference nearly causes me to choke.

He says, "I hope my age doesn't scare you."

"It doesn't," I reply with a hard swallow. "And even if you are forty, you still look darn good for your age. Heck, you look better than most men in their twenties."

No response.

He sips more of his coffee, then asks, "Hypothetically speaking, if we were lovers – not that those are my intentions – but if we were, what would be the main factor that'll cause our fondness to end in turmoil?"

"What's with the off-the-wall question?"

"Would it be my age?"

"Are you serious?"

"Dead serious."

"We just met last night and you're already asking me questions that couples ask after courtship."

"I saw the look you gave when I said my age. Not to say it was negative, but I just want to know my chances with a woman like you."

He was so serious. So direct.

I tell him, "What gives you the inclination that I'm still single and on the market, have yet to sell my share of stock?"

He starts to laugh. Not with me, but at me, says, "I'm pretty sure you're single."

"How can you be so sure?"

He laughs some more, then he tells me, "Just look at the clock. It's only 8:30 am."

"And?"

"And, what man let his woman out of bed on a Saturday morning, before the roosters are finished humping?"

"The type of man who's been humped so good to where he'll sleep till noon."

"Well what about last night. I mean, any man who lets his woman strut the streets of Brooklyn at two in the morning, doesn't sound like much of a man."

"Have you ever thought that maybe he was working late?"

"Working late?"

"Yeah. Working late."

My fabrication comes naturally. Not intending to be malice. Just wanted him to know he wasn't the only dog who was sniffing around this kitty.

He says, "I'm still not buying it. Does this so-called man have a name?"

"Yeah, his name is Kevin," I replied, hollering the first name of memory, the last man of consort.

"Nice try," he says. "But I hope you're a better liar in the courtroom, because you and I both know this Kevin character is no longer in the picture."

"Excuse me?"

"That's right, Angel. Kevin is supposed to be the guy that you dropped in the restaurant, right? So as you can see, I did more homework than you expected."

My brain freezes.

     Cyril Gillion

No longer able to hold my tongue, I ask, "Who are you?"

"Who am I? Don't you recognize me at all?"

"All I know is that you're a man who once gave me a ride home, a man who can't distinguish the difference between coffee and wine."

"Well that's ironic because not only did we meet, but if my memory serves me correctly, I think I served you wine as well. You and this Kevin character."

I added the context clues, puzzled his face with one from the past, asked him, "Were you the waiter that night?"

"Now you remember. Guess I don't feel so stupid after all."

I observe his features once more. His muscular tone. His bald head.

I say, "You can't be the same person. The man I remember had hair. And he wasn't as…"

"As what?"

"Well you know," I said, looking at his biceps. "He wasn't as muscular."

"Funny what clippers and push-ups can do to the average guy walking."

After discovering his true identity, our conversation carried on until noon, felt like it would never come to an end. We talked about everything. Talked about his so-called life as a Christian, and how he didn't have a personal life because of his active roles in the church. He didn't drink or smoke, so he says. And where I was brought up, meeting a man who did neither was more so like meeting a doctor, King Zeus of the Gods. He was also no stranger to education. A student of Morehouse College, he managed to complete a BA degree in nutrition, even though it took him five years to do so. He claims he took off one of those years to try and pursue a career in music, how he once aspired to be a gospel artist, but those dreams went out the window after some woman came into his life. I was waiting for him to tell me how he ended up as a career waiter, wasting his life serving impatient customers. He never spoke on it though. And even when I tried to hint towards it, he'd change the subject every time.

Sad to say, besides Kevin, I don't think I ever engaged in this much conversation with a man, and that lack of experience had me feeling a little eerie, made me want to cut the conversation short and get on with the rest of my day.

Pretending that I had to be somewhere of more importance, I said, "Nice talking to you but I must leave. Have to meet someone at one."

"And who might that be … Kevin?"

"It's actually my professor if you really must know."

"But today is Saturday. What Professor meets with his students on Saturday?"

"One who isn't married. One without reason."

I rose from the table.

He said, "But what about your wine?"

"My coffee?"

"Yeah, you never finished it."

"I never got started either."

I grabbed my purse as if I was in a rush, but while grabbing it, I noticed him reaching for it as well.

I said, "Unless you have $400 dollars handy, I suggest you let go of Ms. Dooney -N- Burke."

He smirks. "I want to see you again."

"How come?"

"Because we never finished our drinks. And I have a phobia of leaving business unfinished."

"Is that what you see me as? Unfinished business?"

"Would you rather I say pleasure?"

I smile, ask, "Let's say we do see each other again, what type of business would I be engaging into?"

He stares at my legs as if he's allowing his eyes to answer that question, gawks me like a prey that's yet to be devoured.

I said, "Think I'll decline on that offer. Angel Inghram doesn't conduct that style of business."

He corrects me. "No sweety. It's not that type of party. I'm only observing your legs because I wanna see if the Angel is equipped to move. How 'bout we go stepping?"

"How 'bout you give me your number and I'll think about it?"

"How 'bout no. All you need to think about is the right shoes to wear and the right skirt to match. Let's go to my spot, Club Down-Under."

No reply.

He says, "I promise you that it'll only be stepping, nothing else. And considering that you've already rejected me once, I think you owe me. Besides, I never had my heart broken twice."

I ask, "When did I reject you the first time?"

"Last night. I asked you if you wanted to visit my church and you looked at me like I'd lost my mind."

"Did I?"

"Made me think I was committing a sin."

   Cyril Gillion

"Maybe you were. You'll be surprised at how many men will use God as a pickup line, as if women are supposed to yield to a man that is religious."

"Works for me every time."

"You see?"

"Just kidding. But on the serious tip, those were never my intentions. Never been the type to use God's sanctuary as a way of crawling into a woman's sanctuary, if you know what I mean. So in all honestly, I'm sorry if I offended you."

"No offense taken."

He pauses, asks, "So what time will you be ready?"

"Ready for what?"

"Club Down Under."

"I never agreed to going."

"Never denied it either."

Contemplating on his proposal, I weighed my pros and cons, realized that the pros were being outnumbered, then cheated myself to where the cons would lose.

"Alright," I agreed, wondering what the hell it was that I was doing. "I guess one night of stepping won't hurt anyone. But don't think about picking me up from my apartment. Instead, I'll just meet you at the club … we clear?"

"Clear."

And like that, we parted.

<u>10</u>

The clock was traveling a mile a minute.

Time wasn't on my side.

In four hours, ready or not, I'll be doing the dating thing with a man who's nearly twice my age, one old enough to date my Aunt Terry. What makes it even scarier is that I wanted this happen, even felt it was a necessity for some strange reason.

I was moving around like a jack-in-the-box, anxious, no idea what a date would be like with a forty-year-old man, no idea what I would wear, no idea what would spark his interest. No fucking idea.

I couldn't call Cuqui. I'd rather sell my soul to the Japanese than hear Cuqui's 29 reasons why I was making a big mistake, and 29 supportive reasons to back them up.

I rushed to the mall and made a visit to my favorite store, had an urge to secretly speak with Victoria. She whispered in my ear, advised me to pick up a black lace thong and a single strapped bra – not to say I would share those secrets with William, but in case that door so happened to open, the room needed to be tidy.

I browsed a dozen stores to look for the right skirt, one that wasn't too short, but short enough to see the light that was running up this tunnel. I went into some no-named store that was at the end of the mall. A store that didn't have a dark face in sight, but the sign that said 25% off was all the color I needed to see.

 Cyril Gillion

Before I could get my hands on the first piece of fabric, a sales woman came flying from the other side of the store. She was Caucasian, late twenties, slim, shoulder-length hair, makeup so horrible to where you would've thought it was done by Stevie Wonder.

She says, "Seems like you're having a hard time looking for something."

I pretend to ignore her, wasn't in the mood to be receiving fashion advice.

She persists, "Something I can help you with, ma'am?"

"That's ok. Just browsing for a last minute dress. But I'm fine."

"I'm sure you are. But at some point, everyone needs a helping hand. So what's the occasion?"

"Well if you must know, I'm hanging out with a couple friends tonight."

She looked at me as if she knew I was a liar, wanted to call me one, but wasn't willing to take that chance. "Let me guess. Dinner?"

"Actually, dancing."

She stood next to me and lined our hips together. "Seems like we both are an even pair. Are you a size 5?"

I looked at my ass, glanced back at hers, and proudly disagreed, "Size 6."

"No problem. I've got you covered. Hold for a moment."

After leaving to cash-out a waiting customer, she comes back with a red polka dot dress that had the word *GoodWill* written all over it. Then, without ever taking off her sales face, she says, "So what do you think? Is it hot or what?"

"Lady, I'm going dancing. Not to the circus. So you might want to put down the clown dress."

She leaves.

I continued to look high and low, going from store to store to find something worth sporting. Nothing around was worth taking a second glance, but after looking at the clock, every skirt in the store had started to look appealing. I soon decided to grab one in black, and I also purchased a pair of white Capri Pants, just incase the mirror decided to have a second opinion about my skirt.

An hour later I was in my apartment, figured I'd take a nap before preparing to meet William. Once awake, I was stricken by another nightmare of my step dad, same gun in my hand, same dripping sweat, pointing it at the alarm clock that read nine o'clock on the dot.

Dammit I was late. And William was probably already at Club Down-Under, his smile steadily diminishing by the minute.

I rushed in the shower, allowed the soap to have its way with every crevice in my body. Upon stepping out, I rubbed cream all over the major parts of my body: legs, buttocks, breasts (every part that has a twin), slid in my thong, skirt, spaghetti-strapped shirt, heels, looked at my butt in mirror, smiled, looked again, smiled, sprayed a whiff of Tiffany's in the air, ran into the particles, sprayed another whiff of Tiffany's, ran into the particles, masked my face in L'Oreal, through on some earrings, white gold necklace, left the house to see the man of the hour, almost forgot the Coach.

I arrived twenty minutes late.

There was William, sexier than he was this morning, sexier than he was last night. A cell phone was to his ear, and he was engaged in a conversation so deep to where he didn't see me approaching.

With a navy blue buttoned up shirt, he was casual dressed. His shoes glistened just as hard as his bald head that was shining beneath the moonlight; shoes clean enough to make me wonder if he treats his women like he does his feet.

Clasping the phone to acknowledge my presence, he compliments me on my gear, tells me that he's glad I made it.

Then, he comes close as if he's about to kiss me on the cheek – but instead of doing so – he embraces me with a light hug, his nicely trimmed facial hair grazing my neck.

I stand strong but want to tremble.

Never met a man who smelled so good. An empowering scent with a soft aroma.

He asks, "Did you have a hard time finding the place?"

"Not really. I would've been here sooner but I kind of over slept."

"Well now that you're awake, let's get inside. I like to get the music while it's fresh, while the DJ is playing ol' school jams."

He aggressively takes my hand, pulls me behind him with a firm grip, guides me through a crowd of about a hundred people, and the bouncer allows us to pass through without ever asking me for identification, acknowledging William as if they were ol' school buddies.

After passing the bouncer, we come to a set of double doors. I think the club is inside, but it's not. And behind those double doors is complete silence, not a face in sight, nothing but a long hallway of red carpet, fluorescent lights, pictures of celebrities like Gabrielle Union, Taye Diggs, and Queen Latifah covering the walls, felt like we were walking the red carpet to a big movie premier; all that was missing were flashing cameras and a set of questions from Wendy Williams.

We head towards a glass elevator.

William presses the *G* button in the elevator, my intention that we're about to go ground level.

I ask him, "Where is this club? In China?"

He laughs, "You'll see."

After a long silent ride to God-knows-where, the elevator doors finally open, and I'm caught off guard from loud music and two more body guards that were bigger than life, both bodyguards wearing Armani suits as if they were protecting the President.

Behind those bodyguards lies paradise. A place that has bright lights, state-of-the-art sounds, gold ceilings, stone walls, four large cages at each angle of the room, and through those cages are four white tigers strolling back and forth, each tiger staring ferociously as if they're anticipating the perfect moment of breaking through the metal and putting this party to rest.

William says, "Wanna tour?"

"Sure."

William takes me through two more rooms that have the same amenities, but those rooms are not necessarily for dance – more so for intimate lounging – rooms where boogying disco has been replaced with soft conversation and baby-making music.

The people in the rooms are of multiple nationalities, a love seat with every race you can imagine. There are Caucasian men pairing with Spanish women. Italian women with Turkish men. Indonesians and Latin lovers. Seems like the United Nations had secretly met at a place where outsiders will never sander.

Most surprising thing I saw was a group of Asian men all huddled up, each wearing suits and ties. Two of them were grouped with black women while one stood by himself, and the single one decided to wink in my direction, gave me the come-here-finger.

I held William's arm tight. Held it like a lifejacket in the middle of sea.

Soon, we were back at square one, the first room of the club. William sits me in the V.I.P section, two feet from the DJ and the bar.

He asks, "You ok?"

"Yeah … I'm good."

We're now surrounded by an older crowd – Williams type of crowd – couples talking about everything from the lighting of the place to the tigers in the corner, about the DJ playing the wrong type of music, about how there's too many people in the club, about topics that were out of my realm of socialization. Unlike me, William socializes with everyone. He introduces me to a gazillion people, every face appearing as one of importance, as if they've known him for years. Shocked me to know I'd be mingling with so many people in so little time, made me wonder how a man who waits tables for a living could have as much clout as William did.

Although I was nervous, I still felt special. Felt like I was a new trophy that brightens a shelf – and at this point, I didn't care if this was only considered *first date* treatment, didn't care if I was his second date of the week, didn't care if he was only doing this to get what was his. Didn't care. Didn't care. Didn't care.

After the dust finally settles, William asks me, "You thirsty?"

"I could go for a drink."

"What would you like?"

Alcohol heals all jitters, I thought. And truth of the matter is, I wanted something strong, needed something strong, but refusing to give off an alcoholic impression, I tell him, "How about you decide."

"You sure?"

"Yeah, whatever you get is cool with me."

He tells the waiter, "On that note, give me a bottled water and give her a sprite. No Ice."

I swallow hard. Swallow as I can smell the liquor in the air. Should've never put the ball in his court.

Dissecting my disposition, he asks, "Is Sprite cool with you?"

I become honest; tell him, "On second thought, I'll take a Long Island on the rocks."

William gives me a disturbing look as if he doesn't like my change of heart, stares at me the way a parent stares at a daughter who just became legal. He tells the waiter, "Very well then. Give her a Long Island, but still give me bottled water. Guess one of us has to be sober and look out for the other tonight."

"Oh trust me, William. No need to worry about me getting drunk if that's what you're implying. I refuse to give you the satisfaction."

The bartender provided our drinks, my Long Island, his water.

William never pays for either drink.

I ask William, "Do you drink alcohol at all?"

"Nope. Not anymore."

"Used to?"

"I used to do lots of things: Drink; smoke, the whole nine-yards. Haven't done any of that stuff in five years."

"Exactly what happened five years ago?"

               Cyril Gillion

"Some things are better left unsaid, at least for right now. There's a right time and a right place for everything."

He sighs heavily. Sighs as if he's been sighing for years, forever being stingy with his past.

Deciding to take the conversation to a new avenue, I ask, "You come here often?"

"I guess you can say it's like a routine spot."

"But why this place?"

"As you can see, at this club I have connections. It's the only club that gives me first-class treatment and considering that my job consists of serving people for a living, it's good to be able to come to a place, knowing that I'm finally the one who's being served."

He shifts the conversation in my direction. "What about you? Do you go to clubs?"

"Yeah, but not these types?"

"What is considered *these types*?"

"The type that has too many rules, not enough leniency. I usually go to clubs that don't require a dress code."

"Sounds like places with juveniles. Places where there's shooting, fighting, and who knows what else."

"Are you afraid of those places? You from the suburbs or something?"

He sneers. "I'm a grown man, born and raised in Brooklyn, never feared no man but God. But no matter how strong a man is, he also wants to be comfortable anywhere he goes, especially if he's with a woman. Nothing is worse than taking a woman somewhere and not being able to vibe because Peanut and his friends are constantly trying to intervene."

Before I could reply, William received a tap on the shoulder. There were two large men standing behind him, two breathing Eskimos. I didn't make eye contact with either one of the men, mainly because it was too hard to see over their broad chests from the angle I was sitting.

William stood from his seat, slapped hands with both men, started to execute that gentlemen thing by introducing the four of us. "Angel, meet a couple of football players. This is Marcus and Tank ... I served them a few times at the restaurant."

"Hey beautiful," Marcus said, shaking my hand. "Where you from?"

"Miami, Florida."

"Miami huh … In that case, you've gotta meet someone." He looks back at William. "You mind?"

"It's cool," William replied.

At that instance, Marcus glances over his shoulder to yell, "Hey Kevin, come on over. We've got a Floridian in the house."

A man comes over, and sure enough, the Kevin is not an ordinary Kevin; it's Kevin Armstrong, my ex boyfriend, the Kevin that has studied me since adolescence.

Stunned to the core, I nearly choked on my drink as I closed my eyes to prepare for this nightmare called *Sight*.

Kevin was staring me directly in the eye, and from the jewelry that glittered on his wrist, it looked as if his football dream had finally come true, after all.

He looked at me. I looked away.

We looked again. Looked away.

And we played that looking game again, and again, and again.

Finally getting some guts, I said, "Nice to meet you, Kevin.

"Pleasures all mine," he replied.

Marcus intervened. "Kevin is one of our new running backs for the Jets. He's also from Florida."

"Is that right?" I replied. "What part of Florida are you from?"

Kevin played along. "Miami. I went to Jackson High, home of the Cougars. Class of 99."

"What a coincidence. I went to Jackson as well. Class of '01."

William started to grow envious; he leaned closer to my side and laid his hand on my lower back to guard his territory from the prowler of the past.

Meanwhile, Kevin bit his lip in a disturbed manner. And although Kevin and I were no longer considered an item, he still gave a disturbed look as if no one was good enough for his little Angel.

Marcus asked, "Do you two know each other?"

Immediately giving different answers, I bid no. Kevin bid yes.

"Well which one is it?"

"We know of each other," I answered. "Kevin was the popular kid in high school. You know, one of the jocks."

"Yeah, and Angel was an academic nerve-wreck. You know, the type of chick that doesn't have time for us jocks. And by the way Angel, are you still trying to be a lawyer?" he asked sarcastically.

"Actually I change my plans, Kevin. Figured I could make more money in the porn industry."

"Woooooo," Marcus replied, choking on his drink. "Talking 'bout skeletons in a closet."

The other friend, Tank, gives a look of elation, and he gawks me as if I was a black Jenna Jameson, the porn star that he's been waiting to meet all night.

Unprepared to adapt to the situation at hand, I quickly made a get-away to the ladies room, left the four of them standing there in disbelief as I headed for the stall to pee out my anxiety.

I must've stayed in that stall for twenty minutes, the toilet becoming my best friend, my consultant, my Johnny Cochran in such a hostile situation.

I had to make a decision. Either walk out the door and face the madness or deface myself from this club entirely.

In the midst of leaving the stall, two women rushed in the bathroom. Screaming to the top of their lungs, they sound like they'd just won the lottery, and from hearing their conversation, it seems as if the screaming was all because of Kevin.

One of them pointed in my direction, came at me like she was having a seizer. "You … you … you actually know him? You know him?"

"Know who?"

"Kevin Armstrong … The new linebacker from the Jets … I saw you with him outside."

"Why is it important that I know him? Are you trying to—"

"Girl, you've gotta put a sista down. I've been wanting to meet that man since he got drafted … with his fine self … did you already sample the booty, 'cause if you did, tell me how was it … I need to know … girl you just don't know what I'll do to that man. I'll suck that nigga's stuff until his ass cave in."

Shocked of what I just heard, my eardrums pop out of my skull, scares me to know that a woman could want a man so much without ever knowing his middle name.

I left the bathroom quickly, headed back into the fire.

The club had gotten darker. Kevin was sitting in the corner, tag-teamed by two women that wanted his John Hancock signed on their bosoms. I looked in the other direction for William. To my surprise, he was on the other end of the club, talking on the phone again. Something told me to go over and meddle in William's business, but instead of giving him that satisfaction, I walked to the bar and grabbed myself another Long Island. Kevin spotted me through the darkness, yelled for me to come and sit with him for a moment. I contemplated on whether I should go, told myself that it was probably a bad idea. But after watching William play *Mr. Telephone Man* on the other side of the club, I decided to reconsider that thought.

"Angel!" Kevin yelled for the second time.

Kevin was still bunged by two women, and one of them were sitting on his lap, her legs spread wide, looked like her intentions was to ride him all the way to the Super Bowl.

"Ok. Now you ladies gots to get the hell off my lap," he said, dismissing them as I entered the table.

Both girls gave me dirty looks before leaving, made me feel like another chick that was eager to get a piece of Kevin's pie.

Kevin said, "Care for a drink?"

"That's ok," I replied, trying my hardest to refuse the $80 dollar bottle of *Krystal*.

He smiles, then he gulps down the bottle of *Krystal*; he's the same Kevin that is a sucker for alcohol. Although he appears to be calm, his expression is a dead give-away for what's soon to come, a lot of questions about my motives for being here with William.

He says, "Looks like you picked up a few pounds since I last saw ya ... You been working out?"

"No ... just eating out."

"Well keep on eating because I like it." He stares at my hair. "Seems like you've also become friends with the hot comb. What made you straighten your hair?"

"Change, Kevin. At some point, we all must change."

He laughs. "*Change.* Now that's a shocking word coming from you. Sometimes I used to think your underwear is all you were capable of changing. That's what I used to constantly tell Cuqui in high school."

I say, "Seems like you still can't control your liquor, so I guess you haven't changed either, except for the women that you're changing by the hour. But then again, I suppose that's the good life of a NFL star."

He sneers. "The good life? Is that what you think? Trust me when I tell you that my life is not what it seems. I still have to wake up everyday and work my ass off at a nine-to-five like everyone else. Not to mention the worries of getting my head ripped apart everyday. There's nothing good about that life, Angel. And you of all people should know it."

He drinks a little more *Krystal*, and says, "Speaking of Cuqui, what is she up to these days?"

"She has her own salon in Miami. Maybe you should call her sometime. She'd probably loose her mind if she knew you were in New York, playing for the jets. Heck, she'd be in front of the television every Sunday watching you play, bragging of how a guy from our projects made it to the NFL."

"And what about you?"

"What about me?"

"Have you seen any of my games?"

"Honestly, I haven't. I've been so busy to where I can't even remember the last time I turned on the television set, let alone watched a football game."

He pauses for a moment, rests in his disconsolation. I could tell he wanted a better response; I could see it in his eyes. Nothing would have floated his boat more than to see me clinging to him with all smiles, doing cartwheels and splits like the rest of the groupies in this club.

Kevin says, "Seems like something else is keeping you from the television set."

"What do you mean?"

"Seems like someone is too busy because their time is being occupied by someone else."

"Seems like someone is beating around the bush, speaking in codes."

He looks to the floor to collect his thoughts, six months of unspoken words, six months of what-if's, and longer than that if you're counting the amount of testosterone that I left him with before we split.

He says, "So after all this time, Angel. All this time you had me fooled. Had me thinking I was losing my mind in that restaurant for being over-protective. I guess you really did like the little waiter after all. But hey, if you're content with being with a guy that makes minimum-wage, then kudos for the both of y'all."

"Think what you wanna think Kevin, but—"

"And just how long you been seeing this ... this—"

"William. His name is William."

"Well how long have you been seeing William?"

I stand on the defense. "Long enough."

"Humph. That's funny. Twenty years of time that I've invested and all of a sudden, a man nearly twice your age comes along and finally pops that little cherry."

"First off, you don't know what you're talking 'bout."

"Hell if I don't, Angel. I see what's going on. I do have eyes and damn good ears."

"Well use those ears and listen when I tell you that you don't know what the hell you're talking 'bout."

At that instance, William tapped me over the shoulder and invited himself at the table. I thought about the length of time that he was standing there, the amount of conversation he'd heard.

As William looks innocent, Kevin gets upset and grabs his bottle of *Krystal*, wasting no more time at the table. He glares at William the way a judge looks at a criminal, and then he bumps William's shoulder without ever acknowledging his presence in passing.

Time stops.

I wait for William to retaliate, wait along with other bystanders that are all anticipating William's reaction – including Kevin – but William ignores the bump as if he's too mature for the squabble, wants to show me that he's a lover, not a fighter.

No longer wanting to be the core of attention, I tell William, "Let's go!"

"What?"

"I want to leave. This club sucks."

"You want to leave already. We never got a chance to step."

"We'll step another time. As for right now, the only place I'm stepping is out the door."

He grants my request without any more questions, without looking at me as if I spoiled the party. We get into the car and ride in dead silence. My tension is flaring; tension that has completely turned this date around, tension that has him on edge – and like a game of jump rope, he's double-dutching the right moment to jump in and say the right words, reaching for the right branch that'll keep this date from falling.

I keep my discomforting look – foreign speaking body language – the kind that leaves him perplexed and precautious of how to respond.

My cellular broke the ice, the ring tone of Cuqui. I could've ignored it, but hell, if he could break the no-cell-phone-talking-on-a-date-rule, then so could I.

"Hello, Cuqui."

"Sup bitch."

"Cuqui, how come every time we talk, you've gots to start the conversation off the same way?"

"Girl quit trippin'. You must be with a nigga or somethin,' cause that's the only reason you'd ever come at me like dat."

She becomes curious, then asks, "Where are you by the way?"

I glance over at William as he continues to drive. "I'm at home."

"Good. Turn the TV on ESPN and look at the person whose being interviewed. Girl, it's Kevin."

"Who?" I asked, pretending as if I didn't know.

"Kevin, bitch. The man you let get away. He's being interviewed right now…[*Screaming*]…Girl, that nigga plays football for the New York Jets … did you hear what I said ho … for the New York Jets … Do you know what that means?"

I let her continue. "No Cuqui. What does that mean?"

"What do you think it means, bitch? It means the nigga that was chasing yo coochie your whole life is now a high-rising millionaire. And you have first-class treatment to that loot."

I look at William. He stays focused on the road, but he would've been deaf not to hear Cuqui screaming as she talked a mile a minute. I stopped her while she was ahead, before she got out of hand. "Cuqui, I'll talk to you later. I'm studying."

"The hell with studying, Angel. The hell with going to law school. Kevin got so much money to where you'll never have to work a case in your life. Not to mention, that nigga can—"

I click the phone. William giggles to himself.

"Sorry, but my friend don't get out much," I said.

"I like her," he replies. "She seems to be very energetic."

"Energetic doesn't fit her profile. That girl's just plain crazy."

"I can tell that the two of you are best friends."

"How so?"

"Every black woman has one person who gets the privilege of calling her that word."

"What word?"

"The one she constantly calls you."

"Are you referring to the word *bitch*?"

He nods shrewdly as if he despises that word in every sense, as if young people has altered its origin, took it to another level.

I say, "Let me guess. You don't curse either."

"What for?" he replies. "It's like you told your friend, Cuqui. What need is there to curse?"

"I only told her that because she does it too frequently. But sometimes, depending on what you're trying to convey, curse words can be convenient."

"Oh my bad. I forget that you're into law. You try to rationalize anything."

"Well it's true. I mean just think about it. If someone owes you money, would you rather tell them, *Hey, give me my money*, or *Hey bitch, give me my damn money*? Curse words declare proclamation in their own little way."

He rebuttals. "Curse words act as replacement words. They are not only offensive, but they handicap a person from using the right words to express their true feelings, which shows a lack of intelligence. That is why they are used so frequently, so unintentionally."

I tease him. "So if I called you a bitch, would you call me one back?"

He doesn't respond.

I continue to joke. "You know you want to say it back. Come on, bitch. Say it. Let the word roll off your tongue."

He laughs it off, shows me that I can't get under his skin with a microscope, and instead of taking my words literally, he takes it as a sign of me being down-to-earth.

He asks, "You hungry?"

"I can go for a bite."

"Good. Because I'm starving ... any requests?"

I didn't want to go too pricy on him, but I didn't want him to think of me as some cheap, taco-eating chick either. So I tell him, "How 'bout *Salinas*."

"*Salinas*?"

"Yeah. Heard they've got some good fish and salmon."

"How 'bout somewhere else? *Salinas* is too expensive."

"Excuse me?"

"In case you haven't noticed, I'm trying to save money here."

"Save money? Haven't your father ever told you to never take a woman out unless you have enough bucks in your pocket?"

"Yeah, but my mother also told me that you don't need to wine-and-dine a woman with money to have a good time. And not to be cheap, but this is not a date. We didn't come to Club Down-Under together. We came separately by your request. Coming separately means that both parties are responsible for their own fees."

I look at him as if he's joking, but his expression tells me that this wasn't a joking matter. And before I know it, he was zipping the car through Steak-N-Shake, letting me out the passenger-side door, and he confidently walked me inside an establishment that was one notch above ridiculous. After ordering, he sits me in my chair, brings over my tray with so much confidence to where you would've thought we were in a first-class restaurant.

 Cyril Gillion

He sets our table. Arranges our silverware like this was the last supper, smooth with lots of class. He uses the napkin like no other. Not like it should be used, but how it could be used. Not for what it is, but for what it's worth. And even through the consummation of fast food, he carries a look of flirtation, chewing the steak-burger as if it's an eight-ounce Sirloin, biting the fries as if they've personally been delivered from the French.

Then we talked. Talked until we were blue in the face. We discussed matters that were most important to us without getting too personal, without engaging into any form of a debate. Unlike Kevin, William knew the art of conversing. He knew when to talk, when to listen, knew when to give an in-depth response, and most of all, he knew how to penetrate me mentally without constant notations of the physical.

An hour later we were sitting in front of my apartment, both running out of words to say. William turned off the radio, took the keys from the ignition and let silence give both of us an ultimatum. It was the time of night where horse playing ends, do or die time. If I let him in my apartment, it was do time for him, die time for me. But to send him home packing would only cause me to die inside, forever wishing I'd done the do; either way I'm dead.

William asks, "Mind using a bodyguard?"

"Excuse me?"

"A bodyguard. A little lady like yourself doesn't need to be walking up the stairs alone, especially in a dangerous neighborhood like this."

I exit the car; tell him, "You already protected me once, even kidnapped me to do it. But just in case you haven't realized it, I'm a big girl. That means I can protect myself."

He comes my way, throws his coat around me, then he leans in close and whisper, "Big girls need protection too."

I give in; let him walk me to do the door, feels like I'm walking a marathon. Once reaching my apartment, I take out my keys to open the door, but the key is not working.

I try again. Again it's not working.

I tell him, "Trust me, I'm not doing this on purpose."

William smirks. "Yeah, I believe you."

The key finally opens the door and I quickly step into my freedom land.

Once turning around, William is waiting on my doorstep like a deserted puppy soaked in rain, tongue hanging out the mouth with slob galore.

He tells me, "It's a long ride home."

"It is isn't it?"

"Indeed it is … you all set?"

"As set as I'm gonna get."

William steps towards me to give a goodnight hug. I accept that hug; allow him to press up against my breasts as his Issey Miyake cologne fills my nostrils.

That hug is never-ending but I'm strong enough to pull away. However, William has a little more hug to give, and just when I think this night is about to conclude, he hugs me tighter, clinching me like a child on the first day of school.

I pull back again, try to remember that I'm the dominate one in this situation, but he strikes me with a stronger hug, and then a strike-of-kiss. This time I push him away; I push away that urge, let him know that any more strikes would send him back to the dugout.

He takes the risk by showing me that he's well-prepared for any penalty or consequence that I'd issue for his actions, and he comes at me aggressively – a man with a vengeance – as if he's holding the persistence torch for all the men that never came this close in the past.

I push away. He moves in closer. I push away. He moves in closer. And before you know it, we're pushing and shoving at the beat of a drum that can't be ceased nor administered.

Our pushing game concludes and William eventually sinks his teeth into my neck, sedating me like a vampire does its victim, dosing me with a poison so deadly to where it calms me, numbs me, shifts through my veins like venom.

I stand strong but want to tremble, weak in the knees, paralyzed from waist down.

He keeps his lock steady, constant sucking on my neck, and he bulldozes the both of us through my front door, through my dining room, makes a left towards the kitchen, moves aside any pots and pans before positioning me on the counter top, all while letting me know that the cooking has just begun.

I tell him to stop; tell him that it's time to say goodnight.

He replies with "NO," and before heading for my bosom, he tells me that he'd rather say good morning.

         Cyril Gillion

I say no more, refusing to put up a fight; I've been fighting this horny sensation for months, and if blue balls existed for women, then my clit would certainly be purple.

He undresses my blouse, unfastens my bra.

My nipples are sticking out, waiting to be devoured, calling for his lips to give them some special attention. He listens to them, communicates with them on a higher level, as if he's literally speaking in tongue, uttering all the words that he couldn't tell me verbally.

He appreciates my breasts. I could tell by the way he takes his time with them, the way he clings to them like a baby who strives for formula, milking them to the point of no return, to the extremity of where he burps tit.

I gain my composure, lean down to nibble his earlobe. I want to show him that I'm not afraid of the moment, want to remind him that I have a bag of tricks of my own. So I kiss him softly, my definition of what's passionate, but in this battle, in this war of the tongues, new school looses to old school, youth looses to elderly, and it's obvious that I'm decades behind him when it comes to oral pleasure.

He shows me his maturity, maneuvers his way down my stomach, down my belly button, down to my panties that sit below the cherry tree, and before removing those panties with his teeth, he makes a deal with Victoria to reveal my secrets.

My legs tremble.

He licks up and down that cherry tree, opening my legs to bite at the forbidden fruit. He teases that forbidden fruit, hisses through the crevices like a rattler in a field of shrubs, blows on my clitoris, nibbles with soft passion, licks it lightly, does it like a magician with two tongues.

His tongue owns this territory. From wall to wall he gives quite the performance, quite the lip service, licks that clitoris like he's getting paid, like I'm his favorite client, making sure I get my money's worth – 100% customer satisfaction – and if I'm not satisfied, he'd refund my cash with the deductible.

As he continues to sex me orally, he talks, "You … taste … so … sweet."

I respond in deep breaths. *Inhale. Exhale.*

He mutters on. "I can … eat my way … to your heart."

At this point I'm too paralyzed to speak, and even though I wanted to say a thousand words, euphoria exists on an island of silence.

William suddenly takes his face out of my pie, lips greasy, takes off his shoes, shirt, pants, briefs, and he pulls out that platinum pecker.

The Other Side of the Pillow

I'm still paralyzed, never seen that type of slong up close, never seen a body so beautiful, one that's been sculptured as a masterpiece by Michelangelo himself.

Then he carries me out of the kitchen and into the living room to allow our saga to continue on the couch. My body is covered by his large mass, a warm physique that feels like butter as he begins to dip his drumstick into my secret sauce.

William holds my body firmly, his rod expanding as he bursts through my pipes. I feel pain. I feel pleasure. I feel pain wrestling with pleasure. I try not to holler, try not to let the pain consume me, want to prove that I'm a big girl and big girls don't cry, but somehow, a moan slips from my lips and the sound excites him more, causes him to progress deeper through the core of my tunnel.

He handles me with care, sets the right tempo so our bodies can move in accordance, and as our private parts become compliant with one another, the sexual pain starts to diminish within me, a pain that is no longer unbearable, my insides adapting to his thickness, my vulva creating space for his organ to dwell within its new habitat.

I like this feeling. Like it more than a kid in a theme park. Like the way he keeps the pushing in cruise control, all while sucking my breasts, grabbing my ass, giving an assignment to any part on his body that can spur the slightest bit of stimulation.

I get courageous by telling him to change positions.

He does. Doesn't hesitate to turn me over, flips me on my stomach with tenacious velocity, an intention to finally start dicking me down, no more dicking around.

Our momentum rises, causing his thrusts to become more vigorous, more relentless, and we're now sexing like wild dandelions, balls bouncing against my clitoris, wicked hair pulling, me throwing it back, wicked ass slapping, me throwing it back, him showing me how the men sex up north, me showing him how the women do it down south, we both giving a tenacious effort of never ending strokes to produce our own sweaty arena.

He talks. "Is it good to you baby … is it good?"

I tell the truth. "Hell yes."

"Tell me that it's good … say it!"

My soprano voice echoes. *"It's Goooooood."*

Talking turns him on, makes his rod stiffer, almost pushes him to that point of release. Our dirty talking heightens, we both expressing the feeling at hand, and if these virgin walls could speak, then their first words would be words of profanity.

 Cyril Gillion

I soon start to feel dizzy, over-stroked.

William's motion changes, his eyes widening as if he's straining not to cum, but he stays in the fire a little while longer to yell, "Do you like it, baby? Tell me that you like daddy's dick."

I don't respond to those words, pretend I didn't hear them, and try to ride this fairy tale until the wheels roll off.

He persists for an answer, yelling, "Tell me you like it. Tell me … how much … you like … daddy."

During sex, I hate when a man says that word daddy. The word is unnerving, makes me want to put something in his mouth to shush him. But William's enjoying the moment too much to be quieted, and as he slaps my butt some more, he repeats, "This thing is good, isn't it?" He growls. "Who is your daddy? Who … is … your … daddy?"

Not able to bear it anymore, I push him into the television and holler, "You're not my fucking daddy!"

<u>11</u>

We sit apart, motionless.

The scents from our naked bodies fluster through the room and I can almost taste the spunk. Although the air-condition blows, it's still foggy in this apartment, and we now have the ultimate greenhouse effect.

William rises to his feet, naked all over, makes his way to the kitchen with a never-ending erection.

This naked man is now raiding through my refrigerator, asking, "You thirsty?"

I don't answer. Nor do I stop him from having his way with the kitchen. Instead, I prop my feet on the couch and curl into a little cannon ball, literally trying to pull myself together to swallow what just took place ten minutes ago.

Inside I am tarnished, like a fish that's been pierced to the scales. And the word *whore* keeps making U-Turns as my head spins with many thoughts.

William observes my body language from the kitchen, watches me in distress. My eyes turn the color of blood, my tears frozen. I pleaded for those tears not to liquefy and drip down my cheek, only because William was in the room. But if he ever left, I'd fill this room with water.

If sex is supposed to conjugate than why do I feel so detached?

                            Cyril Gillion

That was the million-dollar question, a question that only I must answer.

As I sit in misery, William walks over to comfort me as if he's waiting for me to say that usual phrase, *I don't normally do things like this*, but I pull my lips together, refusing to give him the satisfaction.

He asks, "You okay?"

No answer.

"Angel, are you ok?"

I find strength. "Yes. I'm cool … cool as a fan … How 'bout you? Are you cool?"

"I'm cool."

Becoming sentimental, he put his lips to my forehead and tells me, "I don't want to make you uncomfortable. I probably should go."

"Why?"

"Because it's best."

I refuse eye contact, but never refuse my feelings. "I think you should stay."

"You sure?"

"I'm sure."

"Are you very sure? Because if you want me to leave, I'll understand."

"If you leave, don't ever come back."

My ultimatum scares him, and he kisses me on the forehead to let me know that his decision is a no-brainer, that he knows what'll happen if he walks out the door. Meanwhile, my face is still flushed, still dragging a melancholy expression.

William smiles. "I'm glad you told me to stay. Leaving would've destroyed me."

"Why is that?" I replied, walking the line of self-cautiousness.

"Because I'm not into having casual sex. And believe it or not, getting past the sex was the hard part. The rest is easy."

Needing more clarification, I ask, "What do you mean by the word *easy*? I mean … is that how you see me as? *Easy*? One that has no self-respect?"

"Of course not, Angel … you know, just because we had sex on the first night—"

"Second night!"

"—doesn't mean you are easy. Sex is just another way of sharing. Just a deeper version. And to be honest, through conversation, it's quite obvious that we shared a lot … Heck, in 24 hours, I've bonded more with you than I've done with other women that I've known for months.

I knew this wasn't the first time he said those words to a woman. More than likely, a man his age probably rehearses lines like these all the time. But at this point, any type of words would've lifted my spirits. So I pretended that his words were genuine, let them conciliate my licentious behavior, making me feel that a one-night stand has more advantages than just being a slut, after all.

He asks, "Can I use the restroom?"

"Excuse me?"

"Your bathroom? Where is it?"

"Down the hall, to the left."

He jumps to his feet, motions toward the bathroom.

"Wait!" I said, thinking about the period panties that were left hanging in the shower.

"What for?" he replied. "I really have to drain the pipes."

"And I really have to flood the river. So let me go first."

"Fine, I'll let you pull rank since this is your apartment."

I rush into the bathroom to make the necessary changes, grabbed those panties and threw them out of sight, closed the filing cabinets, and right after I fixed the shower curtain, I felt a slight pain between my legs. Darnit. I check my insides to see if he'd torn my uterus, but luckily that area was still in tact, no bloodshed.

When I got out, William was completely dressed. He was circulating around the living room, fiddling with a couple of figurines while staring at my track-n-field medallions and other academic awards from high school.

I watch him. Watch him in motion. Watch him stop in front of the television set and stare at the drawing of my mother, a huge drawing that hung above the television. Analyzing the drawing, he ran his fingers across the paint. Like usual, he was all-smiles, and I could tell that a slue of questions were floating in the air.

The drawing was one that I sketched myself, a picture showing my mother's true disposition, unhappy. Like normal naïve children, I always thought my mother was in high spirits, and nothing could make her day sour: not the beatings from my stepfather, not the fact that she had to struggle as a single mother, nothing. Every year that I've aged, wisdom started to manifest, and every year I revised the picture to unveil her in a more distressing sense, a nature that she's been concealing since I was born, the face she always wanted to show but would've went to the grave before ever showing her child the slightest sign of dysphoria.

William says, "This woman looks exactly like you. Is that your sister?"

I smile. "Mother."

He takes a closer look. "She's beautiful … Got any pictures of her from an actual camera?"

"I have many, but they're deep in my stash. Don't feel like pulling them out."

"Looks like I don't have to worry about you being old and wrinkled in twenty years. Good genes are essential. And if this is an accurate sketch, then the proof is in the pudding." He carries on. "I bet she wouldn't be too thrilled about a man her age fraternizing with her daughter. Does she live in Miami as well?"

"Lived in Miami."

"Where does she now reside?"

"Some say heaven, I say the ground."

He swallows hard. "Forgive me. I thought she was—"

"It's ok. You didn't know. It's not like I ever told you anyway."

He hesitates, says, "And what about your father?"

"Never knew him. Died while my mother was pregnant with me … so I guess when it comes to my family, death is considered a distant cousin."

No response. Only a heavy sigh, and he pauses in a desolation that is too strong to be concealed, as if he once had a lost of his own.

He suddenly takes his eyes from the picture and looks at the clock. Like time, our night is ticking.

William says, "It's 2 a.m. Do you have something to do in the morning?"

"Not really. Just have to study for an exam."

"Maybe I should let you get some shut-eye. Don't want to be the cause of a bad semester." He looks toward my room and asks, "Is that the promise land where I'll be sleeping tonight?"

I point towards the couch. "Your promise land is right there."

"Since when?"

"Since now. But don't take it personal. I have good reasons."

He chuckles. "You've gots to be kidding right. I'm supposed to be a guest."

"Wrong. Used to be a guest."

"Since when did my guest privileges become revoked?"

"The moment you pushed my uterus two inches to the right, that's when."

He lets go of the fight, my assumption that he needed to hear those words for his own male gratification. I toss him a comforter, one of thickness, and I start sauntering towards my bedroom. I can feel him strolling behind me, chasing my shadow for a second round of passion. But when I looked back, he was arranging the comforter while making the couch his new milieu.

He starts to undress, stripping down to his briefs. From the way he undresses, I can tell that he's a man of neatness, a scholar of orderliness, a man who folds his pants crease to crease, hangs his shirt on a thick hanger, organize his paraphernalia in a manner of how they'd be used in the morning.

That frightens me a little. Makes me inquire what his real expectations are of women, if my house is warm enough to make him feel at home.

After cutting off the kitchen light, I gave him one more glance before entering my bedroom, thinking I better hurry up before our sexcapade become a never-ending sequel.

I tell him goodnight, leaving us in total darkness, lying through different doors.

The next morning I awake with killing on the brain.

A pistol lies in my hand, and I'm pointing it directly at the alarm clock, screaming, "I'll kill you … Don't make me kill you!"

Sweat covers me as I stand on top of the bed, discombobulated.

William runs into the room, his eyes widening, and he strips the gun from my arms using some type of military maneuver.

He turns off the alarm clock, holds me tight. "It's ok, Angel … it's ok … was only a nightmare."

My asthma tightens.

Inviting him in my world of struggle, I signal for him to grab my inhaler that's lying near the bed, and I quickly take it to the mouth, inhaling the albuterol while exhaling the anxiety that I possessed throughout the night.

William decides to climb the attentive ladder, and he starts rubbing my back gently. "Breathe, Angel. Relax and breathe."

Doing what he tells me, I breathe strong. Breathe hard. Breathe the beast of breath.

William rubs my back. "You ok?"

"Yes … yes … I'm ok."

I take another puff of the inhaler; let the medicine circulate while William rubs my back some more, my medicine behind the medicine.

Minutes pass.

Whiffs of morning breakfast starts ricocheting from my nostrils, a scent I haven't smelled since mama was alive.

My head is leaned to the floor; I'm too embarrassed of looking up, too afraid of how he'll respond to my outburst of anxiety. Meanwhile, William is all dressed up in the same wardrobe from last night, seems like he's been awake for hours.

He says, "Good morning, beautiful."

His voice is strong. Strong enough to waken the dead.

"Morning," I reply. "What time is it?"

"Enough time for us to grab a bite to eat … You hungry?"

"Starving."

"Good, because cooking in your apartment wasn't easy."

"Cooking?"

He raise me from the bed, carries me into the living room where a shy plate of breakfast awaits me at the table. On the plate sits an oversized omelet, screaming sausage links, buttermilk biscuits, hash browns, another side of two pancakes, and a glass of orange juice that was all waiting to get acquainted with me on a deeper level – one of digestion – a level that causes my sense of smell to become over-zealous and race ahead of the other four senses.

I looked at William, smiled, my cheeks spreading to the back of my skull. "Thank you, but you didn't have to serve me breakfast."

"Did you forget that I'm a waiter? It's my job to serve. Besides, breakfast is the most important meal of the day."

He picks up a magazine from the kitchen counter, starts reading. I'm still in awe, feels like I'm in a five-star hotel, the type where the manager will become your servant.

Digging into the plate like a five-year-old with a sweet tooth, I don't hesitate to eat. The food is good. Tastes better than it smells. The type of cooking that you can only get in the south.

I say, "You really can cook."

"I can't take all the credit," he says modestly. "You have really good skillets."

"Yeah right," I replied, my laughter blending with blushes. "I know the difference between good cooking and good skillets. And this is good cooking."

"Well I'm glad you like it. That's my method of paying you back for inviting me into your home."

"Invited you? Last I remember you forced your way in."

"Did I?"

"And I should have you prosecuted for trespassing, sexual assault, disturbing the peace, and two counts of vandalism."

"Two counts of Vandalism?"

"That's right. One for terrorizing my kitchen. The other for sabotaging Victoria Secrets. It's because of you that I have to go out and purchase a new bra, which is not easy when you have breasts like mine."

He smirks. "Why not go strapless?"

"Huh?"

"Why not free yourself and take it back to Africa?"

"Very very funny."

"I'm serious. Just because you live in America, it doesn't mean you have to be Americanized."

"If being Americanized means covering my tits, then I'm proud to be an American."

He laughs. I continue to eat.

William makes his way towards the kitchen, starts looking around the counter tops.

I ask, "Looking for something?"

"My keys. I gotta head on out. My mother's expecting me."

"Your mother?" I asked in disbelief.

"My mother's in the county hospital. She has a severe case of Alzheimer's that has worsened over the last couple weeks. I see her every morning.

"And what happens if you miss a morning without seeing her?" I asked, becoming bold.

"She'd break my legs and we'll both be lying in the hospital."

I hush.

He continues. "I know it may sound crazy, but out of all my siblings, she's my responsibility."

"So what about your clothes? Do you normally get dressed up to see your mother?"

"I try to see her early in the morning, before I go to church, before I handle the rest of my business. Because she can't attend early morning service, she prefers I bring the gospel to the hospital." He fixes his watch, asks, "Would you like to come with me?"

"To visit your mother?"

 Cyril Gillion

"No, to church."

Straightforwardness leads me to say, "I'll pass on that offer. Never been the churchy type."

Eyes widening, he stares at me like I'm the devil's daughter, and he gives another parental sneer as if I've been spared by the rod, spoiled, raised in a household that lacks values and afrocentric customs. I sit in defense, wait for him to defend his God, wait to tell him all the reasons why church is not for me, why I'm not a fan of God, why my faith was distorted a long time ago.

He doesn't speak on the matter any longer, perhaps because he knows that road only leads to a dead-end, a dispute, nothing but a winless battle. Then his face changes, motion changes, I can feel him changing the subject. "I hope that my strange act this morning didn't frighten you," he says.

"What act?"

"I'm talking 'bout when I came in the bedroom. I'm not sure if you are used to waking up to something like that."

My mind revolts back to that incident, when he burst into the room and witnessed me in distress. I say, "I should be the one apologizing. You were just a man caught in the wrong place at the wrong time, trying to grab a gun from a crazy woman that you slept with last night."

He looks bewildered. "I was referring to the breakfast I prepared."

I pick up my jaw.

He says, "I know the breakfast might be somewhat shocking, but don't be afraid to tell me if I'm stepping out of line or moving to fast."

"Trust me. If you were moving to fast, I wouldn't hesitate to let you know."

He smiles. I smile back.

Our smiles are none stop. And just when I think the parade is finished, my cheeks spread again, another smile evolving, one mature enough to speak figuratively, telling him that he can never move to fast for my appreciative stomach.

He swallows hard, gathers more words. "Well on a more serious note, as far as last night goes—"

I put my finger to his lips to shush him, blocking the remaining words from ever leaving his tongue, breaking his elucidation.

I say, "Last night was last night. And today is today. So let me be a big girl and finish my breakfast. Go 'head and see your mother. I don't want your legs to be broken."

Truth is I was lying to myself. What I really wanted was to be selfish and tell him to tell his mother to get lost, that he was now a toy of my possession and today I didn't feel like sharing. But the truth meant weakness, a spilled bottle of insecurity. So I put that feeling to rest.

He gets up from the table, says, "Maybe I can see you later."

"Later when?"

"Later as in this week, unless you insist on seeing me later today."

We both pause, waiting to give the wrong answer, but knew the inevitable was approaching.

He asks, "Is school the only priority on your agenda today?"

I create a busier life. "Unfortunately, I have to work as well."

"I didn't know you work on Sundays."

"You never asked."

"Where do you work?"

"Huh?"

"Your job? What is it that you do?"

I thought about the facts that would be lined up against me if he really knew what I did for a living, the fact that I was a phone sex operator, the fact that he could possibly mix my personal life with my life at work – wandering if I was a student by day, siren by night – the fact that a tower of words could be floating around in his mind, words like slut, whore, and trick – uninhibited words stacked on top of each other, waiting to collapse on top of me, or rain on this bush that we've burned thus far.

Screw that. I won't let that happen, would drown in this tub of lies before I let our passion run down the drain. Not after what I gave him last night. Not after what he witnessed this morning. Definitely not now.

Thinking hard, I told him, "I work for ABC."

"What?"

"ABC liquor."

"You work in a liquor store?"

"Sure beats working at McDonalds."

He becomes more curious. "What days do you work?"

I grasp for straws. "It depends. My schedule is forever changing."

"Cool. Then maybe I can pick you up again from work and keep you from walking late night on these gruesome streets. What time do you get off?"

"Pick me up … Bad idea."

"Why?"

                    Cyril Gillion

"Nothing … it's just … nothing … I mean … my next door neighbor, Mona, gets off work the same time as me. More than likely I can ride with her. How about you save your gas money and hopefully use it to take me to a better spot than Steak-N-Shake next time."

My humor attempts to break his inquisition, but he's still carrying the look of a detective, investigating the chain-of-events that leads to the truth.

I eat cautiously. Wait for him to find probable cause to convict me of that lie, but he doesn't.

Instead he pleads the fifth, gives a smirk, and flips over the cuffs on his blue-collar shirt, an insinuation that I'm not the only one with tricks up my sleeve.

Then he heads for the door, his silhouette remaining at the table, steadily watching me eat.

12

The next day my tail was dragging.

I sat in class as a totally different Angel Inghram, not caring about my image for the first time ever. I had thrown on a t-shirt, jeans, an old pair of Nikes, pony-tail. Like usual, Professor Stern had given a quiz, a two thousand word paper due at the end of class, one that must be written subjectively detailing the perks and loopholes of the judicial system. My brain was completely fried, traveling the opposite direction of Professor Stern's lesson, speeding down William's Ave.

I tried to shift back in fourth gear, back to the topic at hand. Professor Stern had given us an hour for the task and before I could get into a rhythm, he was already hollering out, "Ten minutes left," leaving me with only half my paper completed.

Those last ten minutes were merciless. So was Professor Stern. He immediately called for the time, requested that we hand in our papers and whoever was still writing would automatically receive an "F."

I wasn't finished. Wasn't closed to being finished. And although I'd been given an order, my pen was still moving, formulating phrases that were unrelated to the topic, far from the usual work of Angel Inghram.

Within seconds, every student had turned in their paper, and the grass was soon cut with only two snakes remaining in the class. Those snakes were me and a black guy named Big Lex, a student who was not only dumb as rocks, but got in college through the power of his parent's Visa.

I kept on writing. Wrote for another two minutes, long enough for me to turn in a paper that was one notch above chicken scratch but still considered finished.

I scurried to write my name because no-named papers received an automatic ten point deduction. In between scribbling the *A* in Angel and the *I* in Inghram, a pale hand stopped my wrist from moving, the pen from bleeding.

I looked up and saw the leopard staring down upon me, an angry Professor that was waiting to attack. He wore huge glasses, lenses powerful enough to see my internal organs, and those four eyes contemptuously stared at me from every direction, binocular vision.

Not giving him any time to speak, I tried to hand over my work but he refused to buy the paper that I was selling.

He said, "When I speak, I have a tendency to make myself clear. For me to see you still writing leads me to think two things. Either a.) I wasn't clear, or b.) I was clear, but was ignored. Now because I hate to be ignored, I'm going to choose option *a* and assume I wasn't clear. So maybe I should say it again, just to be clearer."

He waited for me to speak, yet dared me to speak at the same time. I've been in situations like these before, situations that only take a big butt and a smile to slither my way out of, but considering that this was Professor Stern, the promiscuous route just wouldn't work.

He says, "Ms. Inghram, I hope you're ready for the final exam in two weeks, because in my course, mercy only takes you so far. I suggest you consider this as a blessing."

At 6 pm I was back on the Subway, mentally exhausted. My brain was solid as jello, a brain filled with bifurcated trials and forfeiture hearings that I'd spent hours reviewing in a trial advocacy course. The subway was packed like sardines, and finding a seat was harder than finding a cure for cancer. I stood on my feet for ten minutes, bunged in between two women who were on my ass like headlights. One of the women were Turkish (or so she looked Turkish), carried a scent strong enough to blow through human nostrils, had her hair pinned up. The other women, the one on my other ass cheek, was a short stout white lady who couldn't stay still for five seconds because she was too busy trying to discipline her son who was messing over a carton of milk. On the side of me sat three older men – one Spanish, one Arabian, and a black Rick James look-a-like that almost broke his neck while trying to watch my breasts on satellite.

This whole scenery was New York at its finest. A dozen races carrying different mindsets while riding to a common destination. And I was dead in the middle. Stood out of place like a rose in a vineyard.

The Rick James look-a-like eventually rose from his seat, reached over the little boy to ask me, "Would you like to sit?"

Posing the question to my breasts, his eyes never went past my neck.

I decided to ignore him. Put on the no-talking-to-strangers-face like a kindergarten on the first day of school.

He continues with, "Pretty woman like you shouldn't be standing on her feet."

Knowing that when it comes to a man, nothing in this world is free, including a seat on the subway, I reply, "No thanks. I'm fine."

"No, I insist. Besides, I'm getting off at the next top, 122nd."

At that moment, the woman with the foul odor decided to raise her arm to grab hold of the rail.

I look back at Rick James. "On second thought, I think I'll take the seat," I said, flaunting these young set of D cups before they sag one day and turn into glasses.

We suddenly came to the next stop, 122nd St. The Spanish and Arabian guy decided to exit the subway. I remembered the guy who gave me his seat, the Rick James look-a-like, telling me that this was his stop as well, but he wasn't moving at all to get off. However, the white guy sitting next to me did start to get off.

That leaves three seats empty.

Two seats that were grabbed by a couple of Indian women, and the other seat – the one next to me – was still up for grabs. As the white guy walked towards the exit, he glanced in my direction and slapped hands with Rick James, acting as if it was one of those talk-to-you-later type of slaps, but I knew otherwise.

Rick James grabbed the seat right next to me, pretending to read the obituary section of the Times.

I smiled. Smiled at the power of the vagina, how it has the power to abuse without intentionally being used.

Rick James says, "I guess my conscience was right. The woman really does smile."

In the midst of me smiling, he smiles too, and he shows some teeth that are yellow enough to fill a bowl of margarine.

I tell him, "I thought you said 122nd was your stop?"

"It was. But I figured there'd be no harm in wasting a little time to speak with a beautiful woman."

I say, "Are you always this foolish when it comes to women?"

"Infatuation will cause a man to do foolish things."

"Now that's funny."

"Is it?"

"There are millions of women in Brooklyn. Why would you delay an hour out of your day, just to spark up a conversation with one woman?"

"Like you said ma, there are millions of women in Brooklyn. So the probability of seeing you again is slim to none. And I've never been the type to pass up a good opportunity." He starts back at square one, asking, "So what is your name?"

"Angel."

"Angel huh … I like your country voice, Angel. You must not be from New York."

"I'm not."

"Where are you from?"

"Miami."

 "Cool. How long have you been—"

"Listen up Rick James—"

"Who?"

"Sorry … uum … what is your name by the way?"

"Baby J."

"Baby what?"

"Baby J. But you can just call me J."

"Okay then, J. Look here. I get off at 140th St. That's five minutes away. So that means you only have about three minutes left to skip pass the bullshit of pretending you want to know me and—"

My cellular intervenes. I look at the caller id but I never answer that symphony. For I have no friends at 1-800 #'s.

Rick James, or shall I say Baby J, is sitting on eggshells, afraid of what to say next. He thinks before speaking, but my cellular rings and intrudes once more. Again, I'm not aware of the phone number. However, 305 is a Miami area code. So I pick up.

"Is this Angel?"

"Speaking."

"How are ya?"

"Who's calling?"

There's a pause. Heavy breathing. "This is Kevin."

"Who?" I asked, making sure I heard correctly.

"Damn, Angel. Have you forgotten about me already? It's Kevin Armstrong."

I paused for a moment; started getting my mind together for a conversation I wasn't ready to have. "Since when did the internet start giving out cellular #'s?"

He laughs. "Do you really think I'd stoop so low to where I'd track you down from the internet?"

I thought hard. Thought about who'd be crazy enough to give Kevin my number without consulting with me first.

Then I thought of Cuqui.

I'm gonna kill her ass. She's been dying for me to get back with Kevin, so I knew it had to be her.

Kevin said, "You don't have to worry about me calling you again. Hell, I'll loose your number if that's what you really want. But my main objective for calling was to apologize for the other night. I got beside myself, stepped out of line, and certainly out of character."

"Apology accepted … Is that it?"

His voice crumbles. "Not really."

"Well maybe we can talk some other time. I'm a little busy at the moment."

Rick James's face grows roots of enchantment, his ears glued to the conversation at hand. But on the other end, Kevin is not ready to throw this call into the river.

Kevin murmurs, "Angel."

"Yeah," I replied, my voice now obstinate.

"Maybe we should try this again."

"Try what?"

"After nine moths of not seeing Angel Inghram, I didn't expect for our meeting to be so … so brief … I mean … maybe we should give ourselves a couple hours to catch up on the time we've missed."

William started floating through my brain, his silhouette becoming my conscience. Once again, I weighed my options. Even though Kevin had become a professional football player, my eyes were still fixed on William, still trying to recuperate from all the lovemaking we've done, the talks, the things I never appreciated with Kevin. But then again, to ignore what Kevin has to offer – a man who is damn near worth seven figures – would make me first runner-up for the world's dumbest chick.

Kevin asks, "Are you busy this weekend?"

"Don't know. Have to check my schedule."

"Well today is Monday. You've got till Friday to let me know," he says confidently. "This is my direct number. So if you don't call, I'll know your decision."

I got off at 140th St., two blocks shy of Piedmont Projects, whatever it took to dodge Rick James. By the time I reached 142nd my bikini low-rise were constantly rising up my crack, resulting in my PH no longer being balanced.

I floored into the house, decided to head to the shower for all the right reasons. William has yet to call the cell, so before I hopped in, I checked the caller id. There were two missed calls. One from Cuqui and one from my manager, Dexter, yelling about how he needed an extra girl to work the late-night shift tomorrow. The longer William took to call, the shorter my patience became.

After a two-minute shower, I checked the caller id again. No call from William.

Deciding to stall time, I threw on some PJ's and took a stroll to the mailbox to see if Brooklyn College had sent me anything important. While walking down the steps, I saw Mona's older boyfriend, Pete, walking up the steps with a black woman, a chick the same age as Mona and I. He was drunk and so was she. So drunk to where they were dragging along the banister while steadily groping at each other's throats. Pete wasn't too drunk to recognize me in passing, and as the liquor aroma smelled up the steps, he smirked at me as if he was daring me to tell Mona. Right then and there I wanted to run into the house and grab my camera phone to snapshoot him and his chick, building my own power-point presentation for Mona's personal viewing, just so she could witness how much of a dog he really was.

Then my mind shifts back to William.

If my calculation serves me correctly, I believe him and Pete are the same age, just a difference in color. Like Pete, William could be somewhere right now, licking another chick the way he licks me, fulfilling her with the same pleasure, desperately drinking from another fountain of youth before age swallows his outer features and his thirst for younger women can no longer be quenched.

The thought alone takes me through mind regression, fills my insides with thumbtacks.

Technically, I wasn't his woman. One night of passion doesn't give me the right to be his woman. But technically, considering that he'd already sampled my pearl, means I now have the right to a

The Other Side of the Pillow

different type of right – dick claiming rights – and that alone makes our situation a little more technical. So I stepped outside of the box; stepped outside the Angel that wasn't used to chasing a man.

I dialed his number.

<u>*13*</u>

My intentions were none out of the ordinary, to hang up if William doesn't answer on the third ring.

Nonetheless, a voice answered after that third ring, and to my surprise it was the voice of a woman.

My heart skipped a beat as I thought, *who's the bitch that's picking up Williams' phone*, but the heartbeat resumed on task after realizing that the voice was only the Operator.

I hung up instantly, never been the type to leave messages.

Trying to re-route my mind, I booted up my laptop and started navigating through Netscape to search for a preparation manual that outlines analytical and logical reasoning questions that'll appear on the bar exam. Most websites only provided scenarios of different argumentative techniques and parallel reasoning, but neither contained a strategy that I was unfamiliar with. I finally came across a website that provided the resources I needed, but there was a pricing plan for obtaining it.

That made me upset. Made me wander how psychos can track everything from social security to DNA, but the moment I try getting something productive, it involves a fee.

In the midst of my constant search, a message popped on my computer from AOL.

[*You've got Mail*]

LONG JOHN: Hey sexy.
LONG JOHN: Hey sexy.
LONG JOHN: Hey sexy.

I don't know who the hell *LONG JOHN* was supposed to be, but in just two minutes of being on AOL, he was emailing me non-stop.

LONG JOHN: Hey sexy.
LONG JOHN: Hey sexy.

Usually I ignore instant messages from unknown users, but considering that I didn't have class until 12 p.m. tomorrow, I figured why not have some fun with this guy named Long John, at least until William calls back. So I decide to respond.

Angel: How bout you give me a visual image of yourself.
LONG JOHN: I'm about 6'0, brown-skin, medium build, and a low-fade haircut. Some people say I look like Morris Chestnut.
Angel: lol … lol
LONG JOHN: What's so funny?
Angel: You said Morris Chestnut.
LONG JOHN: And?
Angel: If you look anything like Morris, then take me right now.
LONG JOHN: What about yourself? Do you look as good as you sound?
Angel: You never even heard my voice. For all you know, I could be a man. Hell, my balls could be bigger than yours.
LONG JOHN: I seriously doubt that!
Angel: lol lol.
Angel: I'm 5'8, hair down my back (and yes my hair is real), 75% African American, 25% peanut butter, 34-26-34 measurements, light brown eyes (and yes my eyes are real), lips better than Angelina Jolie, abs tighter than Janet Jackson, bowlegged like Nia Long, pretty toes, no cellulite.
LONG JOHN: Hmmm. Do your lips really look like Angelina Jolie?
Angel: Wanna see a pic?
LONG JOHN: That's ok. Pictures will lie.
Angel: Do they?

                              Cyril Gillion

LONG JOHN: Through the lens of a camera, a person can look like a million bucks. But once you see them in person, you have to do a double-take.

Angel: I disagree. In my opinion, a picture captures detail. It catches what the naked eye fails to pick up.

LONG JOHN: A picture only captures the standstill. But I don't want to see the standstill.

Angel: What you wanna see?

LONG JOHN: Personality. Sex appeal. I love a woman with sex appeal. For me, strong sex appeal is far more attractive than a woman with curves, huge breasts.

Angel: Hmmm. Guess I was blessed with both. I've got the full package.

LONG JOHN: The full package … geez … where I'm from, finding a woman with both is unrealistic.

Angel: Maybe you should get out more.

LONG JOHN: Maybe you're right.

LONG JOHN: Do you stay alone?

In this case, lying is acceptable.

Angel: I stay with my guy friend.

LONG JOHN: You mean your boyfriend.

Angel: Nope. I mean my guy friend.

LONG JOHN: Is your guy-friend supposed to be same guy from a couple weeks back?

Angel: Excuse me?

LONG JOHN: Your guy friend. Is it the same person?

Angel: Do you know him?

LONG JOHN: No. But I know you.

Angel: Who are you?

LONG JOHN: You should already know … We just recently made love.

Angel: Us? Made love?

LONG JOHN: Yes.

Angel: Fantasies are for children.

LONG JOHN: I'm serious. We made love in your apartment complex.

Angel: And what apartment is that.

I waited for his answer. Knew it was a one-and-a-million chance that it could be William, but I still had to be certain.

LONG JOHN: Brooklyn Estates. You stay in Brooklyn Estates.

I busted a blood vessel. I'm sure it was a blood vessel.

Angel: William, is this you?
LONG JOHN: Yes.
Angel: Well the dead have risen.
LONG JOHN: I called you a couple times. Never received an answer.

Liar ...Liar ...Liar

Angel: Maybe you thought you called but really called someone else. You sure you're not confusing me with another Angel?
LONG JOHN: There are hundreds of angels in heaven, but only one in New York. So it's impossible to confuse you with another Angel.

Even on the net, his charm soothes my bitterness, pacifies my ongoing tension. And in any case, whether you're speaking in person or through TPL, charm is still considered charm, and it's a hard bullet to dodge.

LONG JOHN: So what's going on? How's school?
Angel: Forget about school. I'd rather talk about us.
LONG JOHN: Cool.
Angel: Let's talk about Saturday. I know I acted a little crazy during our session, but I have some things going on inside that you'll never understand. However, as far as the sex goes, I enjoyed it.
LONG JOHN: Good, because at first I was thrown for a loop.
Angel: A loop?
LONG JOHN: Yeah, you seemed a little nervous while we were in the act.
Angel: How you figure?
LONG JOHN: The other night, before I started giving you oral pleasure, you were shaking while I was touching you. Looked like you were about to have a seizure.
Angel: lol lol. Don't flatter yourself.

LONG JOHN: It's the truth.

Angel: I was only shivering because your hands were cold.

LONG JOHN: Wish I could put those cold hands on you right now.

Angel: Is that so?

LONG JOHN: No doubt.

Angel: Why so promiscuous? I mean, aren't you supposed to be a man of God?

LONG JOHN: That's right.

Angel: Well from the way you were licking my pie, it seemed like the work of the devil.

LONG JOHN: lol. Guess I got a little beside myself that night.

Angel: I can tell you enjoy giving?

LONG JOHN: Always been a giver. Never been much of a receiver.

Angel: Yeah, sounds like the words of half the men in America.

LONG JOHN: Not this man. I'm genuine when I tell you that.

Angel: Hmmm?

LONG JOHN: I'll lick you more than the post office lick stamps.

Angel: Damn! That's a whole lot of licking.

LONG JOHN: What about yourself?

Angel: What is it you want to know?

LONG JOHN: Are you a giver or a receiver?

Angel: I don't know. I like doing both.

LONG JOHN: What about the giving part? Do you know what you're doing?

Angel: What makes you think I don't?

LONG JOHN: Most women think they know, but they really need training.

Angel: Not this woman. I train the trainers.

LONG JOHN: Really?

Angel: And when it comes to oral, I have a CDL license.

LONG JOHN: What's a CDL license?

Angel: A Certified D$%k Sucking License!

LONG JOHN: LOL.

We both were shit talkers. Both wanted to prove that we were the best at what we do. Truth is I wasn't ready for this conversation and I knew I'd have to live up to everything I said. But at the same time, I wasn't about to sit here and let him intimidate me either. Hell, I did this for a living.

The Other Side of the Pillow   121

LONG JOHN: As far as the CDL license goes, do you really have one? Or are you just bluffing.

Angel: I don't bluff.

LONG JOHN: Ok then. Show me.

Angel: Show you???

LONG JOHN: Yeah, show me how good you are?

Angel: Right now?

LONG JOHN: Right now. How would those lips seduce my long john?

No words.

LONG JOHN: You there?

Angel: I'm here.

LONG JOHN: What would you do first?

Angel: First, I'll kiss you softly on the danus.

LONG JOHN: The danus?

Angel: Right between the rear and testicles. The most sensitive spot on a man. The male g-spot.

Don't ask. Learned it from one of the girls at work.

LONG JOHN: Interesting, why would you start there?

Angel: Instead of going down on a man, I prefer to go up … makes it more enticing.

Angel: Then I'll engage in a foursome.

LONG JOHN: A foursome?

Angel: Me, you, and your two little friend balls.

Angel: I'll tongue-kiss one of them while the other one gets jealous … all in one motion while I'm stroking your long john.

LONG JOHN: Wooooooo.

Angel: Then I'll slide my tongue up the base of your long john. horizontally … then vertically … but never reaching the extremity of your head.

LONG JOHN: Wooooooo.

Angel: After minutes of tongue sliding, I'll give you light licks on the neck of your head … then I'll stop.

LONG JOHN: What? Why would you stop?

LONG JOHN: Why would you stop?

LONG JOHN: Why would you stop?

                    Cyril Gillion

Angel: I'd stop long enough to look your long john directly in the eye.

Angel: I'll make union with the eye … amalgamation.

Angel: And then I'd start throttling it, jerking it, suffocating your long john until the point of release, until it's put to sleep.

LONG JOHN: Wow. Some type of an imagination you have.

Angel: That's no imagination. That's real talk.

LONG JOHN: Well then, I like that stuff you're talking. As a matter fact, I love it.

Angel: Now it's your turn.

LONG JOHN: My turn?

Angel: What is it? Cat caught your tongue.

LONG JOHN: For me, when it comes to sex, I'm the spontaneous type.

LONG JOHN: I love to bring food in bed. Especially cherries.

Angel: Cherries?

LONG JOHN: Cherries can be considered an aphrodisiac.

Angel: And what would you do with those cherries?

LONG JOHN: Squirt the juice all down your back … down your buttocks … let it sizzle between your crack … all over my tongue …. watch you stare down upon me.

Angel: Sssssssss.

LONG JOHN: Start kissing between your thighs … soft kisses … circular kisses around the clitoris … figure-eights … never touching the clitoris with my tongue … and then … and then …

Angel: And then what?

Angel: And then what?

Angel: And then what?

LONG JOHN: Start blowing on it lightly … nibbling … sensual nibbling … light blows and light nibbling … do that thing continuously while you wait for the tongue …

I'd be lying if I said that I wasn't getting turned on. I felt more dampness in my boy-shorts.

LONG JOHN: Can I tell you something.

Angel: Anything.

LONG JOHN: I wanna sex you right now.

Angel: Wow … so direct … are you serious? Right now?

LONG JOHN: Yes, right now.

Angel: What do you want to do to me?

LONG JOHN: You don't want to know.

Angel: Actually, I do. Tell me.

LONG JOHN: I want to bend you over … face down … ass up … an apple in your mouth … cherry in your ass … do it while you're trying to scream my name. LONG JOHN … LONG JOHN.

Angel: Wow. Is that your fantasy?

LONG JOHN: Nope.

Angel: Tell me your fantasy. I want to know.

LONG JOHN: Six women … all virgins … different races … different languages … In Tahiti … on a rainy day … bent over … by the river ….asses up … faces down … humming my name … LONG JOHN … LONG JOHN … apples in their mouths … big apples.

I take my hands from the keyboard. I'm speechless. Boyshorts wetter than a diaper.

LONG JOHN: Angel, you still there?

LONG JOHN: Angel, you still there?

LONG JOHN: Angel, you still there?

Angel: yes … yes … I'm here.

LONG JOHN: What about you. Do you have a fantasy?

Angel: Yes, but I'm not gonna say it.

LONG JOHN: Why?

Angel: You might freak out.

LONG JOHN: Lay it on me. Your ultimate fantasy.

Angel: Okay … wanna do it on a rainy day … on a football field … under the goal post … halftime of the game … everyone watching … I'm wearing a helmet … I'm riding him … slapping him … shoving his head in the grass … Redskin feathers in his mouth.

LONG JOHN: What the hell?

Angel: See, I knew you'd freak out.

LONG JOHN: No, I like it. I love it actually.

In a sense, it was a little juvenile for us to be carrying on like this, chatting online like teenagers. But at the moment, nothing in the world could've made me quit.

LONG JOHN: Can I be the guy in your fantasy? Can I be that guy on the football field, getting his face shoved in the dirt?

Angel: Only if I can be the black girl in yours … and I really like apples. Big apples.

                                Cyril Gillion

Angel: How long can you sex for?

LONG JOHN: A long time.

Angel: Lions can sex for seventeen hours non stop. Can you do it that long?

No reply.

Angel: Long john, you there?

LONG JOHN: Yes.

Angel: What are you doing?

LONG JOHN: Got my hand on the long john … thinking bout that fantasy of yours.

Angel: Are you?

LONG JOHN: You really know how to get a brotha going?

Angel: Feelings mutual. Got my boy shorts soaking wet.

LONG JOHN: Really?

Angel: Yes.

Angel: You hard right now?

LONG JOHN: Hard as a rock!

LONG JOHN: You wet right now?

Angel: Two words … Pacific Ocean.

Angel: Bout ready for you to nose-dive into this Pacific.

LONG JOHN: Nose-dive?

Angel: Dive into it headfirst.

Angel: Then I want you to bend me over, do me from the back, shove that apple into this mouth.

LONG JOHN: Your request is my demand.

LONG JOHN: Can I pull your hair?

Angel: Hell yes. I've got extensions.

LONG JOHN: Can I slap your ass?

Angel: No more questions. Just shut up and put that thing inside.

No reply.

LONG JOHN: Can you feel it?

Angel: Oh yes baby … hell yes.

LONG JOHN: Can I go … deeper?

Angel: Huh?

LONG JOHN: I want to go deeper.

Angel: Go deep … as you … can.

LONG JOHN: "Can you feel it ... can you feel that ... long ... john.
Angel: Yes ... I ... ooooooooohhh ... can feel it.
Angel: Bring it to the left ... a little ... damn ... right there ...
LONG JOHN: Right here?
Angel: Yes ... right ... there.
Angel: Oh yes ... shit ... right there.
Angel: That's my ... spot.
LONG JOHN: Whewww shutz ... your insides feels ... like ... heaven
Angel: Your penis ... can tear up ... hell.
Angel: This ... is ... so good ... so intense.
LONG JOHN: I know.
Angel: You feel ... so good ... inside ... these ... damn ... walls.

No reply.

LONG JOHN: Angel, Can I turn you around? I want you on your stomach.
Angel: Okay, but ... hurry up.
LONG JOHN: Why?
Angel: close to cumming all over this keyboard.
LONG JOHN: You are???
Angel: Hell yes ... hell yes ... keep talking.
LONG JOHN: Can I smack it?
Angel: Ooooohhh ... oooooooahhhhh ... ooooohhh.
LONG JOHN: I take that as a yes.
Angel: Ooooohhh ... ahhhhh ... ooooohhh.
Angel: Harder. I want it ... harder.
LONG JOHN: Is this ... hard enough ... damn.
Angel: Yes baby ... give me more.
LONG JOHN: You want more?
Angel: yes ... keep it coming ... keep it coming ... keep it coming.
Angel: KEEP ... THAT ... THING ... COMING!!
Angel: Oh yes ... right there.
LONG JOHN: Right there?
Angel: Yes baby ... right ... right ... there.
LONG JOHN: You like it ... do you @#g8w ... like that stroke.
Angel: oooooooooooohhhh.
LONG JOHN: Tell me that you ^5*$ like that stroke.
Angel: I ... like ... I ... like ... that ... that ... stro$^#.

Angel: Talk dirty to me baby … talk … dirty.
LONG JOHN: Apples … BIG RIPE APPLES
Angel: ooooooaaaaaaaaahhhh
LONG JOHN: wwweeehhhh.
Angel: ooooooaaaaaaaaahhhh
LONG JOHN: yes … damn girl … you feel so …
Angel: Don't stop … I'm close … shit … don't stop … go deeper
… deeper.
LONG JOHN: This deep?
Angel: Yes … damn … yes … right … there.
Angel: yes … there
Angel: yes … there
Angel: yes … there
Angel: yes … yes … yes … there
Angel: Yes … yes … hold on … oooo … this thing is … shit …
I'm there … I'm there … yes … damn … I'm going to …cum@#^# …
 2qgq2ming2ig4#$^%#@^#mia3womnikbng5l12ktm2qP32cedb2#$^4
eqpp6pppp249820g0944go3q:)

_14_

I sat by the phone waiting for a call from the first man to ever sex me in cyberspace, better yet, the first to ever give me multiple orgasms from just the click of a mouse.

Somehow, I found myself becoming nervous, anxious, more tense than a virgin who was about to be de-virginized, and I kept thinking about the greeting I would use once he calls.

Before I could gather my thoughts, my cellular started screaming. I flipped open the phone, making sure my _hello_ was as sexy as ever.

"Hello?"

"Hi, Angel. Nice to hear your voice."

"Same here. Don't want to say it, but I was anticipating your call."

"Were you?"

"Was five seconds away from hunting you down."

I put the phone on mute. Something was wrong. Something terribly wrong.

This person didn't sound like William, didn't sound like Long John. Couldn't be the John that I longed for. I remembered William having a strong and empowering voice, a voice of thunder. Instead, the man behind the receiver had a feminine voice. High pitched as broken glass.

Skeptical as ever, I asked him for his name again. "Are you sure this is William?"

　　　　　　　Cyril Gillion

Then I heard laughing. Lots of laughing.

"What is so funny?" I asked.

"Angel … you fall for the same thing every time."

"What? Who the hell is this?"

"Bitch, this is Cuqui … the whole time you thought it was William who was emailing you, but it was really me."

"You?"

"Yes Angel… me."

She laughs her heart out as I say, "Cuqui, what the hell are you doing?"

"No Angel, what the hell are you doing? Thought you told me that you were focused on your studies."

"I am."

"Must be the study of dick-ology," she says. "Don't even try to play me, bitch. Who the hell is William?"

"He's no one."

"Who the hell is no one?"

I knew I was already caught. Cuqui was too persistent to let a bogus story stand in the way of the truth. But then again, telling Cuqui the truth was worst than calling a 1-800 number and asking for Ms. Cleo.

So I exaggerated. "I met him a few months back."

"Where?"

"At the coffee shop. And I'm telling you Cuqui, he's far from the usual men that we meet.   He has strong conversation, a sense of humor, and—"

"Whatever, bitch. Let's forget about the small talk and skip to the good parts, like the nigga's appearance … Does he look good? And if his looks are on point, does he also have some good pipe. And if the pipe is good, does he have some good working credit cards inside in his wallet. Those are the three most important questions."

I laughed; told her, "Trust me, girl. He's handsome."

 "More handsome than Kevin?"

"Much more. He's handsome like … like … like Will Smith."

"Will Smith?"

"Hell yeah girl."

"Which Will Smith? The Fresh Prince of Bel-Air Will Smith or the Bad Boys Will Smith?"

"What's the difference?"

"Are you blind, Angel? There's a huge difference."

"Anyways, he looks good. Damn good."

The Other Side of the Pillow

"And what about his pockets. Good looks with no money is an oxymoron."

I think about whether I should answer her, and before the words *he's a waiter* bounces off my tongue, she asks, "Is his money as long as Kevin's?"

"Why do you keep comparing him to Kevin?"

"Because Kevin is not only a provider, but he's a professional football player who just so happens to still be in love with my best friend. So that makes my job very important. I'm the negotiator, the bitch who's responsible for patching you two back together."

"Okay then, what would you say if I told you that William doesn't make as much money as Kevin, but he is still a provider?"

"I'd say he better have an extra dick to compensate for the lack of funds."

We share a laugh.

Cuqui says, "You know I'm just kidding right. Nothing wrong with having a broke-ass nigga, I suppose, if that's what floats your boat. But if you're anything like me, I say you should go for the money man."

I stand in William's defense; tell her, "Money isn't everything."

"Huh?"

"Money is useless if a person is not rich in spirit."

"Huh?"

"Money without happiness is equal to living in a mansion alone."

She laughs. "And good sex would have a woman talking out of character, which is what your ass is doing right now. Girl, what did that nigga do to my best friend? He rape you or something?"

"What? Don't be silly."

"I'm serious, Angel. You don't even know this William guy and he's already got you talking like 'em. As a matter of fact, what is his last name?"

"What? Why?"

"I'm fixing to google his ass on the internet. Need to make sure my friend ain't dating some lunatic."

"Girl you so crazy."

"Oh come on, Angel. Please tell me that you at least thought about it."

"I haven't."

"Well I have. Now what is his last name?"

"Forget it, Cuqui. I'm not trying to go that route."

               Cyril Gillion

"You don't have to, but I can. I'm not gonna let you get involved with some nigga that you know nothing about."

I tell her, "I know enough."

"What?"

"I know all I need to know."

"BS. You only know what he tells you."

"Yeah, and that's probably a good thing because what I don't know won't hurt me."

"No bitch, what you don't know could possibly get yourself killed. Just the other day a girl went missing in Broward County, all because she went out of town with some guy that she thought was a truck driver."

"So what are you saying? That I should hire a private detective, 'cause I'm not trying to be a stalker."

"I'm just telling you to be careful."

"Trust me, Cuqui. William is not that type of guy. Plus, he takes care of his mother, so if he doesn't have anything else, at least I know he has a kind heart. The only thing I don't like is that he seems to be heavy on the religion tip. And you know I don't get down with the religion thing. I mean, the nigga don't even drink. Like he's some type of Mormon."

"Well Hallelujah and thank ya Jesus. Sounds like you got yourself a saint." She laughs. "But if he's cool with you, I guess he's cool with me … How old is he?"

I swallow hard. "What?"

"His age. How old is he?"

"Why?"

"Because age is important."

"Just know that he's very mature."

"Gosh, Angel … How mature is *very*? Older than thirty?"

"Yes."

"Thirty-five?"

I breathe a slow breath. "He's … he's forty."

"What??? Bitch are you insane?" she asks, her voice now twice the volume."

I become defensive. "Forty isn't that old."

"Like hell it isn't. Forty is only ten years from fifty, which is half of a century."

"Darnit, Cuqui. Didn't you just say that it was cool with you as long as it was cool with me?"

"Yeah, but that was before you told me that he was damn near a senior citizen"—She laughs—"Girl, isn't it a felony to go 'round sleeping with men that old."

"Shut up, Cuqui. Besides, me and William are just kicking it. Nothing more."

"Yeah right," she says. "Don't you know that men his age aren't interested in just kickin it? They're looking for something more. Like someone to settle down with, take care of their kids, scare away their baby mama. You know, all the shit you're not interested in doing."

I sit on the phone and listen. Listen to Cuqui recite her five hundred-page book of how to never date an older man, an undiscovered National Best Seller.

In the midst of her rambling, I received a beep on the other line. Wandering who the hell was calling at two in the morning, I click over to answer, but before I could say hello, the call got disconnected.

I clicked back over to Cuqui but she was no longer on the line, one of those females who don't like to be put on hold for more then ten seconds.

My cellular rings again.

This time around, the caller is William. I know it's him because of the special ring tone, *Secret Lovers*, and although it took days for him to call, the ring tone was still music to my ears, enough relief for me to fill the blanks to the unanswered question; the question of knowing that I wasn't some lousy one-night stand that men brag about over beer and poker play.

But I still played my cards right.

Although it might sound crazy, I refused to answer that ringing symphony, didn't want William to think I was some booty call that he could ring in the middle of the night. For there were rules to this game. Rules he had to respect. And no matter how many orgasms he gave me, how sexy he was, how pure, genuine, or charismatic he may appear to be, rules are still rules. And they can never be altered.

I started to shut down my computer, and while logging off, Internet pop-ups kept appearing everywhere. One of the pop-ups read peoplefinder.com, a site where you can find information on anyone alive.

Then I thought about William. If there was anyone who was worth inquiring about, it was him. Maybe Cuqui was right. Maybe I should do my own research on William, just to ensure myself that everything

 Cyril Gillion

about him was legit. There were some unanswered questions that I wanted to know and the Internet was the only source for getting those answers. William speaks relentlessly about his past. He talks about a life-changing experience that happened five years ago, which he refuses to speak on, maybe because it's not the right time for me to know.

I beg to differ.

Although I would never admit it to Cuqui, I wanted to know everything about his life, and what better a time to know than the present, while my feelings are still new – nothing more than that of a seed – before they blossom into a naive plant with roots of embezzlement.

With just the click of a mouse, I took Cuqui's advice, started to Google the name William Randolph on the number one search engine of the web.

Google told me that there were a million William Randolph's, and it forced me to narrow down my search.

After plugging in his date of birth, gender, and ethnicity, I soon found myself becoming desperate for data, no longer a woman with self-restraint.

Was I a stalker?

If I was, it didn't matter at this point. My curiosity had already spun out of control, now circling through a whirlwind of exploration, and if curiosity killed the cat, then I certainly was ready to die.

15

Loud knocks with multiple screams awake me the next morning.

The knocks are coming from the front door, sounded like a kid crying out for help. Considering that this was Brooklyn, I didn't hesitate to reach for my gun, then I placed it inside the back of my boy shorts before covering up with a housecoat. It turns out that the knocker was my next-door neighbor, Mona, carrying two heavy bags in her hands, heavier bags beneath her eyes, my conclusion that her heart was the heaviest.

"Did I wake you?" she asks, her words dragging a melancholy tone.

She wore a white ripped halter-top, sandals, and some turquoise sweat pants that appeared to be bleached to death. Her hair had no sense of direction; hair that was once long and manageable was now preparing its own defense mechanism.

I asked her, "What's the problem?"

"Bill threw me out. He says he don't love me anymore … he … he now loves someone else … he loves someone else."

She begins to cry as if this episode of sorrow is new in her eyes, but in my eyes it's nothing but a re-run. As much as I wanted to slap him for putting her on the street, I wanted to slap her even more for having half a brain. I started to close the door in her face, but I seen my mother in her eyes – a woman that was also put on the street by my stepfather from time to time – so therefore, closing the door on Mona would be equivalent to hitting my mother in the face with the same door.

Aunt Terry used to tell me that everyone needs a helping hand at some point and for every hand that you reach for, God sends you two hands in return. As those words simmer, I look at my one bedroom apartment, look back at Mona, then back at my one bedroom, then back at Mona, and I contemplate on how full my hands would be if I reached out to hers this morning.

"Can I stay at your place?" she asked, tumbling over words. "I promise it won't be for long, Angel. Just need enough time to get back on my feet."

Compassion dwells within me, starts to become her negotiator.

"Fine," I say in empathy. "Is this all your stuff?"

"Yeah, anything left, that creep can have."

I grabbed one of her bag of bodies and dragged it to the living room closet. Mona heads towards the couch after getting settled, excusing herself from the rest of the world. I sat beside her for a brief moment. No intentions on lecturing, just wanted to show her that I was there.

I ask, "Are you ok?"

"Yes, I'm ok … and if I'm not ok, I guess I have no other choice but to be okay … with his lying ass … I mean, why should it matter anyhow, Angel. After all, he's only another man. And men come a dime a dozen, right Angel?"

She looks into my eyes, helpless, a million wrinkles of distress.

I tell her, "That's right?"

"And it's not like I'm some ugly chick either. I mean, don't you think I'm pretty?"

"Of course. You're very pretty."

"And hell, I know I'm not the smartest girl on earth, but I'm not the dumbest either."

"You're very smart, Mona. Smart enough for any—"

"Damn right!" she exploded. "So you see Angel, screw him. The hell with his ass!"

She rises from the couch, paces back and forth with her hands riding her hips. Befuddled by her unpredictable motives, I am no more than a hostage in my own living room and although her anger isn't towards me directly, I still feel the aftermath of her fury.

After minutes of constant pacing, she suddenly freaks out. "My shoes! My goddamn shoes!"

My flesh trembles. "What about your shoes?"

"That freaking liar has my shoes. A hundred dollars worth. He can have that raggedly little slut, but he's gonna give me back my shoes."

She rushes toward the door. I run to grab her before she turns the doorknob, try my best to pin her down. She tries to break free, constantly screaming, "Let me go! I'm getting my shoes! I'm getting my goddamn shoes!" I keep a steady lock on her arm, pulling it like I'm pulling boulders, telling her to calm down, let it go, get a grip – anything to tame this untamed wilder beast from bursting through the door, back into the wild.

A couple more minutes of rumbling and she finally surrenders, her screams diminishing.

She helplessly falls to the floor, disoriented. I try my best to drag her to the couch, to hold her, console her.

She holds me tighter. Holds me the way a child holds her mother after being told the truth about the Easter Bunny, that the person who really hid those eggs was Uncle Earl and not that phony rabbit.

She vents, "How could he, Angel? How could he love her more than me? After everything … after all I've done."

Not wanting to play Dr. Phil, I choose not to respond. Choose not to counsel. Choose not to swim in her sorrow.

Later that night, Mona was still weeping on the couch.

Apparently she had called in sick, and since Dexter needed another girl to work the 8-12 shift at Club Ding-a-ling, he was ringing my phone off the hook, threatening to fire me if I didn't show up. Had this been any other night, I would've told Dexter what to kiss, but at the present time, working a suicide mission was better than letting Mona work my nerves double overtime.

Mona finally rises from the couch and strolls into the kitchen.

"Got anything to drink?" she asked.

Showing hospitality, I tell her, "Look in the fridge and take anything you want."

She opens the fridge and stares at her choices that are lemonade, whole milk, and a half bottle of Vodka that I planned on drinking before my next sexual encounter with William. Hesitant of making a choice, she stares at the lemonade and Vodka like two puppies at a pet sale. From the look in her eyes, I can tell that she's steadfast on going for the Vodka, but before grabbing it, I tell her, "Anything except that

 Cyril Gillion

one," and I give her an evil glare, a hint that my hospitality only goes so far.

After settling for the lemonade, she saunters back towards the couch, lies back in her pool of tears.

I tell her, "Clean towels and rags are in the closet. Comforters and pillows are on the top shelf."

Work turned out to be no better than being home with Mona. Dexter was flying off at the mouth as usual, threatening the other girls of how he'd start docking their pay if they didn't increase their call-time with the clients. He put up a huge chart that displayed the talk-time for each girl, and he gave comparisons of our progress from this month vs. last month. My average call-time had increased six minutes, leaving me at twenty minutes per incoming call, third place. Mona was second place and first was Buster, the transsexual, guy-girl, whatever you call them these days. Carmella and Linda were starting to go at each other's throats, arguing about who was supposed to be the best PSO. Carmella was a Puerto Rican chick in her mid twenties, long curly hair, a butt bigger than mines, breasts like grapefruits, all the assets of a black chick. Linda was Caucasian, mid forties, bi-sexual, looked like she used to be sexy until her stomach started becoming her dictator. The two hated each other in every shape and form. Both of them thought they were experts when it came to pleasing men over the phone and when Carmella noticed that she had a higher call-time than Linda, she ran into her face and screamed, "What you got to say now, hefar? The stat sheet speaks for itself."

"That stat sheet doesn't mean a damn thing," Linda launched back. "It's not my fault that I can make men cum in seconds."

"Whatever you old hag. Thank God those men don't have to see your face, because if they knew what you really looked like, they'd have limp dick."

"Screw you!" Linda blurted out. "Men have been chasing me down before your little butt was even thought about."

"Pa-leeeeze. What men?"

"Black, white, yellow, all types of men. My sister, Karey will even tell you herself."

In need of support, Linda looks towards her younger sister, Karey. She says, "Karey, from the ten years I've been working here, tell this little girl how many stalkers I've come across."

Refusing to answer, Karey gives a dubious expression, as if she knows the truth but is terrified of opening that window due to what lies beneath the curtain. Carmella, along with everyone else in the room, peeps Karey's expression and the truth about her sister is finally unleashed, that Linda is more of a penis repellant than that of a magnet.

Carmella looks back at Linda and taunts, "See what I mean you ol' hag. Even your sister knows how much you can't get a man."

Carmella laughs aloud. Laughter is her victory.

Then she starts to mumble in Spanish, "Puta blanca fea … Usted es basura … Usted es basura."

"What's that supposed to mean, bitch?"

Carmella laughs some more. "Puta Estupida … Usted es basura."

"We're not in Puerto Rico. Speak some damn English!"

"I said you are trash! Poor white trash!"

Linda grows rigid and the conversation escalates to, "Keep talking and watch me kick your little—"

"Try it."

"—ass."

"Go 'head slut. Go 'head and see that it be the last ass you ever kick!"

Linda starts taking off her high heels and earrings, a sign that she was done with the catfight and was ready to start scrapping like dogs.

Before Linda could gather a fist, Carmella cocked back and spit in Linda's eye. "Puta!"

Linda goes ballistic and she leaps towards Carmella to start tussling like she never tussled before, biting, scratching, hair pulling, fists flying at the speed of sound, a ringside showdown between two heavy weights.

"Get your hands off my sister!" Karey screams, jumping into the fight to double-team Carmella. "Let my sister go!"

Dexter storms in from his office to break up the fight. "What the hell is—"

"Get off me. That little whore is mines! Come on you little—"

"Let her go! Let that puta go! Let that puta go!"

Vicki, another employee, tries to hold Linda back; holds her the way an owner holds a pit-bull from attacking its victim.

Dexter grabs Carmella. "That's it. Both of y'all are fired … that was the last straw … the last damn straw!"

Linda hollers at Dexter with a broken nose. "Are you insane, Dexter! That bitch spit on me and I'm the one who gets fired? After

     Cyril Gillion

all the money that I brought in this dump. You've got the nerve to fire me. You better—"

"Only thing you brought me was trouble. You and your damn sister."

Carmella screams from afar, heartfelt words of English mixed with her native language. "I'll kill that old … mataré esa puta … whip that Puta Estupida … let her go … let that—"

"This isn't over yet you little spic. This isn't—"

"—dirty white Puta go. I'll slap your—"

"Take that mess outside!" Dexter yells. "I want both of you to get your stuff and get the hell out my joint."

"You must be crazy!" Linda screams, finally able to break loose from Vicki. "I'm not going anywhere!"

"Oh you're not?"

"Hell no! If you want me out this dump, you're gonna have to drag me out yourself."

Granting her that special request, Dexter charges at her with a tenacious rage, swoops her off her feet, and he carries her outside while she steadily kicks and screams.

Afterwards, Dexter comes back inside like a bull that's out of breath. "And for the rest of y'all … remember that this is a place of business … my business … now get your butts back to work because my phone lines are blowing up!"

<u>16</u>

Our phone lines were literally ringing off the hook, some callers even waiting for twenty minutes to speak with a PSO.

I picked up line four.

It was a guy from Europe, telling me how he never had the chance to screw an American woman. After hearing the name Angelic Puss and knowing I was not only American but also a black female, he started stroking himself to no return, as if a black woman was more than he'd bargain for, double the trouble.

I told him, "I love your accent. What part of Sweden are you from?"

"Lidingo."

"Mandingo?"

He chuckles. "No, Lidingo."

"Ok, Lindingo. Guess we have something in common because I never been with a Swedish man … but I've heard great things about them."

"What things?"

"Unadulterated things…"

"Like?"

"To sum it up, they're supposed to really know how to treat their women."

"Is that so?"

                     Cyril Gillion

"And unlike American men, they work hard to take care of their women too. They'll do whatever it takes to put meat on the table for a family."

"I'll agree to that," he replies in a raspy tone. "I take good care of my family?"

"Hmmm … ever thought about adding some black into that family?"

He laughs, asks, "Would you really want that to happen?"

"Why wouldn't I?"

"Why would you?"

"Ever saw a black and Swedish child? That's why."

Silence rest over the phone. Then he says, "I'll keep that in mind."

"Well don't keep it in mind for too long, suga. This punany is running dry."

He laughs aloud. "You're a piece of work, Ms. Angelic Puss. What time do you get off?"

"Why?"

"Because I want to see you … You never know, maybe we can make that half Swedish child."

"Are you serious? Don't BS me."

"As you Americans would say … I'm as serious as a heart attack."

Leading him on, I tell him, "Cool, how 'bout we meet at the Starbucks downtown in about an hour. I'll be wearing a black leather skirt, pink Stilettos, pink shirt that reads, *Got Milk*."

At that moment, Shiba grabs my chair to get my attention, the woman who sits across the cubicle from mines.

"Baby Puss, what the hell are you doing?" she asked.

"I'm doing my job."

"When you first started working here, what was the number one rule that I told you?"

"Too many to remember."

"No meeting the clients, Angel. Never under any circumstances are you to meet the clients. Don't mix booty with business. Never. And if Dex was monitoring this call, you'd be finished."

"The hell with Dex. Not to mention, I'm not trying to meet the guy for real. I was only jiving with 'em."

"—Angelic Puss, are you still there?" the caller asked.

"Yes sweety. Give me a second."

"Trust me Angel," Shiba said, continuing to ramble on. "Last thing you want to do is go down that road. First it starts off as all fun-and-games and before you know it, you've got a stalker on the loose."

My personal line rings. Coincidentally, it's Dexter, probably calling to capitalize on Shiba's lecture. He says, "Angel, there's a guy in the queue who's been waiting for a red light special. He's requesting to speak with Angelic Puss."

"With me?"

"Yep."

"Who's the guy?"

"I don't know, Angel. But whoever you have on the phone, I need you to get rid of that caller because I've got big dollars waiting on the other line."

"I can't do that."

"Like hell you can't."

"What do you expect me to do, Dex? Hang up on the guy."

"I don't know. But what I do know is that there's an awaiting guy with a red light special, which means more money for you and more for Club Ding-a-ling. And I don't know 'bout you Angel, but I don't like to loose money. So unless you want me to start docking your pay, I suggest you hurry up with your caller so you can answer that other line."

Dexter hangs up.

 Shiba asks, "Who was that, Angel? Dex?"

"Yeah, says he has some guy who's requesting a red light special."

"So what's the problem?"

"I already have a guy on hold, remember?"

She reaches over my desk and presses the release button, disconnecting the caller. "There. Problem resolved, Angel."

Dexter comes out of his office, signalizing that he's about to forward the red light special request to my line. I looked at the time. 9:45 pm. I figured the caller had to be one of my regulars, maybe Tom. His wife gets home at 11pm. So he usually calls to request a red light special before 10 pm.

"Hey Tom," I said, reaching for my earpiece. "Are you ready to finish the honey-jerking lesson that we had last week?"

"Sure. But there's only one problem ... I'm not Tom."

"Who is this?" I asked.

"I don't know. You're the one who's supposed to be the phone expert. You tell me."

I suddenly recognize the voice and timidly ask, "Is this William?"

"Surprised?"

Stunned, I press the mute button and holler the word *shit* in its native language, the way it is spoken when expressing disbelief.

 Cyril Gillion

Shiba says, "Is everything alright?"

I nod yes. "I'm good. Just using a new technique for my callers."

William recognizes my silence and tells me, "Do you mute all the callers before giving them their money worth?"

"No, just the ones who calls the hotline with no motive … how did you know I work here?"

"Actually, I didn't know. When calling, I just crossed my fingers and hoped that Angelic Puss's real name would be Angel."

"William I'm serious."

"Ok … it was your roommate."

"Roommate? I don't have a roommate."

"Then who is Mona?"

"You talked to Mona?"

"Yeah, she told me that you could be reached at this 1-800 number, but when calling, I never expected my options to be, *for blow jobs press 1, for S&M press two.*"

A crossfire of embarrassment and anger speeds recklessly through my veins, one pressing the gas, the other mashing the clutch.

Mona. That bitch. That stupid stupid bitch. Either she better have a good explanation for her uncontrollable mouth or a good doctor to treat her forthcoming bruises.

I told him, "Let's talk another time."

"Why not now?"

"Because I'm at work. And I need to keep the lines open for other callers."

"Your job consists of pretending. So why can't you just pretend that I'm another caller with a fantasy?"

"That's impossible."

"How come?"

"Because we already had sex, which means you already received your fantasy."

William tells me, "You probably don't believe me, but that night I was totally out of character. So let's just forget the night ever happened."

"I wish I could forget, but the soreness between my legs often makes me remember."

We laugh.

I turned the volume down on my phone to keep the other girls from listening in. It's like when one girl receives a red light special, others start to play inspector gadget. I knew it was just a matter of time before William started doing a little inspection of his own, wanting to know why I didn't tell him the truth in the beginning. Something told me not to mention it if he doesn't, but the longer it took me to speak on it, the worse I began to feel. And I'd rather get the monkey off my back right now than worry about it peeking over my shoulder in the future.

So I told him, "Sorry that I wasn't honest about—"

"Save it, Angelic Puss. I don't blame you for lying. Theoretically, you could be like me. A forty year ol' man working as a career waiter."

He says that to lighten my moment, but I still feel like trash on the ground.

He adds, "And if it makes you feel any better, you're not quite the expertise in this field of work. So thank God for that."

"Excuse me?"

"I said you may wanna stay in school. Not everyone has the skills for this type of job."

"My other callers don't seem to think so."

"Your other callers can't think because time you pick up the line, the blood in their membrane has already surfaced to something else."

"What?"

"Men will tell you anything when the snake is in the air."

"Sounds to me like the only thing in the air is jealousy."

"Call it what you want but you can't ignore the truth."

"What truth?"

"That you're not good at this whole call-girl thing. Stick with trying to become a lawyer."

"Okay, waiter-boy. But since you have all the answers, what would you do differently?"

"For starters, you should work on not trying to be so seductive when answering the phone. You must bait your caller. Not every man is interested in hearing an exotic voice. Some men prefer hearing a simple girl-next-door type of woman."

Turning the tables, I say, "Try using your own advice when you're at work serving customers."

"What do you mean?"

"That day we met in the restaurant. You were extremely promiscuous."

"I was only doing my job. Providing good customer satisfaction."

"If good customer satisfaction means flirting with the customers and working double overtime for an extra tip, then you deserve employee of the year."

  Cyril Gillion

We laugh, continue to throw darts at each other's profession, neither one caring about the lack of time we spent not speaking.

After a couple more minutes of him cracking on my call-girl voice, he decides to flip the conversation and tell me, "I want to see you tonight."

"Tonight?"

"Yes, tonight."

"What gave you the inclination that I wanna be tied under some man tonight?"

"Intuition."

"Intuition can be deadly. It could possibly get your feelings hurt."

"Thus far, intuition has been my advocate when it came to you. Besides, is there something that's keeping us from seeing each other?"

"Well for starters, it's already late and I don't get off until midnight. After midnight, the only things open are legs or the ATM. So which one are you aiming for?"

"Which ever one that'll keep my account above overdraft."

We share a laugh.

He says, "And just so you know, I promise not to keep you up all night … promise."

Two hours later I was leaving work, heading home to prepare for William's request.

When I stepped into my apartment all of the lights were on, including the television that was set to a low volume. Voices ran from the living room as I dropped my keys on the kitchen counter. From there, I saw Mona parlaying on the couch with an unrecognizable guy. She was decked out in low-rider denim jeans, heels, black halter top, hair swooped in a bond with Chinese sticks poking out. The guy lounging next to her was dark-skinned, mid twenties, tall and lanky with dread locks that reached his elbows. He was too skinny for a girl like me, but he was all the muscle that Mona needed at the moment, especially after what she's gone through with her man.

Mona's legs were crossed seductively, and the guy's right hand was curled around her neck, as his other hand was lost in her bosom, attempting to find its way towards Nipple Avenue. As much as I wanted Mona to be happy, I couldn't allow her to continue getting her groove on, not when William was expected to show within the next half hour.

Once seeing my presence, Mona's eyes nearly popped out of her sockets. Instantly her company released his hand from her breasts, shell-shocked, as if he was caught reaching for Oreos in the cookie jar.

Timidly turning down the television volume, Mona muttered, "Wassup … I mean, how was work?"

"Same ol' same ol," I replied. "Carmella and Linda were going at each other's throats about who had the highest call time. Turns out that they started fighting and Dex fired them both."

"Thank God. I can't stand that ol' bitch Linda," Mona replied, sucking her teeth. "Please tell me that Carmella kicked her ass."

"She was at first, but then Linda's sister jumped in to help."

"Your job sounds like fun," Mona's company said, jumping into the conversation. "Where do you work?"

I glance back at Mona, we both staring the way partners stare during a table of cards, and she signals not to play that spade of truth. Something told me to put her ass on blast and tell her friend where she work – the same way she exposed me to William – but someone has to be the bigger woman, so instead of going that route, I lie about our jobs.

Mona says, "Amnon, this is Angel. The friend that I was telling you about."

"Hello Angel," he replies, rising from the couch. He comes over to shake hands, dreadlocks swinging with every stride. His locks were just like the guys from my hometown, thick and unkempt. Some were even splitting apart like they were growing in branches, as if insects might crawl up from his four inches of new growth at any given second.

I asked, "How do you spell your name?"

He sounds it out without missing a vowel. "Ammmm-nonnnn."

"That's unique. Does it have any symbolism?"

He gives a slight pause as if he's bobbing for the right apple to fabricate the meaning of his name. "It's biblical."

"Really?"

"Comes from the book of Chronicles, son of David."

Amnon looks back at Mona, smiles covering their faces. Hard to believe that just eight hours ago this same woman was two steps pass being disoriented and one grip away from tearing down the walls of China.

Mona tells me, "Amnon works in the admissions department at Brooklyn Community College."

"Is that so?"

 Cyril Gillion

"He's gonna see if he can pull some strings to get me enrolled for the upcoming semester."

"Well that's very sweet of you, Amnon."

"Yeah, Mona mentioned that she wants to go to school for Occupational Therapy. Luckily, my father is on the board of directors."

Amnon reaches into his pocket, pulls out a wallet and a set of keys. "Mona and I were just about to grab a bite from Flippos Dinery. Care to join us?"

I smirk. "Me … aaaah that's okay. I'm already expecting some company of my own." I glance at my watch. "Company that will be here very soon."

"That's even better," Amnon replies, going through his wallet. "I've got four tickets to Regal Cinemas. Maybe the four of us can grab a bite and later catch a movie. But that's only if your company doesn't mind, Angel."

I started to give his suggestion some thought, but then I thought about the length of time it's been since I was last alone with William and my thighs started to warm.

I said, "Sorry, but he's not that type of company."

"I understand. Well maybe we can do it another time."

Amnon heads for the door. Before leaving, he makes eye contact with Mona to meet him downstairs, leaving her trapped in a never-ending blush with dimples so evolving to where her smile appears as a blur.

Mona grabs my arm after he walks out. "So what do you think?" she asked.

"I think my friend is quite the slut and she has no problems getting over a man."

She chuckles. "But he's so sweet, Angel. I met him on the train while going to Q&Q. When he approached me, he told me that I reminded him of his next girlfriend. And you know that did it girl."

"What? I can't believe you actually fell for that corny line."

"It didn't sound like a line at the time."

"Whateva Mona. Just be careful. I don't need you crying over my shoulder about another man doing you wrong."

"Pa-leeeeze, Angel. Those days of Mona putting her trust in a man is over. Now I'm all about business, seeing what I can get out the deal."

Ecstatically, she swings into the kitchen, starts flipping through the cabinets and bottom drawers.

I tell her, "If you're looking for a spatula, you're fresh out of luck."

She laughs. "I'm not going to have sex with him if that's what you're implying. I'm only looking for my cell phone."

"It's on top of the refrigerator."

"Good. Let it stay there."

"Aren't you gonna need it?"

"Hell no. That cell phone was cock-blocking the whole time that Amnon was here."

"Let me guess … It's Pete. He wants you back."

"Damn straight. Jealous butt was sitting in the car when I came up stairs with Amnon."

"Did he see you?"

"Yep. Him and that ugly piece of shit that was with 'em."

Her cellular rings. "See what I mean. It's him again." She flips open the cellular and I flip it back closed before she can answer. "Bad idea," I told her.

"What are you doing, Angel?"

"Worst thing you can do is pick up the phone. That's what he wants."

"The hell with that," she says, flipping the phone back open. "I want to make his ass suffer."

"Don't make him think that you're available and he'll suffer enough."

"Yeah, but that still won't stop him from coming to your door."

"I'll just tell him that you're not here."

"Screw dat!" she says, snapping out while walking towards the front door. "Just tell him the truth, that another man is gonna be hittin' dis ass for now on. Bet that'll really piss him off!"

The front door opens and just when I think that she's about to leave, she stops in front of the doorway. "Can I help you?" she says to someone.

"Yeah, I'm looking for Angel. Is she here?"

The voice startles me, shifts through my veins like an intravenous. For I knew that voice from anywhere. Could recognize it through a room of mutiny. It was William. William Randolph. Standing in the doorway of my living room, ten minutes before the expectation of his arrival.

The house was a total mess, so was my unkempt hair, and the things I'd do for a bottle of oil sheen was unmentionable. Mona stood in the doorway as if she was stuck in the twilight zone, reluctant to say a word.

William re-iterated, "Is Angel here?"

 Cyril Gillion

Mona finally comes to earth. "Oh, Angel … are you looking for Angel?"

"Yes, do I have the right apartment?"

"Yeah … yeah you do … come inside. She's in the living room."

Before he enters, I dash into the bedroom to set my hair free from ponytail prison, surrounded my edges with some clear gel.

Mona knocks silently on the door. "Angel, you have a visitor."

I crack the bathroom door and Mona stands slouched against the wall with a glare of exhilaration, her fingers twirling the ends of her bleached hair. She whispers, "Who is that guy?"

I hesitate; don't answer.

"Angel, who is he?" she repeats, her whisper rising.

Nonchalantly, I tell her, "He's nobody."

"Who the heck is nobody?"

"Some guy I met a while back."

"Girl, your friend, Nobody, is fine as hell."

"Shhhhhhh. Lower your voice."

"Is that you?"

"No. He's just a friend."

"Well introduce me to that friend."

"Hell no," I said, my voice unintentionally rising with hers.

"Thought you said he was just a friend."

"He is."

"Then what's the problem?"

"It's … it's … he's gay."

"What?"

"He's gay."

"You mean to tell me that that fine ass man in your living room is gay?"

"That's right girl. Tickles more duke than Rupaul."

She ponders over that thought, and just when I thought the word *gay* would turn her off, she mutters, "Gay … well that's even better girl. I hear that gay men are the best lovers."

I look at her with disgust. "Don't you have somewhere to be? Isn't Amnon waiting for you outside?"

She laughs. "Damn, Angel. No need to be so uptight. I was only kidding."

Two minutes later I was leaving the bathroom with Mona trailing my tail.

William was standing in the living room, chin up. He's staring at my mother's painting as though he never saw it before, looking as if he's wandering how I'd look at her age.

He's wearing some light brown Dockers, a cream collar shirt that has burgundy trimming, and some dark brown diesels that had a coordinating belt to match. His shirt defined a whole new meaning of afro-centric. On the front of the shirt was a picture of Martin Luther King saying, *I have a Dream* and on the other side was a picture of Malcolm X saying, *I got your back.*

The shirt was well-fitted and William's pecks were bulging out so much to where it made Dr. King's head appear abnormal.

William looked at me without speaking, our smiles both frozen. Breaking the ice, I ask him, "Were you able to find a parking space?"

"I parked in visitors. Squeezed my bike beside the Tahoe outside."

"I didn't know you had a bike."

"You never asked."

Mona secretly bumps my shoulder, signaled for me to introduce her to William.

William asks, "Is this Mona?"

"Yeah, I assume the two of you were formally introduced."

"Not really," Mona says with infatuation. She comes closer to William and says, "I never rode a bike before. At least not one like yours."

"Well maybe I'll let you ride sometime."

"Is that right?"

"Yeah, everyone deserves a first-time ride."

Mona rides the avenue of that perception and the fascination nearly takes her breath away, causing her forthcoming words to fumble out as, "I'll. Love. To. Ride. Sometime."

She glances in my direction and I quickly put her happiness to an end by giving her a dreadful glare, an insinuation to get her own damn bike to ride.

I tell her, "Mona, don't you have somewhere to be."

She gives a sluttish grin, then leaves.

I lock the door behind her, ensuring that the bolt lock and chain is secured on the front door for no interruptions. William paces towards the bookshelf and the DVD stand. He picks up the Blair Witch Project. Scream II. The Exorcist."

I ask, "Is this supposed to be a movie night?"

"I had that in mind. But after viewing your selection, I'm not so certain anymore."

                    Cyril Gillion

"What is it? Do you not like horror?"

"I don't need another horror flick," he says. "My life is scary enough."

He looks at the bookshelf and grabs the first book on top, author Terry McMillan, *A day late and a dollar short*. "I knew we shared the same interest in something," he said. "I've read this novel twice."

"Don't mean to pee on your parade, but I never read that book."

"How come?"

"I'm not into fiction literature. I'm more of an expository type of gal."

"Really?"

"Yeah, I like autobiographies."

He looks dumbfounded, says, "That's shocking."

"Is it?"

"Something tells me that you don't have the tolerance for reading three hundred pages about another person's crappy life."

"Another person's crap makes my life worth living."

Laughter crashes in our party, eases my skittish state of mind. Williams searches through more DVD's and finds one of interest. "*Rambo*. Now we're talking." He pops in the DVD and mellows out on the couch. Then he unlaces his shoes and positions them neatly in the corner beside the couch. "May I get comfortable?"

"Looks like you already got started."

He pulls off his shirt and places it over his shoes, now left wearing a tank top that is no match for his upper body.

I ask, "Are you hot?"

"Just a little."

I turn down the thermostat and dim the lights, then I snuggle beside him on the couch.

We sit in silence; watch the previews to Rambo, all previews to movies that surfaced from 1983 to '85. Those were my adolescent years but it appeared to be William's prime.

He asks, "Do you remember that?"

"What?"

"It's Mahogany. The flick of Diana Ross and Billie D. Williams."

"Oh yeah, that's right." I agreed, pretending as if I really seen the film. "I loved Billie D. in that flick. I wander what he's doing now."

"Probably nothing. Smoking away his earnings. All the great entertainers have come and gone."

"Not necessarily," I told him. "They've only been replaced."

He chuckles. "Replaced. Some entertainers can't be replaced."

"Like who?"

"Like … Teddy Pendergrass or Luther Vandross. Who's the replacement for them?"

"R. Kelly and Usher Raymond."

"R. Kelly and Usher," he says, laughing as if I'm young and silly. "Are you kidding me? You really think those guys are replacements for someone as large as Luther?"

"Hell yeah."

"Luther Vandross is a world renowned icon. Even Usher will confess to that."

"And R. Kelly is the king of R & B."

"Yeah, that's if R & B stands for raping babies."

We laugh.

Meanwhile, I stop the movie and start flipping through the channels.

William says, "What are you doing?"

"Law and Order is coming on. Gots to keep up with the series."

"Wait!"

"What?"

"Thought I saw Al Pacino on HBO."

He snatches the remote and turns up the volume. The movie Scarface is playing and it's right at the part where Al Pacino is screaming, *I kill for fun*! *I kill for fun*! Williams whirls in mirth and says, "Now this is a prime example of what I'm talking 'bout when I speak of the old entertainers. There's not an entertainer out there that can play a villain as good as Scarface."

"Actually, Vin Diesel is much better."

"Vin Deisel?" he replies in shock, acting as if he knows each entertainer personally. "Vin Diesel is nothing compared to Al Pacino."

Deciding to throw in some humor, I tell him, "What the hell do you know about Scarface anyway? As passive as you are, I bet you never put a scar on someone's face in your entire life."

My humor doesn't amuse him, and his vexed expression shows the man in his eyes, the scar on his face, as if he used to be quite the Tony Montana himself. Subsequently, he aggressively pulls me close to him, biceps circling my fragile waist. He mutters, "I've always been gentle, but never been soft."

Those words are somewhat frightening, but through the terror, his eyes are seducing every orifice on my body. I expand on that notion and it's not long before his aggression becomes our totalitarian, forcing our lips to greet and our tongues to interact.

We lay back in the bed, never breaking the seal of our kiss.

My cellular rings.

I refuse to answer; refuse to ruin the moment.

William says, "Aren't you gonna pick up?"

"If it's important, they'll leave a message."

Kissing persists again. Long kisses. Intense Kisses. Kisses so strong to where I feel lost in his mouth, buried beneath his tonsils, searching my way through a warm saliva cave.

My cellular throws us another ring.

I ignore the cellular, want to put the phone on mute, but this is not a time for multi-tasking.

Touching initiates and he starts stroking my face gently. Then he caresses my lower back, starts kissing me with more passion, more control, breaks it down to a slower tempo, adds a rhythm to those strokes.

We played in that kissing cave for minutes. Felt like hours. I could stay lost in this saliva forever.

My cellular rings. My cellular rings. My cellular rings.

William says, "Aren't you gonna answer it?"

"Why?" I replied in heavy breaths.

"You never know."

"Don't want to know."

We start at it again. Kissing that is. But the cellular continues to persevere, ringing as if it has a mind of its own.

Son.

Of.

A.

Bitch.

Giving in, I answer. "Who the hell is it?"

"Thank God you picked up, Angel. It's Mona."

"What do you want?"

"Can you unlock the front door?"

"Use your key."

"I can't. You have the chain lock on."

"Dammit, Mona. Does it have to be now?" I asked, glancing up at William.

"C'mon, Angel? How else am I supposed to get inside? I need–"

"Okay okay."

I left the bedroom and hurried to unleash the chain from the front door. Before heading back to room ecstasy, I made an arbitrary trip to the bathroom, sprayed a dab of Victoria's Secret on my breasts and thighs, just in case William's mouth got a little watery. But when I came back into the bedroom, William appeared to be no more in freak mode. He was completely covered in my satin comforter, hunched against the wall, and he'd already regained possession of the remote control for the television. I stripped down to my undergarments and curled beside him.

"Is everything ok?" he asked, placing his arm around me.

"Yeah, everything's just peachy."

I move in for another kiss, but instead of meeting me halfway, his finger blocks the kiss from ever reaching its destiny and my lips are left hanging in mid-air, distant, no parachute to save them from plundering.

I try to kiss him again

Again he blocks it.

I whisper, "Something wrong?"

No answer.

He strokes my face as I stare into his eyes, eyes contrasting the color of a vixen. He mutters, "You're beautiful."

"Okay..."

"Too beautiful for a man like me."

"What's so bad about you?" I asked timidly.

"Nothing. I mean … you should probably be in here with another man."

"Huh?"

"You should be in here with a man who's not so serious. One's who's not twice your age."

The sexual moment diminishes as I tell him, "I prefer older men."

"How come?"

"Younger men can't see past my chest."

"And what happens when you meet that young handsome guy that can see past your chest? What happens to that older man?"

"You don't strike me as the insecure type."

"I'm not."

"Then what's with the questions?"

"Life is short. Too short for a forty-year-old man to be having a fling."

I don't take that word *fling* too kindly, never did. So I ask him, "Since when did this become a fling?"

"That's what I'm trying to figure out, Angel."

"Oh, so now you're a forty-year-old that's confused?"

     Cyril Gillion

"No, I'm a forty-year-old that doesn't want to be hurt. And I just … I just don't want any surprises in the future."

I tell him, "Why can't you just let whatever happens happen … you know … flow with the current."

"Sometimes the current can drift you to the deep end."

"And sometimes it drifts you ashore."

This whole thing was surprising. The fact that he's mentioning repercussions about our future at such an awkward time – while we're one step before bumping, two steps before grinding – is unnerving.

He slides his fingers through my hair, caresses my scalp. "Listen Angel, the only thing I'm saying is to give me some assurance. It's no secret that we both are taking a great risk. You may not be looking for something as serious as me, and I've gots to strongly consider that because I don't have much time left for being on the dating scene, so I take the risk of missing out on a woman who might be a little more serious than you. But you on the other hand is just stepping out into the world and have yet to come into your own … don't get it misconstrued. You're very mature. More mature than half the women my age. But you may not be ready to settle down and that's fine because you have your whole life to consider settling down. Therefore, you take the risk of putting your youth on hold. Something that you only get once."

He stares at me. Something tells me that he's awaiting my response, and although he won't admit it, he's prying for me to rebuttal against his practical logic.

Instead of giving him that gratification, I turn the conversation towards a new avenue and make him give it to me bluntly by asking, "So are you insinuating that we should no longer see each other?"

"Definitely not. But I know how important your schooling is and I don't want to be a hindrance of any sort."

"If you were a hindrance, you wouldn't be lying in my bed half-naked."

He smiles, then he unravels the comforter from my breasts, starts caressing my shoulder, pours kerosene on the match to keep our fire flaring.

A half hour pass.

William turns off the television, leaves the room in pitch black. Sight has abandoned us, but our sense of touch picks up the slack. The only thing visual is my white bra that William swiftly removes as well, and through the darkness, he finds my nipples easily, starts to fondle each nipple passionately, connecting the dots as if he's teaching me Braille and I'm his Helen Keller.

A light abruptly flickers beneath the door, a light coming from the kitchen that startles William. "What's that?" he asks.

"Oh … that's no one but Mona," I replied, trying to get back to our lesson.

Suddenly, noises start to ricochet through the wall and a squirming masculine voice is now moaning the words, *Oh yes … right there*, and the obscure voice is intertwining with a mixture of slurping sounds.

William giggles. "Seems like Mona's midnight snack is a ballpark frank."

The slurping sounds increases volume and the moaning becomes more headstrong. I become embarrassed. To embarrassed to claim residence of this apartment. But as long as my name is on the lease, there'd be no moaning of another bitch's name.

I rise from the bed. Frustration sits around the corner.

William asks, "Where you going?"

"To get some silence."

"You sure you want to intrude?"

"As long as I pay rent, I'm sure."

I flick on the light, throw on a pink tank top, walk towards my bedroom door with an urge to put these noises to rest.

William says, "Wait."

"What for?"

He turns on the television and turns up the volume. "See. Problem resolved. Now you don't have to go out there and act like Laila Ali."

I release the doorknob. Don't want William to think I'm ill-tempered.

As I head back to bed, I hear a loud bang through the door and more noises are coming from the kitchen.

The hell with this, I thought.

I go to crack the bedroom door and Mona's new friend, Amnon, has her bent over the kitchen counter with her head in the sink. Because of her, I already had to replace three spatulas and I'll be damned to let her ruin another kitchen utensil or any appliance for that matter. As I turn on the light, Mona pulls her head out the sink and Amnon jumps into the stove with eyes big as plums.

I look at Mona; tell her, "Respect my house or get the hell out! Your choice!"

Giving her no chance to speak, I shut my bedroom door and head back to bed for the third time. William refuses to comment, and he gives the look of someone who's being held in confinement.

                              Cyril Gillion

We lay in silence; watch the ceiling as a trio of embarrassment, horniness, and frustration is racing through me, each emotion sticking their chest out for first place.

William steps out of confinement and asks, "Not that it's any of my business, but is there a reason why she stays with you?"

"Her man lives downstairs. He threw her out the house … Can you believe that? A man throws a woman out and he's the one that's cheating."

"Well from the looks of it, she sure doesn't have a problem with moving on."

"That's the sad part about it. She's only screwing him to get over her ex."

He laughs. "Seems like Jerry Springer paid a visit to Brooklyn."

"I'm serious, William. I mean, what does it take for a woman to realize that a man doesn't give a damn about her?"

"The same thing it takes to get a baby to wipe their butt."

"Stop it, William. I'm serious."

"So am I."

"What does a baby's ass have to do with my friend?"

"It has everything to do with it. You can give a baby the whole role of toilet tissue, but the chance of seeing that child wipe his butt is slim to none. The same thing goes for adults. No matter how much knowledge you try to equip a person with, people still won't change unless they see the light for themselves."

"Is there anything that you can't rationalize?"

"A great book once said, 'In all of your getting, get understanding.' I guess I tend to apply that logic to my everyday living."

I smile. "Interesting. What book is that?"

"One of your type of books."

"Expository?"

"Yeah. The book of Proverbs."

"Hmmm. Never read it."

"I know. But maybe we can work on that."

I hesitate, then I ask him a question that I've asked before, but only in different words. "So tell me, William … what was your light?"

"Excuse me?"

"You said that people don't change unless they see the light for themselves. But five years ago, something changed your life … what was it?"

"God … it was nothing but God."

"That's a generic answer."

"That's the truth."

"Actually, that's the reason behind the truth … was it a tragedy?"

"Huh?"

"That day in the coffee shop, you also told me that in order to honor the good times, we must first honor the bad – the tragedies that comes before the enchantment … So if you're living a life of enchantment, then what was the tragedy?"

"I told you that it was nothing but God. And whenever God is in the midst, it's never a tragedy. Only a blessing."

He says that as if that's the conclusion, end of discussion, conversation finished.

Little does he know, this conversation might be finished, but my inquest will never be complete, not until I get answers that are worth my liking.

I had my own sources. A background report that would soon be in the mailbox, compliments to peoplefinder.com

I hate to admit it but Cuqui was right. No matter how good of a man that William may appear to be, he is still a man. And behind every good man lies a cryptic past.

One way or another, I will know his past. Know the truth. Know the man behind the man.

17

Morning came sooner than expected; insanity was right on time.

The bed is a sweaty arena.

The alarm clock is my adversary.

Although I'm awake, the nightmare presumes, and there's still enough time for me to shoot the murderer and restore the past, keeping mother alive.

I try to reach under the bed for the pistol but it's missing.

Knocks raid the bedroom door. "Angel are you ok? Are you ok?"

It's the voice of Mona. The antidote to my morning's insanity.

I reach for my asthma inhaler to give myself another dose of lungpower. Regulate my breaths. Strategize my oxygen intake.

"Angel are you ok?" Mona asks, knocking on the bedroom door.

"Yeah. I'm good Mona … I'm ok."

The mirror reflects the breathing battle between my lungs and the albuterol. Puffy eyes. Clammy face. Sleep around the mouth.

Eager to freshen up, I head into the bathroom and after nearly busting my ass from someone leaving the toilet seat up, I realized that William had not only vanished, but in his absence he left a note lying under a bottle of potpourri:

Angel, sorry that I left this morning without saying bye, but unfortunately I had to attend to some unfinished business. However, before we continue in this rendezvous, there's something I need to

The Other Side of the Pillow

share. Don't panick! Think of it as a surprise. If you have some time today, meet me at 632 Lane, StoneEdge Apartments, #321. 6pm. My place in case you're wandering.

With the note in my hand, I sit on the toilet.

I never liked surprises. Don't know whether to be happy or scared.

Two p.m. rolled around like clockwork. The last two hours were spent in the coffee shop working on my laptop. The bar exam seemed to be right around the corner and I was researching different torts and contracts that cover the substantive part of the exam, along with cramming in a diagnostic analysis that was due for Professor Stern.

I sat in the back of the coffee shop, right next to a black and Latin couple that was bickering about some unsettled differences. Usually at this time the coffee shop is quiet, but their constant bickering made up for the lack of noise. The woman said, "I cooked for you last night and you didn't come home until 1 a.m."

"I came at 12:30," the man reconciled.

"12:30. 1 a.m. No difference."

"Who are you supposed to be? My probation officer?"

"I'm your wife. So you at least owe me an explanation."

"Fine. I gave Terricka a ride home. You happy now?"

The woman snaps. "You a damn lie."

"I'm not lying. She didn't have her car and she had no other ride home."

Well you must've driven her to Dick County because that's the only ride that takes two hours."

The man looks around, then back at her. "Lower your voice," he pleads. "We're in a coffee shop."

"I don't give a damn where we're at. Come home on time and you won't need to hear me bitchin."

Temper extends from brow to brow as he tells her, "You see what I mean, Vickie. That's why we're having so many problems. You're forever over-reacting."

"Over-reacting … I'm over-reacting. You stay out all night with God knows who, screwing some other woman, and I'm the one who's over-reacting. That's enough for any woman to over-react."

My mouth drops to the floor, ears becoming supersonic. The woman recognizes my attentiveness and says, "You tell me sistah. What you think about that?"

"About what?" I replied, acting oblivious to their conversation.

  Cyril Gillion

"What would you do if your man stayed out all night after you spent two hours preparing a meal, when he knows he has kids at home and a horny wife that hasn't been done in months?"

The guy steps in. "Leave her out of it. This is between me and you only."

The woman perseveres. "Shut up and let her answer. Maybe you need to hear another woman's opinion since you think mines doesn't matter."

My mouth remains wide open, the cat still holding my tongue with a firm grip. In just a couple minutes, I've been promoted from stranger to mediator and their future kinship is now riding on my response. I quietly sit as a judge – her prosecutor, his defense – but somehow, I'm the one who's been put on trial.

My cellular rings, posts my bail for the situation at hand. It's Kevin Armstrong, a person that I refuse to talk to, but his voice was as sweet as pie at the moment.

Kevin asks, "Did I catch you at a bad time?"

I look at the couple argue their way out of the coffee shop. "Your timing is perfect."

"Good ... so did you give our last conversation some thought?"

"What conversation?" I asked.

"About a month from now, on the 29th, the football team is having a function for me and a couple more rookies. I want you to be my escort."

"Escort?"

"Yeah. That's if you're not busy of course."

William runs through my mind. "Bad idea."

"How come?"

"I'll be busy."

"It's not until a month from now. How do you know you'll be busy?"

"I just know ok."

He sighs. "Let me guess ... it's William?"

"No. Not exactly."

"No or not exactly?"

"No ... I have exams in a few weeks."

"So?"

"So I have to study."

"You have all the time in the world to study, Angel. Besides, I want you to meet a friend of mine that is scheduled to be there as well."

Looking at the phone as if he's crazy, I say, "I'm not into meeting any more athletes."

"He's not an athlete. He's an attorney. One of the top attorneys in New York. You're still looking for an internship, right?"

"Yeah."

"Well I got you covered."

"And what are you looking for in return?" I asked, questioning his motives.

"What makes you think I want something?"

"Because men don't believe in giving freebies. Especially men like you. Besides, I'm sure there's a long line of Brooklyn women that are waiting to be your escort. So what's the urgency in taking me?"

"You and I have history, Angel. History that goes far back as 6th grade, before I was a lottery pick, before the NFL was nothing but a dream. And if that's not a good enough reason for me to take you to a banquet, then I don't know what is."

His words rubbed off my shoulder like sweat. History my ass. It was obvious that his intentions were far greater than just taking me to a banquet.

"So what's it gonna be?"

"That's ok, Kevin. I'm good."

"Come on girl. After all we've been through. Besides, I know how much it means for you to get an internship and believe me, this attorney can get you one that pays."

"Pays?"

"Oh what … I know you didn't think I'd waste my time hooking you up with some BS non-profit gig. The internship is paying $22 an hour."

Those words alone had changed the conversation. Made me want to reconsider. Hard to admit it but he was right. I've been trying to get an intern for months, and finding one that actually compensates was twice the battle. Plus, if I did so happen to get the gig, I could kiss the call-center goodbye, no more spending my nights talking to old perverts.

Following Kevin up on his offer, I asked, "When did you say this banquet would—"

"The 29th," he quickly replied. "And oh, the dress code is probably gonna be formal. So if you can, wear the dress that I used to dig."

"What dress?"

"The all black one with the little slit in the back."

 Cyril Gillion

"Actually, I ditched that dress last month."

"How come?"

"Let's just say the little slit turned into a big split."

His voice rises. "You ripped that dress? Angel, don't you know I paid five hundred dollars for that dress."

"Sorry Kevin, but mother nature didn't approve of that dress."

"Mother nature?"

"Yeah, in case you haven't noticed, she gave me an extra cup size within the last few moths."

He laughs over the phone, gives a stimulating giggle instead of one that's intended for mirth.

Suddenly, a beep interferes on the other line. It's William. "Hold on for a moment," I said, my heart skipping a beat. "A call is—"

"I know I know. You've gots to go."

I tell him, "The 29th right?"

"Yeah, and just so you know, Angel, as far as Mother Nature goes, I've definitely noticed."

Kevin hangs up. William's call is missed.

I wrapped up my belongings and left the coffee shop to prepare for William's undisclosed surprise/confession, whatever the hell I was about to witness. William told me to meet him at six. However, I didn't feel like studying any longer, so I decided to go a couple hours early. From the directions on the letter, William's place was about three blocks up from the coffee shop. I started walking a block, but later hopped on the subway after seeing that my edges were starting to sweat.

A half hour later I arrived at William's apartments, *Stone Edge*. The apartments were the most rundown apartments that Brooklyn had to offer, so old to where a single blaze could cause them to come tumbling down. Somehow, before approaching the stairway, I didn't remember William's apt # and Nextel was giving no reception as usual. There was nothing else to do besides play pick-a-face and hope someone around might know William.

I spotted a woman and two middle-aged men sitting on a bench nearby. The three of them were drinking Heinekens and sharing a cigarette. Each was taking a couple puffs of the cigarette and passing it along, consuming every drop of nicotine from going to waste. Neither three seemed like the people that William would affiliate with, but considering their age bracket, I figured that one might at least know William's apartment number.

"Are you lost or something?" the woman asked in a scratchy voice.

"A little … I'm looking for someone who supposedly stay in these apartments."

The cigarette makes its rounds into her possession. "Man or woman?" she asks.

"A man. About 6'0, brown skin complexion."

"You've just described half of this entire block," she replies, blowing ovals of smoke.

One of the men intervenes. "How old is he?"

"Forty, but he can pass for thirty. His head is bald. Muscular build. Light brown eyes."

The woman laughs. "You've got the wrong apartments."

"You sure?"

"Trust me when I tell you, sistah gal. Ain't no man that fine gonna come through *Stone Edge* and go unnoticed. I've been staying in this dump for twenty years and I know everyone and their mama."

She consumes another puff of the cigarette and passes it along, never breaking its stride. Then she coughs; the cough of someone whose been smoking for years, lungs as fragile as branches. "What is his name?" she asks.

"His name is William."

Her eyes widen. "Hold on there. You talking 'bout Trouble."

"Who?"

"Trouble."

"Thought his name was William."

"That must be the name he goes by in the professional world, when he's around y'all uppity people. But around us, he's known as Trouble. And he's my baby brother."

"You're his sister?" I ask, controlling my state of shock.

"Can't you see the resemblance?"

She gives an over-zealous smile, gums reflecting the color of tar, crooked teeth that wanted to wage war against the dentist. Biting my tongue, I say, "Yeah, you do favor him a little. But he never mentioned an older sister before."

"Half sister," she said, correcting me. "We have the same mother, Mama Earl. It's a whole damn football team on their side of the family, and to be honest I can't stand any of those Hooligans, none of them except William of course. But as for those other bastards: Esther, Ruth, Uncle Tony … they can all rot in hell. Especially that Uncle Tony. I can't stand that old hag. Had it not been for William and Mama Earl, I probably would—"

"Pam, for Christ's sake. Shut the hell up," replies one of the men. "This woman could careless about your damn family tree. Just tell her where Trouble stays so she can go 'bout her business."

Pam snaps. "Kiss my ass and pass me the damn butt … besides, it's not often that I get a chance to talk about Trouble."

She takes another puff, then she gives me a scrutinizing sneer. "Who are you anyhow and what are you to my brother?"

"I'm just a friend," I answered. "My name is Angel."

"Well if you're looking for Trouble, he stays on the third floor. Apt. 321."

Curiosity leads me to ask her, "Where does the name Trouble come from?"

"Gal, you mean to tell me that you don't know," she says, looking at me as if I've been in the dark the whole time. "When he was younger, his lil' ass was forever staying in trouble. Trouble in school. Trouble with the law. You name it and he was in it. Had it not been for Devilla coming along and setting him right, who knows what other type of trouble he'd be into next."

Wandering who the hell Devilla was, I ask, "Who did you say?"

"Devilla."

"The devil?"

"No, I said Devilla. She's the love of his life. The reason why Trouble turned his life around."

My heart collapses like a cloud in the sky, falls into my liver.

Hesitant of asking the question of death, I say, "Is that his wife???"

She laughs. "Humph. She might as well be the way she controls him. Devilla has been with Trouble for five years and he's been clean ever since."

My blood solidifies. Thoughts turn into ice.

I think and think and think and tell her, "Pass me that damn cigarette!"

"What?"

"Hurry up! I need to take a hit."

She hesitates to pass it, but I quickly snatch it from her hands, and as I take the puff of a lifetime, I try to use the cigarette for all its worth.

Cough … Cough … Cough

"Easy gal," she says. "You okay?"

"Yeah, it's just been a long time, that's all."

She snatches it back. "Good. Because the next time you want to experiment with those virgin lungs, try blowing on someone else's shit instead of wasting mines."

Regaining my composure, I ask her, "Do you know if this Devilla chick is up there right now?"

"More than likely she is. Trouble can't be without his lovebird for too long or else he'll go insane."

I thought about turning around and heading home. That would give me enough time to develop the perfect murder diagram, the massacre of all massacres. But I can see the apt. # 321 from where I'm standing, and although my feet are stationary, it feels like I'm already walking towards the apartment door.

Curiosity becomes my dictator.

The truth.

I wanted to know the truth right now, for myself, the hell with waiting for tomorrow.

I look at his sister and thanked her for telling me everything, and then I walked away.

"Wait!" she screams, talking to me while my back was turned. "Let me walk you up to Trouble's apartment."

"That's alright. I can find it myself."

"No, let me take you there. I could use the exercise anyhow."

I give into the devil's advocate; wait for her to lead me to hell that sits on the second floor. The trip is never-ending, each step equivalent to that of a stumbling block, as if gravity was preventing me from progression forward, pulling me back to ground zero. Although the walk is slow, anxiety runs through me like a ghost, and my lungs break a record setting pace as I get closer to William's door.

We finally reach our destination, apt. 321.

William's sister smiles as she rings the doorbell of doomsday.

"Who's there?" William answered.

"Open the damn door, Trouble. It's your big Sis."

A face looks out the window. The face is blurry but the lengthy hair tells me that it's a woman.

I look away before the woman can catch my stare, not ready to lock eyes with the woman of mystery.

William yells, "Come in, big Sis."

She responds to his request and I watch the door fling open. I can now feel the air conditioning blowing inside. It's cold. Very cold. Almost as cold as my conscience that's pleading for me to stay outside, and before I enter, the air exits with a billboard that reads, "ENTER AT YOUR OWN RISK."

William's sister says, "Don't be shy gal. Come on in and make yourself at home."

 Cyril Gillion

We enter the living room and this Devilla chick is nowhere in sight, but you can bet your ass that I was looking around. William's sister makes her own domicile on the couch, pulls out a cigarette to continue what she's mastered.

A voice rings from afar, "Be right there, Sis. You need anything while I'm in the kitchen?"

"Got some E&J," she replies, preserving her last couple puffs.

Skeptical of my surroundings, I stand behind the couch like a fish out of water.

Observation distracts me.

The inside of this apartment far exceeds the exterior. Everything in the living room is the color of black and it gives off a dismal perception. A forty-inch plasma television is the center of attention, makes me want to question what it is that William really does for a living. Tile covers the floor. Marble exterior with a spider-web design runs from all different angles. The walls are filled with black-and-white pictures from medieval times, and in front of those pictures are four sculptures, all going in a perfect formation. From the looks of it, the sculptures appear to be African women that were once slaves, and the four of them stare at me from every corner of the room. Four Mona Lisa's with corn rolls.

In comes William. The man of the hour. The unmarked man. A dead man walking.

The kitchen follows him. Smells of garlic and pasta is blending in with cigarette smoke from his sister.

A glass of lemonade is in his hand and a God-forsaken smile sits on his face, the same deceitful smile that he carried in the coffee shop that morning. After spotting my presence, that smile unfolds and quickly evolves into a dazed reaction, as if he'd locked eyes with the Grimm Reaper.

He says, "What a surprise, Angel. I wasn't expecting you so early."

"Well Mr. Trouble, I guess you're not the only one who's full of surprises."

I say his name with disgrace, the way it should be said by women of all ages; the way I should've said it before he took away my precious jewels, my flower, my damn womanhood.

He tells me, "I see you and my sister have already got acquainted."

"That's right," his sister adds. "I was just telling her how you used to be such a badass when you were little, tearing up everything but the Son of God." She laughs an aggravating laugh, then goes to take another puff of the cigarette, but somehow the flames have dissipated, menthol has lost its stamina, and there's no more nicotine to burn.

William turns his attention towards his sister. "What do I keep telling you about smoking in my house?"

"Well don't have a damn fit, Trouble. It's not like you're gonna die from second-hand smoke anyhow."

He shakes his head in disgust. "Don't you know that second-hand smoke can be more harmful than the person who's actually smoking?"

"Really? Well thank God that I got to it first," she replies, twirling in amusement. "And by the way, where is Devilla. I could've sworn you said her name."

William doesn't answer.

His mind is elsewhere, eyes overlooking his shoulder to see if anyone is coming down the hall. Never making eye contact with me, he turns his glare back towards his sister, tells her that he needs some privacy for him and I to talk.

His sister leaves and after he locks the door behind her, fury shines through me horrendously, layering my face like a pile of makeup.

Playing on that fury, he says, "Care for anything to drink? Iced Tea. Cranberry Juice."

"How 'bout some Vodka," I reply. "Vodka without a chaser."

He smiles. "If I was a drinking man, I'd have no problem letting you—"

"Skip pass the bullshit ok!"

"Excuse me?"

"What are you supposed to be, Mr. William? One of those old little men that's trying to re-live there youth by screwing with younger women?"

"What are you talking about?"

"I'm talking about Devilla. About your conniving ways. I'm talking bout how you're a damn liar."

"I didn't lie to you."

"Really? Then what would you call it?"

"I told the truth. Just not all of it."

"So I guess that makes you a partial liar, huh. Same difference."

He moves in closer, tries to put his hand on my shoulder to calm me, but I swipe away his hand and instantly clasp my fist. "Don't you dare touch me!"

He backs up. "Just hear me out, Angel. I can explain."

"Explain what? What the hell can your ass explain to me? That you're a sicko? That you need therapy? Explain it to a psychiatrist.

Explain it to your God. And besides, your gossiping sister already did the explaining for ya."

"My sister?"

"That's right. Your goddamn sister."

He shakes his head. "You actually listened to my sister? Those cigarettes got her so whacked out of her mind to where she doesn't even know what's going on."

"I'd love to agree but her mind worked pretty damn good when it came to speaking of Devilla … that's right William … she told me everything."

"Everything huh?   Well did she tell you that Devilla was away for the last six months? Did she tell you that?"

"That's bullshit."

"That's the truth."

"No, that's bullshit. And you can't bullshit a bullshitter. Just admit it, William. You were playing this game the whole time. Probably plotted the whole thing from beginning to end. Go 'head and say it."

"Say what?"

"That it was you who set those guys up in the alley, pretending to kidnap me so you could move your way into my life. Wasn't it?"

"What? What makes you think I'd do something so absurd?"

"Because you're a sicko. And sickos specialize in doing sick things. Hell, you probably lied about your occupation too. A waiter my ass. What is it that you really do for a living?"

"I do what I said I do."

"You're lying."

"You wasn't completely honest about your occupation either, Angel. Did you forget about the phone sex thing? How you lied about that. How the truth had to come out from your—"

"That's different!"

"No difference, Angel. A lie is still a lie."

"BS! Men are always trying to flip the script when they have no way out."

"I'm not flipping anything."

"My job pays my way through school. Puts food in the little refrigerator that you ran your stinking hands through. So don't try to compare that to your indelicacies."

"My what?"

"You heard me goddammit. Indelicacies."

"What indelicacies?"

"Oh what? So now you have amnesia!"

"What are you talking about?"

"I'm talking 'bout your wife."

"My wife?"

"That's right, William! Your. Mother. Fucking. Wife. You think you're so damn slick. Trying to find some younger girl so you and your wife can live out your sick swinger fantasies, your sick threesomes, or whatever the hell y'all do in your spare time. Well you found the wrong Miami chick to mess with. As a matter of fact, why don't you bring that little slut out the room 'cause I know she's in there." My anger shouts towards the bedroom. "Come your ass out the bedroom! Come out the room you little dike!"

Suddenly, a little girl appears from nowhere, a girl no older than five years of age, and she's carrying a black doll in her hands.

She points her finger at me and says, "Daddy … daddy … she said a bad word! She said a bad word!"

William runs to the little girl, and hugs her. "Devilla, go back to your room!" he demands. "Daddy is busy."

_18_

The cat dies from curiosity, a slow and gruesome death.

My mouth has become a lethal weapon that has turned against me in tenfold.

William is pacing back and forth, his hands folded in the back of his head. I would open my lethal weapon to speak, but I refuse to give it more ammunition.

William never breaks his pace, and his stride is now towards the front door. Turning the doorknob, he says, "Be right back."

"Wait! Where you going?"

"Be right back."

The door slams.

I'm left standing in his living room extremely perplexed. The walls are closing in. All four of the African Mona Lisa's continue to stare, and their glares have now turned hideous, as if I'm the evil massa that's taken over their premises.

William comes back in.

Not being able to hold back my feelings, I say, "Sorry William. I didn't know that—"

"Shhhhhh," he replies, his index finger to his lips. "Let's just start all over from scratch."

"Huh?"

"I'll start first. My name is William. Some people call me Trouble. And your name?" he asks, reaching out for my hand.

I smile, looking at him as if he's gone nuts. "Stop it, William. This is silly."

He proceeds. "Do you not know your name?"

"Fine. My name is Angel."

"Well Angel, I'm from New Jersey and I'm forty years old. I work as a waiter in the busiest restaurant in New York City. I make $8.50 an hour, tips included, and I try to save every bit of it."

He swallows hard, then goes on. "I have a daughter. Her name is Devilla and she's the love of my life, the reason why I save the little dollars that I've collected so far. She's five years old, somewhat feisty, and she loves to read, dance, and act ... Now Angel. Tell me about yourself."

Presuming this game of honesty, I say, "I'm an ordinary law student from Miami, Florida. I came to New York a year ago to finish my last two years at Brooklyn College. Since financial aid only pays for my schooling, I work as a phone sex operator to pay the rest of my bills." I swallow hard and tell him, "The first guy I had sex with was two weeks ago with a guy named William, and since then I—"

"Hold right there," he says. "You mean to tell me that you're a virgin."

"Was a virgin?"

"Why didn't you tell me?"

"What for? Would that have stopped your penis from rising?"

"No, but at least I would've tried to have more restraint. It's already bad enough that I fornicated, but to tarnish a young woman's purity ... that's just ... that's just ... that's twice the transgression. I mean ... it's as if I've taken advantage of you or something."

He shakes his head as if he committed the impartable sin and hell is waiting to greet him with a cup of Folgers.

I look at him in empathy. "Okay, truth is ... I wasn't a virgin. You were actually the second guy I ever had sex with. But even if I was a virgin, why would you feel so bad? It's not like you forced yourself upon me. I wanted it to happen. And besides, isn't your God supposed to be—"

"Understanding."

"—lenient. And if God is what he's perceived to be – the Alpha and Omega, the ruler of all – then shouldn't he be more forgiving?"

   Cyril Gillion

"Yeah, but before there is forgiveness, one must be remorseful. And before that, one has to"—he shakes his head in frustration—"never mind. Some things just have to be self-taught."

I give him time to pull himself together; watch him as he looks into my eyes with a solemn glow, making me think that he has more transgressions to spill. He says, "Stay right here. I want to show you something."

He strolls into the bedroom and brings out his daughter, the five-year-old girl, Devilla, the one I foolishly called a dike, all because of my lethal weapon.

She stands beside William with a doll in her hands. Her skin is a fiery brown, William's nose to match. Her head is full of hair, hair so tangled to where it's committing an insubordinate act. It's a little curlier than William's, the type of texture that makes me want to inquire about the mother.

William says, "Devilla, this is Angel. Why don't you tell her hi?"

She hides behind her father.

I tell her, "Hello pretty girl. How are you today?"

William hugs her tighter. "She's a little shy right now."

"No I'm not!" she replies, snapping back.

She looks into my eyes to prove her bravery. Her glare towards me is evil, the fifth Mona Lisa in the room. She has William's eyes and his same serious expression. The resemblance between them is creepy. But what's even creepier is being able to see myself in her eyes. She's a splitting image of me when I was five.

She asks me, "Where are your wings?"

"Excuse me?"

"You said you was an Angel. So where are your wings?"

"Well darling, I haven't received my wings just yet."

"How come?"

I try to think of a legitimate answer that is satisfactory to a five-year-old. "I have to wait for God to give me a pair of wings."

She questions my answer. "Is that why you're not in heaven, because you couldn't fly there?"

"No," I replied, choking on my next set of words. "It's just that … it's just that … God wanted to leave me here on earth for a little while."

"That's not what Daddy says. Daddy says that most angels are in heaven and the others are with the devil. He never said anything about some being left here on earth."

She stares at me with the debater's eye, waiting to demoralize me with any response that I dare to give. I hold my breath, tongue-tied, a polished author with writer's block.

William throws me a lifejacket by saying, "Honey, she's here to look after you. So think of her as your guardian angel."

I finally breathe.

Devilla's face is full of bewilderment. She says, "So you mean to tell me that there are guardian angels as well … shutz … this stuff is so complicating."

She throws her arms into the air and strolls back into her room, her intellect increasing with each stride.

I smile.

William says, "I already know. She's a handful."

"Seems as if she's just like her dad."

"And what is that?"

"A spiritual freak."

"Trust me. That has nothing to do with me. While other children are requesting to hear a Winnie-the-Pooh bedtime story, she prefers hearing stories about the bible"—he laughs—"so I guess Christ works through children as well.

I say, "She's very pretty. She must take after her mother."

"Funny. Very very funny."

My lethal weapon loads and I can't help but to ask, "Do you have good ties with the mother?"

"Used to. But she died."

"Oh … I'm sorry."

"It's fine," he says, trying to conceal his pain. "She died while giving birth to Devilla on Christmas Eve. Doctor warned me that she wasn't capable of having a baby … said her uterus wasn't strong enough … we prayed about it and God answered that prayer by giving us a miracle … little Devilla … we call her the miracle baby … and what's crazy is that I'm the one who convinced her to have Devilla … heck, I knew what was at stake. We both knew. But she still decided to take that chance. Regardless of what the doctor said, she still took that chance for me, only to give me what I wanted … I mean it's like … sometimes I feel as if I killed her myself."

He sighs hard, no words. It seems like he's about to break at any given moment, like he's giving the eulogy at a loved one's funeral.

But he doesn't break. He stands strong. Too much of a man to be broken.

          Cyril Gillion

William turns his glare towards a picture that lies on the shelf. "Look … this is her right here."

I stare at the picture. Stare at the woman of mystery that's supposed to be Devilla's mother.

The woman has a pale face. Too pale to be a woman of African descent. And while the photo throws me for a loop, I want to ask the million-dollar question.

I murmur, "She looks to be very light-skinned."

"She's mixed with black and Italian descent. That's where Devilla gets her hair."

"She's extremely pretty."

"I know … that's her when she was about your age."

The picture continues to grab his glare, perplexity becoming his auxiliary.

He says, "You know it's strange that the bible tells us to rejoice when one dies and to cry when a baby is born. Funny that we tend to do the opposite … for some reason, I used to think that I was getting punished when God took her away. But it didn't take long for me to see the truth. That even though God decided to take a life, he gave two lives in return. Not only did he give Devilla, but he gave me a new life as well, a better life from the one I used to live. It's now that I live for my daughter. I live through Devilla."

His words are beyond genuine, as bone chilling as frostbite. I ponder over those words. Ponder over the situation. For William to be raising a daughter by himself, especially under these circumstances, was quite the Herculean task, enough to have respect demanded.

But with respect comes jealousy.

And that jealously swam in my blood.

I wasn't jealous of William, but more so of Devilla. She has the father that I always wanted. The father that any girl would want. One that lives his life for his child, will die in her place, would look a bullet into the eye before ever letting it scrape his daughter. To me, that's love beyond comprehension. Love I never had. Love worth being jealous over.

A knock intrudes through the door.

William yells, "Devilla, your godmother is out here to see ya."

A woman enters the living room. The woman is very pretty. Prettier than Devilla's doll. Damn near a walking goddess.

She stands 5'9 with the body of a swan. Her breasts are a decent size. Not bigger than mines of course. But she's ahead of me when it comes to the booty. She has a dark mocha complexion. No makeup.

No blemishes. Her black hair sits midway down her back, but there's no doubt in my mind that it's a weave – the expensive synthetic type – and she keeps flipping it over her shoulders as if it's really hers, as if there's no receipt to match those costly extensions.

I peep out her wardrobe. She's dressed in business attire on a Saturday afternoon, bottled water in hand. Either she's a dedicated entrepreneur or a woman who doesn't get out the house much.

William says, "Courtney, meet Angel. She's into the field of law as well."

We smile at each other enviously, fake smiles, two leopards on the same terrain.

I ask her, "So what type of attorney are you?"

"Civil attorney. I've bounced around a little bit, but I've spent the last four years partaking in torts, invasions of property. That's more of my realm."

She sips more of the bottled water. "What about yourself? Has litigation taken you through a number of turns?"

"Actually, I'm still in law school," I tell her.

"Really?" she responded in disbelief. "And just how old are you?"

"Twenty-four."

"Twenty-four?"

"Yes … twenty-four."

She looks at William scornfully, as if he should be hung by the neck or held in court for contempt. William smiles to overshadow her ignorance, and through his smile, I can tell that history lies between them, a score of unsettled differences. Courtney glances back at me with a two-faced glare, half-filled with resentment while the other half smiles, a checkerboard face of nice mixed with nasty. "Law school huh?"

"Yes, third year at Brooklyn Law."

"You take the bar yet?"

"Hopefully in February."

"You ready?"

"I'm prepared for the worst."

She says, "That's a bad way to think."

"Is it?"

"Preparing yourself for the worst is no different than preparing for failure. Trust me, I know."

"Know what? That you're a failure?"

"No," she replies, her half-nice face now filling with nasty. "I know that a person should never plan for failure."

William interrupts the tension by saying, "Angel wants to be prosecutor."

"Is that right?" Courtney replied. "I started off in criminal law as well. Wanted to prove myself worthy of the challenge. But you'll be singing a different tune in a couple years. The workloads in criminal cases are just too strenuous."

"Interesting," I tell her, feeding off her words of indolence. "That doesn't sound like the attitude of a persevering woman. Or in your words, a woman who doesn't plan to fail."

"Youngin, perseverance is what got me to this point."

I smirk. "And what point is that?"

"The point where you'll hopefully be someday."

She says that as if she's already won the battle (as if there was ever a battle to coexist), and without words, we stand nose-to-nose, competition facing competition, two gang leaders squaring off at the end of a block, reading each other's disparaging thoughts.

In this little moment of contention, a world that could never be understood by male intellect, we try to detect each other's flaws, both studying the imperfections that will give the other woman an advantage.

As much as I hate to admit it, she was right. My whole purpose of living was to soon be where she was at. To walk around someday in the flashy suits, the dark briefcase, Zephyrhills bottled water, like I'm King Zeus of the Gods (or Queen Zeus for that matter), perceived by others as a person who makes a difference, a spot in society that the average person envies.

But with every advantage comes a disadvantage.

With every asset comes a defect.

As diminutive as it may sound, her defect was age, maturity working in her favor yet tearing her down at the same time.

From the looks of it, I was at least ten years her junior. Ten years that she could never retrieve. And it's obvious that she had to envy that youth, because in the two minutes of us meeting, my age was all that she had room to critique, enough room to wander why I was in William's apartment.

Before either one of us lions could roar, Little Devilla comes running out the room, coming between our silent tussle. She's still carrying the black doll in her hands and the warm smile on her face. Devilla hugs her godmother with passion; hugs her as if God himself has literally entered the building.

William asks Courtney, "Are you getting Devilla for the night?"

Courtney gives William an indecisive glare, as if that wasn't apart of the plan.

Devilla yells, "Please mommy please. Let me stay with you tonight. Daddy won't let me watch TV."

"And why won't I let you watch TV?" exclaimed William.

Frightened, Devilla looks down at the floor, looks long enough for William to repeat, "Tell Courtney why you can't watch TV."

Groaning, Devilla says, "Because I said a bad word."

"That's right," William said. "And you've gots to learn what words to say and what words not to say."

Adding fuel to the parental fire, Courtney says, "Devilla you're supposed to be a big girl. And big girls don't say bad words."

"Well what about the word *dyke*?" Devilla blurted out. "Is that a bad word too?"

Courtney snaps. "Yes, and don't ever say that word again!"

"But Ms. Angel said it. She told daddy that I was a little dyke. And isn't she a big girl too?"

Courtney glances in my direction, disgust beaming in her eyes, and embarrassment floods my veins as I get ready to suffocate a five-year-old.

William steps in. "Honey, Ms. Angel was trying to say the word *bike*. Isn't that right, Angel?"

"That's right, Devilla. I was trying to say, *Bring out that little bike. Maybe we can ride bikes together someday*."

"For real?" she asked, becoming elated. "When?"

"When you're big enough to ride without training wheels," William said. "Now let daddy have a hug before you go."

William reaches into his pocket to hand her five dollars. "And this is not for her to spend on candy," William said to Courtney.

They leave together. Exit like mother and daughter.

William asks me, "Have you had enough surprises for today?"

"Too many to grasp."

"Well, if you don't want to see me again, I'll understand."

"Why would you think that?"

"Because a child is not something you bargained for. Women tend to flee like roaches when they usually meet Devilla."

"Not all women."

"Trust me. You are an exception."

"What about Courtney?"

"What about 'er?"

"Is she an exception too?"

He laughs. "Courtney is practically like a little sister."

"Well that little sister must be into committing incest, because she almost had a conniption when I mentioned my age."

"That's just the way her attitude is. Over protective of me. We both are like that towards each other. Maybe because we've known each other since high school." Then he gives a soft giggle. "It would bring my mother back to good health if she knew that me and Courtney got together, but truth is, we don't look at each other like that. My daughter, Devilla, only refers to Courtney as mama because that's the only mother she's known since birth. But when it comes to me and Courtney's relationship, I assure you that it's strictly platonic. She's more into athletes and men that are making six figure salaries."

I wasn't buying the bullcrap that he was selling, but I refused to question any further. I knew the truth. Something like a woman's intuition. And even though Devilla's mother had died, I was still in for baby momma drama with Courtney.

It wasn't long before William took the conversation for a U-Turn and started questioning my views of children, asking if I wanted any in the near future. My answer was that I could date a man with kids, but having any of my own was out of the question. His opinion was different, so different to where it reflected our difference of ages. While I saw children as an interference, he sees them as inspiration. While I value them for what they are, he values them for what they're worth.

Between those differences lies a dilemma.

Devilla.

His daughter. My ultimatum.

William refused to let me walk out the door until I gave this threesome some clarity, if Devilla would be the roadblock that splits us in two different directions, our little demise.

I gave it to him straight, that I was willing to strengthen our bond as long as there was no stepmother role involved in the contract. He laughed at first, but behind the giggle was an expression of relief, as if he'd finally found that understanding woman, the only woman in the city that was willing to sign on the dotted line. Then he puts his arm around me and looks tenaciously into my eyes, we both finally knowing our place amongst each other. For I was officially his woman. Signature signed on the dotted line. And as we locked eyes in the present, I locked eyes with the future.

Our future.

The eerie notion of knowing the unknown.

The Other Side of the Pillow

<u>19</u>

The next day I was back at William's place, walking through his front door.

Smells of garlic flustered through his apartment as Little Devilla was laid across the living room floor with a coloring book.

Timid of spoiling her focus, I ask, "Hi Devilla. Where's your dad?"

She didn't speak, answered with an evil glare.

A voice yells from the bathroom. "Devilla, is someone out there?"

"It's no one but Angel," she replied, turning up her nose in my direction.

I dropped my purse on the couch, headed down the hall to look for William. He came out the bathroom with his usual serious demeanor. "Devilla, thought I told you to leave the coloring book alone and get prepared for dinner?"

She pleads with him. "Please daddy. Just one more page."

"What did I say?" he demanded.

Devilla throws a hissy fit and storms into the kitchen.

"That includes you too," he sarcastically added, smiling in my direction.

He comes closer to kiss me on the cheek. "You hungry?"

"A little."

              Cyril Gillion

"Good, because I cooked your favorite dish, lasagna. Figured you needed a good meal after such a long drawn-out day."

I've come to realize that William is always on time with the meal plan, a man who thrives at gaining your heart from whispering to your stomach.

While heading into the kitchen, I saw Devilla sitting at the table with her hands folded. I sat across from her. The two of us were adjacent to the big empty chair, William's chair, like two serpents waiting to yield to a king.

William was still trying to put the finishing touches on the meal, and he turned his focus away from the stove to ensure I was already seated, also checked to see if Devilla was misbehaving.

I smiled at him. Smiled at the man who cooks for me, caters to me, and most of all, the man who trusts me around his daughter.

"Ouch!" William yelled.

"What is it?" I asked.

"Burnt myself on the front eye of the stove."

"You want me to get you some—"

"I'm fine," he said, refusing to let me obstruct his presentation. "Dinner will be ready in a sec."

Sweating ferociously, he eventually brings out the pan of lasagna, a meal large enough to feed pharaoh's army. Continuously reaching her four-foot frame over the table to fill her plate to the rim, Little Devilla started digging in before we could pick up the silverware, and she carelessly got sauce all over her shirt and arms.

William snaps. "Devilla! How many times I gotta tell you that grace is to be said before every meal? And where's your cup?"

Devilla responds to her father by saying, "Dang it", and she also comes out the mouth with, "how come I have to drink out a cup but Ms. Angel gets a glass?"

"That's because Ms. Angel is an adult ... and what I tell you 'bout speaking out loud?"

Devilla looks at me scornfully.

We bow our heads to say grace, to give reverence, or whatever people do when they call themselves blessing a meal. Truth is I haven't bowed my head since the age of sixteen, since staying at Aunt Terry's.

After a minute had gone by, William was still saying grace, had blessed everything from the food on the table, to the funds that purchased it, to the hands that prepared it, even thanked God for the fifteen percent discount that he received for the purchase. I started to tell him to cut it short, but I knew the relationship that William had with God, and I didn't want to disrespect that, especially in his household. As he went on, I opened my eyes, giving my eyelids a break from being closed for so long. Devilla was twirling her hair around and after looking into my direction, her eyes widened, then she yelled out, "Oooohhhhh. Ms. Angel's eyes are not closed! Her eyes are not closed!" That interrupted William's prayer, and the word *Amen* came sooner than expected."

William snapped. "Devilla! You must really wanna get it!"

Defensively, she says, "Ms. Angel's eyes were open."

"So what?"

"You told me that you should always close your eyes when praying to God. You said that—"

"Enough!" he demanded. "I don't want to hear your mouth for the rest of dinner. And if you weren't so busy with your eyes open, you wouldn't know what was happening on the other side of the table with Ms. Angel."

Devilla puckers her lips. The doorbell rings.

"Come in!" William yells, never asking who the knocker was.

In the living room comes a heavy-set guy with a mini afro, large boots, Heineken in his hand."

William looks over his shoulder and yells, "Be right there Rob!"

"Uncle Rob!" Devilla screams, running to jump into the man's arms.

"How's my baby doing?"

I look at William. "That's your brother?" I whispered.

"No, Angel. That's my neighbor. Devilla just calls him Uncle."

"Oh."

William says, "I have to step outside right quick for something that's very important. If it's not too much, will you keep an eye on Devilla for me? Make sure she doesn't choke on the lasagna. And if she gives you problems, I'm right outside the front door."

I accept the challenge, not because I want to, but to show him I can handle his daughter, even if she is the child from hell.

William leaves.

Silence resides at the table between Devilla and I as she keeps sticking out her tongue, rolling her eyes, trying to get my attention. I ignored her and started manifesting my lasagna. Garlic bread sat in the center of table, a couple inches beside Devilla's plate. As I reach for a piece of bread, Devilla blocks my hand. "Don't!" she demanded. "That garlic bread is mine. Get your own!"

Smiling, I tell her, "Devilla, part of being a big girl is learning how to share. Now if you want, we can split the bread so both of us can get a piece."

"No. My daddy makes garlic bread for me and me only. So move your hand old lady. Get off the—"

"Look here you little runt!" I snapped, taking another approach to the parental handbook. "First off, I'm not old. Secondly, I'm not here to replace your godmother, auntie, or anyone else in your damn family. I could careless what your daddy normally does, because I'm getting that garlic toast whether you like it or not. Now Ms. Angel is very stressed at the moment. And right now, she don't need no snotty nose five-year-old giving her more stress. So take your hand off that dinner roll, sit that ass up straight, and you've best not say another word!"

William comes through the door.

Devilla runs into the arms of her father, holding him before he can ever sit down.

William asks, "Is everything ok?"

Smiling, I take a large bite of the mouth-watering garlic toast. "Everything's fine," I said. "Me and Devilla was just having a conversation about garlic bread. Isn't that right, Devilla?"

She timidly shakes her head in agreement. "Right."

Later that night, after Devilla was put asleep, William and I talked about everything under the sun.

He says, "Mind if I ask you for a favor?"

"What type of favor?"

"My mother gets discharged form the hospital tomorrow and I want to see her tonight."

"Thought you only see her in the mornings."

"I do. But I had to work this morning, which means I missed a day. Figured I'd make up for it tonight."

"So what are you saying?"

"I want you to come along."

"Come with you while you see your mother?"

"That's right."

"Probably not. I'm not ready for that meeting."

"Come on, Angel. It's not Algebra."

"I know. It's more so calculus. I mean, don't you think it's a little early for me to be meeting your mother? Hell, I just met Devilla."

"It's not even that type of ball game, Angel. All I want you to do is ride with me to keep me company while I make a quick visit. Heck, if you're uncomfortable about coming into the room, you can stay in the lobby."

Somehow, in the midst of saying how much I wasn't going, I still found myself getting ready to make that trip.

I kept telling him that she better not be one of those disrespectful mothers – the kind that shut you out before you even get a chance to speak, but then I remembered that William said she had Alzheimer's, and that was a good thing because a sick woman is not necessarily a threat.

William went into the room to check on little Devilla before we left. Sleeping beauty was knocked out.

Once reaching the hospital, I took off my earrings and bracelets from my wrist.

"What is it?" William asked.

"Don't you think I'm a little over doing it for a hospital visit?"

"No, Angel. You're fine."

I become paranoid. "Give me your jacket."

"What?"

"Give me your jacket. I don't want your mother thinking I'm a whore."

"How many times do I have to tell you that you have nothing to worry about? Besides, she's probably sleeping."

We walk into the elevator. I hold the door for a middle-aged woman and a little boy that appears to be her son.

"Eighth floor," she requested.

As William presses the button, the boy swats his hand away. "Let me do it!" he demands, mashing all the buttons on the elevator.

"Timmy, why'd you do that?" his mother says. "Apologize to this man."

"Hell no!" the boy replied, launching back while puckering his lips. "Daddy lets me do it!"

My mouth drops to the floor.

People start to fill the elevator as we go from the floor to floor, tormented by the little boy who's wearing the pants in his household.

William says, "Angel, If Devilla ever embarrasses you in public, you have my permission to make sure that she never does it again."

We soon reached our destination. Floor eight. Intensive Care unit."

Cyril Gillion

We passed a flower stand on the right and I decided to purchase some get-well flowers for William's mother, figured that any sort of flowers were better than none.

"What are you doing?" William asked.

"The least I can do is bring flowers."

"My mother doesn't like flowers."

"Every woman like flowers."

"Very well then. Your choice."

We entered her room – room 422 – and just like William said, his mother was sound asleep. Relieved, I released the deep breath that I'd been holding since the elevator.

The nurse was in the room before we entered, looked like she was on her way out. "How's she doing?" William asked her.

"She's good. I just gave her a dose of Zyprexa about a half hour ago."

"Zyprexa?"

"Yes, it's a cholinesterase inhibitor."

"A what?"

"A cholinesterase inhibitor."

"In case you haven't noticed, I'm not a doctor."

"I'm sorry. Zyprexa is one of our most recommended medicines for Alzheimer's. It'll reduce some of her hallucinations."

William still looks befuddled.

The nurse says, "Don't worry, she's gonna be fine. Are you her son?"

"Yes."

"Well visitation hours ended at 9 p.m."

William sneers. "And?"

The nurse doesn't reply, and she quickly exits.

After the nurse leaves, I'm left standing there with a perplexed William and an old woman that looks like she's been asleep for years. It's cold in this room, the temperature dropping lower than a freezer full of corpses. William stares hard at his mother, the stare of a person that's witnessing a miracle. He has her nose; the same nose that's been passed to Devilla. She's also darker than William. Very thin. Seemed to be a peach in her younger days before her long hair turned grey and brittle.

As we watch her, she breathes heavily. Breaths of volcanic eruptions.

I say, "She's beautiful."

"I know. Don't we make a perfect pair?"

"A pair?" I asked sarcastically. "You must take after someone else in the family."

"I take after my mother. People tell me all the time."

"Well daddy must've been creeping because the two of you look nothing alike."

"I heard that," his mother said, raising her brow from her sleep.

I swallowed my tonsils. "Hello … hello Ms. Randolph."

"You mean Mrs. Randolph," she said, correcting me. "I may be old but I'm still married."

I look at William. "Thought you said your father was deceased."

"He is. She's talking 'bout my stepfather."

Ms. Randolph lets out a cough. "What you mean stepfather, boy? Trouble don't you know that man took care of your mama for thirty years … the least you could do is call that man daddy."

William smiles. "Momma, this is Angel. Angel Inghram."

I tell her, "Nice to meet you, Mrs. Randolph."

"What did you say her name was?"

"Angel."

"Well well well," his mother says. "Thank God your mother named you appropriately … 'cause believe me honey child, not all Angels are beautiful. And I know because I've met some Angels in my life that looked like Lucifer's little sister ya hear."

"Well thank you for the compliment."

William intervenes. "Mama, Angel brought you some flowers."

"Oh did you?"

"Yes ma'am."

She turns her neck to William. "Well let me see 'em boy," she said, demanding William to raise the flowers into the air.

I swallow hard as she observes the flowers from every angle, analyzing them up and down, back and forth, as if she was calculating the value of each stem.

A smile finds its way to her wrinkled cheeks. "Those flowers are beautiful, child. Just plain beautiful."

"Why thank you."

"And what was your name, suga?"

"Angel. Angel Inghram."

"Angel … well that's a beautiful name … thank God your mother named you appropriately … 'cause not all angel are beautiful … And did you buy my flowers?"

"Yes ma'am."

     Cyril Gillion

"These flowers are beautiful. And they ain't cheap. Did you pick 'em out yourself."

"Yes."

"Man o man are these flowers beautiful … and they ain't cheap. 'Cause I know cheap … now those flowers you see people buying in the hospital … that's what you call cheap … cheap as can be."

I swallowed again. "Thank you Ms. Randolph. I just hope you feel better."

"Well thank you, Angel," she replied, finally remembering my name. "Something told me that it was you who paid for my flowers. I knew it couldn't be Trouble's cheap ass. That boy wouldn't pay for his own funeral if he could afford it. He's nitty. As nitty as they come. Don't get me wrong though; he has a good heart. Lawd knows my baby got a good heart. But he ain't coming out that pocket. Lawd knows my baby ain't coming out that pocket. Hell, he'll pay for you to get in the movies, but you can forget about popcorn, because he'll leave yo ass high and dry."

I laughed at her hysterically. "Yep, that's him alright."

She continued with, "That's right, honey. And you know who he gets it from?"

"No ma'am."

"His cheap ass father. Now that was a cheap bastard. Honey child, if that man could, he'd prevent us from paying for his own funeral."

I continue to laugh as she looks towards William. "And where's my little suga pie?" she asks.

"She's with Courtney?" William answered.

"Who?"

"Courtney."

"Who the hell is Courtney?"

"Devilla's godmother. Remember? She just came to see you the other night."

"I don't know any Courtney. But make sure you say something to my suga pie for me."

"I will mama."

"And by the way, how old is she now?"

"She'll be six on Tuesday."

"Tuesday! My lil' snugums will be six-years-old and you haven't brought her by here to see me yet?"

"She was just here yesterday, mama. I brought her and Lachelle."

"Who?"

The Other Side of the Pillow

"Lachelle. That's your other granddaughter. She's the—"

"Boy, don't you think I know who my own granddaughter is … I tell ya Trouble … lawd knows I should've never been drinking when I had yo butt."

William goes over to his mom, kisses her on the cheek. "Well mama, we're about to head on out."

"Already?"

"Yeah, just wanted to stop by before I picked you up tomorrow."

"Well see ya later, baby. You and your friend, umm—"

"Angel," I reminded her.

"That's right," she said.

20

William's mother wasn't the last Randolph I'd have to face.

It was little Devilla's birthday, and believe it or not, I got forced into going to a six-year-old party, all because I pinky-sweared to Devilla that I'd attend.

Thinking that I would run into a hundred snotty-nose children that were throwing Frisbees, I ended up touching ground at a party that had more grown-ups than children, more liquor than freeze pops.

William said, "Just to let you know Angel, I have a crazy Uncle Tony who loves to talk. So no matter what he asks, just smile and nod your head yes."

I told him, "If I can survive your mom, I can survive anyone."

The party was at a park that lied in the middle of Flatbush. There must've been about a forty people here. Most people were over fifty, a whole gang of William look-a-likes that almost covered the park. Kids were on the loose playing games – not your usual typical games – but games that dealt with slinging rocks and pulling rope. One of them little bad asses almost hit me with a rock, came five inches from giving me a nose redder than Rudolph. When I looked up to see who threw it, I saw little Devilla and one of her friends laughing on the swings – the Devil and the Devil's helper – each of them glancing over their shoulder to see if I'd notice.

A few ran up to William to ask him for money, kids that were sweaty from playing in the dirt. He let two boys split a five dollar bill, but apparently that wasn't enough because they tried to test their luck even further by asking me for more money, they all crowning me the name of Auntie Angel.

The older side of the family was gathered under a wooded pavilion that needed some serious reconstruction. I looked for familiar faces. Looked for William's mother and his sister. Neither was present. From where William and I stood, it seemed to be mostly men engaging in a game of cards. Some were drinking liquor. Others were just laughing and talking.

"Eh Trouble?" yelled one of the guys from the card table. "Get your butt over here."

I walk into a beehive of strangers.

Once touching base, you would've thought William was a celebrity because the men were either throwing him high-fives or giving him pats on the back. At first I thought they were just happy to see him, but the truth eventually came out when one smiled in my direction, saying, "Nephew, you sure did strike a goldmine with that one."

"And good afternoon to you too," William replied, tapping me on the shoulder to ensure me that this was his Uncle Tony.

Uncle Tony is a splitting image of William in twenty years. He's missing his left arm, but somehow, he's still able to multitask with his right, doing everything from drinking, to eating, to playing cards with his other brothers. He's a little lighter than William though. A pop belly. Salt and pepper hair that had a lot more salt than pepper.

One feature that is common amongst all of them are those light brown eyes. Those were the alluring eyes that swept me off my feet, and now those same eyes are watching my every move from each part of the family tree.

Not wanting them to think of me as being stuck-up, I said, "Hello fellas."

"Hellllllooooooo," they all said in congruence.

William said, "Everyone, this is Angel.

"Hellllllooooooo," they re-iterated.

William takes me around the table to introduce me to each one of his uncles, flaunts me around like a trophy that was hid in the basement.

"Angel, this is Uncle Henry."

"Hey Sweetness."

"Uncle Sal."

Cyril Gillion

"Hello my beautiful sistah."

"Cousin Riley."

"Welcome to the family."

"And Uncle Tony."

"Good God almighty!" Uncle Tony yelled. "Lord knows he knew what he was doing when he decided to make a thing like you."

"Why thank you," I said, watching him continuously shake his head while gawking me up and down.

Then he looks over at William. Looks back at me. Then back at William. Back at me. He says, "Boy, where the hell you get a pretty little thing like that? She's 'bout the best-looking gal I every saw you bring up in here." He looks over to his brother and says, "Sal, is she not the best-looking gal that Trouble ever had or what?"

"You ain't lying," Uncle Sal agreed.

"Boy you know you out did yourself this time, nephew. That girl is not only a piece of work, but she's got a good depadition."

"You mean disposition," Cousin Riley said, correcting him.

"No, I meant what I said. DEPADITION. Look it up in the dictionary."

Uncle Sal tells William, "Nephew, you still working over there at that restaurant?"

"Yea," William answered. "I also picked up a gig on the side."

"I see why," Uncle Tony interrupted. "A woman like that would have you working three or four jobs at a time."

"I know that's the truth," replied Uncle Sal.

I watch them work. Watch how William communicates with his family. Watch the way he watches his family watch me.

Uncle Tony continues. "So now that you're working an extra job, give your uncle a couple bucks."

"I'm broke," William replied.

"You lying boy."

William gives an uncomfortable giggle. "Seriously, I don't got it this time. Maybe next time."

"Well damn, nephew. What's happening? Don't tell me that this young bristle is already taking your money."

I smile at him and say, "I'm not that type of woman."

"I hope you're not, because if you were, you'd be one upset cookie when it comes to Trouble. My nephew ain't never been a cake daddy."

"So I've heard."

"Yep, and he learned from me. Never give a woman all your money. A woman never respect a man who can't say no. Ain't that right, Sal?"

"That's right."

"Because women would use ya … they'll use ya good … leave ya hangin' high and dry."

"He ain't lying," Uncle Henry agreed.

"That's why I taught my nephew how to be a pimp at a young age. I told him too—"

"Stop it," William demanded. "It's obvious that you had too much to drink."

"Naw, Trouble. Go 'head and let the girl know the truth. Let her know that you're a pimp just like your uncle. Besides, we're all grownups around here, so I'm sure she doesn't mind."

I laugh aloud as Uncle Tony continues with, "I'll even prove it. I'll prove that my nephew's a pimp." He looks over at his brother, Henry, and says, "Henry, what was the name of that one lil' girl that Trouble used to be with?"

"What girl?"

"You remember? The same girl that Trouble took to the skating rink that time. What was her name?"

"Tyra."

"That's right. Tyra. Now that's one girl I'll neva forget. That girl was—"

"No," William interrupted. "You've told that story for the last time."

"Don't be scared, boy. Let me tell the girl the story."

"She's not interested in hearing your story."

"Yes she is."

"No she's not."

"Go 'head and tell the story," Uncle Sal said, adding fuel to the fire.

William shakes his head in disagreement. "Save your story for another time. Angel is not interested in hearing it."

Uncle Sal looks in my direction. "I say we let her decide. Babygirl, do you want to hear the story or not?"

Not wanting to spoil his joy, I said, "Why not?"

"See there, boy. Told ya so."

Uncle Tony clears his throat, preparing himself for a story that he'll take to the grave. He says, "I'll neva forget it. My nephew was only fourteen years old, still wet behind the ears … that boy came up to his uncle, talking 'bout he needed some money … twenty bucks I think it was … so I'm like, what the hell a fourteen-year-old boy need twenty dollars for, and Trouble was like, to take a girl to the skating rink. Now I'm not the type to give out money, but when it comes to my nephews, I don't mind, because that's just type of uncle I am. A man that—"

"Hurry up and finish the story," Uncle Henry said.

"Kiss my ass, Henry. This is my nephew and I take as long as I like … But anyways, to make a long story short, I gave him the money right – just because I wanted him to have a good date at the skating rink. But when he came back, that lil' nigga was smiling his ass off … So I was like … nephew … what the hell you smiling for. And I'll neva forget it … I'll neva forget it … That boy looked me straight in the eye, chin-up, and said, 'Yep. I got some tail. And I'm finally considered a man.' God knows I could do nothing but laugh my ass off."

William's uncles die in amusement as William stands their embarrassed, disgusted as if he'd stomached this story too many times. Although the story wasn't nearly as funny as I thought it would be, I pretended to laugh along, worst thing you could do is not laugh at an elderly tale.

While laughing, it felt good to know that I was actually here with William, we both mingling with his peeps without any drama, kind of made me feel like I had an extended family of my own.

William asked, "You thirsty?"

"I could go for a soda."

"Cool. I'll be right back."

"You crazy? And leave me hear with these hooligans. You must be out your mind."

"Ok then. How 'bout you go grab the drinks … get me some ginger-ale."

As I walk towards the drinks, I can still hear William's uncles carrying on about me.

The drinks were sectioned off into two coolers, one containing soda and water, and the other container was filled to the rim with Heinekens. A table sat above both coolers, and on top was a 2-liter coke, Jamaican Rum, Hennessey, some gin, and many other alcoholic beverages. I reached into the cooler to scoop up some ice, filled three-fourths of my cup with coke. My conscience told me to bypass the Hennessey and walk away, but my sub-conscience became more of the aggressor, forced me to add in a little liquor until William said, "Angel, let me introduce you to someone."

I settle for Coca Cola.

Walking back to the table, I see more excited faces, the women of William's family. I saw Devilla's godmother, Courtney, and she was joined by three other women, two appearing to be in there fifties and the other in her thirties. The older two lounged beside William's uncles while the younger woman curled around William's cousin. Courtney was the only one by herself, but from observation, I could tell that she was the life of the party. She was dressed in her normal attorney attire, still slinging that fake weave as if it was her own, and I knew my mood would be messed up from the moment she planted her eyes with mines.

"Hello Angel," she said, giving a fake smile.

"Hello," I replied, waiving my hand to acknowledge all of the women.

I immediately felt tension at the table. Tension between me and the four women.

They never spoke. Never even tried to acknowledge my presence. But their hideous glares were cursing me out silently, staring at me like I was an escaped convict. I could tell that Courtney had already briefed them on me and William. Jealous bitch. She was already setting up building blocks between me and William's family.

William said, "Angel, this is my Aunt Erva, Aunt Beth, her daughter Jewels, and you already know Courtney."

"Nice to meet ya," I replied.

"Ain't she a beautiful thing?" Uncle Tony said to his wife, stirring up the waves of jealously. "That's how you used to look until you kept messing with all that pork."

"I'm not the only one who gained weight," his wife replied.

"What did you say?"

"I said your ass is as big as mines so you have no room to talk. Only thing you do is sit around the house and eat."

"Woman, I'm a sixty-five year ol' retired man."

"And? What's that supposed to mean?"

"That means I've earned the right to sit around the house and eat. Hell, I'll fry your big ass on the skillet if it could fit."

Everyone laughs.

While William's uncle is having his way with his wife, his cousin Jewels tells me, "Angel is the name right?"

"Right."

"Do you also work at the restaurant?"

"No. I have a part time job."

"Part-time?"

"That's right," William said, intervening. "And that's only because she's a student at Brooklyn law, the same school that Courtney once attended."

Cousin Jewels says, "How splendid. Law school and a part-time job. Sounds like you have a full load."

"Well I try to make time for things that are important."

"Such as?"

I think hard. "Such as family. Nothing should be more important than family."

"Well you're always welcome in this family," replied Uncle Tony. "You just gotta know how to work with a deck of cards. Do you play spades?"

"Of course I play spades. That's all we do in the south."

"Okay then. You and Trouble can battle me and my wife."

William says, "That's alright, Uncle Tony. Angel's only purpose for coming was to wish Devilla a happy birthday. That's it."

"Yeah yeah yeah. Whateva you say, Trouble. Why can't you just shut up and let the girl have some fun. It's only one game of cards."

"I agree," Courtney adds. "I'm sure Angel doesn't mind playing a game or two. That's if she's not afraid of a little competition?"

I look that bitch in the eyes and say, "What competition?"

"Well I'll be damned," replied Uncle Tony. "A beautiful gal that's not afraid to talk shit. Now that's what I call a catch."

It didn't take long before William agreed to playing a game of spades, we both sitting across the table as partners, our first act of unison in public. Our opponents were supposed to be William's Uncle Tony and his wife, but for some reason, she was not in the mood to play spades.

"I'll take her spot," Courtney said, quickly jumping in the chair to become my contender.

The cards were soon dealt.

Courtney said, "Two-of-hearts is the highest card."

Confused, I said, "Two-of-diamonds is supposed to be the highest."

"That might be how y'all play down south, but you're now in Brooklyn, and in Brooklyn, a two-of-diamonds is the lowest card in the deck."

"Don't matter," I replied, showing her that my knowledge of the game goes far beyond a single card.

When it was time to call-out our books, William's look was nowhere near confident. He said, "I've only got two books. Possibly three."

"I've got five," I replied, picking up for his lack of hand.

"What about you?" Uncle Tony asked, looking over at Courtney. "I hope you got somethin' 'cause my hand is dry as turkey."

Courtney proudly says, "I've got seven. Seven and a possible."

"Seven? Are you sure, 'cause I don't want to get set back? Uncle Tony ain't used to losing."

Courtney stares at me from out the corner of her eye, giving me a challenging glare. She said, "Trust me, Uncle Tony. Just like in court, I don't loose. So like I said, we're going an even seven."

"Well that's good enough for me," Uncle Tony replies, writing it down on the paper. "Seven it is."

Intending to top her, I say, "Me and William are going for eight."

As we arranged the cards in our hands, William's other relatives kept circling around the four of us, peeping what each one brought to the table.

"Damn, Beth. Let the girl breathe," Uncle Sal said, pulling his wife from over my shoulder.

As this horse race sets off, both teams achieved two books apiece. Each book either came from Courtney or me, and instead of Courtney paying attention to what she had in her hand, she was paying more attention to me and William, observing how we interact amongst the family.

Uncle Tony plays a queen-of-hearts. "Come on wit it," he said. "Show us how y'all get down in the south."

"Like this!" I said, slamming down my king-of-hearts to top his queen.

Courtney tops me with an Ace and tells me, "Not so fast, Southern bell"— then she gives me an evil scowl. I give her one back.

This is a war.

The intensity started to rise, and one of William's relatives yelled, "What's the score over there… Tony, are y'all on top?"

"Of course we are," Courtney replied, throwing the card down forcefully to take the lead.

Another book is played and the game is now tied at four books apiece. I silently communicated with William from across the table. He let me know he was out of clubs, but he also gestured that Courtney still had another diamond, which is what I would have to play in order to turn this game around. I knew that Uncle Tony had diamonds too,

          Cyril Gillion

and that wasn't a threat because I was still carrying the king-of-diamonds and the ace had already been played.

Uncle Tony says, "I hope you're not playing clubs because my partner is waiting to cut."

"Good, because I hope she's not waiting on this?" William said, playing a ten-of-diamonds."

"No. But I am," replied Uncle Tony, beating William with a jack-of-diamonds.

I roughly dropped my king on table and said, "Sorry Mr. Tony, but in a case like this, my king must over-rule your jack."

"Yeah, but sometimes the queen has to do what's best for the kingdom," Courtney said, beating me with her queen-of-spades and glancing over at William, her evil lips puckering.

I knew that she wasn't referring to cards. I could see it in her eyes. Her attention was more so focused on winning William than winning this game.

She wanted this war. She wanted it bad. And I had no problem giving it to her.

"Pow Yow!" Uncle Tony screamed, throwing down his ace-of-spades. "You've gots to come better than that!"

Courtney looks befuddled at Uncle Tony, tension rising in her eyes. "What are you doing?" she asked.

"What does it looks like I'm doing? I'm playing cards."

"You mean to tell me that you had an ace-of-spades the whole time and you're now deciding to throw it down."

"Don't worry about what's in my hand. You just worry about yours. Now lets play the game. Shoot. I've been playing cards before you were runnin' in pampers."

The dispute between them continues to escalate, causing them to loose focus. That paves the way for me and William, and now, the game is at six books apiece, one card left to play.

We dropped our cards at the same time.

"Darnit," I said, thinking that my two-of-hearts had lost us the game. Then I remembered what Courtney said earlier, how the two-of-hearts is used as the highest card to play. And in this case, my two-of-hearts supersedes her two-of-spades."

"Hmmm, I think I like the way y'all play in Brooklyn," I said, looking over at Courtney to give her that radiant smile that she despises so dearly.

She says, "I wouldn't speak too soon. That's only the first game, 70 points. You still have 230 points to go."

The next couple of games got more intense, and as the score continued to grow, so did the reactions of William's family. Uncle Tony and Aunt Beth had even started to make bets, they both acting crazy as if we were at a world-renowned poker tournament.

William and I continued to prefect that perfect chemistry. The perfect team on and off the table we were.

Truth be told, I could care less about winning or losing this game of cards at the moment. My attention was more so on William. On his sexiness. While his family continued to bump their gums about this useless game, I was more so fantasizing about bumping something with my partner, kept envisioning myself as his queen-of-heart being slammed on the table by the royal King.

I couldn't help it. Couldn't stop having a dogfight with my imagination.

Lord knows I wanted to kiss him, for I had not kissed him all day. Lord knows I wanted to mess up his white t-shirt before his daughter got birthday cake all over it, or even further, we could leave this birthday party altogether, and go to a sacred place where he'd place me into a birthday suit of my own. Lord knows I wanted to pause this game of cards and jack his diamond spade until he spit clubs of spunk.

Lord knows.

Lord knows.

Lord— "Angel, what the heck are you doing?"

"Huh?"

"Why are you playing diamonds?" William asked.

I come back to earth. "Oh … I thought hearts were the last card that played."

"Can't take it back," Uncle Tony said. "Once the card hits the table it's written in stone."

I got myself under control, took my mind from the gutter, and as this game continued to roll, two little girls ran over to the card table, they both gasping for breaths.

"What y'all want?" Uncle Tony asked. "Can't ya see that grown folks are playing cards?"

Stuttering, one of them said, "Uncle … Uncle William?"

"What is it?"

"Devilla … Devilla is—"

"Spit it out!" Uncle Tony demanded.

"Devilla is on the playground fighting. She pushed Precious against the monkey bars and—"

"No she didn't!" the other girl intervened. "Precious pushed her first!"

"No she didn't!"

"Yes she did!"

William rises from the table as the kids continued to bicker, leaving the game to go settle the dispute.

"Guess I'll grab myself a beer in the meantime," Uncle Tony said.

"Me too," agreed Uncle Henry and Cousin Riley.

In just the blink of an eye, the men had left the table, leaving me stuck with William's aunt, his Cousin Jewels, and Courtney. Although we were all women, I somehow felt out-of-place, and something told me to get up from the table and grab a beer with William's uncles.

Aunt Beth fired up a cigarette and passed the lighter to her daughter, Jewels.

Suddenly, Jewels asked me, "So how did you meet my cousin?"

She says the word *my* as if she's establishing ownership, already demanding her stamp of approval.

I tell her, "We met at grand central."

"Grand central? Now that's surprising."

"Is it?"

She reads me like I'm a wall full of hieroglyphics – her and her mother too – they both acting as if they're getting ready to solve the DaVinci Code. Courtney was also scoping me from across the table, shuffling the deck of cards as if she was preparing for a cross-examination. The three of them looked like the wicked witches of the west; all that was missing was a broom. Each of their expressions let me know that I was sitting behind enemy lines and my only ally was too far out of reach, too busy protecting his daughter on the playground. I'm not afraid of these women, but I am afraid of the moment. Feels like I'm a black Martha Stewart behind prison bars.

Depending on what I say or how I react, this moment could be the closing stages between William and I. Could be our demise.

"You know what," Courtney says, steady shuffling those cards. "Usually William would go on and on about the women he meets. It's strange that he never mentioned you … not until now."

"Maybe he just wanted to hide me from you."

"Is that right?"

"That's right."

"And why would he want to do something like that?"

"I'm not sure. Guess you'll have to ask him."

It was obvious that she was jealous. Even Stevie Wonder could see it. But what's funny is that I should be the one who's jealous of her. After all, she's supposed to be the established lawyer. The bitch with the big career. But me, I'm nothing but a law school student that's struggling with a part time job, still residing in the projects. So why envy me? Why envy a chick that's half your age, half your worth of revenue.

Not letting up, she says, "So what are you and William exactly?"

My safe response is, "We're just friends."

"Friends as in *mutual friends* or friends as in *we get down to business* type of friends?"

"Friends as in *none of your business* type of friends."

"Honey, don't take it personal," his cousin added. "She's only asking because of my wedding that's soon to come. We're doing something special for couples and we need to make sure we have enough invitations."

"Really?" I replied, thinking to myself, *don't try to patronize me.*

She says, "The wedding is in three months."

"Well congratulations."

"Thank you."

"I'm honored to know that you'll want me at your wedding."

"Oh girl it's nothing. Any person who's a company of William is a company of ours. Besides, the more women the more strippers."

"Strippers?"

"Damn skippy. I hope you don't think I'll jump across that broom before jumping in some tail? Girl, I'm gonna have the bachelorette party of the century. Ain't that right, Courtney?"

"That's right," Courtney agreed. "And I'm gonna see to it."

Jewels said, "Courtney is in charge of the bachelorette party. The women have already put in their requests for the type of men they want at the party. Do you want to put in yours?" she asks, placing me in between a rock and a hard-shell. I didn't know if she was serious or not, but whatever the case was, I treated her question as one of rhetorical. Refused to answer. Had to remember that this was still a war and I was thoroughly being watched.

Jewels said, "Come on, Angel. You don't have to act shy because of William. Tell Courtney the type of strippers that you want at the party."

I tell her, "It doesn't matter to me. I don't have a preference."

"Humph, wish I could say the same, but unlike you, I do have a preference. I already told Courtney to make sure each stripper is 6'0 and taller. Nice pecks. Bald heads. Must be able to dance. Can't be older than forty."

"I thought we agreed to forty-five," Courtney said.

"Hell naw, girl. A man shouldn't be stripping after forty. I'm not trying to see anything wrinkled slinging around my party."

They laugh.

Courtney says, "Don't worry, girl. I got ya covered."

"I hope so, 'cause I haven't seen another naked man in ten years. And I'm on the verge of drowning in my own wetness."

"Too much information."

I felt sorry for her. Felt sorrier for her soon-to-be husband. Anyone could tell that her marriage was already on the rocks before she even reached matrimony, and if infidelity was based upon the consumption of lust, she'd be a first-degree cheater, a female Wilt Chamberlain. She looked at me, then over at her fiancé. He was drinking a beer with Uncle Tony, smiling back in her direction.

She says, "Just look at 'em girl. Don't we look good together?"

"Y'all do," I replied. "The two of you actually look alike."

"I know. You start to look like your man when you've been with him since high school; it's like the man turns into your twin. Hell, sometimes I feel like I know that man like the back of my hand."

"Yeah, I bet you do," remarked her mother. "You and every other woman."

"Don't start, ma."

"Jewels, I'm serious," her mother replied. "I keep telling you that you're making a big mistake."

"Ten years of faithful love is not considered a mistake. Besides, marriage is what you make of it. Those were your words, right? And considering how much we made it already, I'm sure we'll do just fine."

"That's what you say now. But marriage is not that simple. If you ask my opinion, I don't see y'all lasting a year."

"So what are you supposed to be? A psychic?"

"No, I'm a mother. Been yours for thirty-five years. And if I don't know anything else, I know my daughter. Probably know you better than you know yourself."

Blowing each other off, they turn their cheeks as if they've been bickering about this forever, a kinship that could never reach a common ground. I envy that. I envy that connection. I'd give up the world if it meant getting another chance to argue with my mother. Would literally kill for her advisement.

"How 'bout you, Angel? Is there a spot for marriage in your future someday?"

"Hopefully," I replied.

"Hopefully?"

"Yes … once I'm all settled."

"Do you see my nephew as the type of man that you'd want to marry? Do you think he's—"

"Dang mama," her daughter intervened. "You're already asking the girl about marriage and we've yet to establish if they even have a relationship."

Her mother snaps, "I don't have to establish anything because I already can see what's going on. That girl has love written all over her face and to be honest, I don't think I've seen Trouble this happy in six years, the day that Devilla was born."

"I agree," Courtney said, playing the role of a puppet. "You've gotta admit that William has been looking a little content lately. And now that we know why, it's only fair to ask what Angel's intentions are."

"Fair enough," I said, letting her know that I'm not afraid of this conversation. "I think William is a good man. Any man that can raise a daughter by himself is a man worth considering. But as far as marriage is concerned, I'm not thinking about it right now."

"What about kids?"

"Kids?"

"Yeah, like those little badasses on the playground. Do you like kids?"

"They're ok."

"Just ok?" Jewels asked. "No love for children?"

"Is that vital?"

"Damn right it's vital if you want to date my nephew?" her mom said, jumping in. "Not every woman can tolerate his daughter."

"No offense, Mrs. Beth, but I think I have a lot of tolerance, especially when it comes to a six-year-old."

"I hope so, because Devilla is a handful to deal with and when it comes to her father, she's very jealous. That means I don't want any controversy between the two of you"—she pauses—"and believe it or not, it took a child to get Trouble to even respect women the way he does now, 'cause I can remember how Trouble used to be, always running from one woman to the next. Never could find a woman that was equivalent to his mama, so he kept searching for the right one. Thank God that boy finally decided to settle down."

     Cyril Gillion

No reply.

She goes on, "By the way, do you know how to cook?"

"If needed, yes. I'm not a gourmet chef, but I can hold my own."

"Good, because Trouble can cook. And not every woman can put up with a man who's better in the kitchen than she is."

"I don't mind a man who can cook better than me," I told her. "I'm not the old-fashioned type."

She snaps. "Old fashioned? What do you mean by old fashioned?"

I swallow hard; tried my best to take back those words. "I didn't mean old-fashioned as in—"

"See that's the problem with you young girls. You know nothing 'bout taking care of a man. All you want to do is run the streets and be fast."

"Sorry, but I don't run the streets."

"Bets not," she said, firing up another cigarette. "Cause Trouble doesn't need another trollop in his life."

Not knowing what the hell a trollop was, I opened my lethal weapon to say, "Excuse me, but what did you just call me?"

"I said, my nephew don't need—"

"To be hurt again," Courtney said, intervening. "That's all she's trying to say. William doesn't need to be hurt."

Honesty overshadows my intentions of being polite, and I tell them, "William is a grown man. I think he knows how to make decisions for himself."

"You're right," Courtney replies. "But although he's a grown man, he's still our pride and joy. A woman has already ruined his life once and we don't plan on letting another woman do the same, considering that he just got back on his feet. You know, we're not trying to scare you, but just know that we're watching you, Angel. We're watching you very very carefully."

"Well don't watch too hard because I don't swing that way. I'm strictly—"

"Heeey!" William said, coming back to the table. What is my beautiful family over here talking about?"

"Nothing," Courtney said, masking that fake-ass smile. "We all were just discussing Jewels wedding."

"I hope not," William said. "I don't need y'all scaring Angel, giving her any ideas."

William's Aunt Beth is steadily grilling me from across the table, biting her bottom lip as if this war is far from being over. Jewels give the same expression as her mother, they both puffing evil blows of smoke from their cigarettes, family sticking together.

If I were the designated driver, I'd leave this park right now with William, would grab my wizard and escape this Land of Oz.

But I couldn't. I knew that William wasn't leaving anytime soon, especially since it was Devilla's birthday party.

Instantly, I rose from the table and walked over to William, tongued-kissed him so the wicked witches could see.

"Is everything alright?" he asked.

"I'm cool. Think I need another drink, though. Y'all got any more gin, I mean, ginger ale?"

"Yeah, but what about food? My Uncle Tony is getting ready to put some hamburgers and hotdogs on the grill."

"I'm not that hungry."

"You sure, girl?" Uncle Tony yelled while pouring kerosene over the charcoal. "You won't find barbeque like this in the south."

I spent the rest of the party keeping to myself. The only time I ever spoke is when Devilla was blowing out the six candles of her cake, and that was only to tell her happy birthday. After it was all over, Devilla told William that she wanted to ride home with Courtney, wanted to end her special day by going to Chucky Cheese.

"I just gave you a birthday party," William told her. "Isn't that enough?"

"Lighten up, William," Courtney said, jumping in. "Birthdays only come once a year."

"Fine, but make sure you have her home before eight. School is tomorrow."

Tension sat on my face as William took me to his place. Our ride started off in silence, but William somehow found a gospel song on 94.3 FM, decided to raise the volume to eights bars.

Irritated, I tried to turn it down, but I accidentally changed the station.

William asked, "What is it? You don't like my type of music?"

"I have a headache."

"That headache may have come from my uncle and his loud talking. I know he made you a little uncomfortable, but I warned you about his character."

     Cyril Gillion

I start to comment but he grabs another set of words before I could speak. "Not to mention, your headache could've come from an empty stomach. I mean ... you didn't eat the whole day."

"Food wasn't the problem," I said, finally speaking my mind.

"Then what was?"

"You—"

"Me?"

"No ... you as in ... you can't take me to prison and expect to give me room service."

He hesitates and says, "So you see my family as a prison?"

"No."

"Then why'd you say it?"

"Prison is an understatement. Sitting at that card table was more like sitting on death row. Had you left me there a little longer with those women, it would've been on. Would've been the second fight you would've had to break up today."

We approach a red light as he gives me a bewildered gaze. "Am I missing something?" he asked.

"After you left to go check on Devilla, your aunt and cousin damn near harassed me to death."

"What?"

"That's right, William ... Trouble Trouble Trouble. That's all I kept hearing the whole time. Each one of them threatening me, talking crap about what they'd do if someone hurt their little Trouble. For Christ's sake, you're supposed to be a grown ass man. Forty years old. But me. I'm the one who just broke out of a five-year relationship. So if there's anyone who should be worried about getting hurt, it should be me. I'm the one who's—"

"Well just hold on for a second, Angel. How did all of this start and who said—"

"Oh don't act surprised! Don't act like you didn't know the drama you'd stir up when bringing me to that godforsaken party." I catch my breath. Air is my only source for remaining calm. "And who is this infamous woman they were talking about?"

"What woman?"

"The woman who supposedly ruined your life."

"That woman?"

"Yeah ... that woman."

His eyes widen and he lets go of the steering wheel, as if he'd suddenly seen a deadly past through the rearview mirror.

Another red light is approaching us, causes him to slam on breaks.

I tell him, "Watch the road godammit!"

"What did they say?"

"Oh, so I guess they were telling the truth after all. And to think I thought they were just pulling my leg the entire time. That's just fantastic."

He snaps. "What the heck did they tell you, Angel?"

"What I just said."

"No, give me specifics."

"You've answered my question, so there's no more to say."

"No godammit! There's more."

His hands start shaking over the steering wheel, his body language making me think that he's about to have some type of attack.

I say, "What's wrong with you?"

"Nothing."

"Then why are you shaking. Why are you—"

"Just tell me what—"

"—acting out of character."

"Never mind how I'm acting. Now tell me what they said."

"Why is it that important?"

"Because it is ok. It just is!"

"Do you still love this other woman?"

"No!"

"Am I some type of replacement?"

"That woman is already behind me. Long gone."

"Then forget about it. Forget that I ever brought her up."

"I can't do that!"

"Why not?"

"Because you already spoke on it."

"Well I'm not speaking anymore. I'll just sit here and be quiet."

"Too late. Now tell me what they—"

"No, William. I don't wanna stir up any bad memories."

"They're not bad memories!"

"Then why are your hands shaking all over the steering wheel?"

"I'm not shaking!"

"Yes you are. You're all—"

"Darnit! Stop fucking around and spit it out!"

"Red light!"

"What?"

"There's a red light!"

"Don't you think I see the darn—"

"Breaks!!"

                    Cyril Gillion

<u>21</u>

"Dammit! Where did y'all learn how to drive?"

"Us? Your stupid husband is the one who can't drive."

That was my voice, an upset woman who was arguing with the wife of the driver who just hit our car.

You would've thought that William would be cursing out the driver instead of me cursing out the wife, but instead, William's only focus was trying to close the dented trunk. Meanwhile, I was acting like the mad wife in the middle of Lexington and 46th, bickering with a heavyset white woman who was strutting around on one leg and a pair of crutches.

"Shutz," the driver said from afar. "I just got this truck out the factory yesterday."

"Don't your man know what a red light means?" the woman yelled."

"Don't yours?" I yelled back. "And the light wasn't red. It was yellow."

"Yellow means slow the fuck down!"

"What you say?"

"The speed limit is forty-five. Y'all were going almost sixty!"

"We were going the flow of traffic."

"Flow of traffic my white ass! My husband makes a six hundred dollar payment a month for this Explorer. That's too much money to let some drunk driver and his—"

"My husband doesn't drink!"

"Could've fooled the hell out of me!"

She hops over to my side of the car and raises one of her crutches into my face. She tells me, "Now you listen to me and listen good. You and your—"

"Bitch, if you knew what was best, you'll get your crippled ass in the car before I beat you with those damn crutches!"

"Dorothy, get in the car!" her husband hollered, coming between the two of us. Then he steps in front of me. "Sorry about your car, ma'am."

"Sorry. Sorry isn't going to fix our rear-end."

"There!" William yelled, finally able to close the trunk. William steps into the dispute and shakes hands with the other driver.

"I say we handle this in a civilized manner," the man said. "I have full coverage insurance. It'll pay for the damages."

"Cool," William agreed. "Let me get your contact information."

Stalling, the man reaches into his pocket for his cellular.

William asks, "What are you doing?"

"Calling the police."

"Bad idea."

"What?"

"There's no need to get the police involved."

"Why not? It's best that we do this thing by the book."

"That's ok. Let's just forget about this whole thing."

Looking at William as if he's bumped his head, I say, "Are you nuts? What do you mean forget about it?"

"Angel, it's nothing but a bump."

"Nothing but a bump. For goodness sake, William. Look at your car!"

"It's ok, Angel. I know someone at Rover's Automotive."

"So what are you suggesting?"

"I'm saying we should leave. He'll fix this for me in no time. Therefore, no one comes out the pocket."

"So let me get this straight. They hit our car, but we're the ones fleeing the scene. What the hell is this supposed to be? A get hit and run."

"Are you sure?" the man asks, eager to pull out his insurance packet.

                          Cyril Gillion

"I'm sure, but thanks for your gratification," William replied, walking back to the car. "God bless."

Our ride to William's house was silent. I don't know what was on his mind, but I was still thinking about our conversation before the wreck. Once getting inside, William sat me down on the couch and told me that he was a little tired from being out all day, asked me if I wanted to crash at his place for the night.

I said, "You sure that Devilla is going to be cool with that?"

"Why would you ask that?"

"Don't know. Just didn't want to cause any static. I know how jealous your daughter can be."

"Last time I checked, I was the father. And Devilla is gon' stay at Courtney's tonight anyway."

"Courtney huh," I say, sucking my teeth.

"What is it? Oh let me guess. Courtney also had something to say at the card table. Didn't she?"

"Forget about it, William."

"Why do I get the inclination that you're still thinking about that other woman?"

"Like any woman, I don't want to feel like leftovers."

"Having feelings for someone else doesn't mean you are leftovers. This was a woman that I was married to. She's an ex wife. So there's going to always be feelings involved."

I looked surprised and all I can say is, "Your wife???"

I know it's startling."

"Thought you were only engaged to Devilla's mother."

"That's all that I told you thus far. Devilla's mother is all that I wanted to claim as a wife. But truth is, there was another woman that came long before Devilla's mother"—he pauses—"Her name was Kay. Short for Kaylin. I can honestly say that she was the first woman who genuinely loved me. Taught me the true meaning of love. But I took that love for granted. Abused it for all its worth."

I have a gazillion questions to ask. Questions stacked on top of question marks.

My conscience tells me to stop right there and seal that book of questions, but post-mortem causes me to turn another page and ask him, "So what caused y'all to split?"

"Split? Us splitting would be an understatement. Our relationship more so became tormented … you may not know it, but I used to be a

The Other Side of the Pillow

truck driver, always on the road, never had time for quality time. Not to mention, I was still trying to live the bachelor life, which means I would be picking up a different woman every single trip. Kaylin's girlfriends would tell her of my indiscretions, but they never could prove it. So all she had to go on was suspicion … but then …"

"Then what?" I asked, trying to milk out the rest.

He clears his throat, creates a word passageway through that congested corridor of grief. "Then there was the day I'll never forget. I came home from delivering a package from Nevada that took two days … my front door was unlocked, and some noises came from upstairs … noises coming from the bedroom … I saw two wine glasses sitting on the living room table, following some Don Parigon on a bucket of ice … That's when I glanced upstairs, but used all the strength that God gave me to keep from walking up those steps … so instead, I sat on the couch and told myself that I'd wait for them to finish whatever it was that they were doing, figured I'd sit on my couch and enjoy one last episode of CSI at the place where I pay rent … That was the only way to keep me from bursting down the door and tearing up that room … Then, twenty minutes passed and I was still in the same spot, hearing the godforsaken noises upstairs. I decided to reach across the table and pour myself some of their Don Parigon, because CSI just wasn't enough to keep myself under control … Not knowing whether to stand or sit, I blocked myself out from the television and starting drinking as much wine as possible … That was my breaking point. The point where everything started to come to life, and it was only then that I thought about those times that I mistreated her, all the women I'd fornicated with on the road … Worst part about it was that I felt no envy towards her at the moment, even though I was getting ready to witness the average man's nightmare … Then I got impatient … Very impatient … I could no longer wait for them to finish, couldn't let another minute pass without opening that door and seeing the man who was screwing my wife … So I took my chances by walking up stairs and silently pulled back the doorknob, only to see that there was no one in the room at all … not a single face in sight … and the loud noises was coming from the television set, which was a pornographic tape that she'd left in the VCR … I turned off the TV and later saw a note on top of that VCR. … All the note said was *Trouble, you should consider yourself lucky. You could've seen worse* … And that was the end of it … That was the last time I ever saw or heard from Kaylin, my ex wife, until she mailed me some papers a year later, saying how she wanted a divorce … I eventually signed those papers, but it took two

   Cyril Gillion

days before I could even pick up the pen … In her eyes, I was signing away all of my rights, freeing her as a woman. But in my eyes, that signature served a different purpose … I made a promise to myself that I would never treat another woman like I treated her and those women that came before her … Just so happened that God was willing to send me another woman, which was Devilla's mother, and I promised to give her twice the love that I lacked to give Kay … I did just that too … I loved her with all my heart … But then she died, and to be honest, I haven't been seriously involved with another woman ever since … It's like my heart has been completely void, and I've yet to find a woman that could fill that empty space."

I tell him, "Maybe God will fill that empty space one day."

"Or maybe he's already working on it," he replies, giving me a warming gaze.

I stare back into his eyes. Eyes carrying enough fire to light a match.

At this moment, I could care less about that woman from his past or how many times he was unfaithful to her … hell … bitch probably deserved it anyhow.

William asks, "Can I say something?"

"Anything."

"Do you want this?"

"If only you knew."

"No. Not physically. I mean, do want this relationship? I'm talking about a real commitment."

What he didn't know is that I was far passed wanting a commitment and my commitment had already started from the first time I opened my legs. Although that wasn't for him to know, I told him, "Yes, a commitment sounds good."

"You sure?" he asked. "Because there's more."

"Ok."

"I've been doing a lot of thinking. And I've decided that I wanna go a different route."

I wander if he's gonna tell me the unthinkable, that he could possibly be gay, but unless he wants to meet death before his time, he wouldn't dare.

I ask him, "And what route would that happen to be?"

He grabs my hands, kisses one of my knuckles. "Celibacy."

"Excuse me?" I said making sure I heard him correctly.

"I want to try celibacy."

"Celibacy?"

"Yes."

"For what? I mean, since when?"

"Since now," he says. "I just realized something. I'm constantly asking God to put the right woman in my life, to bring me my soul mate, but then again, I can never keep that woman. Something tells me that there's a reason why."

"And you actually think it's because you're having sex?"

"Could be."

"Since when did love-making become a sin?"

"Fornication is a sin. Forbidden by God. We tend to ignore the repercussions because we do it so often. So how can I expect God to give me a wife if I constantly have intentions on sinning?"

"What?"

"I know it seems a little over the top. Especially considering that we already engaged into the act. But I know that God is telling me to wait."

"What?"

"Are you listening?"

I was listening, but I wasn't comprehending, and as he hoaxes me into thinking he'd have a first-class ticket to hell, I ask him, "For how long?"

"Excuse me?"

"How long do you intend to practice this celibacy thing?"

"Hopefully until marriage," he says, shifting my hormones out of sequence. "I want to give my wife – whoever that woman will be – everything. Now I know this could put a strain on our relationship, but one thing I do want to ask you is … is this something you think you can handle?"

First thing that came to mind is our first date, how he had my ass high in the air, asking me to call him daddy on my living room couch. Now all of a sudden that so-called daddy-talk has gone out the window and has suddenly turned into a daddy-daughter lecture.

I want to gag on that notion. A perception that is too hard to swallow, even harder to digest.

It's probably easy for him to practice celibacy; especially considering that he practically screwed every woman on the northern hemisphere. But here I was, that woman who finally got a sample of the dazzler, that same woman who finally found a man worth sleeping with, and I now have to put those desires on the backburner, all because of some agreement that he made with his God.

How selfish of him?

　　　Cyril Gillion

I mean, does he really expect me to gift-wrap my vagina, store it somewhere safe, and pull it back out on my wedding day, after it's been sitting around for how ever so long, doing nothing but getting old and collecting dust.

Run like hell Angel.

Run like hell Angel.

Run like hell Angel.

That was my conscience talking. Looking after me the way it normally does.

I didn't want to appear as a slut by sending him on his spiritual journey, but then again, I wasn't up for hanging around and suffering through some type of nymphomania disorder either. So I told him what any woman would've said when her back is against the wall. I looked him dead in the eye and said, "I have to think about this."

"You sure, Angel? 'Cause this doesn't have to be your battle. It's mine."

"If this is supposed to be right by God, then why would it be considered a battle?"

He doesn't reply. All smiles.

Nightfall came right around the corner. I was lying in William's bed wearing a long t-shirt and panties. Despite the perception of most men, William's room was neatly organized. The only clothes out of place was a long-sleeved collar shirt and dress slacks, both neatly hanging from a two layer rack that sectioned his undergarments on top, t-shirt and shorts on bottom. An old desk sat in the corner of the room and the quantity of books on top was over-flowing. Wind blew from an open window, blew down one of the six pictures of Devilla that sat on the window seal, looked like there was a picture for every year that she was alive. William had a full-size bed, a little shy of the size that I expected for a man of his magnitude, but it was doable.

As we lay on common grounds, our minds appear elsewhere. While my head was buried into a litigation book for Professor Stern's class, William was reading one of his theological pamphlets. He was lounging at a ninety-degree angle, wearing nothing but briefs and a pair of reading glasses.

The comforter.

It separated the two of us, became the intermediary of our sexual fixations. I flip back the covers, hoping my bare legs would stir up some tension, but William doesn't react, doesn't even break a stride through his reading.

A half hour pass and reading time is soon over. William rises from the bed, rests his glasses near the lamp.

He asks, "Would it bother you if I turned off the light."

"Makes no difference to me."

After flipping the switch, he undresses in the dark. A light from the window flickers down on his chest as he takes off his shirt and undergarments. Adding insult to injury, he also takes off his briefs, and the light from the window decides to flicker between his legs, giving me a glimpse of paradise.

"No fair," I told him, immediately turning on the lamp and seeing his package up close. "You're now playing dirty."

"What do you mean?"

"Unless you want to loose your religion, I suggest you cover up that cobra."

"Oh this," he replied, pretending to be nonchalant. "Sorry, but I'm used to sleeping naked."

"Whateva."

"I'm serious."

"So am I."

"Ever since I was little, I slept in the nude. My mother couldn't afford any fans, so this was my way of staying cool and breezy. Guess it developed into a habit that's hard to break."

"Well you're no longer little and neither is he. And most importantly, I'm not your mama."

He laughs. "Cool. I can respect that, especially considering the conversation that we had earlier. So to alleviate any type of arousal, I'll just sleep on the couch. You can have the—"

"No."

"What?"

"Sleeping on the couch is not necessary," I said, telling him anything to preserve my package. "Besides, I have a better idea."

"Yeah?"

Right then and there, I slid off my panties, tossed my bra to the side, and slithered into his bed completely naked, a flesh waiting to be annihilated. Then I lay at a ninety degree angle, put an arch in my back, let him see what he'll be missing if he considers taking this celibacy thing seriously.

He says, "On second thought, maybe we both should sleep covered … completely covered."

     Cyril Gillion

<u>22</u>

The next morning I awoke in peace, no nightmares.

Although no action occurred between William and me, he still managed to hold me the entire night. I turned over to the side of the bed to greet my morning sunshine, but like always, he'd already risen before I could awake. Then I felt a tongue, a slippery sensation sliding around my toes.

"And good morning to you too," I murmured, looking towards the ceiling.

His head was under the covers, positioned at the end of the bed, but I couldn't see his face, and as he licked the crevices between my toes, I could only thank God for finally answering a prayer, allowing William to have a change of heart about this whole abstinence thing.

While he masters that foot fetish craft, I relish in the moment.

I mutter, "You've did this before haven't you?"

He doesn't answer, a mouth too full to speak.

His tongue goes faster.

And faster.

And faster.

As he reaches his pinnacle of speed, I moan harshly; give echoes loud enough to ricochet from hilltops.

He then mutters, "Good morning."

Unable to open my eyes, I say, "I see that you finally came to life down there."

"Angel, I'm over here," he says, tapping me on the shoulder."

"You're what?"

"Wake up, Angel. You were dreaming."

"Dreaming? I wasn't dreaming. You were just giving me special attention."

"What?"

"Why did you stop?"

"Stop what?"

"Licking my toes."

He laughs. "Hard to believe that you can wake up with such a sense of humor."

"Stop screwing around, William. Now why did you stop? And how did you get across the room so fast."

"You really are serious aren't you? I'm telling you Angel, you were imagining things."

"I wasn't imagining anything. You were just below the covers, licking my toes."

"Only thing I licked this morning was the bottom of my plate. I just came in here to offer you some breakfast that I made earlier. Figured you might of wanted some considering that—"

"Where is Ivanna?" Devilla screamed, storming into the bedroom. "Where is Ivanna???"

"Who?" I asked, surprised to see that Devilla was here.

"Go into the living room," William told her. "Daddy will be out in a second."

"Hi, Ms. Angel," Devilla said, walking out the door.

William tells me, "Ivanna is her puppy."

"Puppy?"

"Yeah."

"You mean to tell me that there's a dog in here!"

I flip back the comforter, and sure as heck, there's that fury beast of hell.

I run into the shower and turn the hot water on full blast.

"What's the problem?" William yelled from outside the bathroom door.

"I hate dogs!"

William laughs. "That's not what you were saying earlier. Thought I heard you moaning about how good the dog was licking your toes."

I flip William the bird and I start scrubbing my feet intensely.

         Cyril Gillion

The shower exceeded well over an hour. By the time I got out, William was packing Devilla a lunchbox and they both were feeding the dog a treat before Devilla went to school.

Devilla yells, "Ms. Angel, come and pet Ivanna."

"That's ok, Devilla. I don't think it's a good idea."

"Please, Ms. Angel. She's only a puppy. I promise you she doesn't bite."

"That's right, Angel," William said sarcastically, continuing to laugh. "Besides, didn't the two of you already get acquainted?"

I walk through the living room like I'm walking through mud, giving William an evil glare at the same time. The puppy, Ivanna, licks her chops in my direction, stares at me as if she's ready for a round two, eager to show me that although she may look like a dog, she's equipped with human tactics that goes far beyond my comprehension.

William's cellular rings, saving me from reacquainting with the puppy.

He talks in a high voice. "Are you downstairs … no … what do you mean you have a convention … so what am I supposed to do … I have to work tonight … no … never mind … forget it Courtney … fine then."

Click.

"Daddy, was that mommy?"

"Yes, Devilla. Daddy's gonna have to take you to the play tonight."

"Why?"

"Because Courtney has to be somewhere that's very important."

"But daddy, she's supposed to help me with my rabbit makeup."

"Oh don't worry, Devilla. Daddy can do your makeup."

Devilla gets upset, storms into the room.

"Devilla!"

"Leave me alone!"

William feeds off her emotions and they both get upset. William makes his way towards the couch. "Darnit!"

"Everything ok?" I asked.

He shakes his head. "What am I supposed to do, Angel? I know nothing about dressing a little girl up as a rabbit. Let alone putting on makeup. For Christ sake, why tell a child you're gonna do something if you know you can't do it!"

Volunteering for a mission impossible, I tell him, "Maybe I can take her."

The Other Side of the Pillow

"What?"

"Don't even worry yourself. I can help her prepare."

"Don't you have a class later today?"

"My last class ends at three."

With doubt, he says, "You sure you'll be ok with this, because I can call-in from work if I have to. Heck, I've done it before."

"I'm sure, William. Just tell me where the school is located and the time she has to be there."

The whole time William contemplated on whether he was making a good decision, I asked myself the same question: If I would still be alive after keeping his daughter? No easy decision for either party, this was a gamble for us both. But I realized that if I was gonna be committed to William, I'd somewhat have to commit to his daughter. Can't get the package without the package deal.

William tells me, "Thank you, Angel … I'll be home at four, so in case you change your mind, make sure to call before then."

Four o'clock rolled around like clockwork.

I was in a rush to get back to William's apartment; the play would start at 6 p.m., but Devilla needed to be there at 5:30 for rehearsal.

Trying to appear as the motherly type, I wore a black suit. Lavender blouse underneath. Closed toe wedge heels. Accessorized myself with a couple of silver figararo bracelets. Even decided to flat-iron my hair for the occasion.

William's expression staggered me when coming through the door, made me feel like I was overdressed.

He said, "All of this for a children's play."

Didn't know what to expect."

"Well you look good. Darn good."

Devilla's costume was laid out on the living room couch, an orange lion-looking outfit with footies.

I said, "Where is she?"

"Bathroom."

He pulls out his wallet and hands me forty dollars.

"What's this for?"

"Gas. Her school is in Secaucus, New Jersey. Patterson Plan Rd. Claradon Elementary."

"Why so far?"

"It's an all *A* school. And since I want Devilla to have the best education, most schools in Brooklyn just don't cut it."

          Cyril Gillion

He continues with, "If you run into any problems with the car, make sure you call me immediately. Here's my work number."

I ask, "Are you on your way out?"

"Yeah. My shift starts at 4:30."

He goes into Devilla's bedroom to hug her; tells her that he'll see her later tonight.

And just like that he vanishes – long gone – leaving me standing in an apartment alone, no one to give me guidance but the puppy dog that kept licking its tongue in my direction.

"Daddy, are you still there?" Devilla yelled from the bedroom.

I walk into her domicile, and there she is, balancing an unlighted candle in the air. Her room is full of colors, multiple rainbows within a five-foot radius. There are toys and stuffed animals thrown everywhere you turn, so many to where you have to watch your step. The walls have a couple drawings of weird-looking angels, crosses, and there was a large stick-figure man that she'd drawn, my assumption that it was supposed to be Jesus.

I tell her, "Your dad has already left."

"Man shoot!" she replied, displeased.

"What is it?"

"He left before handing me the torch."

"Torch?"

"Yeah, he was supposed to hold my torch so I can work on grabbing it."

"Oh that's ok. I'll hold it for you."

"Ok, stand right there," she says, handing me a long candle.

I raise the candle in the air, shoulder length for her reaching.

"Higher," she demanded. "You have to raise it to where I can barely grab it."

Listening to the warden, I raise the candle higher, bar length to the top of the dresser. Devilla slowly walks over to grab it from my hands, and with much enthusiasm, she struts towards the end of the room, a ballerina without the golden slippers.

She blurts out, "For we are your kingdom!" And then she smiles in my direction as if she's waiting for some sort of applause. Although I had no idea what the hell she was doing, I still acknowledged her work.

I tell her, "Seems like you're ready for the play."

"I am," she replied in excitement. "I just hope I'll be very pretty. Guess what I'm going to be?"

"What?"

"A lioness."

"Wow," I replied ecstatically. "You're going to be a lion. King of the jungle."

"No, Ms. Angel. Not a lion. A lioness. There's a big difference."

"Well Ms. Lioness, I'm going to make sure you're the prettiest lioness in the jungle."

"Yes! I can't wait."

She pulls out an orange jar of kiddy makeup, glitter, and a thin brush for designing her whiskers. She reaches for a picture from the dresser, her interpretation of the perfect lioness.

She asks, "Can you make me look like this?"

"Of course. I can make you look better."

While putting on her makeup, I became a nervous wreck. Felt like I was giving Oprah a makeover.

After twenty minutes of fingers trembling all over her face, I hold my breath as she looks into the mirror.

She hollers, "What the heck is this, Ms. Angel. I look like a cat!"

"You look fine."

"That's what you say now. But all the children will be laughing at me later."

"They'll only laugh because they're jealous. Now trust me Devilla. You look just like a lioness. Just a darker tone."

Not buying it, she takes a harder look at the lioness on the picture; then she looks into the mirror, looks back at the picture, then back at the mirror, and now at me.

She cries out, "I look nothing like the picture."

"Yes you do."

"No I don't."

"Yes you do ... just look ... if you turn to the side, the whiskers are exactly the same."

Set in our own opinions, we go back and forth like political parties down the stretch of a campaign. I tried my hardest to vouch for my work, but no matter how hard I tried, those whiskers never resembled the ferociousness that she was trying to convey, and after hearing her constantly complain, I contemplated on changing her little butt from a lioness to a bear.

I was heartbroken.

My first task and I was already halfway out the door, already prepared to relinquish the role of parenting – and the more I designed her, the more I noticed how much she resembled her father. Despised imperfection like he hated profanity.

       Cyril Gillion

Fifteen minutes passed. Fifteen minutes of trying to make her look like the perfect lioness.

After redesigning her whiskers for the third time, she was finally pleased with my artwork.

"Now this is what I call a lioness," she said, mimicking the picture.

She runs into the living room to grab her costume, steps into the bottom half that includes feet and tail.

I say, "Take that costume off Devilla. Your dad says you can't wear it right now."

"Why not?"

"Because you have to wait until we reach the school."

"Come on, Ms. Angel. Just let me put it on for a little while."

She gives those pleading eyes. Irresistible eyes like those of her father, impossible to turn down.

I say, "Ok. I guess you can wear it for a little while. But you must take it off before we leave."

I fasten the top half of her costume and straighten up her lioness tail. While doing so, she feels the need to show me one of the pictures that she drew on the wall. "Look Ms. Angel. There goes an angel just like you. But only that Angel has real wings."

"I see. And who's the man beside the angel," I ask, pointing at the stick-figure artwork.

"That's daddy."

"Really."

"Yep."

"Why does he look so sad?"

"Because that's how he always looks. My teacher told us to draw our mom and dad the way we're used to seeing them … so that's him."

Those words are shocking, to know how much children can recognize anger, how they possess the ability to express unforgettable images on paper.

From looking at Devilla's expression, I can tell the picture causes her pain. Hurts her to know that her dad is hurt.

A picture says a thousand words, ignites a thousand questions.

I ask, "Why do you think your daddy is always sad?"

"I don't know. I think it's because of grandma. Every time he comes from seeing grandma, he sits on his bed, crying with a box in his hands."

"A box?"

"Yeah … a little black box."

My curiosity flusters. "What's in the box?"

"I don't know," she replies, shrugging her shoulders to give the perfect cover up. "All I know is that he tells me to never go near it."

I repeat. "So you have no idea what is in the box?"

"No."

"You promise?"

Looking suspicious, she replies, "I promise."

They say that honesty lies only in children. No other human is more straightforward. Somebody must've lied.

I ask Devilla, "Think you can show me where daddy's box is located?"

"No … I mean … I don't know."

"No or you don't know?"

"Daddy puts it high in his room where I can't reach it. And he tells me not to ever go in his room when he's not home."

I know it was a low thing to do, seeking the truth from a six-year-old child. But the truth is still the truth, and no matter the source it comes from, I still wanted it badly.

I try to make her a bargain. "How 'bout we play a little game?"

"What game?" she replies, all ears.

"If you show me the place where daddy stores this little black box, I'll take you somewhere fun after the play … a place that's very very fun."

With excitement in her eyes, she says, "Really? Where?"

I mention every kids dream. "McDonalds."

"McDonalds?"

"Yep … all the French fries that you can eat."

Not being able to control her excitement, she prances around the bedroom as if she's already won the lotto with Ronald McDonald.

I say, "Not so fast little one. First you gots to show me where this little black box is located."

"Promise me you won't tell my daddy."

"I promise."

"Pinky swear."

"Ok," I reply, raising my finger so she can swear me into oath.

We head into William's bedroom, and it takes her forever to remember where she saw this so-called, little black box.

"There!" she says, pointing her finger towards the top of the closet. "He keeps it right there."

I fumble threw stacks of clothes, in desperate need of the box. It's no where to be found. No where on the shelf.

               Cyril Gillion

Something tells me she jinxed me so she could go to McDonalds, but then I saw the attic, and finally stumbled across home base.

In slow motion, it drops from the attic. The little black box. Sullen and dismal as its name.

"There it goes right there," Devilla says. "See it?"

"I do now," I reply, opening the latch.

I place my hand in the box before actually looking inside; better to get a feel for the terror before staring it in the eyes. Once touching it, I felt a feeling like no other.

Handle.

Glock.

Trigger.

Gun.

I flip closed the box before looking at death, placed it back into its proper place.

"What's in there?" Devilla asked.

"Nothing," I replied, damn near falling from the shelf. "Let's just get out of this room."

"Well are you still taking me to McDonalds?"

I don't answer. Can't think. Too frantic of what I might see next, or furthermore, what I might touch.

"You promised me McDonalds," she said.

"I did?"

"Yes you did."

"Oh yeah ... that's right," I replied, the gun still triggering inside my head. "McDonalds it'll be."

Energized, she struts around the house in glee, half human – half lioness, screaming, "YES! I'm going to McDonalds! I'm going to McDonalds!" In the midst of jumping into the air, she splits her lioness costume and the tale becomes detached.

Right then and there, her screaming goes from being over-joyful to yelling, "My tail! I broke my tail!"

My mind goes into overdrive and I wander what William would say if he knew what just happened, how this whole ordeal went down.

Devilla continues to pout. "My tail! My tail!"

"Your tail is going to be fine."

"No it's not! Now I look like a rabbit."

I tell her, "Stay here. Don't move."

I dash around the apartment, flipping through drawers, dressers, cabinet doors, the sink, any place where I can find something sticky. I finally get my hands on some krazy glue, some that was stashed under one of Devilla's stuffed animals. She's still crying, snot beginning to pour from her nostrils.

I say, "Stop crying. You're going to ruin your makeup."

"It's already ruined!"

I grab the tail of the lioness, using half the bottle of krazy glue. She watches from the bed, watches me like she's watching a magician, and as I re-attach the tail, her crying stops immediately, tears evaporating like sweat.

I say, "There. Now you no longer look like a rabbit."

Reaching Devilla's school was like reaching Disney Land. There were hundreds of kids with parents – majority white – and me and Devilla looked like foreigners on American soil. There was a different animal costume for every child, and it must've took an hour for them to get the kids situated in the auditorium. Devilla was one of the smallest children in the play, the only lioness to appear as a cub.

"What grades are these children in?" I asked one of the administrators.

"Most are in fourth and fifth grade. Few are in kindergarten."

"Figures."

They seated us in an orderly fashion, first by level of importance, then by who arrived first on time. My crew, the parents who got there late, was dumped in the last three rows in the back, and the school faculty told us to get in where we fit in. From the looks of it, I was the only single parent there (or at least I felt like a single parent), and my seat was in the mid section, right next to a heavyset loud-talking couple who was a little over-ecstatic to see their child perform.

"Our child is the hippo. Which one is yours?" the woman said.

Seeing that I was the only black adult in the audience, I told her, "I'm sure you'll figure it out."

Once the play started, each parent clapped for their child as their scene approached. Some of the kids forgot their parts. Others were just too petrified of the camera. Thinking that Devilla would also be shy, she surprised me after she got on stage, showed bravery that I never thought she possessed. Although William wasn't there, I stood up and applauded her for the both of us, applauded her like a child of my own.

"Sit down so we can see!" yelled one of the parents.

"Screw you!" I yelled back. "That's my little girl up there."

Devilla was supposed to be the lioness that Simba fell in love with, the one who kept getting him in trouble. Holding my fingers, I was hoping she wouldn't forget any of her lines, but more importantly, I was paranoid of her tail coming a loose.

"Why don't you just come back to Lion Kingdom and do it your own way."

"Never! My father Mufasa would never allow it."

That was also Devilla. The lioness that supposedly convinced Simba to ignore his father and reunite the lions with hyenas for a greater cause. She was hitting her lines right on queue, kept her head up the entire time. Best part came at the end of the play, when all the animals walked on stage and Devilla was finally able to act out her favorite scene, the one where she gets to walk with the torch. Raising fire in her hands, she smiles at the audience and screams, "We are your kingdom!"

With a standing ovation, the crowd leaped to their feet, applauded her like she was an undiscovered actress, the next Ramon Samon in the making.

After the play was over, the principal eventually brought out all the children. A bunch of lions, giraffes, and elephants; the whole animal kingdom came running offstage as a stampede, each child eager to run into the arms of their parents. I looked up for Devilla but she was held hostage by the principal and a couple more children, all of whom that were acknowledging her performance. Once spotting my presence, she embraces me with a hug that I never anticipated.

I tell her, "You were excellent."

She celebrates like she just received an academy award and the principal comes over to give her another pat on the back.

Devilla says, "Look, Ms. Angel. They told us that we can keep our costumes."

"That's great … now you can be a lioness everyday."

"Are you the mom?" the principal asked.

I look at Devilla with a sensational feeling, like we did this together and I'm half responsible for her success.

I answer with, "I am her mother tonight."

23

I used the play as a relaxer for the gun I'd seen at William's place, funny how kids can relieve a person's mind.

The whole way to William's house, Devilla kept bugging me about going to McDonalds, pointing at any symbol that looked like a Ronald McDonald. I kept my word. Let her order anything she wanted on the menu; watched as she ate two burgers, a super sized order of fries, and a strawberry milkshake that she gulfed down like a contestant in a shot-glass contest.

William was already in the house once reaching our destination, his face stuck in a newspaper.

Ecstatically, Devilla tells him, "Daddy, the principal said I was the best lioness she ever seen before."

"Were you?"

"Yes, and all of the other kids were coming up to me, asking for my autograph."

"Sounds like we have an actress in the family," he said, sitting her on his lap.

"And you should've seen it daddy. At the end of the play, I held the torch in the air and screamed, "We are your kingdom! I screamed it loud as possible."

"Well don't scream it too loud honey. We have neighbors."

William looks my way and smiles. That smile says a thousand words, establishes a trust I've yet to receive, a trust that shows how dependable I could be when it comes to his little girl.

He whispers the words *thank you* and turns back to his daughter. "You know what, Devilla? One day you're gonna get another chance to shout, 'We are your kingdom,' but the only difference is that you're going to be in a real kingdom."

"Really?"

"Imagine a place where you can have anything you want."

"Grandma's house."

He laughs. "No honey. Not grandma's house. I'm talking 'bout a much bigger kingdom. One that has streets of gold and fountains of juice."

"Really? What place is that?"

"Heaven. The greatest kingdom there is."

Devilla asks, "Can we go tonight?"

"Maybe? It all depends on the time the master will open the kingdom doors. But he'll only accept children that put him first. Those children that listen to their parents and pray every night."

Devilla presses on. "How big is the kingdom?"

William stretches his arms into the air. "It's this big ... big enough for all of us."

"Can Ms. Angel come too?"

William smiles back in my direction. "She sure can."

"Good. Because when we go to that kingdom, I want to dress up like a lioness, just like I did in the play, and I want Ms. Angel to do my makeup because she drew me with really big whiskers."

"Did she?"

"Yep. And she knows magic."

"She does? What type of magic?"

"Before going to the play, she did magic on my costume and patched my tail back together."

"Wow!"

"And before that, we played a game.

"Did y'all really?"

"Yep. And I won."

"What type of game did y'all play?"

"Ummm—"

"Shhhhhhh—" I gestured, trying to silence her behind William's back, knowing that she could possibly spill the beans about the gun.

Devilla says, "I can't tell you daddy."

"Why not?"

"Because I pinky-sweared."

"You what?"

"I pinky-sweared not to say anything."

William turns his head towards me, then back at Devilla. "Tell me, Devilla. What type of game did you play?"

Interfering, I say, "I told her I'd take her to McDonalds if she promised not to cry on stage."

William stares at me again, studies my body language. He wants to believe me, but after looking back at Devilla's expression, it's obvious that the truth is elsewhere."

He says, "Devilla, is that what really happened?"

"Yes," Devilla answered with an I'm-lying-type-face, far from the actress that I saw in the play.

William goes on. "You sure, Devilla. Don't lie to daddy."

"I'm not lying."

"Remember what I told you about lying, Devilla. Do you remember?"

"Yes daddy … I remember."

"What happens?"

"You … you hurt people when you lie."

"That's right. Now do you want to hurt daddy?"

"No."

"Then tell me the truth."

I give her another gesture. This time more threatening. Let her see that along with lying, there are consequences for telling the truth.

She says, "I can't tell you daddy."

"Why not?"

"Because I just can't."

William puts his foot down. "Tell me right now, Devilla!"

"Uuum ….uuum … I can't daddy. I'll get in trouble."

"No you won't. Not if you tell me the truth."

She glances at both of us, juggles for the lesser repercussion, devil or the devil's advocate.

She tells William, "We were in your room. But Ms. Angel forced me to show her—"

"What? Show her what?"

"Show her where you keep your black box."

Instinct makes me want to strangle her, but twenty-five-to-life sets in.

Williams says, "Is that the truth?"

 Cyril Gillion

"Yes daddy. That's the truth."

William gives his daughter an upsetting sneer, the glare of a parent who's just been hoaxed.

He tells her, "Devilla, go to your room … go there right now."

"I thought you said I wouldn't get in trouble."

"You're not in trouble. Just go to your room."

The questionnaire is over, beans spilled all over the floor, and a indescribable fury shines on William's face, fury thicker than alligator skin, the type of fury that'll take a lifetime to put into words.

That fury juggles with my nerves. Never seen this type of rage in him before. Never been this close to anger.

He jumps up from the couch, heads toward the living room door. "You. Outside!"

I try to explain, but before I can give any type of clarity, he tells me, "Get up right now. You can't stay here tonight."

"I was only trying to—"

"Save it Angel! Just get out my house."

I pretend to walk out the door upset, but I'm really panicked inside, shaking like I've just committed murder and the feds are right on my neck. Not saying anything, I walk down the stairs, but he grabs my arm midway and turns me around.

I stand up to him and say, "Grab me like that again and it'll be the last arm you ever grab."

"What the hell is your problem, Angel? I leave you alone with my daughter for a couple hours, and you already have her looking at guns."

Something tells me to run. I should've ran a long time ago, before he got upset, before Devilla's play, before ever seeing the gun.

But instead, I stay and gamble with death. Not because I want to, but because I needed some answers. He at least owed me some answers. And even if we did so happen to argue, he still owed me the quarrel.

I said, "First off, I didn't know it was a gun in the box. And secondly, she never actually saw the gun."

"Doesn't matter!"

"Huh … What do you mean it doesn't—"

"You had no right going into my personal assets, let alone exposing my daughter to that type of danger."

"I wasn't trying to put your daughter in danger."

"Could've fooled the heck out of me? What if the gun had accidentally fired off?"

"It wouldn't have."

"How the hell do you know?"

"Because the safety lock was on the trigger."

He repeats. "How the hell do you know?"

"Cause I know guns. Even took classes on how to shoot them."

"What … what the heck are you? Some type of deranged Charlie's Angel?"

"I'm deranged? Last I checked, I'm not the one who's keeping weapons around a child."

"Just because you keep a gun under your pillow, it still doesn't give you the right to go around sniffing out others."

"I didn't have to sniff out anything. Devilla already sniffed it out for me."

"Leave her out of this!"

"What for? You're the one who—"

"Keep my daughter's name out your mouth you little—"

"Go head and say it! Call me a bitch so I can bitch slap your ass right off these steps."

Devilla peeks her head out the front door.

"Devilla, go back into your room!" he yells. "I'm not gonna tell you again!"

"Don't yell at Devilla because she aired your dirty laundry."

"Oh, so now you're supposed to be her mother."

"Never said I was."

"What type of grownup tries to pinky-swear a happy meal for exchange of a gun?"

"Doesn't matter 'cause I'm not her mother."

"Thank God you're not. I leave my daughter with you for a day, and you weren't even responsible enough to keep her out of harms way. No wonder you don't have any children"—his voice rises—"thank God you don't have any children, 'cause if you did—"

"I don't have children by choice."

"I know. You choose not to endanger their lives. Good choice!"

Fire builds in my lungs and my next set of words comes out in flames.

"Fuck you.

Fuck you.

Fuck you.

Fuck you.

Fuck you.

Fuck you.

And you know what else? Fuck you some more."

"Like I said Angel, Good choice!"

I trotted down the stairs, rushed towards the first underground that'll put me on the subway.

I kept talking to myself the whole way home, didn't know whether I was cursing myself out or cursing him.

Once getting on the subway, I immediately called up Kevin. Figured the only way to take my mind off William was to converse with someone else.

Kevin answered with, "I knew you'd call."

"Yeah," I replied, huffing and puffing. "I guess it's like you said earlier. We have history."

"So does that mean you're down?"

"With going to your football convention?"

"Yeah, it's going down tomorrow."

I juggle with the decision, but all that keeps going through my head is the way William disrespected me earlier.

I tell Kevin, "Yeah … I'm down."

"Aiight then. I'll pick you up tomorrow. Say about … 8 pm."

"I'll be ready."

<u>24</u>

Next day.

I was entering the steps of my apartment, just coming from grabbing the few belongings that I'd left at William's place. There were no exchanging of words between us, and when I got there, he already had my belongings waiting to greet me at the door, a transaction that was quicker than the ATM.

Kevin would be coming to scoop me up for tonight, and the whole way home I was piecing together the outfit that I'd wear.

Once opening my door, Mona was still in her pajamas, laid in the living room watching the next top model on television.

The house was a total mess.

Not only had she devoured all the pistachios, but the lemonade was a glass away from its fatality. For me, that was the final straw that caused her to overstay her welcome, and all I could think about was William's words, how he told me to never let another person become your burden.

I picked up the shoes from the living room floor and turned off the television.

Mona looks befuddled. "What's your deal?"

"You're my deal," I replied, handing her the shoes. "You have to go."

"Huh?"

"You can't stay here any longer."

"Why?"

"Look around, Mona. The house is a total mess. You eat all day. Sleep all day. And not to mention, you screwed some nigga in my kitchen. And that's just … that's just … no respect at all."

Dumbfounded, she tells me, "That happened almost a month ago."

"I don't care. It still happened."

"Are you forgetting that this is a one bedroom apartment? Where else was I supposed to go?"

"I don't know, Mona. In the car. In the bathroom. Anywhere besides my goddam kitchen … Besides, you embarrassed me in front of William."

"Who?"

"William. He stayed over that night. Probably thought I was running a whore house."

"You mean the gay guy?"

"What?"

"William … that's the gay guy, right?"

"Yeah."

"Why do you care what a gay man thinks?"

"Because he's not gay."

"What?"

"I said he's not gay!"

"That's not what you said earlier."

"I was lying okay. He's far from gay. I only said that so you wouldn't intrude."

"Intrude? You're supposed to be my girl, Angel. Why would I do something like … ooooh … ok, I see where this is going. I hope you didn't take me seriously when I asked him if I could ride his bike."

"I didn't."

"Then what's your problem?"

"You've overstayed your welcome."

"I've what?"

My cellular rings. It's Kevin.

I don't answer.

The apartment plant seeds of tension as me and Mona bickers our way through the living room, we both not caring what the other has to say, and as those seeds grow into roots of anger, Mona starts picking up her belongings, and she dumps them into a huge suitcase, her whole life in one bag of leather. "Screw you, Angel … You want me gone. I'm gone!"

The Other Side of the Pillow

I storm into my bedroom. The front door slams.

There was a message on my cellular, Kevin saying he'll be here to pick me up in half an hour.

I called back to request fifteen more minutes of preparation time and advised him to meet me downstairs instead of knocking on the door.

Before heading into the shower, another message popped on my cellular, a message from Cuqui. I started to ignore it and call her later, but she was screaming on the voicemail, demanding that I call her back ASAP. Once calling her back, she screamed, "Bitch, where yo ass been the last four hours? I've been calling like a junkie on crack."

I turned down the speaker volume. "I've been sleep. Why?"

"Whateva," she replied. "The only sleeping yo ass been doing is sleeping with Mr. Senior Citizen."

"Whatever, Cuqui. What do you want?"

"I want you to cancel your encounter with Kevin tonight."

"What encounter?"

"Don't play me, Angel. You and I both know that you're going out with Kevin so don't even front. Aunt Terry even knows."

"What?"

"That's right. He's been calling everyday, telling Aunt Terry how you were the one woman that got away, asking what he could do to steal you back from this William guy"—she laughs—"I was trippin girl 'cause it was so sad to see a nigga as big as him, crying like a lil' punk. Girl, you must have some serious kryptonite in that little coochie."

"Is that why you've been blowing up my phone? To tell me that garbage?"

"Actually, no. I've been blowing up your phone to tell you that he's already engaged."

"What?"

"That's right, girl. Engaged. Soon to be married. Sowing his royal oaks."

"How do you know?"

"This past weekend, he was in Miami, flaunting his bitch around on South Beach. That hefar had a ring on her finger so big it nearly blinded the hell out of me ... you would've thought that bitch was Halle Berry from the way he was flaunting her around. But if you ask me, she's ugly as hell. Looks like the bottom of a Converse sneaker."

"Did he see you?"

"Did he? The nigga looked me dead in my eyes for so long to where I could've took his photo, and then he tried to play it off by

                    Cyril Gillion

introducing me to his little slut. So you know I had to shine on that nigga right.”

“Cuqui, don’t tell me you got crazy?”

“Crazy ain’t the word. I told that nigga he could keep his money and his raggedly ass ho. I told that nigga that you already had a real man that was sexin’ you good like—”

“Cuqui?”

“What?”

“You actually said that?”

“Damn right I said it. And he’s been blowing up my phone ever since, leaving messages about how he really loves you and how he’d throw away his woman if you gave him another chance.”

“So he’s married?”

“Might as well be. All that’s missing are the papers and a priest. And to think he actually had the audacity to try and two-time my friend. Hell no. I’m not having it.”

“Be cool, Cuqui. I can handle it.”

“I’m trying to be cool Being cool is what kept me from whippin him and his bitch on Southbeach, ’cause you know a bitch just got off probation right and I ain’t tying to catch another charge. But you Angel … you should whip his ass.”

“Naw … I’ve got bigger fish to fry. So I’m cool.”

“You what?”

“Going off on him is not gonna prove anything. That’ll only bring him satisfaction.”

“And beating his ass can be your satisfaction. The satisfaction of seeing him bleed.”

Somehow, in the midst of hearing Cuqui ramble, I wasn’t surprised at the allegations. Athletes are forever hiding some wife in the alley, sniffing out the next piece of ass that they can get their hands on. It explained Kevin’s behavior to the utmost degree. Explained why he was so destined to get at me, chasing my panties like he chases the football.

Cuqui wanted me to cancel tonight’s rendezvous and expose Kevin for what he’s worth. I had different intentions. Truth is I could care less about Kevin being engaged or if he’d been married for twenty years. My focus was more on his friend, the lawyer. And if I could get an internship out the deal, then dealing with Kevin for one night was a contract worth signing.

I took a shower and threw on a skirt that I haven't worn since undergrad, the get-a-man skirt. It was still tailored the way I like it. Dull white. Thigh width. A strapless miniscule masterpiece.

I prioritized my makeup, went light on the cheeks, lighter on the eyes. Pantene moisturizer was swimming in my hair. I pressed it out four times; would've gone for a fifth if it wasn't for those J-Renee heels that took forever to squeeze into.

Disobeying my request of waiting downstairs, Kevin knocked on my door right on time. Less dressy than I imagined, he was wearing some dark brown Dockers. Solid white muscle shirt. Brown casual shoes.

On his wrist was a bragging black Rolex, one so glittery to where it made his low-priced clothes appear expensive.

He said, "I see that Brooklyn has brought you up a notch. You're looking sexy."

I pretended to smile. "You don't look so bad yourself."

He threw his wrist into the air and looked at the time, his way of making sure I noticed the bling. "We're late," he said. "Guess we better get going."

As we walked to the car, I turned my cell-phone on silent, just in case William decided to play bug-a-boo.

Kevin's car was beyond flamboyant, looked like a modern day batmobile that was parked in the ghetto. It was a nicely painted silver LX 600. Lamborghini doors. Chrome rims so large to where you couldn't see the tires. The dashboard on the inside was also chrome. Gold steering wheel. Leather alligator seats that were waiting to bite my butt.

It's hard to believe that this was the same guy who used to sport me around in a broken down 1986 Honda.

Being cordial, I said, "The car is nice, Kevin. Must've taken a while to find what you wanted."

"Oh this piece of junk," he says nonchalantly. "I'm thinking about giving it to one of the niggas back home. It was actually given to me from the president of the jets. Supposed to be a welcoming present that came with the contract."

I ask, "Your contract involved a car of this caliber?"

He smirks. "You serious? This is nothing. Other first-round players have gotten mansions, acres of land, things you wouldn't imagine."

"Damn. Sounds like they need an NFL for women."

He laughs, asks, "So when's the last time you've been home?"

"I don't recall. You?"

"Last weekend."

"Bet you received a welcoming like no other."

"You can say that again. And I refuse to go back."

"How come? Is the price of stardom too overwhelming?"

"Overwhelming isn't the word. Try suffocating. I can't even sit in a movie theatre without a chick coming to sit on my lap, trying to get paid. The same stuck-up broads that could care less about me in high school are the same broads approaching me everyday, acting as if Prince has entered the building … money money money … that's all everyone wants. Even my family is hunting me down for a piece of the pie, a hundred million cousins that I never seen in my entire life, they all telling me a sob story to get some dough"—he catches his breath—"I mean, what people fail to realize is that a cat doesn't become rich when he first hit the NFL. Just like you, my rent is due on the first. But unlike you, I'm put in a higher tax bracket. Not to mention, I have to put my mom in a bigger house and give her the things she wants. Hell, I was better off being some broke cat with a football dream."

Kevin bends the corner roughly on 156th, nearly knocks over a pedestrian while doing so. The person yells, "Watch it you asshole!"

"Watch this!" Kevin replies, flipping up the bird.

I switch up the flow of the conversation to talk about business. "So what about this friend lawyer of yours?"

"Dan Quintera. Now that's my nigga," he replied.

"Is he black?"

"Actually, he's Spanish"—he laughs—"But he's still my nigga."

"How well do you know him, and is he a reliable source?"

"He was reliable enough to get me off."

"What do you mean, *get me off*? You telling me that you were actually in the penal system?"

"I was for a week; it happened about a year ago … You remember Bernosetronique?"

"Who?"

"Bernosetronique. Jason's friend."

"Yeah, you talking 'bout the boy from Zimbabwe. The boy who never talks."

He sucks his teeth. "Correction. Used to never talk. Six months ago, his no-talking ass almost talked me into getting a damn prison sentence. Now that nigga is the biggest drug dealer in all of Miami."

"What? No way."

"Yes way. Fifteen kilos stashed in the back of my Suburban, all while I was trying to get up in Club Rolex with Jason. Them pigs pulled us over, searched the car like they were searching for Sadaam Hussein, and when they checked the back of the truck, they found so many bricks to where they could've built me my own prison. Those pigs were slapping fives because they thought I was Bernosetronique, but I soon found out that the nigga had fled the country because he had so many warrants. So they locked me and Jason up. Tried to prove that I was involved and my only intentions for coming to Miami was to get my hands dirty. I looked at them pigs like, how the hell could the coke be mines when—"

"So what about the attorney," I asked, forcing him to make a long story short.

"Dan Quintera. Hell, he was awesome in the courtroom, would've thought he was Johnny Cochran's little brother … It turns out that Dan was able to get Bernosetronique's girl under oath, and everyone knows her ass can't hold hot water. Plus I only had two misdemeanors on my prior record so the stat sheet spoke for itself …. I won that case, and since then, Dan Quintera has been handling all of my issues… Just so happens that the night that I saw you in Club Down-Under, I thought about Dan and how he could get you that internship."

Our destination was 21st St. and 6th Ave., right in the prime of spot of NYC's nightclubs.

We parked valet.

Once getting out the car, Kevin warned the valet attendant, "Watch how you handle the whip, partna … I mean it … one scratch and that's your job."

The outside of Kevin's football social palace was beautiful, even more beautiful inside. There were chandeliers hanging from the high ceilings. Limestone floors. Cocktail waitresses doing their thing from each corner of the room.

Jitters ran through me as we started to make our rounds.

Kevin muttered, "If you can, try to partake in as little small talk as possible, because these people are the nosiest sons-of-bitches I ever seen. Remember that you're here with me. So all you have to do is smile."

Smiling is what I did. Not because of Kevin, but because I wasn't trying to socialize with a bunch of huge hunks that ate and slept football all day, they all staring at me as if I was Kevin's wife, Mrs. Armstrong.

Soon, I sat at a table with other women, women that were more horrendous than I expected. Half of them were groupies, a bunch of slut-buckets that crept in from the lobby to get a taste of the players. And the ones that were actually with the players were clinging to their shoulders, afraid to use the restroom for fear that another woman may snatch-up their man. I talked to a few of them, but every conversation was a testimony of how lucky they were, each of them mapping out their future years of how to be the perfect stay-at-home wife while their husbands bring home the rings.

An hour later the veteran players were preparing a toast for Kevin and other rookies on the team. It was then that I noticed him in the room. The man that I came for. Kevin's attorney.

He looked to be in his late thirties, forty at most, demeanor as strong as Kevin portrayed him to be.

His hair was slicked back. Clean cut. Could've passed for one of those mafia type guys. Balanced a cocktail in one hand. Cell phone in the other. Wore an Armani suit with no tie underneath. Also wore a lavender collar shirt that never reached the top button.

Never letting go of his cocktail, he gave Kevin a warm greeting, and then hung up with the person on the cell-phone.

Kevin said, "Dan Quintera, this is the woman that I've been telling you about … Angel Inghram."

I go to shake his hand, but he kisses me on the cheek instead. "I bet you're ready to get the hell from out this place," he said.

I smile. "Actually, this place isn't so bad. There's an upside to everything."

"Yeah right," he replied. "You don't have to pretend for this Kevin chump. What's the upside in listening to a bunch of muscle-heads talk about the next touchdown that they're going to score?"

I tell him, "I'd rather hear them discuss their next set of touchdowns than hear them boast about the ones from last week. Better to plan for the future than harp on the past."

He smiles. That was my initial spark, my breaking-of-the-ice for a first impression that I hoped to carry mileage.

Mr. Quintera takes another sip of his cocktail, then he shakes his finger at me and says, "Your response tells me that you're a good bullshitter. But that's not a bad thing. I like that. Every courtroom needs a good bullshitter. Shows me that you can think quick on your feet."

I took his words as a compliment, as if there's a course on bullshitting that I've aced, even though I'd indirectly been called a liar.

Kevin leaves as Mr. Decker grabs another cocktail. Pulling me up a seat beside him, he says, "Quick question … and this time don't try to give me a bullshit answer … Do you think that formal justice should be a legitimate component of court proceedings?"

"Definitely not," I answered.

"How come?"

"Because formal justice only opens the pathway to plea bargaining."

"And what's wrong with that? Don't you feel that plea bargaining is a proponent of procedural due process."

I tell him, "In my eyes, plea bargaining is only an antecedent of injustice."

He kicks his leg into the air, places it over the other. He says, "I don't know what Kevin told you, but the majority of students within this internship are linked to defense attorneys. And we train students on special tactics that are used for defense cases. Sounds to me that you should reconsider an internship that develops you with working beside prosecutors."

He gets up from his seat, reaches to shake my hand. "Nice to meet you anyway."

Bewilderment takes a seat beside me, and I tell him, "Is that it?"

"Yep."

"You've yet to even ask me for a portfolio. Grades. Nothing."

"A portfolio wouldn't be necessary," he replies. "I already know enough. So good luck."

Not taking no for an answer, I tell him, "Sit down!"

"What?"

"I said sit down. This so-called interview isn't over just yet."

I clear my throat and I prepare for the beg of a lifetime.

I tell him, "Now if you don't want to hear anything else, try hearing this. I'm a dedicated student. Been wanting to be a prosecutor all my life. Not because I want to, but because it's a necessity. Don't ask. Just know that it's personal. Therefore, I need this internship. Want it more than any other student you'll ever come across. Hell, I'll even do a few extra service hours on the side if I have to. So if you're thinking about turning your back on me, try thinking about seeing me on the other side, assisting another attorney with helping you loose your first case."

He says, "I thought you weren't in favor of plea bargaining."

"I'm not."

     Cyril Gillion

"Could've fooled the hell out of me," he replied, sipping away at his cocktail. "This case hasn't even been open for two minutes and you're already begging me to hear you out, already asking for a plea bargain ... So now you see. Now you see how it is to be put on trial, viewing justice from a criminal's eyes. When a convict – or any person for that matter – is down in the hole, back up against the wall, a plea bargain is always worth considering. So in our case – the case between Attorney Inghram and Attorney Quintera – you loose, I win. Case dismissed."

I look at him as if someone has tapped his cocktail with some PCP.

He sits back in the chair, legs folded. "I like you, Angel. I like you a lot. As far as the intern goes, I'd be crazy not to put you on ... Now listen up because time is an essence and the only time I repeat myself is when I'm speaking to a judge or jury ... You'll first have to complete a group training session, underlying the fundamentals of court proceedings and police procedures. After that, you'll link up with me and I'll instruct you on the intricacies of investigations. Your investigations will primarily consist of interviewing a wide range of social and economic backgrounds, preparing exhibits for court presentations and serving subpoenas. On my team, we work, which means there are no slackers and no time for slumber. Slacking will get you a warning. Slumber will get you put out the door."

Whether he was kidding or not, his answer worked for me. I smiled at him and mutated back into that reserved Angel, the one before the plea bargain test. Not wanting to come straight out and inquire about hourly wages, I told him of my current condition and fabricated my school expenses. He told me that we'd discuss it in a week, but ensured me that it would certainly be enough for me to quit wherever it was that I was currently working. I never mentioned my job as a PSO. Hell, no girl in their right mind would admit that. But one thing for damn sure is that I was not only hours away from kissing Club Ding-a-ling goodbye, but time I get back to work, I was gonna pack up my things and tell Dexter what to kiss.

Mr. Quintera finished his cocktail and took down my contact information along with issuing the address of his private practice. I was scheduled to show next week wearing a business suit, hard shoes, and as he would say, *An extra brain.*

By the time we finished talking, the convention for Kevin's football team was ending. Instead of taking me straight home, Kevin wanted some extra quality time, saying how Mr. Quintera stole it all at the banquet. Not wanting to give him the impression that I was using him for just an internship, I decided to go with the flow.

Our next destination was Times Square.

A Broadway play was showing in five minutes, and considering that I've never seen a show on Broadway before, it was certainly worth the treat.

People were packed like sardines, a line so long to where the tail was out of view. As Kevin and I walked through VIP, the line opened up. Most people recognized who Kevin was. Others just recognized a 6'4, 260 pound guy, which was enough for anyone to create some space for passing.

Once approaching the door, the ticket man never looked our way for compensation, and we waited in the hallway for them to open the main doors for seating. Meanwhile, Kevin made an arbitrary trip to the bathroom but got caught up in a conversation midway. I stood along the wall next to a mother and a crying aggravating child who kept yelling because the show had yet to start. Chaos was going on outside. Security had to kick two teenagers out the front of the line, due to a suspicious ticket theft. One kid was Spanish. The other was black.

"I paid for those damn tickets myself!" the black kid yelled.

"You're lying," the ticket man replied. "Show me your pockets."

He empties his pockets, but no tickets are found.

The investigation is now pointed towards the Spanish kid and he has to empty his pockets as well, causing the line to become more congested, people screaming, "Stop holding up the damn line!"

I looked closely at the people that stood behind the chaos and from where I was standing, I saw a familiar face. The face was that of Courtney, little Devilla's godmother. I first wrestled with the conception of whether it was really her, but after seeing the woman's hair, I knew it was Courtney because I could spot those extensions from anywhere.

I took a closer look and there was little Devilla standing beside Courtney, pouting because she was too short to see the chaos in the front of the line. I turned my stare from making eye contact with either two. Not because of Courtney, but mainly because of Devilla. Had that little brat saw me with Kevin, she'd be running to her daddy, blabbering of how she saw the guardian Angel at Broadway with the incredible Hulk.

Kevin appeared behind me, placed his hand softly on my shoulder. "What's all the commotion about?" he asked, looking at the security guards.

                                  Cyril Gillion

"Seems like some teenagers stole some tickets."

He laughs. "Same ol' same ol' drama every time I come to this place ... well let's get situated. They're starting to seat people inside."

The inside of Broadway is a clear view for outsiders to see, but before going inside, I kept hearing my conscience, Devilla ratting me out to her daddy.

Stopping in mid-strive, I told Kevin, "Let's take a rain check on Broadway."

"Huh?"

"This play. They say it's expected to be three hours long. And it's already ten o'clock."

"So what? Last I checked, you're too old to be worried about it being a school night."

"Actually, I'm more concerned about falling asleep on a three hour play. I say we check out a movie or something."

I look over my shoulder to see if William's watch dogs have recognized me, but their heads are turned opposite. Then I smile back at Kevin to camouflage my fretful state.

Kevin reacts nonchalantly. "Ok, Angel. We don't have to see the play. But no movies. I have something else in mind."

We head for the exit and I let Kevin lead the way, never questioning his motives. While leaving, security was still frisking the teenagers, ordering them to come out of their shoes. People were starting to get out of control, and as the crowd grew larger, the ruckus was louder than boots stumping at a protest. In the midst of walking towards my freedom, management decided to close the back doors and they advised any insiders to exit through the front entrance, the same entrance where Devilla and Courtney were waiting to purchase a ticket. I slowly strolled behind Kevin, allowing his 260 pound frame to block me as we approached the exit.

"Ramsey! No one is to leave the building," a policeman ordered.

Security stepped in front of us and blocked the door, blocking my stride to freedom.

"I told you that I didn't steal anything," the black kid screamed again.

"Turn around!" the security guard demanded.

The commotion in the line begin to heighten, people screaming, *"Don't you pigs have anything else to do besides antagonize innocent people."*

Kevin held me tight.

Security grabbed another guy and girl, both suspicious of stealing tickets. "The two of you. Empty your pockets right now. I need to frisk you both."

The girl snapped. "Are you blind or something? Does it look like I have any pockets? For Christ's sake, I'm wearing a skirt!"

"Then empty your bra!"

With frustration beaming on her face, the girl reaches into her bra and pulls out a stash of hundred dollar bills, enough dollars to cover Times Square. She throws it at the cop and says, "Frisk this you pervert! I have my own damn money!"

The money goes everywhere, and before one could blink, people started raiding exits and diving to the ground as if it was raining Benjamin Franklins.

Paving our way towards a back exit, Kevin grabs my arm. Luckily, valet parking still has his car on standby. "Let's go," Kevin said, reaching for his keys.

We start riding towards an unknown destination, dashing lights, cutting lanes, speeding down Saxon Blvd.

"What the hell just happened back there?" Kevin asked.

"I don't know. But never piss off a woman in a skirt."

After bending a right on McGriff, we made a stop at a Citgo gas station, and after seeing Kevin's gas tank as being half full, I figured he might be stopping for another reason.

"You want anything?" he asked, getting out the car.

"I'm cool. Still full from the banquet."

"Well hang tight," he says, carefully caressing my hand and giving me a seductive wink. "Be right back."

My cellular rings. The ring tone of William.

I didn't want to pick up. I was still mad at his ass from the other night, but for some reason, for some strange reason, he kept calling.

Short-tempered, I pick up the phone. "What do you want?"

I had to be fierce. Had to be vicious. Had to remind him that this war of ours was still in the midst of battle, no matter his reason for calling.

"Hi," he mutters. "I just wanted to make sure that you made it home safely."

"Are you kidding me? I left you more than four hours ago."

"I know. But you know how I feel about you and the subway. You already know how over-protective I can be."

"By the time you get here to protect me, I'd already be buried alive."

     Cyril Gillion

"So I take it that you're safe."

"Oh trust that I am," I reply, looking at Kevin pump the gas. "Bout as safe as I can be."

"Well if I may ask, where are you?"

I instantly thought of Devilla and Courtney. Thought about how Courtney could've possibly seen me with Kevin. It hasn't even been ten minutes and she's already running back gossiping.

Going on the philosophy of being innocent until proven guilty, I tell him, "I'm out with Mona. Figured we'll make it a girl's night out since we never go anywhere."

A huge breath of air goes through the phone waves as William says, "You're with Mona … humph … now that's an interesting duo."

"What makes you say that?"

"She just doesn't seem like your type … well, at least from what I know so far."

"There's a lot you still don't know."

"Is there?"

"Yeah, I'm sure you can relate to that."

"Are you hinting at something? Beating around the bush?"

"You built that bush."

He hesitates, says, "Yeah … well maybe I can—"

"Call me some other time. I gotta go."

I hang-up as Kevin opens the car door.

I swallow pain. Although the storm is still strong between me and William, I still wanted to call him back to spark up some more thunder, wanted that weather no matter how the wind may blow.

Then I shake off those feelings; convince myself that I'm now in the car with Kevin. Don't want to be. But I'm here.

When Kevin gets in the car he carries two bottles of water, a stick of Rolaids, and lotto tickets. He laid the bottles of water beneath my legs. "Just in case you're thirsty."

Looking at the lotto tickets, I say, "You actually play that stuff?"

"Damn right. Started playing 'bout a year ago. Now it's like an addiction."

I shake my head in disbelief.

"What is it?" he asked. "You never saw a millionaire play the lotto."

"Not lately. It's like seeing a candle in the sun, just doesn't mix. Besides, the lotto is just another way of keeping a black person broke."

He laughs. "I forgot how analytical you could be at times."

"It's true. That's the reason why Aunt Terry never had any money. She had too much of a lotto addiction."

He says, "Better an addiction for the lotto than one for gambling."

"Not in my eyes," I reply. "At least if she gambled, the odds of bringing money into the house would've been better."

We come to a red light. I place my hand on the armrest. Kevin drops his palm on top of mines and say, "Whether we know it or not, we all have an addiction towards something. So besides the study of law, what's become your addiction over the last few months?"

Something tells me to be frank with my answer and tell him the truth, that although he's the millionaire, another million-dollar man has stepped into my life with no expense, and in my eyes, the real addiction lies at Stone Edge apartments, door # 321. But instead, I tell him, "Some things are confidential."

He laughs. "Really? Are you referring to things like being a PSO?"

"What did you say?"

"A PSO. Phone Sex Operator. Is that considered confidential?"

My heart becomes a brass instrument at its highest peak, thumping out of control.

I ask, "Who told you that?"

"Why does it matter?"

I repeat. "Who told you that? Did Cuqui tell you that?"

"Honestly, no one did. I found out myself. You'll be surprised what you can find with technology these days."

I snap. "So what the heck are you? Some type of NFL stalker."

"I wanted to surprise you at work with some flowers, Angel. It was my way of apologizing for our encounter in Club Down-Under last week."

Rage runs through my body as I tell him, "Make a right on 109th."

"Huh."

"Make the right on McGriff right now."

"Where are you going?"

"Home."

"But I was—"

"Don't say shit to me. Just make that right turn."

He says, "The hell with this," and he flicks on his hazard lights, stops the car in the middle of the road.

I ask, "What are you doing? Thought I told you to drive me home."

"Try driving your little stuck-up butt out of my ride," he replied. "I don't need to take this any longer."

The light turns green but Kevin never goes. We're now holding up traffic, cars blowing their horns at Kevin in passing, each driver cursing to express how they feel about us blocking one of the busiest streets in Manhattan. One driver yells, "Where the hell did you get your driving license from? Kmart."

Kevin flips up a bird.

"Asshole."

Kevin looks my way. "What the hell are you still doing in my car? Thought I told your butt to walk!"

"With pleasure," I replied, grabbing my purse.

While exiting Kevin's ride, a million eyes witness my humiliation. Embarrassment swims the breast stroke through my body, and I'm forced to stoop to an immature level, telling him, "Make sure you loose my number. Mines and Cuqui's. And just so you know Kevin, our encounter tonight was only business. Far from personal."

"Yeah. Yeah. Yeah. Tell it to another nigga 'cause I could care less. And while you're getting out, try not to scratch up my paint with those cheap-ass heels."

I slam the passenger door, watch him drive off in the night.

There is a long walk to Brooklyn Estates, and walking on East 86th Street was no cakewalk.

I couldn't call William. We were still at war. And even if we weren't, he'd be asking too many questions of why I was dressed in a skirt, wandering the streets at this time of night. I started to call a cab, but in this neighborhood, I had a better chance at waiting for the tooth fairy.

While walking that green mile, it dawned on me that I was expected to work the 10-2 shift tonight. I tried to reach for my cellular to call-in sick, but before I could speak, Dexter was already chewing me out, telling me how I better be there tomorrow, sick or no sick, or he'll have my cubicle boxed up when I arrived on Tuesday.

By the time I reached my apartment I was passed sweating, breasts going into cardiac arrest. Mona wasn't there. She'd left the house key on the kitchen counter, also left her shoes in the corner.

I picked up the phone to call her, told myself that I needed to apologize for going off on her earlier.

She said, "Why are you calling? I already left your spot. Left the keys on the table."

"I didn't call for that."

"Then why did you?"

"Your shoes. You left your shoes by the front door."

"Keep them."

"Keep them?"

"Yeah, I'll no longer need 'em."

I take another look at the shoes. Hazel Stilettos. The only kind she ever wears.

Making sure she wasn't high, I told her, "You sure?"

"I'm sure. I left them there on purpose. My method of showing you appreciation for letting me stay. Besides, it's the only way I know how to thank you."

I tell her, "You know I didn't mean what I said? About you leaving and all. I was just upset about William … and … lets just say you were in the wrong place at the wrong time. But you're welcome to come back if you want."

"That's ok. I found a new home."

"Where?"

"Southside Bronx. Amnon finally got himself a place. Luckily, he just moved in yesterday."

"Well congratulations, I suppose. Hope everything works out for you both."

"Yeah … you too ... hope everything is going swell for you and the gay guy. Or should I say, William."

She laughs. Her laughter heals me. Opens my heart so I can feel better.

Then she hangs up, we both ending the call on a good note.

Before heading for the shower, I opened the fridge to pour myself a glass of lemonade. Knocks raid my front door, interrupts my swallow.

I dropped the glass of lemonade, decided to look out the peephole, and hoped it wasn't some little brats trying to hustle me again with some Girl Scout cookies.

To my surprise it was Kevin. Kevin Armstrong. Satan standing on the other end of that door, probably here to beg for my forgiveness.

Wanting revenge against the stunt that he pulled earlier, I snatched the door open and told him, "If this is where you try to apologize, try saving your begging for the next bitch."

I slam the door in his face, but he blocks it from closing. "Wait Angel … Now I'm sorry for what happened back there, but you provoked it."

I go for the gut; tell him, "It doesn't matter, Kevin. I'm expecting someone anyhow."

 Cyril Gillion

"What?"

"You hard of hearing? I'm expecting someone."

"Who?"

"None of your damn business. So as you would put it, get off my doorstep before I kick you in the face with these cheap ass heals."

As I close the door, he blocks it again, and this time, he steps in uninvited.

Fear goes through me as I tell him, "Get the hell out!"

"Not until you give me an explanation."

"Get the hell out my apartment!"

"It's that punkass nigga William isn't it. Oh what, you can give him some ass, but I'm not worthy?"

I become paranoid, no words, and I reach for my cellular to dial 911, but he quickly grabs it from my hands. "You're not calling anyone. Now whether you like it or not, I'm going to get me some pussy. Nine months of pussy that I've yet to get."

He reaches for my skirt and strong-arms me at the same time. I try to swap his hand away, but hitting him is no greater than hitting a wall.

I scream. "Let go of me!"

"Not until I get mines!"

"Let fucking go of me!"

"Scream all you want, but I'm getting mines!"

He doesn't listen. Doesn't let go. So I cock back and slap him in the face.

He rips my skirt. Rips it with ease.

I punch him again … and again … and again.

His 260 pound frame becomes immune to my punches, is equivalent to feeding a dragon some tick tacks.

He grabs me again. "C'mon, Angel. I'm taking you to the bedroom so we can sex like real lovers!"

He drags me to my bedroom, a place that has now become a dungeon.

It's dark. Lights off. The only light beaming is the light coming from the window, and he pins my face against that window, breaks the glass, and as I kick and scrap to break free, I see a face from across the hall, Mr. Rutherford, peeping through my window from his balcony.

I try to scream, but Kevin covers my mouth, and he slings me on the bed, yelling, "Open your legs you teasing little whore!"

He grabs my thighs, repeats, "Open those legs!"

"Get … off … of … me!"

"Shut up, Angel! You brought this on yourself!"

"Help! Please … help … someone…"

I reach for one of my little figurines that sit on the dresser and try to beat him upside the head as many times as possible.

He takes it from my hands, raises the figurine in the air. "I should beat you over the head with this thing. Is that what yo ass want? For a nigga to get put in jail for somethin' petty… huh, Angel? Is that what ya want?"

He throws the figurine to the floor and grabs me by the throat.

He snaps. "Let's see you try to grab something now!"

I kick, scream, jerk, punch. "Please … stop it … please … please don't!"

"Too late for begging!"

I gasp for breaths, not able to kick or scream any longer.

He forces his hand beneath my skirt, holding me relentlessly with the other.

He drops his pants. "Take it like the little whore you are!"

He tries to force his way inside of me, screaming that same old tune. "Take it like the little whore you are!"

Tears pour down my eyes and I start to see mama; start to see the nightmare. Mama is getting beat relentlessly by my stepfather, struggling for her life, crying for me to go into the room, shrieking in disarray, a god so selfish, a devil so relentless, pain beyond borders; no one there to protect her, but me; no one here to protect myself, but me.

That nightmare ends but the present is never-ending.

I suddenly find strength, enough strength to knee him between the legs.

"You little bitch!" he screams, holding his nuts in agony.

I rush towards the floor in search for my pistol, had to find it before the monster came back to life.

My room is darker than the color black, clothes scattered everywhere, and finding my pistol is more difficult than Ray Charles running through Times Square.

I see the shadow of the enemy. Then feel the hand of the enemy, Kevin sliding me back towards the bed, pulling me through the comforter, back towards the devils playground.

He yells, "Trying to go somewhere?"

I kick him again in the only spot where I can cause injury, the spot below the stomach where no man can stomach.

He jerks, aches, releases my leg.

Then I'm back at square one, underneath the bed looking for the gun, searching for my salvation, my liberation. Luck guides my

                    Cyril Gillion

fingers through the darkness, towards the root of the pistol that lies beneath a blouse, towards death, and soon as I get my hands on the gun, Kevin gets his hands on my right foot, but adrenaline gives me enough force to kick him in the chest, causing him to plummet on the other side of the bed.

I rise to my feet, gun in my hand, holding it the way a mother holds a newborn, ready to wage war against the enemy if he dares to invade, nervous and anxious all at once.

I point the gun towards Kevin as he stands in shambles, his chest rising and falling like a Godzilla that just received CPR.

We now have a dilemma. Can't rewind time. And the queen-sized mattress is now the intermediary between a catch 22 that's too late to be reconciled.

I see paranoia in his eyes. Godzilla is afraid. But he still comes at me boldly, allowing his fear to become his obsession.

Getting a good grip on the pistol, I tell him, "Back the hell up! Back up right now."

"And just what do you plan to do with that gun? You gon' shoot me?"

Those were the same words as my stepfather, and I don't hesitate to tell him, "Don't think I won't godammit. Don't you dare think I won't!"

He takes another step towards me; impulse forces me to cock the chamber of the gun, daring him to cross that white line of chalk.

Tears welt in my eyes as I tell him, "You tried to rape me!"

"I'm sorry, Angel. Just let me—"

"You animal! You tried to rape me!"

He comes closer, attempting to push his way through my corridor of aghast. "Come any closer and I'll kill you!"

"You really want to kill me? Then go 'head. Pull the trigger. Your pussy is worth the bullet."

He steps closer. Puts one foot in the grave.

He sneers. "Worth the bullet!"

"Back the hell up!" I demanded with the gun trembling in my hands.

Playing on my hesitance, he decides to invade enemy territory, and he tenaciously tries to strip the gun from my hands.

A scuffle breaks out.

I try to clinch the gun for dear life, but the pistol slips from my hands, sets off a trigger, and I suddenly hear the sound of death, a gunshot bursting through Kevin's chest.

The Other Side of the Pillow   *251*

My soul collapses like jello.

BLOOD.

Blood is everywhere. Blood dripping from Kevin's chest. Blood dripping down my shirt. Sheets. Pillows. Mattress. Comforter.

Kevin is on the ground, barely breathing. Lights blind me. Flash lights are coming from a pale wrist.

"Get your butt on the ground!" the voice demanded.

I reach for my asthma inhaler.

"Lady, get on the ground right now!"

I surrender. Fall to the floor. Lay the gun aside.

Voices continue to ring out. "Slap the cuffs on her! Hurry up!"

"I got her, Steve! I got her pinned!"

"Grab the gun!"

"I need my asthma inhaler! I need my inhaler from the dresser!"

"Tony, get her asthma inhaler!"

"Keep her pinned!"

I puff. Breathe. Puff. Breathe.

"Get up. You're going to jail!"

"Check his pulse! Make sure he's—"

"He's not breathing! He's no longer breathing!"

"Call an ambulance!"

"What?"

"Call a fucking ambulance!"

"Haul her in the car!"

"Get your butt in the car and lock those little fingers!"

<u>*25*</u>

I sat in the back corner of the coffee shop distraught.

I was studying for the MBE, the multiple-choice section of the bar exam, and considering that it deprived of 200 questions, I was only on question 10.

Questions 11:   "Plessy vs. Ferguson, The Dred Scott Decision, Brown vs. the Board of Education.   Which case was the most influential?"

That was the question, but neither of these cases could hold a match to the one that I was in store for.

Kevin Armstrong. Dead. Died under my hands. DNA all over my apartment.

I'll choose answer d.) Brown vs. the Board of Education.

The preliminary would start tomorrow. Truth is I wasn't ready for the preliminary. Wasn't ready at all. I was still traumatized about the visit from the doctor, sample evidence of Kevin's semen being found inside my cervix.

After the cops hauled me into jail, I remained there for a couple days, long enough for William to come up with ten thousand dollars that I needed for bail. I have no idea where he got the money, and because I was so grateful to be out on bail, I dared not to ask.

On the same token, Professor Stern was nice enough to find me an attorney named Silvia Dawson, a heavyset woman with a dark complexion, big fierce eyes, one of those sistahs that put you on eggshells when they first enter the room. With a record of two wins and three losses when it came to murder trials, she was not the best lawyer in town, but at this moment of urgency, she was definitely good enough to do for me.

When she found out that the opposing counsel was a guy named Tony Decker, she charged me a price that would take months for me to collect, but luckily, William had the money stashed away in the same black box where I saw the gun, and though he claimed it as being a savings plan for Devilla, he gave it to me because he was more afraid of me going to prison. He even raised an offering at his church, telling people that a friend of his was in need for a dignified handout. He says they pronounced it as the Angel offering and it would be in my best interest to make an appearance, at least once, telling me how I need to acknowledge God for sparing my life through a situation that so many other women has died from.

Though it was hard, I acknowledged what he was saying. Not saying that God exists, but after replaying the episode with Kevin, it felt like there was more than a pistol that was protecting me that night.

I can still see the bruises when I look in the mirror. The spot where Kevin had choked my neck, plus a mark on my hip that caused pain every time I bent over. Through time, my neck has healed its course, but the mark on my hip still exists.

I even abandoned my apartment for fear of stepping into my bedroom. Before I sleep in that apartment another night, I'd rather sleep in hell and wait for Satan to crash in on my slumber. For the time being, I packed my belongings and stayed at William's place. There, I was welcomed with all arms and William was eager to show me the meaning of *Mi Casa Su Casa*, although we've yet to speak about the gun that was in his house. The last couple weeks I've been sleeping on the couch, primarily because I wasn't ready to lie beside a man at all. And William was very cool about letting me have my space.

Everyday I was fed. Not once, but a three course meal three times a day. Little Devilla didn't know the true reason for me being there. William had given her the watered down version, but no matter what version he gave, it still didn't matter in her eyes. All she knew is that I was interfering with her scheduling of the Disney channel, and she was already strategizing a way to get me out the house.

My true happiness would come next week, the day my best friend, Cuqui, would arrive in New York. Attorney Dawson agreed that it was a good idea for Cuqui to testify, especially since she was the only person who had evidence of how Kevin really felt about me, heartfelt words that Kevin left on her voicemail. Unlike Cuqui, Aunt Terry never agreed to make the trip to New York, but she did call me after the incident to say how much she loved me and never stopped praying for my subsistence.

After going through forty more sample questions of the MBE, I packed my things and left the coffee shop, only to see Attorney Dawson waiting for me outside.

She embraces me with a hug and says, "How you feeling?"

"I'm good."

"Did you eat?"

"Not yet."

"Good. I'll take you to one of my spots. Hop in."

We get into the car, in her black Chevy Suburban, and we notice men gawking at us from all different directions, enough men to nearly turn my stomach, they all reminding me of a bunch of Kevin's in action.

I tell Attorney Dawson, "Never mind the breakfast. I don't feel like eating."

"You sure?"

"Yeah. Just had a lost of appetite."

She hesitates; says, "Well I picked you up for a reason … you feel like making a stop?"

"Where?"

"To the crime scene."

"You mean my house?"

"That is the crime scene isn't it?"

"What's the reason for going? I already told you that the gun went off by accident. I didn't kill anyone."

"I know, Angel. And that's the story that we're sticking to. But if I remember correctly, you also told me that you saw a face staring in your window, a man who supposedly saw you during the assault. Who was that person?"

"His name is Mr. Rutherford. He's an elderly man that lives across from my window. But he's not a reliable source."

"He is now. He's our star witness."

I tell her, "Bad idea."

"How come?"

"You have a better chance at winning the lotto than getting a person in my apartment complex to witness anything."

"Well, guess we're just gonna have to shoot for the lotto, 'cause believe it or not, that old man has more leverage on this case than you know. And besides, why would he be staring through your window? Is he a peeping Tom or something?"

"Probably so. That wasn't the first time I've caught him staring."

"So he likes you … that's good … that's even more of a reason why he'd probably want to testify."

As we knocked on Mr. Rutherford's door, it took him forever to ask who it was, even longer to open the door. Soon, this old wrinkled Caucasian man, completely bald, gangrene on his arm, cane in his hand, cracks open the door and fear sat in his eyes when he saw me on the doorstep with Attorney Dawson.

Panicking, he said, "If you're looking for my nephew, you won't find him here."

I'm afraid of making eye contact with him. Afraid of seeing any man that views me as a piece of meat, no matter the age.

Attorney Dawson holds me close to her side, gives Mr. Rutherford a friendly glare. "Sorry for the disturbance, Mr. Rutorford. We're here to—"

"Ru—ther—ford. Get my name right, lady. It's Mr. Rutherford."

"Sorry, Mr. Rutherford. Just to let you know, we're not looking for anyone. Instead, we need—"

"Well who the hell are you?"

"My name is Attorney Dawson and this is Angel. Nice to meet you," she says, reaching for a handshake.

Mr. Rutherford refuses to shake her hand and he tells her, "Well if you do run across those people who are looking for my nephew, tell 'em to leave us be because we don't know where he is. You people keep popping up every damn day and it's causing my wife's blood pressure to rise."

Finding the strength, I raised my face and said, "Mr. Rutherford, I stay in these apartments as well. Right across from your window in apartment 214. Don't my face look familiar?"

"Hold on a minute," he says. "Let me get my glasses."

He comes back out with huge bifocals, tilting his eyes toward my breasts.

Those eyes open wide and he says, "Yeah, you and that woman look just alike."

"That's because I'm that woman."

A smile stretches on his wrinkled face and he adjusts his overalls. "Well don't just stand out there. Come on in."

      Cyril Gillion

We step inside his domicile, a house that smells like it's been closed up for years. Scents of mothballs are filling up our nostrils, plus the living room is full of shrubbery, every plant that you can imagine alongside a pool of flowers.

Pictures cover all the walls of Mr. Rutherford's living room, more faces on the walls than that of Hollywood. Most of the pictures are from the 60's, a time where cameras were spitting out black-and-white images instead of the color of the rainbow. He poses on most of the photos with his wife, and together they look so happy, like they were born to be together, bonded from the beginning of time. One photo shows the two of them at Fresno State, and the headline says, *1941, the year I met my sweetie.* Other pictures are from war, him and old buddies sharing snapshots on top of enemy territory. For every war picture, there's a gold plaque or medal that's hanging beside it. On a few images, he's receiving recognition from government officials, the mayor, and I even thought I saw him posing beside the president of the United States, but then again, who's to say that wasn't a look-a-like of Franklin Roosevelt.

Seeing Mr. Rutherford's accomplishments kind of had me thinking about life, wandering how a person can achieve so much on this earth, but still be looking in the bottom of the barrel, residing in an apartment that was one notch above section 8.

Mr. Rutherford yells from the kitchen, "Mind if I offer you girls something to drink?"

"Yes," Attorney Dawson replied. "I'll take a glass of water." Then, Attorney Dawson steps in front of one of his shrubbery, a blossom known as the herbaceous flower. She tells him, "Your plants are beautiful," and after reaching over to touch it, Mr. Rutherford tells her, "Leave that plant be. You'll run up my wife's blood pressure if she saw you touching her plants."

He comes from the kitchen, brings Attorney Dawson a glass of cranberry juice instead of the water that she requested.

Breaking the ice of my uncomfortable state, I tell him, "So you're a war veteran, huh?"

"That's right," he says. "I'll be a marine till the day they lay me to rest." He glares at the picture on the wall, stares for seconds, seems like he's reminiscing on those bloody days of combat. "Yep, 1942 was an unforgettable year … People's mentality of war was different back then and the country not only used to appreciate war, but they knew the meaning behind it."

Next, he steps into my face, the breath of a corpse, teeth looking like they've also fought in combat.

He says, "You see young broad ... nowadays, you people know nothing about courage and what it takes to defend a country."

"What people?" I asked, thinking he just insulted my entire race.

"Young people," he clarified. Them young punks in the army that's wasting the government's money for school, paraphernalia, everything except for what it's intended for."

"And what is it intended for?"

"Haven't you been listening, thick tits? It's intended for battle. Nuclear warfare ... When China attacked us in World War II, we dropped that bomb on Hiroshima with no remorse, giving them an ass whippin that soap and water couldn't cleanse. Osama Bin Laden's narrow ass wouldn't stand a chance in those days. That's the country I used to know. The America I used to represent. Nowadays, everything has changed. People don't understand the value of war and what it takes to be respected as a nation."

Right before Mr. Rutherford starts feeling it, Attorney Dawson steps in and tells him, "Basically Mr. Rutherford, we're here because we need your help."

"Help?"

"Yes sir."

"Well you better not be looking for a handout. I already did my good deed for the day. Two dollars to the bomb sitting on the bottom steps."

"Mr. Rutherford, do you remember the last time you saw Angel?"

"Who?"

"Angel. This woman beside me. When's the last time you saw her?"

"I never seen that woman in my life!" he exclaims, looking my way.

Attorney Dawson says, "What about the woman from the balcony. The one with the big breasts. When's the last time you saw her?"

"Oh, that woman ... dunno ... been quite some time since I seen that youn' tender thing. Ever since her husband moved in she's been keeping the window blinds closed, which means I can no longer catch a peak."

Attorney Dawson looks bewildered. "Husband?"

"Yeah, her husband had her propped against the window, fondling her like they were auditioning for hustler porn. And like always, I had

     Cyril Gillion

the perfect view. Kinda reminded me of how my wife and I used to be in the fifties, before my pecker shriveled up like a grapefruit seed."

Attorney Dawson winks in my direction as if she's finally got the parrot to talk, then looks back at Mr. Rutherford.

She says, "Mr. Rutherford, if it would be of no inconvenience, can you lead us to the balcony and describe exactly what happened while the woman was screaming?"

He guides us to his balcony, what looks to be a perfect view to my bedroom. The balcony is somewhat congested, more pottery and plants everywhere you step. Although it took some time, Mr. Rutherford was able to recall exactly what happened on that night, from quotations of me screaming to precise details of how Kevin was choking me against the window.

When asked if he would testify to the incident in court, he said, "You must be out of your mind. I have parking violations."

"Don't worry about those," Attorney Dawson replied. "I can sort them out."

"I'm still not buying it," he replied, refusing to bargain. "You people can't be trusted. You always say what you can do, but when it's time for the doing, you do nothing."

Attorney Dawson sits the half-finished glass of cranberry juice next to one of the pottery bowls and Mr. Rutherford's eyes start to widen. "Lady, are you on the pill or something? My wife's blood pressure would shoot to the sky if she saw that drink lying beside her pottery."

"Yeah, I bet so," Attorney Dawson replied. "And if I told her the truth about you sneaking around, lusting after another woman from the balcony while she thought you were watching television, I bet that'll also cause her blood pressure to rise, wouldn't it? So do we have an agreement or must I go find Mrs. Rutherford and have a talk?"

He looks dumfounded, glares at Attorney Dawson like she's an evil sergeant on a battlefield.

"Thought so," Attorney Dawson said, walking back into the living room.

While riding to William's house, Attorney Dawson started telling me key points of what the case would consist of, along with a briefing of what to expect from the courts during the preliminary tomorrow. She gave it to me straight. Told me that since Kevin was a rookie football player, it was no secret the case would seek media attention, and some people would categorize me before the case even goes to trial. Since we were in Brooklyn, a place where the population percentile consists of sports fanatics, Attorney Dawson thought it was best that we try to seek a change of venue from the judge, at least to a place outside the boroughs.

Once approaching William's apartments, she reached into the glove department and presented the portfolio of my case, word for word of my testimonial, exhibits of my apartment, and images of my neck right after the incident.

She asked, "Does this cover everything?"

Skipping pass the photos of my face, I say, "The Angel's missing."

"Excuse me?"

"The angel. Remember? The little figurine in my bedroom that he beat me with. I tried to use it as a defense mechanism."

"Dammit" she replies.

"What is it?"

"I remember having that bagged for prints. There was blood on it. Must've left it back at the lab while talking with the forensics."

"What do you mean left it? That's one of the leading factors in the case."

"You let me worry about the leading factors. You just try to relax and get your mind right for the preliminary tomorrow. Are you ready?"

I sit with my head down, think about how *not ready* I really am.

I tell her, "Yeah … I'm ready."

"Good, because tomorrow you're gonna have to be strong in there for the entire defense. So try to get some rest. I'm gonna head back over to your place to prepare some more exhibits."

     Cyril Gillion

26

Later that night I was stretched on William's living room couch with a thick comforter.

It was 2 a.m. and the nightmares were nonstop, but only this time around, they were of Kevin and not my stepfather.

William's bedroom was just a few steps away and I suddenly possessed an urge to lounge beside him. A light shined beneath his cracked bedroom door. I thought he would've dozed off to sleep by now, but after creeping through the door, his eyes were glued into some reading material.

Lying beside him, I said, "Don't mean to interrupt. Just wanted a little company before the case tomorrow."

He takes his stare away from the book, smiles to acknowledge my presence.

"What are you reading?" I asked, picking up the book from his lap.

"It's called The Dark Ages."

"At two in the morning. Must be quite some book."

"It's a book of theology. One that gives predictions of how it's going to be in the last days of time, how people are going to be forced to accept customs against their free will."

"And what happens if they don't?"

"They'll be prosecuted."

"Sounds like the holocaust all over again."

The Other Side of the Pillow

"Precisely, but only to the second power ... During The Dark Ages, there will be brothers turning against brothers, mothers against daughters, all sorts of horrible things."

"And what makes you think that there is truth to any of the stuff you're reading?"

"Because the truth is all around you. I mean just think about it ... nowadays, you've got terrorism, a hundred different political parties, endless discussions about the discontinuing of affirmative action, murder every time you turn on a television, all signs prepping us for the Dark Ages, or as God will call it, *The Last Days*."

I ask, "So what's your opinion on these Dark Ages? Do you think it is right by God?"

He frees his glasses from his face, placing them on the desk. "I think it's nothing but a test."

"A test of what?"

"A test of faith, Angel. If your faith is weak, you'll succumb to what the devil has in store. But if it's strong, you'll be able to weather the storm."

"How can a person's faith be tested if there is nothing to test?"

"Meaning?"

"Not everyone has faith. I haven't possessed it in eighteen years, since March 2, 1989, the day my mother died. My faith ended at that very hour."

"No, Angel. Your faith in God ended at that very hour. But faith doesn't necessarily mean trusting in a higher being. Faith is simply a matter of belief. Whether that belief is in God, Allah, or in just an ordinary conception, it's still considered faith.

He sets forth a kiss to my forehead and mutters, "What happened?"

"Huh?"

"What happened to your mother?"

"I don't talk about my mother."

"How come?"

"Because I don't."

"Because it hurts? Don't let pain come in between your joy. Pain is only a glass wall to felicity."

"What's with the therapy approach? Are you supposed to be a psychologist?"

"No, I'm a man who cares? So please, Angel ... tell me what happened? I need to know."

I hold in my sigh. "Well it's not what happened. It's what didn't happen ... what didn't take place ... and I'll tell you this, William.

                    Cyril Gillion

When it came to the death of my mother, faith couldn't prevent the inevitable, nor could it rewind time. Faith may have resurrected Lazarus from the dead, but my mother is still six feet under."

"Faith is what got you this far?"

"And how far is that? To a point in my life where I have no mother, no father, and is a countdown away from spending my life in prison."

"Yes, but on the flip side of things, you're a beautiful woman who made it without a mother, nor a father, and aside from thinking you may go to prison, you're actually only a year away from finishing law school and sending others to prison. That's got to be worth more than a *God-please-kiss-my-ass speech*. It gots to mean more than what it appears to be on the surface. Now I'm not telling you to have faith in God. But at least have faith in yourself. Faith that you'll prevail for other victims that have faith in you."

I sit up in bed, in the physical form, but mentally, I'm buried in the crevices of William's words; words that seemed ravishing at the moment. Although William never mentioned it, I knew he was using this Dark Ages book to refer to the rape trial tomorrow and the number of women who weren't strong enough to testify about their case – women like my mother – those women who put their faith in me to speak on their behalf. That made me feel good. Made me feel like there was something in this trial worth getting, even if life-in-prison was at stake.

I harped on that perception. Rode his words to sleep. Drifted into the morning as I curled in William's arms.

27

Stepping into the courtroom was like stepping in hell.

The judge, Judge Hawthorne, was a Caucasian man who looked to be in his mid fifties, wore a long beard that grazed his suit, and from what I read, no one has ever been acquitted for murder in his courtroom.

The prosecution, led by Attorney Decker, seemed to be discussing some matters at first, but when I passed his way, he looked into my direction and smiled. It felt like Kevin was sitting next to him – the ghost from the past – both plotting schemes on how to bury me behind bars.

But it wasn't the ghost that scared me the most. It was seeing the face of Kevin's fiancé, some Latin chick who sat next to Attorney Decker. She was tall pale and skinny, hair reaching her butt. A totally different woman than me, there was nothing about her that said *Kevin's type* whatsoever. I remember Cuqui telling me that she doesn't speak good English, but I could've sworn I heard her mumble some English curse words when I passed by. My lawyer, Attorney Dawson, told me not to look her way. I tried to listen, but ignoring her glare was quite the battle.

The defense consisted of all women: Me, Attorney Dawson, and another Attorney that was assisting her, a young Vietnamese woman who went by the name of Denai Tasuese. Denai never did much

                    Cyril Gillion

talking, often stood behind the scenes to gather evidence for Attorney Dawson. Surprisingly, Professor Stern sat behind the three of us, and he let me know that he'd try to be there from the beginning to the end of this trial.

William never showed up; told me that he had to work. And above everyone, I wanted him there the most.

When Judge Hawthorne ordered the bailiff to shut the doors of the courtroom, I nearly defecated in my seat, wasn't prepared for a court that was now in session.

It was now that I started thinking about how I should've asked for a plea bargain. For if there was ever a time I needed a bargain, it was right now, while my back was against the wall, head stuck in bob wire.

The Defense and Crown started battling back and forth, trying to determine whether my case was strong enough to go to trial.

Attorney Dawson lost that battle. Lost by a long shot.

And that was the beginning. The beginning of a trial set for May 16, two weeks from the present, two weeks from Doomsday.

May 15, the day before the trial, it was a war in process. The media was on a rampage everywhere I turned, reporters chasing me down like Martha Stewart, photographers snapping pictures, people breaking their necks to get a word from Attorney Dawson and me. The change of venue that she requested was denied and the trial was set to go at a court outside of Brooklyn, perfect for the press. Attorney Dawson ordered me not to speak with any reporters and I should avoid entering any places that may attract me to the public eye that included transportation such as catching subways and buses.

In lieu of what she told me, I did make a trip to LaGuardia airport to pick up Cuqui. Cuqui was not only here to testify, but more so to inquire about the man that I've been spending long hours with. Because William didn't want me getting smothered by any reporters, he decided to drive me to the airport himself.

The time was 2 p.m. Cuqui's plane had landed at 12:30. Once calling to ask her for the gate that she'd be waiting at, first thing she said was, "Bitch I'm sorry, but I'm gonna be another fifteen minutes. They've got us all cased up."

"Where are you?" I asked.

"I'm just passing the person who collects the jewelry."

"You mean to tell me that you still haven't passed inspection?"

"Yeah, or whatever you call these nosy people with metal detectors."

"What's the hold up?"

"Hell if I know bitch. I think they saw an Arab on the plane, so now they got all of us practically butt-ass naked." She screams to someone. "Nigga, give me back my damn bracelet! You have any idea how expensive that is?"

William laughs as Cuqui's voice continues to rise over the phone.

She says, "Girl, I don't know if I'll be able to handle these northerners. A bitch just stepped off the plane and I'm already on the verge of flowing someone."

"You'll be fine. Just make sure you call us when you reach your gate. We'll be outside the American Airlines exit. Look for a white Taurus."

She hangs up.

By the time we reached the airport, Cuqui was nowhere to be found. Because of the no parking zone, we had to keep riding pass the American Airlines exit to see if she had made it out. After passing through for the sixth time around, I spotted her standing in front of Delta Airlines, Gate 7. "Stop the car! There she goes."

"You sure?" William asked.

"Trust me. There's not too many women walking around with a tube top that reads, *DADE COUNTY FOR LIFE*."

As I step out the car, William throws on the hazard lights and pops the trunk. Cuqui is busy cursing out a taxi driver, yelling, "Be careful how you handle that fucking bag! That's coach!"

I sneak up behind her and tap her on the shoulder.

"Wassup Girl!" she screamed, turning around ecstatically.

We hug each other tightly, embracing twenty years of reliable friendship. It's been nearly a year since I saw her, but that wonderful smile still beams from her dark complexion. Other features on her have rather changed. Her natural hair is now shoulder length and she's gained a pound here and there. She's also picked up a couple tattoos. One is a dragon blowing fire down her legs and the other is two eyeballs on her lower back, following a sign that reads, *I SEE YOU LOOKING*.

She tells me, "I miss you so much girl. You ok?"

I nod yes. "I'm good. Just had a couple rough weeks. But I'm holding up ... By the way, do you have the recording?"

"What recording?"

 Cyril Gillion

"The recordings of Kevin's conversation. You told me that you recorded it."

She hesitates, says, "Oooh. That message. I'm sorry, Angel. I just switched contracts from Sprint to Alltel, so I no longer have that message."

"What?" I replied, wanting to slap her. "Cuqui, thought I told your ass to keep that recording for the trial. Don't you know how much evidence you just got rid of? Without that recording, how are you supposed to testify?"

"Damn, Angel. I told you that I'm sorry. Besides, you know how a bitch gets when it comes to these phone contracts. This month I'm with Alltel, next month it'll be Cingular, and I'm thinking about crossing back over to Sprint, 'cause they now have free roll-over minutes ... but don't worry girl, your best friend is here. And I'll be damned to let them put you away for that asshole."

No reply.

"And girl, you wouldn't believe the rumors that are spreading around ... Remember them whoes Ciara and Tanya?"

"Who?"

"Ciara and Tanya. You know, those bitches from Hialeah."

"Uuum—"

"Well anyways, they've been going around stirring up lie-after-lie about you and this whole thing with Kevin. Just so happened that me and Shae ran into them whoes at the movie theatre while they were with a couple of niggas buying soda and nachos. So you know a bitch wasn't gonna let that shit ride, right. Niggas around or not, I had to put them bitches in their place. Girl, not only did me and Shae beat them whoes senseless, but we dumped their nachos right on top of 'em. Bitch, we covered them whoes in so much cheese to where you would've thought they were a couple of quesadillas."

We laugh. She always makes me laugh.

Changing the subject, I said, "I like your new look. The hair. I see you finally lost the natural."

"Yeah girl, I was tired of having to maintenance this stuff all the time. Figured I'll shock the men with something else."

Next, she circles around me, observing my features to see if anything has changed. That's what we do. Always making sure each other is intact.

She says, "Damn girl! You've got some ass!" Then she laughs aloud as though she's going into cardiac arrest. "I can't believe this here ... my girl finally got some ass ... and a proportioned ass at that."

William steps in, intruding right at the point where Cuqui asks, "Are you the man who gave my girl that junk in the trunk? You William?"

William gives a puzzled expression. "I guess that would be me. But I can't take credit for Angel's butt. She had that before we met."

They laugh and shake hands.

"Damn," Cuqui says. Strong hands to go with a strong voice. Hmmm. Do you have a brother?"

William smiles. "I don't."

"What about a cousin. Perhaps an uncle?"

"Cuqui get in the car," I said, placing her bag into the trunk.

For the time being, Cuqui was set to reside at my place. Once reaching Brooklyn Estates, I told William he could leave, that I was now comfortable since Cuqui was here. He kissed me before leaving, told me to rest up before trial in the morning, all while informing me that he wasn't going to make it for the second time.

After he drove off, I decided to check the mailbox before entering my apartment.

I had mail for days. Mail for weeks. Mail like a celebrity.

In fact, there was so much mail to where they stopped trying to stack the mailbox and decided to drop it on my doorstep.

Cuqui, said, "Angel, you have a note on your door."

"From who?"

"Dunno … looks like it's from the landlord."

"Well what does it say?"

She stares at the note for a brief moment, then pauses. "Damn!"

"What is it?"

"It says, *72 HOUR NOTICE OR PACK YOUR SHIT.*"

"What?"

"Look."

Thinking she was just kidding, I snatched the note from her hands, but to my surprise, it was just as she had read, word for word.

I placed the note on top of the huge stack of mail and dropped everything on the living room couch once going inside.

First thing Cuqui did when entering my apartment was head to the fridge. I opened the windows to allow the closed-in apartment smell to air out. Cuqui said, "Damn, bitch. Do they not have grocery stores in Brooklyn? Your refrigerator looks like it has HIV."

"There's some cheetos in the top cabinet."

She grabs the bag of cheetos and invites herself to a glass of juice; makes her way to a XXL magazine that sits on the dining room table.

Meanwhile, I turn my glare to the bedroom. Although William came in here to clean up earlier, I couldn't get pass the visualization of how the room looked a few weeks ago with Kevin, a bed once turned lopsided, broken picture frames, the window with all the busted blinds. I went towards the window and shut the blinds, tried to see if I could face the past.

At that moment, I heard Cuqui talking to someone in the living room, and I also heard the television.

After going to check on her, there was no person at all, and she quickly changed the channel when she saw me enter.

I ask her, "Were you talking to the TV?"

"Yeah, but don't worry about it. I was only tripping on the girls from that show called *Flava of Love*."

She was lying. I can always tell when Cuqui's lying.

I said, "What were you watching?"

"What?"

"Turn the channel back."

"To what?"

"To what you were just watching."

Reluctant, she grants my request, and channel six is showing a synopsis of the trial that was set for tomorrow. They were currently interviewing the head coach of the jets, and the coach was talking a whole lot of mess of how Kevin's death is such a tragedy and it's insane that I'm not behind bars already. "Whateva!" Cuqui screamed out to the television. "That's for the jury to decide." They went on to interview other football fans about the issue, and it just so happened that all of the guests were men, everyone saying how it's ludicrous for a young rookie football player to loose his life, all because of some jealous ex-girlfriend. They kept flashing my picture alongside Kevin, had to be the worst looking picture I ever took. All my life I imagined myself on that television screen doing a good deed, and now my breakout photo is no more than a criminal mug shot, as if I was the FBI's biggest achievement. Not being able to stomach it any longer, I told Cuqui to turn the channel, and I dropped my head in dismay.

Comforting me, Cuqui says, "Sorry Angel, but you already know how people can get. They're idiots."

"I know. I'm just waiting for this whole thing to be over."

The next couple hours, Cuqui did everything in her power to take my mind off the case. Talking like we used to talk in high school, she briefed me on what was happening back in Miami and how she was contemplating on staying in New York, finally getting the urge to take the GED. That conversation carried on till nightfall and before you know it, she was lecturing me on my future plans with William and how I shouldn't let a child stand in the way of us being together. Since Cuqui is usually the type that doesn't believe in a person going outside the norm, it was strange to see her give William such praise, telling me that we're a perfect match.

But then, after all the praise, she asks me, "So are you gonna open the report?"

"What report?"

"This report," she said, grabbing an envelope that was buried beneath my huge stack of mail. "Isn't this the background report?"

"What … give it here," I said, grabbing it from her hands.

I stare at the envelope. Stare at a white rectangular-sized paper that has the word CONFIDENTIAL written on top, the background report that I've been waiting to retrieve of William.

Across the top are black-and-white stripes, the same stripes of imprisonment – and right now, at this darkest hour, this featherweight envelope is heavier than a ton.

Cuqui says, "Damn girl, can you take any longer to open it?"

I hesitate; tell her, "I can't do this."

"What?"

"I can't do it, Cuqui. William has been very good to me. And nothing in this envelope is gonna change that."

"But don't you at least wanna know? Don't you want the truth?"

Truth is I did want the truth. But even after finding the truth, it still wouldn't negate the other truth – truth that I'd fallen for a man for all the right reasons; a man in my life that I can actually classify as a man.

With that in mind, I repeated those words back to Cuqui. "I can't do it."

"You can't, but I can." And right then and there, she snatched the envelope from my hands, tore open the seal, and pulled out some folded documents all in one motion.

She stares hard. Stares strong. Stares at the document for nearly two minutes, as if William is a man of her own.

Meanwhile, I can do nothing but wait. Wait on Cuqui's response. Wait as if I'm waiting for a verdict.

Another minute passes and Cuqui says, "Here … check it out."

Not wanting to look, I told her, "That's okay … not interested."

"You sure?"

"Positive."

"Okay well—"

        Cyril Gillion

"Wait!"

"Huh?"

"Let me see it."

"Thought you said you weren't interested."

"I'm not … I mean, I am … well … hell, since I'm looking at prison charges, I guess it doesn't make a difference anyhow."

I reach for the document; reach for a truth that once seemed unreachable.

Once viewing the report, there was a full description of William's life, going back to the last ten years:

2005 – '07	Employee at Le Bernardin restaurant
August 22, 2006	Traffic Infraction
2002 – '04	Employee at Chicken and Waffles
2002 – '03	Employee at Foot Locker
May 23, 2001	Drunk Driving; Misdemeanor
June 16, 2000	Alimony
April 24, 1999	Alimony
1999 – 2002	Employee at Cheesecake Factory
August 12, 1999	Reckless Driving
1999 – 2000	Moors Range
August 2, 1999	Traffic Infraction
June 6, 1999	Traffic Infraction
May 4, 1999	Traffic Infraction

After looking at the report, Cuqui asks me, "You satisfied?"

"Yeah … now it all makes sense."

"What makes sense?"

"The gun that I found in William's apartment."

"You found a gun?"

"Yeah, came across it while watching his daughter for a day. But according to this background report, he used to work at Moors Range, which is also called Moors Gun Range … I know because it's the same range I used to shoot at every week."

Looking bewildered, she mutters, "Okaaaay … so?"

"So, that explains why he had the gun. Since he used work there, I'm sure he was licensed to carry it for good reasons."

"Let's hope so," Cuqui replied. "But in the meantime, where's your bathroom? I think it was something inside those rotten-ass cheetos."

As Cuqui went to handle her business, I called up William; had an urge to hear his voice before the night ended, before I went to trial tomorrow.

William never answered. Only the voicemail.

While the Operator told me to leave a message, I glanced back at the background report that lies on the dining room table.

This time around, I decided to leave William a message, and although the message was only a few words, it was considered a mouthful for a woman like me.

I told him I love him.

Cyril Gillion

28

Before the opposing counsel, Attorney Decker, started his opening remarks, the courtroom was so quiet to where you could hear a mouse peeing on cotton.

Wearing a shiny silver suit that could be recognized through eyes of cataracts, Attorney Decker stood upright, hands cuffed in his pockets.

After pacing the courtroom a few times, he tells the jury, "I'm not here to prove the guilt of Ms. Inghram. I'm only here to present the truth. Truth that Kevin Armstrong was invited into Ms. Inghram's apartment instead of allegations of trespassing. Truth that the marks in which Ms. Inghram endured was strictly from self defense of Mr. Armstrong. Truth that Ms. Inghram shot Mr. Armstrong because of jealousy and envy of Mr. Armstrong's fiancé, and I will prove that the gunshot wasn't accidental. Not only that, but—"

"Bullshit!" Cuqui blurted out, saying exactly what I was thinking. "Angel could careless about that damn skeezer!"

As all eyes went to Cuqui, she quickly noticed where she was at, realizing that this is a courtroom and not some block in Miami where she usually shoot dice.

The judge looked sternly in her direction and said, "Excuse me ma'am, but you're gonna have to reframe from such comments while court is in session."

The Other Side of the Pillow   273

Following both counsels's opening remarks, the judge was given an order to part for recess and the trial would resume at 1:30 p.m. Attorney Dawson spent most of that time preparing exhibits and quizzing our first witness, Mr. Rutherford, giving him a test cross-examination for questions that Attorney Decker might throw at him.

When court returned back in session, the judge asked, "Is the defense ready to summon the first set of evidence?"

"I am," replied Attorney Dawson.

"Then let's presume."

The first set of evidence was circumstantial, enlarged laminated photos of my neck a day after the incident, following images of my pelvic area. She went over to the jury pool and placed the photos inside their hands. For each time she waved a photo in the air, a slight pain waved down my spine, pain hid beneath the burrows of facial expressions.

When the old man, Mr. Rutherford, was called to testify to that beating, he approached the panel with a great stand of diligence, and he saluted the flag with his left hand while holding a cane in the right. Standing as a proud war hero, he takes forever to sit down, and he puts on a pair of glasses so thick to where he could see back to Vietnam.

"Do you swear to tell the truth, the whole truth, and nothing but the truth so help you God?"

"Pardon me?" Mr. Rutherford replied.

"Do you swear to tell the truth, the whole truth, and nothing but the—"

"I heard you the first time godammit … Yes I accept."

Accommodating Mr. Rutherford with a slow speech, Attorney Dawson said, "Mr. Rutherford, can you tell us your place of residence?"

"Yep. I live in … Brooklyn Estates."

"Are you familiar with the apartment number, 214?"

"Yep."

"How familiar?"

"I can see the window of that apartment from my balcony. There's a young gal who stay in that apartment." He smiles. "And she's a young sweet tenderoni."

"Sweet huh?"

"Sweet as apple pie."

"Is that young tenderoni in the courtroom right now?"

"Yep … she's right over there," he says, pointing in my direction.

     Cyril Gillion

Attorney Dawson says, "Mr. Rutherford, the night of October 2, you wrote in a statement that you had problems sleeping. Tell the courtroom what transpired that night to keep you awake."

He gathers his words carefully. "No problem ... I was sleeping beside my wife when all of sudden I kept hearing a lot of commotion. At first, I thought it was my neighbor's dog ... that little son-of-a-bitch will bark until he can't bark no more, and not even a bone will shut 'em up ... but I eventually awoke, and while going to take a leak, I heard a loud bang and lots of screaming ... It was coming from the patio ... and that's when I noticed it wasn't the damn dog ... it was a gal, the young gal across my balcony. She was howling like I never heard a woman howl before, and there was a big black Shaq-looking man who was strangling her against the window, slapping her around like a piece of meat."

Attorney Dawson pulls out a picture of Kevin and says, "Mr. Rutherford, did that Shaq look-a-like look like this?"

Mr. Rutherford gives a strong stare, takes his time, and says, "Yep. That's him alright ... that's definitely him."

"Mr. Rutherford, what did you do after you saw this guy slapping around the defendant?"

"What the hell you think I did ... I called the police ... put it in the hands of the law ... I mean, I hope you don't think I was supposed to run over and fight in her defense, 'cause if so, you must be out your damn mind ... I mean, had this occurred thirty years ago when I was a US Marine, I would've showed Shaq what happens when you put your hands on a woman ... but I've gotten old ... can't do it like I used to."

Attorney Dawson smirks as she looks over to the prosecution, satisfied of the mark that she's planted. "No further questions your honor ... no further questions."

When the opposing counsel, Attorney Decker, stood up to cross-examine our witness, I thought he'd come out the blocks like an angry sprinter.

But he didn't.

Instead, he gave Mr. Rutherford a long drawn out stare – no words – as if he was allowing silence to do the damage.

He plays on that silence. Use it to his advantage.

Making sure all eyes were on him, Attorney Decker smiles at the jury like a polished attorney that's ready to have his picture snapped for the press.

Then he turns to Mr. Rutherford. "Mr. Rutorford, how long have you—"

"Rutherford okay! It's Mr. Rutherford!"

"Well Mr. Rutherford, how long have you been living in Brooklyn Estates?"

"I've lived there for thirty years ... No actually, thirty-five. But back then, they weren't called Brooklyn Estates."

"So I guess you're something like ... the neighborhood overseer."

"I've been given many names."

"Really? Would one of those names so happen to be, Peeping Tom?"

"Objection!" Attorney Dawson snapped.

The judge sneers at Attorney Decker and says, "Counselor, that's strike one."

"Sorry your honor." He turns back to Mr. Rutherford and says, "Mr. Rutherford, if I may quote you word for word, you told us that the defendant was pressed against the window, howling for her life. You also told the jury that it happened while you were sleeping ... Do you normally sleep with your glasses on?"

"Sleep with my glasses on? What for?"

"You're right, Mr. Rutherford. What for? And along with that *what for*, it's safe to say that you weren't wearing your glasses at the time of the incident."

"No. I wasn't but—"

"So if you weren't wearing any glasses, how can you be certain that you seen what you thought you seen?"

"Because I have eyes. Damn good eyes at that."

"Really, well how come your medical file begs to differ. Records show you as being extremely far-sighted, and you have astigmatism in not only one, but both of your eyes."

"That doesn't mean a darn thing."

"Technically, that means you're as blind as a bat ... So tell us, Mr. Rutherford. How is it that a person with impaired vision able to descriptively see an image from over ninety feet away? Furthermore, how can we even be sure that the woman you saw was Ms. Inghram?"

"Are you kidding me? I may have not been wearing glasses that night, but I'm still not blind! I could've spotted them tits from the other side of the toilet!"

"Not according to your doctor you can't."

"Listen here, kiddo. I don't care what you think you may have gathered from the doctor, but I only need my glasses for driving at night."

"If that is so, then prove it. Let's put your vision to a test."

"What?"

"I'll stand thirty feet back from where you're sitting ... How 'bout you take off your glasses and tell us the number of fingers I have in the air."

"Objection!" Intervened Attorney Dawson. "Your honor, this is argumentative."

"Over-ruled," replied the judge. "Bailiff, please remove the glasses from Mr. Rutherford."

Once the glasses are removed, Attorney Decker steps thirty feet back from the witness. Giving the courtroom quite the entertainment, Attorney Decker flashes his middle finger into the air and Mr. Rutherford squints his eyes as he stares at the finger, acting as if he's staring through a maze.

Mr. Rutherford answers with, "Two."

"Excuse me?"

"You're holding up two fingers."

The courtroom giggles.

After the embarrassment, Attorney Decker glances at Attorney Dawson and the rest of our bench, portraying a taunting grimace. He says, "No further questions your honor."

29

**It was only two weeks into the trial and we were already down in the
hole, losing by a landslide.**

Our star witness, Mr. Rutherford, had screwed up tremendously,
and the only way to recover from that blow was to return the favor,
shutting down whatever evidence Attorney Decker might of think he'd
gathered. Like always, Attorney Dawson carried a confident look on
her face and she kept reminding me that the case was still in my favor.

She remains calm. So do I. But just like a child depends on their
parent during a drastic situation, my calmness depends on her.

The next person to appear on the stand was Dexter, my manager
from Club Ding-a-ling. Why Attorney Dawson threw him in as a
witness was beyond me, but her reasoning behind it was that any sort
of evidence could be good evidence, and the more evidence provided,
the more room there is for reasonable doubt.

Even on the stand, Dexter carried his usual fierce demeanor, as if
he was still on the job, ready to evaluate each girl's talk-time.

When Attorney Dawson asked him to state his name for the jury,
he proudly said, "Dexter Thornton. And I'm the manager for Club
Ding-a-ling."

"Mr. Thornton, at Club Ding-a-ling, how well would you say you
know the girls?"

"Well enough."

"Would you consider Angel as one of the top PSO agents?"

"Yes, she has only been there four months and already has a higher talk-time than other girls that's been there for years."

"Records show that she talked to you an hour before the tragedy, which was not long after Kevin threw her out his car. Can you tell us what she was calling for?"

"Yes, she was calling to tell me that she wasn't coming to work and Monday would probably be her last day. But that wasn't the first time one of my girls mentioned quitting. I hear those words everyday. However, it was strange to hear it from Angel, especially at a time when her commission was starting to increase."

"Did she ever say why she was quitting?"

"No, they never do. All she ever said was that she couldn't do it anymore. At first I blew it off and told her to have her butt on the next 10-2 shift tomorrow night. But then I detected her voice being a little solemn. It sounded like something I never heard before. Something told me to send one of the girls to check on her, but I was too busy trying to find a replacement for her shift."

"Mr. Thornton, in Angel's four months of working at Club Ding-a-ling, has she ever received a no-show?"

"No."

"Has she ever been absent at all?"

"No, she's been late a gazillion times due to transportation problems, but she'd always eventually show up."

"What about Angel's personality? Did you know her on a personal level?"

"Yeah, I knew all of my girls very well. As for Angel, she was definitely a quiet girl. I had to open her up a little, got her say what was on her mind. She never had a father. So I kind of played that father figure."

"In your span of knowing her, do you ever recall her having mental trauma of any sort?"

"All of the girls had their share of problems. Most of them come from broken homes. But while other girls were letting their problems consume them, Angel used her problems as motivation."

"Mr. Thornton, if someone told you that Angel Inghram killed someone, how would you respond to that?"

"I'd say they were out of their rabbit mind. Violence was nowhere in Angel's ballpark."

"Thank you, Mr. Thornton. No further questions your honor."

Silence floored through the courtroom as the judge asked, "Would the defense like to cross?"

"Certainly, your honor."

Doing his usual routine, Attorney Decker remains in his seat for a brief moment as if he's allowing a nervous state to swim through Mr. Thornton's veins. Once standing up, Attorney Decker adjusts his tie, puts on that evil glare, and says, "Mr. Ding-a-ling … I mean, Mr. Thornton, exactly long have you been the manager at this … this … sex place of business?"

"Objection your honor. Are those comments really necessary?"

"Sustained," the judge replied. "Attorney Decker, we don't have time for you to ridicule the witness's place of work."

"Sorry your honor."

Dexter spoke out, "I've been the manger for ten years. And club Ding-a-ling is not necessarily a sex place. It's a place of revision."

"Well at this place of revision, you mentioned earlier that Angel Inghram was one of your top PSO's?"

"That's right."

"Exactly what qualities are determined in being a top phone sex operator?"

"Time management."

"Time management as in what girl can make a guy climax the quickest?"

"No. It's actually the complete opposite. The sooner a man climaxes, the sooner the call is ended. Our objective is to try and keep a caller on the phone as long as possible."

"And what would you say is a good talk-time for a PSO?"

"Anywhere between twenty-five to thirty minutes."

"Are there certain bonuses that PSO's receive after having such a long-lasting talk-time?"

"Yes, after an hour a red light appears on their line. We refer to it as the red light special. Once that red light appears, a PSO will receive double for the call. A caller can also request a red light special with a PSO that really interests him."

Attorney Decker looks astonished. He says, "You mean to tell me that guys actually sit on the phone and talk to these women for over an hour?"

"Most certainly. Some of our top reps have even kept callers on the line for two hours or more."

 Cyril Gillion

"Jeez," replied Attorney Decker, bringing laughter into the courtroom. "Sounds like I need to get introduced to some of these women."

"Well you see … what people fail to realize is that our agents spend the least of their time discussing sex. When men call into Club Ding-a-ling, they're mainly calling for some type of understanding. This type of understanding cannot be received anywhere else. Not even at home with their wives."

Attorney Decker laughs, and says, "So in a sense, I guess it's safe to classify your girls as … psychiatrists. All that's missing are their clothes and certification."

"If you say so."

The courtroom follows that laughter.

"And what about relationships?" Attorney Decker asked. "Are there any personal relationships amongst the callers and your reps?"

"No."

"Are you sure? I mean I would think that after spending nearly fifty bucks on a red light special, a guy would at least wanna meet the woman that he was speaking with."

"Precisely. And that's what keeps them coming back, the fantasy of wandering what the caller looks like. But I encourage all the reps to never get personally involved with the callers."

"You encourage them not to, which means you don't know for sure if they are involved with the callers or not."

"No I don't," Dexter replied. "But if there were any personal relationships, they certainly won't be discussing personal talk through the hotline, because I monitor all the calls. And if I sense a personal call coming in, I automatically disconnect the call."

"What about Angel?"

"What about 'er?"

"Has Angel Inghram ever had any personal calls?"

"No. Not that I can recall."

"No or not that you can recall."

"No. But then again, I don't work everyday. So I can't say for certain if she ever received one or not."

"Yeah, but aren't all of the calls recorded?"

"Yes."

"So if there were personal calls coming into your hotline, the big bad boss man would still have record of it … right?"

"Objection your honor! The witness has already stated that the defendant didn't receive any personal calls."

The Other Side of the Pillow

"Sustained. Counsel, please get on with it."

"Mr. Thornton, did you ever have a personal relationship with Angel Inghram?"

"Yes, I already clarified that I had a personal relationship with all the girls. We all were—"

"Save it, Mr. Thornton. I'm strictly talking about a relationship that was physical."

"What?"

"Did you and Ms. Inghram ever have a physical relationship?"

"What do you mean by physical?"

"Sex. Screwing. The Wild Holy Mollie."

"Why would you ask a question like that?"

"Just answer the question!"

"No. We never did."

"What about phone sex. You never tested her PSO skills for your own pleasure? You never—"

"Now you've best stop right there, Mr.! I already told you that Angel was like a daughter in my eyes."

"Yeah, and committing incest is not the best start to parental guidance."

"Your honor!" screamed attorney Dawson.

"Mr. Decker, I will not allow that in my courtroom. Now either you prove these allegations or you keep your slanders to yourself."

"Very well your honor."

Attorney Decker walks over to his assistant to pick up a folded document of what looks to be a tape. "He says, "Your honor, I would like to present exhibit *A* to the jury."

Attorney Dawson steps in and says, "Your honor, this tape was never inserted on the initial role of evidence."

"Correction!" retorted Attorney Decker. "It was entered in this morning, and I intend to prove that Mr. Thornton's viewpoint of Angel is bias and his testimony should be discredited!"

"No your honor! He intends on trying to humiliate my client!"

"As if he hasn't already humiliated himself!"

"Enough!" the judge demanded. "Counsel, approach the bench right now!"

As both attorneys waged war against each other, another battle existed within myself, nervousness of what could possibly be on that tape. Moments later, the judge allows Attorney Decker to release the cobra from the bag and the tape is reviewed for evidence. Attorney Decker looks at the jury and says, "What you will witness on this tape

 Cyril Gillion

is the defendant, Angel Inghram, and the witness having a father and daughter conversation on the same line that is used for business purposes. Although this tape can get quite graphic, I strongly encourage you to pay close attention, because when you get finished viewing it, you'll definitely see why this wasn't your average father-daughter relationship."

[The tape plays]

"Hello caller. You've reached the right girl at the right place. This is Angelic Puss. And who am I speaking with?

"Hey, Angelic Puss. Don't you know my voice by now baby."

"Ooooh. Is this Al?"

"That's right baby ... do you miss me?"

"Hell yes. I'm still having flashbacks from our last encounter ... can I change your name from Al to Big Al."

"Ooooh ... I like it."

"So are you home alone?"

"Yes. My wife stepped out to pick up some Dunkin Donuts for a late night snack."

"Hmmm, why go out for Dunkin Donuts when there's a Dunkin stick waiting at home? If I was your wife, I'd have that Dunkin stick for a late-night snack every night."

"You would?"

"Damn right I would. And I'd wash it down with some milk that's pulsating from that stick."

"Is that so?"

"Yes baby. I can't go a day without that Vitamin D. Gots to keep my bones and teeth strong and full of calcium."

"Damn baby. You're so direct. I never met a woman who was so ... direct."

"That's because you never had a real woman. Angelic Puss never has time for games, and she won't hesitate on letting you live out your ultimate desires. Anything you want, I can fulfill."

"Anything?"

"Of course baby ... anything."

"What about spanking?"

"Is that what you like? You want to spank me."

"No, I want to be spanked. My wife never does it. I don't want to come out and tell her, only because I know she'd freak out. But I love being spanked."

The Other Side of the Pillow   283

"No problem, baby. Angelic Puss will give you a lashing like never before. All you have to do is toot that little butt in the air ... do you have the paddle?"

"I don't want the paddle. I want your raw hand."

"Whatever you say, Sweetie. Go 'head and ease off those tighty-whities so I can give you this—"

[The tape stops]

Butterflies run through my stomach as the jury sits upright, appalled of what they just heard. Doing everything possible to milk this cross-examination for what it's worth, Attorney Decker turns to Dexter and says, "I'm sure you can explain this, Mr. Thornton. Can't you?"

"Explain what?"

"Explain how the guy on this tape, Big Al, has a voice identical to yours."

"I don't know. Must be a conspiracy."

"I bet. The same way it's a conspiracy that this same man, Mr. Big Al, managed to call your place of business twenty times, requesting a red light special from the defendant, twenty times; twenty calls that were never monitored, ten of them that were made on the same days in which the big boss, you, so happened to be on vacation."

Dexter says, "My cell phone was reported stolen during that month. This so-called guy named Big Al must've got a hold of it."

"Is that right?

"That's right. You can call Sprint yourself. Hell, they should have records of me reporting a stolen phone during the month of July."

"Mr. Thornton, do you understand that you're under oath?"

"Are you calling me a liar?"

"The repercussions will be a lot less if you just come out and say it."

"Say what?"

"That you're a nymphomaniac. A stalker. That the only thing you were monitoring in that call center was the size of Ms. Inghram's breasts!"

"Objection your honor! He's badgering my—"

"Screw you!" yelled Dexter, screaming with evil in his eyes. "You damn right I monitored those tits and I don't feel bad for doing so. Let's see you try to go five years without touching a woman, knowing that you're the manger of a place that consists of women talking dirty all the time, and your nuts are going haywire from constantly seeing a blowjob being emulated by a girl in her twenties, and all you can do is

     Cyril Gillion

watch her personify those things that you can only dream about, knowing that the chance of it happening to you is once and a lifetime. Try doing that for a day or two! See that it drives you insane!"

Attorney Decker looks back at the defense, smiling as if he's licked the final stamp of this case. He says, "No further questions your honor … no further questions."

30

Later that night I was a total wreck.

Still trying to recuperate from Mr. Rutherford's testimony, I stayed up the whole night drinking tequilas and watching old re-runs of Goodtimes.

Although William never showed at my trial, he'd spent the whole day trying to console me, trying to piece together the little hope that was left inside, but I was so far gone to where his words were non-effective.

Him and Cuqui had left my apartment an hour ago. William needed to watch little Devilla, and Cuqui was hanging out with some guy that she met in court. Although I was on my ninth shot of tequila, I was nowhere near drunk, and all that kept running through my mind was the look on the jury's face after the prosecution dragged the truth out of Dexter, a truth that was impossible to recuperate from.

Moments later, I received a surprise knock on my door from Attorney Dawson. I instantly poured the tequila down the drain so she wouldn't see me drinking, but her first words when entering was, "You've been drinking haven't ya?"

"Yeah," I replied. "At the moment, liquor is all I can rely on."

She takes the glass from my hands. "C'mon Angel, you should be getting some rest, getting yourself together for next week."

"What for? I'm not the one who's getting paid to convince a jury of a person's innocence."

"What are you saying?"

"What I just said."

"Be more specific."

"We either need to find another witness or call in the dogs. Is that specific enough?"

She looks appalled by my comment. But I didn't care. After all, I was the one who was on trial. Not her.

She says, "The jury is still in our favor."

"Are you blind or something? How come everyone can see what's happening in that courtroom except you?"

"And what is that?"

"The prosecution is whipping our ass … that's what."

Acting as if everything is under control, she says, "One lousy testimony is not enough for paranoia, Angel. Cases like these are forever going back and forth. I've seen it happen a million times before. You've gotta trust me. We'll bounce back tomorrow."

"And how are we supposed to bounce back? You plan on pulling some magic out of a hat?

She looks at me as if she's the teacher – I'm the student – and I'm pass stepping out of line.

Realizing that I'm going to still need a lawyer no matter how angry I become, I transitioned back to that reserved Angel, and I tell her, "I'm sorry. It's just this whole trial has got me nervous and I can already see those prison cells. I mean … going to jail was already bad enough, and I'll be damned if I have to eat another lunch beside another girl named Dynamite."

She sits me down on the couch, no words, giving me time to relax.

After a moment of resuscitation, she says, "You've gotta trust me, Angel. I'm not gonna let anyone send you to prison. Not after what you endured."

I tell her, "I know you have good intentions. You don't have to convince me of that. But my only problem is … I just wish you could understand the frustration of knowing you're getting blamed for a crime, but in all actuality, you're supposed to be the victim."

"Believe me, Angel. I already know what you're going through."

"Correction. You think you know but you really don't. Do you know how it feels to get raped? To know you're lying on the floor, squirming helplessly, waiting for a man to not only take your body, but also mind and spirit, the little spirit you have left. And worst of all, you—"

"Stop right there!" she said, cutting me off. "You're not the only one who's suffered grief."

"Huh?"

"Like you, I was also raped."

"You were?"

"Happened when I was twelve years old … and you know what, it wasn't by some stranger or ex-boyfriend either. It was by my own family, my perverted uncle. The same man who's been coming to our house every week to eat Sunday dinners was the same man who used to sneak me in the bathroom, forcing my legs wide open. And you know what … you know what … that bastard got me pregnant as well. Can you imagine that? A twelve-year-old carrying a baby from her uncle, and even though your mother knows it, she tries to cover it up by forcing you to get an abortion because of fear that it might ruin her brother's reputation. Can you imagine what that'll do to a twelve-year-old? Huh? Can you?"

I stare at her as nothing but terror pulsates through her eyes. Terror beyond conception.

Through her terror, I can see myself. Ten years older. Forty pounds heavier. Not a pretty sight.

I ask, "Have you told anyone else?"

"No, Angel. And I'm surprised that I'm speaking to you about it."

"Why haven't you gone to the police?"

"Police," she says, sucking her teeth. "How does a twelve-year-old go to the police? I was too afraid. And just when I built enough courage to say something, he convinced me that no one would believe me. So I decided to take matters into my own hands … I killed 'em."

"You what?"

"That's right. I murdered 'em. Did what God should've done a long time ago; put that son-of-a-bitch out his misery … I poured gasoline around his bed and burned his house down while he was sleeping and dressed it up as if it was one of his drug pals. My sister knew what happened that day, but we swore to keep it confidential. Till this day, we're the only ones that know the truth … and now you."

At this point, I didn't know whether to tell her, sorry for what happened or sorry but you have to exit my apartment. Either way, I was sorry for ever asking in the first place.

I glance at Ms. Dawson; watch her as she drowns in pain. She is no longer my attorney, no longer that woman with the expensive suits,

 Cyril Gillion

the intimidating woman with years of law experience and how-ever-so-many alphabets that stand behind her name. She's now a little girl. We're both little girls. And no matter hold old a gal gets, no matter how successful you become, pain will always be pain. Will always be overpowering.

Asking her the question that I constantly ask myself, I say, "Don't you feel any type of remorse for what you did? Any regrets?"

"I did at first. But that was until I realized I wasn't the enemy. And then it became easier for me to deal with it. I wasted twenty years of my life thinking about what I should've done, how I should've locked him up rather than take his life. But then I realized that prison would've been too easy for a man like him. Too little of a punishment. So he got what he deserved. Capital punishment. Something I could never see myself doing, but it was the only solution for keeping my sanity. Had I confessed to that crime, I'd probably be in jail right now, hoping for a lawyer to come along and get me off the hook, making it appear as temporary insanity. And for what? All for some no good family member who couldn't keep his pants zipped up. Hell no! I did what any twelve-year-old would've done with her back against the wall … I adapted."

She stops talking. Stops the madness. And as silence rest between us, we realize how much our past consists of common grounds.

I have more questions to ask, but due to the situation at hand, I hold my tongue.

Then I think about William.

William once told me that God would never put more on a person than they can bear, and no matter how bleak the road may appear, there's always another driver in the far lane, another person traveling that same rugged road. It was strange to see Attorney Dawson as that other driver. Not only has she walked in my shoes, but she'd worn them out completely, the only other 7 ½ that could slide into these pumps.

We were two killers without evil intent. Two murderers that weren't actual murderers. For if there was ever a word to describe us, it would need to have multiple parts of speech, a meaning so irregular to where it'll create its own thesaurus.

Ms. Dawson says, "I'm thinking about bringing Mr. Rutherford back on the stand."

My mind does back flips and I tell her, "Hell no. That old man is not getting back on the stand. Attorney Decker will eat 'em alive."

"Angel, that old man is the only witness who can attest for that night. Without re-examining him, this case can possibly turn for the worst."

"And what if he freezes up again?"

"Guess we just have to take that chance."

"Take a chance?"

"Yes, it's our only hope."

I take in her words and swallow hard. Swallow the possibility of imprisonment.

I tell her, "The hell with that."

"Huh?"

"That old man is not the only person who can attest for that night."

"You telling me that someone else was there?"

"No, I'm saying I should testify."

"You testify? Uh uh. Bad idea."

"How come?"

"Like I told you before Angel, it's too risky."

"It's been risky already. And what can be riskier than Mr. Rutherford?"

She nods her head to disagree, then says, "Putting you on the stand will give the prosecution exactly what they want."

"Then give them what they want. Heck, switch up the routine a little. I'd rather take a chance on myself than let some old retired war hero determine my fate ... I'm beggin you Ms. Dawson. Let me testify. And if it's meant for God to send me to prison, then so be it."

She drops her elbows on her thighs, contemplating the advantages of my proposal. "Fine," she says. "I'll put you on the stand. Maybe it will increase the sensitivity of the jury. But you are to keep your statements brief ... very brief ... if you try to elaborate on anything, I'm sitting your ass down."

<u>*31*</u>

Court would presume in thirty minutes.

Trying to regroup, my head was to the floor, and I was sitting on a bench in the hallway, by myself, no reporters around.

Once looking up, I made eye contact with a woman in a wheelchair. It was Mrs. Armstrong, Kevin's mother, a blind woman that had 20-20 vision. She was strolling her wheelchair in my direction, and in her lap was a briefcase. Due to the circumstances, I was hoping she'd keep rolling by, but although she was blind, she still looked in my direction as if she wanted to make eye contact.

I stuck my face back into the floor.

"Angel?" she said. "You can't speak?"

"Oh I'm sorry, Mrs. Armstrong. I didn't see you come up."

She laughs. "How can't you see me but I'm the one that's blind?"

She finds a spot next to me, and she rolls back into her wheelchair, adjusting it so we both are facing parallel.

One can never phantom the remorse that I feel right now. Sitting next to her. Looking into her eyes. The mother of a man that I used to care about, knowing her only son was killed in my arms.

I don't know what to tell her. Don't know where to start.

Not only was I on trial for murder, but I was now facing a life of conspiracy in her eyes. Even if she knew the truth, I still felt she'd never truly understand it, a truth that will always stay buried beneath a rock, covered by grains of sand.

I ponder over those thoughts. I am those thoughts. And those thoughts alone do circles around my conscience. Hunts me like vengeance hunts karma.

Clearing the airways, I put it out there by saying, "Mr. Armstrong."

"Yes child."

"No matter what happens to me, I want you to know the truth ... truth that I didn't kill Kevin intentionally ... it was an accident ... I promise it was ... swear it on my mother's grave ... and although it doesn't mean much now ... I just want to say ... just want to tell you sorry ... I'm sorry Mrs. Armstrong ... sorry for everything that happened ... sorry for what I put you through ... I didn't know the gun would go off ... didn't know it was loaded ... you've gotta believe me Mrs. Armstrong ... it's important that you and you only believe me."

"I do believe you, Angel."

"You do?"

"I believed you before you even said it. I know you're not a murderer. And most importantly, I know how my son felt about you. You're the one who's been dealing with this constant burden ... people with cameras ... false accusations ... strangers approaching you with evil looks ... you're the one that deserves an apology."

She stares at me with open arms, eyes without vision, and she embraces me like a second mother.

I tell her, "I don't wanna go to prison."

She laughs. "Prison ... Yeah right, honey ... God doesn't place people like you in prison, Angel. Just keep having faith and you'll see what he really has in store for you ... And how are you doing in school?"

"One more year and I finish Brooklyn Law."

"Law school huh? Seems like it was just yesterday that you and Kevin was arguing about who was gonna be the most successful. Now you're all grown up, representing young black women like you should be. God knows if your mother could see you right now, she'd be so proud of what she left behind. Did you know that your mother was supposed to go to law school as well?"

"Was she?"

"Uh huh."

"I thought she stopped at her third year in undergrad."

"Are you kidding me? Like you, your mother was Suma Cum Laude in undergrad. She went to some school in Georgia."

                    Cyril Gillion

"How do you know all of this?"

"Cause I was supposed to go with her but I never went ... I didn't have the drive like she did, and back in those days, going to college just wasn't the thing to do ... You know it's funny ... I remember your mother coming home every summer with a young man ... His name was Dennis Inghram, your father. She was so overjoyed when they were together, and you could tell her life was going good. The last summer she came home she got pregnant. Pregnant with you of course. And during that same summer your father died in a car accident ... Believe me when I tell you that your mother was devastated ... Hurt her like hell ... But because she was a fighter, she still went back to school. She didn't come home quite often, but the last time she came, she was back to her usual self, all smiles, and she brought back some handsome guy from up north ... That guy was your stepfather; a businessman who always dressed in flashy suits, always gave your mother whatever she wanted. And before I lost my vision, I remember them always having fights because of the other women that wanted a piece of your stepfather. Though your family confided in him, I always knew there was something about him that just wasn't right, and it wasn't long before I found out that he was a drug dealer, used to be one of the biggest dealers up north. I never told your mother about it. Never wanted to spoil her happiness. But then"—her eyes start to water— "that's when I heard the news ... that he'd killed her ... killed her over a drug deal, while you were in the house, and tried to dress it up as an accident ... Then they sentenced him to second-degree murder, but that didn't mean a thing because he was killed in prison five years later ... I remember the whole city of Miami being in an uproar about your mother's death, and I cried myself to sleep every night – not because she died, but because of me not being a better friend ... Eighteen years later, I still carry around that guilt ... I should've told her about your stepfather ... should've been there for your mother."

Something told me to respond, but I refuse to speak on the past. I've already spent years trying to sweep away that dust.

Mrs. Armstrong says, "Can you do something for me?"

"Yes."

"Reach down there and grab my briefcase."

"What's in it?"

"You'll see."

I flip back the latch and in the briefcase lies a raggedly stack of papers, thick as a book, they all bunged together in rubber bands.

The Other Side of the Pillow

"What are these?" I asked.

"Letters. All letters from Kevin to you."

"Excuse me?" I asked, looking at the stack again.

"Kevin was devastated when y'all broke up. He would constantly call me for advice, asking how he could tie y'all back together. I told him to move on. Told him what any mother would say to her child in a situation like that … But he never listened. He still considered you as his wife, even after you rejected him in that restaurant. And ever since, he was too afraid to give you a call, so he wrote down his thoughts. He wrote down each conversation as if he did call, as if y'all had really spoken."

I skim through the letters. Three hundred pages of cursive anguish.

She tells me, "Make sure you give those to Attorney Dawson. Tell her that you came across some new evidence."

"Excuse me?"

"These letters can help you with your testimony."

"That's ok, Mrs. Armstrong. I refuse to put you through that kind of misery. I've already put you through enough."

"If you don't use this for evidence, you'll be found guilty. And whether you want to admit it or not, these letters are your only ticket to freedom."

"But what about—"

"My son."

"Yeah. I mean … it's like you're testifying against Kevin."

"You think I came up here to watch you go to prison … Never … I came here to make sure you don't go and I'll do everything in my power to keep you as a free woman. I have to do what's right, Angel. And to let them send you to prison … now that's … that's … that's just not right."

As we sit in a solemn state, I saw a shadow coming down the hallway, a familiar stroll.

To my surprise, it was my comforter, William Randolph, dressed in a charcoal suit, walking though a swarm of people that has now flooded the hallway. Beside him is his daughter, Devilla – a little devil in a Cinderella dress – walking beside her father like a bride that was waiting to be given away.

Nothing surprised me more than to see William coming to the trial, finally giving me the support that I needed, and although I didn't know his motive for coming, I was just elated to know he was here.

After seeing Kevin's mother and I sitting together, he gave a look of shock, but he played it if off by kissing me on the cheek. "Hey baby."

"Hey, what are you doing here?"

"Can't I be here to give my woman some support?"

"Yeah, but you've yet to come before, and I didn't think—"

"That I'd ever come … Well I'm here now. The both of us are."

Turning back around to Mrs. Armstrong, I tell him, "I was just talking to a friend of mines. Meet Kevin's mother, Ms. Armstrong."

"Hello Mrs. Armstrong."

"Hello Mr.—"

"Randolph. William Randolph."

She turns her head towards Devilla. "And who might this little one be?"

Devilla stands behind her father, but courageously says, "My name is Devilla."

"Devilla. That's such a pretty name."

"I know … my daddy gave me that name."

"Did he?"

"Yes … Are you blind?" she blurted out.

William snarls. "Devilla!"

"No its okay," Mrs. Armstrong said. "Yes suga. I'm blind. But when you're blind, God gives you other powers."

"He does?"

"Yes … For instance, you're on the right side of me. Angel is on the left. And your dad is in front."

"How could you know that when you can't see?"

"Like I told you, God gave me other powers."

Moving to a different spot, Devilla gives the glow of an audience that's awaiting another trick from a magician. "Okay … what about now? Can you see me now?"

Mrs. Armstrong laughs. "She's so sweet … Do you think she'll also be sweet enough to escort an old woman to the water fountain?"

"Yes ma'am," Devilla replied, jumping behind the wheelchair.

William joins them, but he kisses me again before leaving. "See ya inside, Angel … I'll be sitting on the back row."

As they leave, Attorney Dawson walks up. "Come on, Angel. We need to be on the floor in a few minutes."

"Okay … I'll be there."

Attorney Dawson leaves, never noticing the stack of letters that I had from Kevin.

The Other Side of the Pillow

I take a look at my surroundings. A garbage can sits beside me, one in arm reaching distance.

I stare at that garbage can. Stare back at the letters that sits in my lap.

I think and think and think. Think of how I can't do this. Don't have the heart. Don't have the guts to use this for evidence.

Then I stare at the garbage can once more; stare back at the letters.

Although this could be my fatality, I throw away the letters, disposing myself of those written words.

Soon to be written memories.

Cyril Gillion

32

Ten minutes later I was being sworn into oath, sweating like I'd already been convicted.

Wearing a dark blue suit with my mother's pearls around my neck, it felt like I was about to become the bird's eye of the prosecution, the cross examiner's chop meat.

Attorney Dawson told me to just speak from the heart and let my emotions run free, but it was no use in trying, because soon as I took the stand, the emotions were overflowing internally, and speaking those words were equivalent to spitting gasoline on heightened flames.

I looked into the audience; saw a blur of William's face as he sat in the back row with Devilla in his arms. A comforting beam gleamed on his face and his words continued to seep through my cerebrum, *Angel, have faith.*

Attorney Dawson was trying to work the jury by asking me a bunch of rhetorical questions, but then she took the testimony into full throttle by saying, "Ms. Inghram, in your own words, can you describe what happened after Mr. Armstrong came back to your apartment?"

"We were coming from a theatrical play at Broadway, and while riding to our next destination, we got into a huge argument. I told him to take me straight home and I guess he didn't like it because he put me out of his car in the middle of an intersection, told me I better walk the rest of the way home. But when I reached my house and finally got settled, there he was again, knocking on the door. I no longer wanted anything to do with him and I opened the door to finalize us, to make it clear to him that we were over. He apologized for throwing me out of his car and wanted to make-up right then and there. I tried to tell him to leave, but he refused, and just like that, he bulldozed his way through my apartment. That's when he started coming at me sexually, saying how I owed him for setting me up with an internship. As I reached for the phone to call the police, he took it from my hand and said he wasn't going anywhere until we had sex … he ripped my shirt and started to grab my breasts … I slapped him but he still wouldn't let up. He pulled me to the bedroom and threw me against the window seal … kept slapping me as I could do nothing but scream help … He was strong … very strong … He threw me on the bed and after slapping me a couple more times, he started fondling me, ramming his fingers up my skirt, and suddenly started penetrating me … Eventually, I was able to find enough strength to knee him in the groin and I was able to break loose for my gun … I pointed the gun in his direction, just to scare him, just so he could leave. He charged at me to take the weapon and we started tussling back and forth, him trying to strip the gun from my hands, and me doing whatever I could to keep it in my possession … Eventually, the gun exploded, and after that everything just happened so fast … Kevin was on the floor … blood everywhere … and it wasn't long before I was in handcuffs."

Whispers floor through the courtroom before Attorney Dawson could continue, some turning their heads in disbelief, others sweeping my sadness beneath the rug. Attorney Dawson says, "Ms. Inghram, how many times did Mr. Armstrong come to your house before the night of the killing?"

"That was his first time coming. Before that, he never knew where I lived."

"The night that you saw him in the club, were you with someone else?"

"Yes," I replied, making slight eye contact with William. "I was there with a friend of mines."

"And can you tell us what Mr. Armstrong's reaction was when he saw you with that friend?"

"Objection!" Attorney Decker shouted. "These observations are redundant Your Honor. It's impossible to say for sure what Mr. Armstrong's attitude was like that night."

"Over-ruled," the judge replied.

"What? How can you over-rule this—"

                    Cyril Gillion

"Over-ruled counselor … Ms. Inghram, proceed."

I clear my throat. "Kevin was a little perturbed when he saw me with someone else. I guess after five years of disappearance, he expected to see me alone. We tried to speak about it, but it later escalated into an argument and we couldn't come to terms of an agreement."

"Ms. Inghram, how long has it been since you and Mr. Armstrong broke up?"

"About a year."

"And since the breakup, have you two ever had a physical relationship of any sort?"

"No. Not even close. After he got drafted, he called a couple of times. But we agreed to keep our relationship platonic. Nothing more than friends."

After Attorney Dawson sat, Attorney Decker rose abruptly. Never blinking, he was studying me with all senses, as if I was the last assessment that would conclude his premise. He says, "Ms. Inghram, the night of the murder, you stated that Kevin knocked on your door right after he made you walk home from throwing you out of his Lexus."

"Yes I did."

"But you also stated that you and Kevin's relationship was strictly platonic … nothing more than friendship."

"That's right."

"Do you usually go to banquets with your friend guys?"

"Besides Kevin, I never had a guy that I'd consider as a friend, so I can't answer that question for certain."

"But you can say for certain that Kevin was someone special, considering that he was the only guy to break that wall of friendship."

"If that's how you want to interpret it, then yes."

"Would you say that you knew his character quite well?"

"I thought I did. But then again, you never really know a person."

"I agree with you on that. It's impossible to fully know someone. However, what you did know is that Kevin's friendship for you had progressed into feelings, especially after the way he acted when seeing you with another man in Club Down-Under. You do know that don't you?"

"Objection!" retorted Attorney Dawson. "Your honor, my client has already stated that she didn't know this man's character."

"Sustained."

"Very well then … Ms. Inghram, since we all agree that you didn't really know this man, Kevin Armstrong, why would you let 'em into your home, especially after he threw you out his vehicle, showing you the character of a deranged man; a character that you claim you didn't know."

"I didn't let him into my home. He forced himself in uninvited."

Chuckling, he says, "Ms. Inghram, if I'm not mistaken, you're supposed to be a student of law, always have been in the top percentile of students in your class. And from what I've gathered, you have a huge problem with trust. You agree?"

"Agree."

"So why would a woman like you – a woman with trust issues – decide to even open the door when you knew it would do nothing but generate another problem?"

"Because I had to get some clarity."

"Clarity on what?" he asked sarcastically. "Friendship?"

"Clarity that I wasn't some rubber band that could be flipped back and forth. Clarity that you can't embarrass me one minute and try to make it right the next."

"So what, you open the door to slam it back?"

"Haven't you ever had an argument so badly to where you had to get some understanding, no matter how long it lasted?"

"Yeah, but I've never come in between a ready-made household either. So I guess that makes us two types of people, doesn't it."

"Objection your honor! He's badgering my darn witness!"

"Sustained! Attorney Decker, that's enough!"

"Sorry your honor … Ms. Inghram, you mentioned that you had no intentions of shooting Mr. Armstrong, and your revolver accidentally went off after Mr. Armstrong ran into it. Before the so-called accident occurred, did you know that there were bullets in the gun?"

"Yes I did."

"Did you know that it was loaded?"

"No."

"You sleep with a gun under your pillow every night, but you don't know when it's loaded?"

"No. I usually know when it's loaded."

"So let's get this straight … you usually know when your gun is loaded, but you didn't know it was loaded the night you murdered Kevin … how come?"

"Easy … must've forgot."

"No, Ms. Inghram. People forget to take out the garbage. They forget to feed the dog. They forget to turn off an oven from burning. Normal people don't forget to lay their head next to a loaded gun, knowing it could fire at any given moment."

"I'm a fulltime student, plus I work late night at a tiresome job. Sleep – if I ever get some at all – is the last thing I do. So as you can see, there are many reasons why I could've forgot."

"Would one of those reasons so happen to be engaging in shooting courses?"

"What?"

"This is what," he replies, walking over to his assistant. He picks up a hard copy article and heads back my way. He says, "Your honor, I'd like to present exhibit *C* to the jury … What I'm carrying is not only a certificate of completion from the Tactical Range Shooting Academy, but it's also a 4th place prize, one awarded to Angel Inghram for her outstanding precision with firearms."

Wandering how the hell he ever got his hands on that, I say, "I don't care how much homework you think you may have done, I still didn't kill anyone intentionally."

"Why don't you tell us Ms. Inghram. About how many participants start off training in this Tactical Shooting Range course?"

"Why does it matter?"

"How many???"

"I don't know. Maybe a hundred or more."

"And out of those hundred or more, how many actually finish the class to get a certificate.

"No more than twenty. Twenty-five."

"Wow. And you came in 4th place."

"What are you trying to pitch? That I should be prosecuted for learning self defense?"

"No. I'm saying that it's almost impossible for an accident like this to occur for a person that's been trained so thoroughly with a firearm. According to the academy, you're skilled at handling a revolver, a .22, an AK47, and who knows what else. Heck, you could probably shoot the hair off a ferret's fanny if given the chance. So don't you dare sit there and tell us that shooting Mr. Armstrong was some sort of accident."

"I'm telling you the truth!"

"No you're not, Angel. You're only saying what your lawyer told you to say. Be honest, Angel. Tell the truth and maybe the jury will sympathize with you. Tell the jury that—"

The Other Side of the Pillow

"Objection!"

"Tell the truth, Angel. You were jealous of Kevin's fiancé weren't you? And your world came tumbling down when you found out the truth, that someone else was getting the riches that you invested so much time into. You couldn't—"

"Objection!"

"You killed him on purpose didn't you? Say it, Angel! Tell the jury that you killed him because you couldn't kill her! Tell the truth, Angel. Tell the jury that you wanted him dead! Tell us that it was—"

"You damn right I wanted him dead! That son-of-a-bitch deserved it. And if I could, I'd kill 'em a thousand times more and spit on his fucking grave!!!"

33

A month passed.

We were driving in William's ride. Me, Cuqui and Little Devilla, all suffering from the burden of William's early morning gospel music, Kirk Franklin screaming the song *He's Able* through the speakers.

I'd finally got the urge to visit William's church. It wasn't for him though. This was my own decision.

The jury was ready to convict me tomorrow and after doing all of this soul searching, after trying every method of relief, I felt a need to try something new.

William started singing, "He's aaaaable! He's aaaaable! Oh yes he is! Oh yes he is!"

Little Devilla sung along with her dad as Cuqui and I sat in the car, imprisoned in their awful symphony.

Cuqui whispered to me from the back seat. "What the hell is his problem? We haven't even got there yet and he's already acting as if he's caught the Holy Ghost."

"Just relax, Cuqui. He loves his music."

Somehow, in the midst of us riding forwards, I felt myself going backwards. Back to the place that I'd abandoned all my life. Back to the route in which I clearly crossed off the map.

Back then, when I was a child, it was easy for me to accept this type of music, or even greater, to accept God for what he was and relish in his many blessings. It's like church was delivered to me with a silver spoon, placed on a platter. But now it's different. Now I was digging into that same plate with forks and knives, straining to regain the acceptance that I possessed as an eight-year-old child. And no matter how hard I tried to make the music move me, it just wasn't working.

Once reaching our destination, William told Devilla, "Hand me my coat."

Looking good as usual, William wore a grey tailored suit. Black hard-bottoms. Checkered vest with the tie to match.

If heaven was based on dress-code alone, then William could've ushered his way into the pearly gates.

He helped me pick out my dress as well. A red petite crepe flounce dress that was hemmed below the knee, the final dress that we agreed on after trying on seven others. From the many times I switched dresses, you would've thought I was auditioning for some big time performer, but according to William, if you can't look good for God then no one else is worth looking good for.

William's church was in the most gutter part of town, right next to the crack house on Martin Luther King Blvd. A couple gang banger look-a-likes were sitting on the front steps of the church, baggy jeans, chains around their necks, and both were peeping Cuqui and I like vultures. Just like when we were kids, we stuck to each other like Siamese twins when starting to pass their way.

"Good morning my beautiful sistahs," they said, extending their right hand of fellowship.

"Morning," I mumbled.

William said, "You young men ever plan on coming inside?"

"Nah partner. We're straight."

"You sure? We have a prolific speaker that you might wannna hear."

"Man I told you that we're straight. Maybe some other time. Isn't that communion thing supposed to be going down next week?"

"Yes."

"Well then … guess we'll be there next week."

"Why then?" William asked.

"Because that's the only time the church is serving wine. Why else?"

They laughed.

William shook his head and grabbed Devilla's hand, escorted the four of us inside.

Stepping into church was equivalent to stepping into the courtroom. The pastor was just like the judge, the elders resembled the jury, and the congregation was the same but only larger.

The church was packed. Sardine packed. Only seats left were those in the second row, right behind the deacon heads and a bunch of older women who wore hats larger than the planet Saturn. We were extremely late, but the pastor didn't hesitate to acknowledge our tardiness, and the moment we got into our seats, the pastor was speaking into the intercom, yelling, "Welcome! Welcome to Mt. Sinai! Church of the living God."

It wasn't long before that same *welcome* turned into, "We'd like to welcome all the visitors. Will all the visitors please stand?"

It was at that point that I wanted to hide in my seat, would've dove under the pew if it wasn't for the pastor looking me directly into the eyes.

I looked over at Cuqui. She was just as scared as I was.

I whispered, "Cuqui?"

"What?"

"Cuqui?"

"What girl?"

"Are you gonna stand?"

"For what?"

"Because he's talking to us. We're visitors."

"Uh uh baby. You're the only visitor up in here. I've been a Christian all my life. Bapized twice."

"Shhhhhh. No stupid. We're still not members of this church."

"Like I said, I'm a faithful member at the Christian church back home. And once you're a member in one Christian church, you're considered a member in every Christian church around. So you see girl. He's talking to you."

I look over to William. "Do I have to stand?"

"Only if you feel the urge, Angel."

"Looks like we have a visitor in the front!" the pastor yelled, putting me on blast.

I looked around the church. All eyes were on me. And right then and there I wanted to run to the pulpit and strangle the pastor with the microphone.

"Come on sistah," the pastor persisted. "Stand up and acknowledge yourself."

At that moment, William grabbed my hand and stood from his seat, forcing me to stand as well.

Addressing the congregation, he said, "As you all may know, my name is William. And here with me is a good friend, Angel Inghram, visiting for the first time."

I stood there and smiled, counting down the seconds of when I could sit back down.

Pastor Walden said, "Angel Inghram … the young woman from the trial? Is that you?"

"Yes sir," I softly replied.

"Well isn't God good. Man o Man o Man. Sistah we are so glad to have you up in here today."

"And I'm glad to be here," I replied, not knowing what else to say.

"Stay right there so Pastor Walden can come down and give you a hug," he said, trotting down the steps of the pulpit with a microphone in his hand.

After making his way pass the pianist, he reached over the pew to embrace me. Then he gave me a long stare, smiling as if I was the chosen visitor of the month.

He looked into the congregation and said, "Now you see church. This is exactly what I'm talking 'bout … Young people … Young people like Ms. Angel standing strong for the lord, doing his work … Angel, tell us what church you're from."

"Excuse me?"

"Your church. What church are you bringing greetings from?"

I stood there dumbfounded, palms sweaty, couldn't read a script if it was placed before my eyes.

"She's bringing greetings all the way from Miami, Florida," William said, jumping into the fire to save me once more. "She's yet to find a church but she's happy to be here today."

"Florida, huh?" Pastor Walden said. "Well I hope you brought some of that warm weather?"

"I'm actually looking to bring some of this cold weather back home," I answer, throwing in a joke to pretend I wasn't uncomfortable.

"Well Angel, we commend you for all the perseverance that you showed during the trial and no matter the outcome, you remember that God loves you and you're always welcome at Mt. Sinai."

The pastor hugs me tight, sweat dripping through his gown, felt like he just finished wrestling with the devil.

Although the hug was a little sticky, I can't deny that it made me feel good, like everyone around had wanted to see me prevail.

The service carried on and so did my interest. There were lots of singing, touching testimonies, and some poetry was also thrown into

 Cyril Gillion

the service – a middle aged woman who recited Maya's Angelou's *Ain't I a woman* in sign language.

The ushers came through a couple times to take-up offering, and each time William gave me some dollars to place into the offering plate. As the ushers made their rounds for a third consecutive time, Cuqui looked at one of them said, "What the hell? Y'all must think money grow on trees."

By the time the pastor stood up to speak his sermon, it was already 2 p.m. Cuqui was steadily complaining about the heat and little Devilla was snoring on William's lap. One of the members behind me had tapped me on the shoulder to offer a bible so I could follow the pastor with the scripture reading.

The pastor said, "Can you please turn your bibles to the book of Hebrews, Chapter 11, verses 1-39."

Opening that bible was like turning pages of Greek. I had no idea where the book of Hebrews was and I even found myself looking in the wrong testament.

"Right here," William said, pointing at the right verse to save me the humility.

I said, "Jeez … All of this. Verses 1-39 is a whole chapter."

William gives me an evil stare.

The pastor's sermon was entitled, "Keeping the faith," a title that he so readily prepared with scripture after scripture. From 39 verses of consecutive reading, he spoke about these so-called great people in the bible, how each person was able to move mountains once they placed their faith in God. From Noah, to Enoch, to Abraham, they all had inspiring stories.

But I wasn't some Noah. Wasn't some Enoch. Wasn't Abraham either.

I'm Angel Inghram.

And with all of their faith combined, it will still never be strong enough to erase my past, 1989, the year my mother died.

The pastor then spoke of how some people's faith in God has been replaced with other things that were more sensible – things like school, careers – all the things that seemed practical to the naked eye, people who can't accept God for who he is because the whole notion of faith is to illogical.

Slowly but surely, I started to realize that I was one of the people that he was talking about. For I was that pragmatist, that woman who views everything conceptually, constantly scoping the scales through the belly of the fish.

The sermon soon turned into an appeal, one in which the pastor was asking the congregation to come to the altar and lay down their burdens based on faith.

God knows I had enough burdens to lie; had enough transgressions to fill this entire room, and even though the pastor was afar, it felt like he was whispering in my ear at the moment.

Although that inner voice was pleading for me to come, I still strained not to go; told myself that it was going to take more than faith to raise me from this pew and send me to that altar.

But God moves people.

That's what the Pastor said. God has a tendency to move people when they never plan on being moved.

And just like that it felt like I was being moved, couldn't put my finger on it, but something was pushing this little body inside.

I became extremely confused. Torn between good and evil. A candle burning at both ends.

I don't know what to do.

In my eyes, faith is considered impractical. Spiritualism is considered impractical. But thus far, the most practical things in my life has turned out to be over-bearing, which is why I am at this point right now, reaching out for the impractical, the unreasonable, *faith*.

"Come to the altar," he said. "Have faith and let God fix those problems."

Faith tried to set in, tried to push its way through my barriers.

"Pick the lock," the pastor pleaded. "Open that door. Give God a chance."

Was I opening the door for God or was he opening the door for me? Was I giving the church a chance or was the church giving me one?

Whatever the answer was, it was a door I was willing to open. A chance I was willing to take.

I walked to that altar.

Cyril Gillion

<u>34</u>

The next day, tomorrow, was still my yesterday.

I had not slept. Haven't pulled an all-nighter since first grade, Christmas Eve, when Cuqui and I were arguing about whether Santa would come down the chimney or walk through the door.

I was sitting in the courtroom wearing my Sunday's best, and since this could possibly be the last decent outfit I'd ever get to wear, I wore my Dolce & Gabbana with dignity, figured I'd spray on the whole bottle of Tiffany's before sniffing those prison walls of funk.

This time around the jury appeared to be confident when entering the courtroom. After taking their seats, voices floored amongst the twelve of them, sounded like footsteps circling around an unmarked grave.

For some reason, I wish they'd get this over with and convict me already, while this mental massacre is cruising through the preliminary stage of burden, before it spins into overdrive.

Forget about prison. My penitentiary had already started. The only thing missing was the orange jumpsuit and the straggly slippers.

I glanced at my dream team that sat behind me: Cuqui, Professor Stern, and now William and Devilla that was sitting in the back row of the courtroom, all of whom which was just as nervous as I was.

When the judge told everyone to rise, Attorney Dawson clasped my palms that were sweating like never before.

The judge asks, "Has the jury reached a verdict?"

"Yes we have your honor … In the case of Angel Inghram vs. The State of New York, we hereby find the defendant … not guilty of first degree murder."

35

It was six pm, thirty minutes before the settling of dusk.

Two weeks had passed since the verdict, four weeks if you're counting the stress that I had to go through with the press. The case had gone mainstream media. Journalists were around every corner.

I'd even received a couple invitations to appear on the Montel Williams show, O'Reily Factor, and most surprising, Oprah – all who wanted my side of the story, or even greater, my panorama of sexual assault in general. I declined the visit on all of their requests. Why? Well it's quite simple. I felt like my personal life was already broadcasted enough, and at this moment, my main objective was to put this whole thing behind me and finish law school. Cuqui told me that I was crazy; you know, declining on the Oprah show and all. She loved Oprah like a parent loves a child and after telling Cuqui that I had no intentions of appearing on the show, she threatened to drag me on Oprah herself, bickering of how she'd never let me ruin the possibility of meeting her idol. In a sense, it seemed as if this case was benefiting everyone in some way or another. Especially Attorney Dawson. Since the case ended, she had clients who were willing to pay her almost double the amount of her usual asking price, triple the amount of what she initially charged me.

Right now, I was heading to Professor Stern's house. He said I'd be in for a surprise and it was urgent that I show as quickly as possible.

The Other Side of the Pillow　　　　311

Considering that Professor Stern has never invited me over his house before, I knew there had to be something major about this visit or strange might I add. At the same time, William and I had our own plans tonight. So with that in mind, I told Professor Stern to make this visit short and sweet, because nothing was going to interfere with the plans I had with my lover … nothing.

Professor Stern stayed in a condo in the upper Eastside of Manhattan, minutes away from the Metropolitan Museum of Art.

Stylish to the core, his condo is a replica of what I wanted in five years, looked like a place that was purchased from years of pennies being saved.

The living room was equivalent to Wonderland. Photos of some of the most prestigious lawyers around are covering the walls of his living room that are made of nothing but granite; lawyers like Nina Shaw, Teresa Rosenborough, and Bart Williams (to just name a few). There's a long antique hexagonal piecrust table with claw feet in the center of the room, and behind it lays a few camel-colored sided armchairs that were upholstered in a quilted diamond-shaped pattern, each chair giving the perfect view of a fifty inch plasma television. There are tall vintage table lamps everywhere you turn and a long stairway leads to a balcony that has a panoramic view over New York City.

As I walked through his palace, I saw a girl leaving out. Her face appeared to be a little flustered, and after saying hello, she ignored me and continued to walk out the door.

I looked towards Professor Stern. "New student?"

"No, I just got finished telling her that she'd have to find herself a new professor."

"What is it? Are there only a certain type of students you teach?"

"It's not that. I'll teach any student. Any student that is willing to learn. But in this case, I'm moving."

"Moving?" I replied astonishingly.

"That's right. I'm retiring. Moving back home to Boston to lay my head. I'll be gone on Saturday. Sunday at most."

"I thought you said you were from Florida."

"No, Angel. I only used to work in Florida, but Boston is my home, born and raised. Besides, my mom is very sick. She's developed lung cancer and I'm the only one who can take care of her. That's my main purpose for moving."

"I'm sorry to hear that … You gon' be ok?"

He smirks. "Who me? Professor Stern will always be okay."

                    Cyril Gillion

He reaches for a cardboard box that lies near the sofa, starts stuffing it with plates and silverware. "Care for any?" he asked. "I'm trying to get rid of it."

"That's ok," I replied, thinking this wasn't the surprise I expected.

"But don't worry, Angel. Before relocating, I made sure you were taken care of."

"What do you mean taken care of?"

"You've been looking for a paid internship, right?"

"Yeah."

"Well..."

"Don't tell me you got me an internship."

"That's right. I got you an internship at a firm that I used to work at."

"Stop kidding."

"Have you ever known me to be the kidding type? All you have to do is show up dressed properly with a portfolio. And make sure you bring a briefcase. Attorney Hackensack always judges how serious a person is from their briefcase."

"Who?"

"Attorney Hackensack. He's the lawyer that you'll be working beside. Luckily, one of his assistants quit and he needs a fill-in expeditiously. He's a prosecutor. Deals with probate. He was hesitant about accepting you at first, mainly because of what you've been through with the trial. But I convinced him that you were a hard worker and basically told him what he'd be missing if he got another student."

"You did that for me. Why?"

"Well don't be so quick to count your chickens before they hatch, Angel. He told me that he was in need of an intern and I can tell that he's interested in you. But before he gives you the job, he still wants to interview you, just so he can get your views on certain legal matters ... But it's nothing to be nervous about. Don't worry about trying to make a good impression; just make sure you're honest and straightforward with him. Like me, he can always detect when you're not being straightforward."

"Thank you, Professor Stern. But I'm not so sure if I can accept this internship from you. After the incident with Kevin, I'm trying to stay away from receiving certain helping hands."

"We all need helping hands, Angel. You'll quickly learn that in this field of work. And besides, you deserve this intern."

After accepting the offer, he tells me, "Why don't you grab me two of those boxes behind you, the ones lying on the dresser, top shelf."

The Other Side of the Pillow

I start to carry the boxes his way, one that reads, *bathroom accessories*, and the others reading, *DVD's and VHS*. Thinking it would be my only assignment, he kept giving me more tasks as if we were in the classroom.

In the midst of me going back and forth, I soon started to become more observant; I saw something that nearly scared me, something that forced my thoughts to become retroactive.

Along with the other attorneys that hung from the walls, I noticed Professor Stern having a picture of Attorney Banniker, the same prosecutor who handled my mother's case after she died.

Full of questions, I became confused. What business did Professor Stern have with Attorney Banniker, and even greater, why was he on the wall, shaking hands with Professor Stern, smiling as if they were friends for a lifetime?

Professor Stern said, "What happened, Angel? Are you giving up on me?"

"Actually, I was just observing some of your photos. Who is this person right here?" I asked, grabbing the picture.

"Oh, that's Attorney Banniker," he replied delightedly. "Me and him go way back."

"Exactly how far back do the two of you go?" I asked, not caring if I crossed that line of inquiry.

Professor Stern says, "We go back over forty years. I'm talking back to my last year of law school ... Attorney Banniker is special to me. He was a much better lawyer than I was. Only lost one case in his entire career."

I ask, "And what case was that?"

"A murder case ... it happened a long time ago, might've been his second or third case ... come to think about it, I still have the file of that case." He points his finger towards the dining room and tells me, "Would ya grab me that huge box in the corner? The one marked important files."

I ask, "Care if I look at it first?"

"Suit yourself. It should be the last file in the bottom of the stack. The file that reads, *Ross vs. the State. 1989.*"

As he said my stepfather's last name, I almost panicked, felt like I was stricken by a shock wave. Then I started to dig deep into the box like I was digging up a grave, or even greater, digging for the contents of my soul.

"You ok?" he asked. "You're moving like you're on speed."

I don't answer. For I was too concentrated on looking for that file, too busy trying to pick the lock to my mother's post-mortem.

It didn't take long for me to get to the bottom of the stack. Ross vs. the State. The unsolved case.

I flipped open the file and a picture lied inside.

It was my mother.

The air that I breathe. Breath that was stripped from my lungs.

She was dressed in a dark suit, smiling in her usual idyllic state, and behind her was a picture of my stepfather, the murderer. I glanced at his picture and quickly turned my stare back to mama.

Professor Stern said, "That's Anna Brown and her husband, the defendant … Do you know her?"

"No I don't. She just reminds me of a woman I used to know. However, I do know a little about this case. I remember reading about it in high school."

"Yeah," he replied, taking the picture from my hands.

He sighs while staring at the picture. "I remember hearing about this case like it was yesterday. The defendant was supposed to receive capital punishment, or life without parole … God knows that bastard deserved it … But word got out that one of the jurors in the case was a former high school classmate of the defendant, and he convinced the other jurors of lessening the charge to second-degree murder. It wasn't until a couple months after the verdict that the courts realized the correlation between the defendant and the juror, and by then it was too late … I mean, you'll think that a person who deliberately kills his wife would receive stronger justice than a lousy ten-to-twelve year sentence. But I guess justice doesn't always prevail."

I picked up the picture of my stepfather, stared at the face that I haven't seen in eighteen years, the image that I see every night but just in a different world. Then I saw the black ring on his finger, the same ring that he used to bruise my mother's face – and it made me want to tear open the picture frame and bring his photo back to life, just so I could re-write the past and send him back to a watery grave.

I said, "If you ask me, God gave that asshole the death that he deserved. So at least justice was served in one way or another."

"Death?" Professor Stern asked astonishingly. "What death?"

I grunt. "Death in prison. They murdered his ass in prison."

"No, Angel. We must not be talking 'bout the same case."

"Yes we are," I tell him, remembering the trial like it was yesterday. "You're talking about Travis Ross. The murder trial of 1989. And the opposing counsel was Attorney Samuel Davis."

"You've got the right case, but Travis Ross didn't die in prison."

"What?"

"Travis Ross served his full ten years, went to the work-release center for a few months, and was completely released in May of 1999."

"What?"

"I know. It sickens me too. Like many trials, it makes me want to take justice into my own hands." He shakes his head, then he goes on to say, "That bastard is probably on the streets right now, looking for another woman to terrorize."

I swallow my stomach. Swallow what's left inside, and before he can elaborate any further, I tell him, "You don't know what you're talking 'bout. Don't you dare tell me that he was released … Travis Ross is dead … He was killed in prison by a former enemy on the outside."

"Trust me Angel when I tell you that he was released. Some people say he left the country for a couple years, perhaps because he knew his life would be in danger after getting out. But last I heard, he had changed his identity completely, and he was living back in the states … Cheyenne, Wyoming is the last place he was seen. But that's been a couple years back, so I'm sure he must've relocated by now."

Instantly, I start to question my belief, start to question my whole life, and I suddenly make eye contact with those two words that hunts me so dearly: *WHAT IF*.

What if what he's saying is true, that my stepfather really did get released and I just wasn't aware? What if Aunt Terry knew the truth all along, and the whole time she was concealing that truth with some prison-death story, perhaps to make it suffuse my heavy burden inside, so I would never want to know where my stepfather was at, or even greater, so I wouldn't go looking for him in the near future.

That would make my whole life a cover-up, nothing but an endless tale of lies.

With anger exasperating though my soul, I looked at Professor Stern and said, "What's the name of that juror?"

"Excuse me?"

"The juror in the case? You mentioned him being a classmate of the murderer, Travis Ross. Tell me his name."

"Calm down, Angel. Now what's the importance? And why do you—"

"Just tell me his name ok!"

"Antonio Smith …geez, Angel … His name is Antonio Smith."

   Cyril Gillion

I grabbed both pictures and headed for the door, left Professor Stern standing there puzzled.

Rushing to get back to my apartment, I kept saying son-of-a-bitch all the way home, and I called my sweetie, William, had to cancel our plans for tonight.

William didn't answer; he left me with the voice of an answering machine. I dropped him a brief message informing him that I'd be on the next flight to Cheyenne, Wyoming to handle some unfinished business.

First thing I did once reaching my apartment was boot up my laptop to Google the name, *Antonio Smith*. Through my search, you wouldn't believe how many Smith's there were in the computer, would've taken me hours to find the one I was looking for. After narrowing down my search to *Antonio Smith's in Florida*, I was left with 136 addresses and 112 phone numbers to go along with it. I charged up my cellular and promised myself that I'd call 112 different Antonio's if necessary.

After the first hour, I had already called thirty-one Antonio's and none of them admitted to knowing a Travis Ross or even knowing of the case from '93. Eight of those calls took me directly to voicemail and you could bet your ass that I was still going to leave a message. Six of them hung-up after hearing an unrecognizable voice, and three were giving a busy signal. By the time I reached the 67th Smith, a knock appeared on my door. It was William and little Devilla, both dressed as if they were going somewhere.

I told William, "I take it that you didn't receive my message."

"I did get it. That's why I'm here. To make sure that you're ok. You sounded a little flustered on the voicemail."

"I'm good. But right now, I've got some important business to handle, and I'm fixing to be on the next flight to Wyoming."

"Wyoming? Is everything alright?"

"Everything's cool."

"Oh look daddy," Devilla screams out, running over to my laptop. "She has a mini computer."

"Don't touch that!" William demanded. "Go into the living room and watch some TV or something. Daddy need some quiet time with Ms. Angel."

Putting my stringent call-search on hold, I try to exit out from Google, but the computer froze before I could close out, and William notices the listing of names on the monitor. Smiling, he asks, "Who is Antonio Smith? Are you trying to replace me already?"

I could've told him a lie, but lying would be harder than telling the truth. Besides, if this is supposed to be a relationship, than I should be able to tell him anything.

He sits next to me on the bed. "You don't have to pretend, Angel. I know something's wrong."

He gives a pampering stare, eyes strong enough to make a woman confess to her indiscretions.

I ask him, "In your opinion, how important do you think honesty is in a relationship?"

"Well … I guess that depends on the relationship."

"What do you mean, *depends on the relationship*? I thought honesty was considered honesty, no matter what."

"Not necessarily, Angel." He lowers his head as if he's gathering a thought. "Honesty is supposed to be the cure to all wounds. But in some instances, pouring honesty on a wound can be equivalent to pouring salt."

"Yeah, but if time is supposed to heal everything, then pouring salt shouldn't be so bad … right?"

He hesitates, says, "Some wounds never completely heal, Angel. And if they do, a scar remains forever. So to answer your question, I feel that honesty is most important when it comes to the love of a spouse, simply because a spouse can be replaced at any given time. But when it comes to a parent and child – like me and Devilla – honesty has to be examined very closely. That type of relationship only comes once and a lifetime."

He comes my way and kisses me on the cheek. "And just to let you know, I've yet to erase your message."

"What message?"

"This message," he says, pulling out his cellular.

Going through his voicemails, he puts the phone on speaker, and there I was on his answering machine, muttering that I love him, the same night Cuqui arrived in New York.

He smiles. "Though I never said it, I love you, Angel. Love you like I should've loved a woman a long time ago."

"I love you too, William. Or should I say, *Trouble*. I love you too."

"Speaking of trouble, give me a brief moment to go and check on the little one. Let's hope she hasn't redecorated your living room."

He rises from the chair, and just like that, the pain I had earlier is starting to lessen. As he heads for the living room, my eyes go towards the laptop. In the midst of shutting it down, I noticed a missed call that appeared on my cellular, an unrecognizable number.

 Cyril Gillion

Verifying if the caller was one of the Antonio Smith's, I checked my call Rolodex.

Indeed it was.

Intuition caused me to call the number back, and faith allowed someone to pick up the phone. "Hello?"

"Yes," I replied. "I was trying to reach Antonio Smith. Is this him?"

"Why? Who's asking?"

The voice is that of a middle-aged man, carried the voice of someone from my homeland, Miami, Florida. His pitch was nowhere near friendly, probably thought I was a bill collector of some sort.

I didn't want to scare him away by giving my real identity, so I told him, "My name is Kelly."

"Kelly who?"

"Kelly Burgess."

He pauses, then goes on to say, "Okay Ms. Burgess, can I help you?"

"I'm looking for a Travis Ross. Would you happen to know 'em?"

"I know of him. But I haven't seen 'em in years. Why?"

A shockwave goes through me, almost detaches my hand from the receiver.

I ask, "Are you familiar with the trial, Ross vs. the State? You were supposed to be one of the jurors in the case."

"I don't know 'bout no trial. And if you're looking for Travis, look elsewhere. I'm going to hang up now. Have a good—"

"Hold up please. All I want to know is … have you seen Travis Ross. That's it."

"I don't know of a Travis Ross."

"Thought you told me that you knew 'em? Now where is—"

"Forget what I told you, lady! I don't know of any Travis Ross."

"Well what about Anna Brown?" I asked, saying my mother's name with conviction. "Have you ever heard of her?"

He blows a hard breath over the phone, discouragement going through the airways. "Who are you?"

"I told you. My name is—"

"Why don't you assholes just leave him alone? That man has already served his time. You damn journalists never seem to stop do you."

"I'm no journalist! I'm the daughter of Anna Brown, the woman he killed. And right now, you're talking to Travis's stepdaughter."

"Bullshit! Travis never had a step daughter."

"He did too. Her name was Angel Inghram and this is her. So please, just tell me if you saw my stepfather."

"Listen here, lady. I don't know who you are, but I haven't seen Trouble in ten years."

"Who?"

"Trouble. Travis Ross. The guy you're looking for. I haven't seen him in years, couldn't recognize 'em if he was staring me face to face. So make this your last damn call okay! This is a family household and we have little children!"

Click.

I dropped the phone and fell to my knees, the world weighing heavily on my shoulders.

When I looked up, I saw him dead in the flesh. I saw William. Saw Travis Ross. Saw my step dad.

SAW TROUBLE.

With features that resembled the ghost from the past, he stood through my bedroom door with the face of a corpse, stood as my nightmare's worst nightmare.

And then I saw the ring.

The same ring that was worn for beating my mother is the same ring that's wrapped around his finger. 22 Karat Gold. Sterling Silver.

That.

Same.

Fucking.

Ring.

Insanity falls on my shoulder and there's only one option remaining, one straw for me to pull. That straw is the pistol, the colt .45 that's lying beneath my bed, waiting to be used for what it's worth.

I instantly reach for the .45 as if I'm reaching for my salvation; point it towards the man who deserves to die.

Motionless, the devil asks, "Angel, what are you doing?"

"What I should've done a long time ago. You bastard ... you mothafucking—"

"Put down the gun, Angel."

"You killed my mother didn't you? DIDN'T YOU???"

"Your mother?"

"Anna Brown ... eighteen years ago."

"Please, Angel. Put the gun down. Let's relax so we can—"

"ANSWER THE DAMN QUESTION!"

He hesitates, "Yes, Angel ... I ... I killed her ... but ... but it was an accident ... the gun slipped from my—"

     Cyril Gillion

"Accident my ass!"

He motion towards me, fear pulsating in his eyes. "Calm down, Angel … please calm down so I can—"

"The hell with calming down! All this time, William, or Trouble, or whatever it is that you answer to. All this time I've been waiting to see your face. I thought you were dead. Thought they finished you off in prison a long time ago … How could you do this to me … I was only six years old … how could you goddammit??? All this time you knew the truth and you … you—"

"I didn't know, Angel … I didn't—"

"—LYING SICKO! How could you try to come into my life after what happened? How could you try to—"

"Daddy! Daddy!"

"Devilla, go back into the living room! Ms. Angel and I are having a talk."

"No daddy! I won't leave you!"

"Devilla, do what daddy says and go back into the living room … now put down the gun, Angel … come on baby … we can fix this … just put down the gun … please… God knows we can—"

"Too late for screaming God!"

I cocked back the .45. Cocked the life of the chamber while holding the gun for dear life.

Tears welt in my eyes. Tears I've been waiting to mourn. Tears I've been waiting to plummet.

I closed my eyes and released the ammunition…

…To be continued

FOR ADDITIONAL COPIES OF

THE OTHER SIDE OF THE PILLOW

$15.00 + 3.95 FOR S&H
BOOK QTY________

NAME ____

ADDRESS ____

CITY ______________ STATE ________ ZIP __________

PLEASE MAKE CHECK OR MONEY ORDER PAYABLE TO:
CG PUBLISHING INC.
P.O. Box 21318
Tallahassee, FL 32316

Or Pay Online @ www.cyrilgillion.com